W9-BOM-824

DISCARD 2/13

DISCARD

DISCARD

DISCARD

DISCARD

COLUMBUS AVENUE BOYS

Avenging the Scalamarri Massacre

David Carraturo

IUNIVERSE, INC.
BLOOMINGTON

Columbus Avenue Boys
Avenging the Scalamarri Massacre

iUniverse books may be ordered through booksellers or by contacting:

iUniverse
1663 Liberty Drive
Bloomington, IN 47403
www.iuniverse.com
1-800-Authors (1-800-288-4677)

ISBN: 978-1-4697-7828-0 (sc)
ISBN: 978-1-4697-7829-7 (hc)
ISBN: 978-1-4697-7830-3 (e)

Library of Congress Control Number: 2012903069

Printed in the United States of America

iUniverse rev. date: 3/30/2012

COLUMBUS AVENUE BOYS

Avenging the Scalamarri Massacre

Also by David Carraturo

Cameron Nation

CONTENTS

Part 3. Hit the Fan

Introduction

LA FAMIGLIA SCALAMARRI

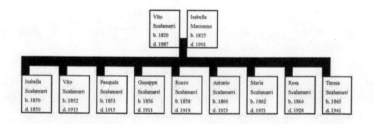

RISORGIMENTO WAS THE NINETEENTH-CENTURY political movement for Italian unification that led to the establishment of the Kingdom of Italy. This rising was inspired by the realities of the new economic and political forces spawned by the French Revolution of 1789 and the ideas of eighteenth-century Italian reformers and *illuminista* (enlightened ones).

The *Risorgimento* had two distinct phases. The first was idealistic, romantic, and revolutionary; began in 1815; and climaxed in the revolutions of 1848–49. The second was pragmatic, diplomatic, and practical and transpired in the 1850s. This phase culminated in the creation of a united Italian kingdom by 1861.

As a manifestation of the nationalism sweeping over Europe at the time, the *Risorgimento* aimed to unite Italy under one flag and one government. For many Italians, this meant more than political unity. The common denominator was a desire for freedom from foreign control, for liberalism, and for constitutionalism.

There was agreement on the need for unity among the various states and for constitutional guarantees of personal liberty and rights. Disagreements arose on whether unity should be under a confederation or a centralized form of government. There was further disagreement on whether a united Italy should be a republic or a monarchy.

It was on these issues that the revolutionary initiatives of 1848–49 floundered. Radicals distrusted moderates. Unitarians and federalists disagreed. Republicans condemned monarchists. Such distrust and disagreement undermined attempts to create an Italian legion (common army) and to agree on a preliminary constitution applicable to all parts of Italy. Above all, it prevented the ability to present a united front against common enemies that were embodied in the Austrian armies under the supreme commander of the region, Field Marshal Radetzky.

Everywhere, Italians joined in what they felt to be truly their *Risorgimento*. From Sicily to the northern states of Piedmont-Sardinia, Lombardy, and Venetia, people took to the streets against the Austrians and native rulers.

Ideological and dynastic rivalries prevented a united effort. The Neapolitan king Ferdinand II and Pope Pius IX withdrew support from the common war against Austria, and plans for an Italian league and army collapsed. The army of Charles Albert, King of Piedmont-Sardinia, was twice defeated by the redoubtable Radetzky, and the revolutionary republics established in central Italy and Venice fought their battles alone. By 1849, Italian insurgency had collapsed and the Roman Republic fell to French forces. The heroic, revolutionary phase of the *Risorgimento* was over, but its legacy and lessons paved the way for the cautious deliberate diplomacy of Count Camillo Benso di Cavour.

Count Cavour was the prime minister of Piedmont-Sardinia after 1852 and the founder of the original Italian Liberal Party. He was able to use the threat of potential revolutionary resurgence to persuade conservative opinion that a united Italy under the House of Savoy and the dynasty of Piedmont-Sardinia would be a force for stability.

After 1849, Piedmont-Sardinia was the only Italian state with a constitution and an elected parliament, and Cavour exerted a powerful attraction for the large majority of Italian nationalists. By 1859, the French military had given support to Cavour in a war against Austria. He also secured the support of the Italian National Society.

As a result, Austria was forced to cede Lombardy to Piedmont-Sardinia. This was followed by a series of upheavals in the states of central and southern Italy to overturn rulers, including a successful campaign in southern Italy, led by Giuseppe Garibaldi.

In Turin, on March 17, 1861, the Kingdom of Italy was proclaimed, and by 1870, the aims of the political *Risorgimento* had been achieved. The parliament was composed of elected representatives from all parts of Italy with the exception of Venetia. Venetia remained under Austrian rule until 1866, and Rome stayed under papal control until 1870.[1]

Italy's southern region had remained impoverished and possessed a virtually feudal society. The bulk of the population consisted of *artigiani* (craftsmen), *contadini* (sharecroppers), and *giornalieri* (farm laborers) who all eked out meager existences. For reasons of security and health, these people typically clustered in hill towns away from the farms. Families typically worked as collective units to ensure survival. Each day required long walks to family plots, which added to the toil that framed their existence.

The impact of the 1870 unification was disastrous to the people of the southern region. The new constitution had heavily favored the north, especially in its tax policies, industrial subsidies, and land programs. The southern region's hard-pressed peasantry was forced to shoulder an increased share of national expenses, while attempting to compete in markets dominated more and more by outside capitalist intrusions. These burdens only exacerbated existing problems of poor soil, absentee landlords, inadequate investment, disease, and high rates of illiteracy.

An exodus from the southern peninsula began in the 1880s and soon became the source of more than 75 percent of immigration to the United States. The regions of Calabria, Campania, Apulia, and Basilicata started a wave that later spread to Sicily. From 1876 to 1924, more than four and a half million Italians arrived in the United States. This initial movement dispersed widely across the country, and New York soon became home to millions of Italian immigrants. The first phase consisted primarily of temporary migrants who desired immediate employment, maximum savings, and quick repatriation. This movement was predominately

---

1   www.ohio.edu/chastain/rz/risorgim.htm, accessed January 15, 2012.

composed of young, single men of prime working age (fifteen to thirty-five years old) who clustered in urban centers. Multiple trips were commonplace, and ties to American society, such as learning English, securing citizenship, and acquiring property, were minimal.

During the second phase, they brought with them *campanilismo* (family-centered peasant cultures) and fiercely local identifications. They typically viewed themselves as residents of their hometown villages, not as Italians. The organizational and residential life of early communities reflected these facts, as people limited associations to *paesani* or fellow villagers. Gradually, *campanilismo* gave way to a more national identity as they became acclimated and others soon regarded them as simply Italians.[2]

One family was sired by Vito Scalamarri, the oldest son of Rocco and Maria. Vito was born in 1820 and had spent his days on the farm, laboring as a *contadini* in Mileto, a *comune* in the Province of Vibo Valentia. Located within the region of Calabria near Catanzaro, the city was founded not far from the site of the ancient Medama by Greek fugitives from Miletus in Anatolia.

Vito married Isabella Marzuno in 1848. In 1850, their firstborn, a daughter who was named after her mother, died soon after birth. Heartbroken, the young couple persevered. Over the next thirteen years, they were blessed to have eight additional children; the first five were boys, and the last three were girls. Of the Scalamarri children, all of the five sons ventured off to find a better life in America. One descendant of this family even became president of the United States—but that is another story.

2   George Pozzetta, "Italian Americans," Everyculture.com, accessed January 15, 2012, www.everyculture.com/multi/Ha-La/Italian-Americans. html#ixzz1ahBGuoDH.

Prologue

BUGSY

June 20, 1947

NIGHTMARES FROM THE BATTLES he had fought in across the Pacific would be forever engrained in his memory. They had taught him to always be prepared for any engagement. After being away for twelve long years, the early morning train heading east could not come soon enough. Ready to head back home, he had one last mission to complete. Then his weapon would finally be lowered for good.

The M1 Garand, resting comfortably across his chest, was one of his spoils of war. To go along with two Arisaka rifles and six Type 94 pistols, he possessed three additional M1s from his campaigns on the atolls and islands of Guadalcanal, Tarawa, and Saipan. These souvenirs had already been shipped home. The meticulously maintained .30 caliber was all he would need tonight.

The retired Marine Gunnery Sergeant had carefully planned this mission, and his confidence level was high. He stood up and stretched for the first time in eighteen hours. If this had been the jungle, he would never have stood completely erect this close to the front, but on a sweltering, star-filled night behind a detached garage in Beverly Hills, he believed he was safe from enemy attack.

His olive-green T-shirt reeked with sweat. But if all went according to plan, he would be wearing a fresh set of clothes in less than an hour. Crouching low, he made his way around the side of the detached structure and then peered into a living room window of 810 Linden Drive. Oblivious to his fate, the target was less than ten feet away, seated in a lounge chair and reading a newspaper. The assassin exhaled, smiled slightly, and then squeezed off eight successive rounds. The shattering of the glass was barely heard over the loud pinging as the spent clip ejected.

Benjamin "Bugsy" Siegel's murderous life had come to an end.

The recently deceased had earned his nickname, which had been acquired early on in his criminal career, because he had a tendency to "go bugs" whenever angered. While it would not be an issue any longer, the gangster had actually despised the nickname, and anyone who spoke it to his face risked certain bodily harm. It was always safer to call him Ben or Mr. Siegel.

Still officially a married man at the time of his death, Mr. Ben Siegel was living in a home rented by his movie star girlfriend, Virginia Hill. They had had one of their famous fights, and she had fled to Paris to give him time to cool off.

The first shot penetrated Bugsy's right cheek, exiting through the left side of his neck. The next shot struck the right bridge of Ben's nose, passing behind Mr. Siegel's left eye before exiting directly behind the zygomatic bone, where it met the temporal bone. Overpressure from that bullet's striking and passing through the skull blew his eye out of its socket. The ruthless gangster was hit by several more bullets, including shots through his lungs.

Grasping the rifle across his body with both hands, the assassin retreated. With the assistance of an overturned wheelbarrow, he climbed over a six-foot-high fence and landed on the maintenance road that hid the garbage pickup in this fashionable California community.

Crouched low, he traversed north half a click before climbing over a neighbor's fence. Hidden in the dense tree line separating a tennis court to the left and a bean-shaped pool to the right, he stashed the weapon under the floorboards of a pool house. Then he galloped across the colossal backyard. This pattern of retreat continued as he serpentined among the darkened mansions of Linden and Greenway Drives. The meticulously manicured suburban landscapes provided the perfect cover for his escape.

Less than eight minutes later, he reached the seclusion of the eleventh green at Los Angeles Country Club. With moonlight and memory for his guide, he located a waiting duffel bag tucked deep in the mini-forest growing in the middle of the exclusive private golf course. Out of breath and sweating profusely, he stripped from his soiled assassin clothes and then tossed them into an already prepared hole. He changed into a blue floral short-sleeve button-up shirt, tan slacks, and black wingtip shoes before covering the discarded garments with dirt and brush.

The next phase of his retreat took him in a southwesterly direction. He passed over the undulations of the greens, tee boxes, and fairways and exited onto bustling Wilshire Boulevard. He walked at a casual pace for twenty minutes before entering the campus of the University of California at Los Angeles. It was now almost an hour since the incident. Police cars were streaming in the opposite direction. He turned south to Westwood Village and blended into the student population dawdling about.

After reaching the parking lot of the deserted facilities management building, he bent down behind a row of flannel bushes for a hidden basswood Hartmann suitcase. Then he walked casually with the luggage to the student library. The building was locked and closed for the weekend, but he had left a window unlatched the day earlier. After checking the surrounding area, he opened the window and shimmied in. He entered the first floor of the darkened library then closed the window. He swiftly made his way to the lavatory. Another change of clothes; this one consisted of a pair of blue high-cut trousers and a crisp white dress shirt. With a straightedge razor and a can of Barbasol, he shaved the two-week growth of dark brown stubble off of his face.

Feeling like a new man, he rubbed the smoothness of his cheeks. Then he lifted his suspenders over his shoulders and neatly knotted a bright red tie. His ensemble was complete after clipping cufflinks in place and checking his reflection in the mirror. After adjusting his jacket and black fedora hat, he quietly exited the library the same way as came. It was after midnight now. He walked back toward Wilshire Boulevard, where he caught a cab to Union Station. The 7:00 a.m. *Super Chief* to Chicago awaited.

Part 1

Revelation

1

FOXWOODS

January 11, 1996

IF YOU ARE DEALT lemons, you make lemonade. Sal and Tony advanced higher than others in their crew because they always had that uncanny ability to simply never let a crisis go to waste. The TV weather guys called it the New York City area's worst storm in fifty years, but the two business partners had put their heads together a week before the first flake had even fallen to maximize the event. While many in their crew's money-making opportunities were limited, theirs were not.

Even though they had already received upfront payments from snow-plowing customers well before Christmas, an extra bonus was now warranted, especially if the owners of the residential and commercial buildings wanted their tenants to see the light of day before March. The two bruisers unofficially held the snow removal rights in the area, and there was very little chance of a brave upstart in a four-by-four and shiny new plow muscling onto their turf. It was not major-league baseball, and it was very unlikely that a scab would cross this picket line.

The veteran mobsters believed it was totally justified. With the unemployment rate under 6 percent, everybody had plenty of cash. All told, they ended up taking in an extra forty large over the three days of anticipation and panic before the storm, making a $19,000 profit after kicking up ten grand to their captain and surprising the worker bees (who did all the work) with a taste.

The storm did not disappoint. Twenty inches of the white stuff reportedly fell on the ground over the two-day period. Unless you had a plow attached to the front of your truck and removed snow for a living, life ground to a halt. Having been cooped up in their respective one-bedroom apartments with wives and infant sons for the entire time, the two men decided that a celebratory day trip to Connecticut was the perfect venue for a sunny but still bitterly cold Thursday.

Noting his arrival by pressing the buzzer to 2E2, Tony left the lobby of the Consulate and went back to the heated comfort of his Chevy Tahoe to wait for his buddy to come downstairs. He was laughing out loud with his eyes closed to one of Howard Stern's radio bits and did not mind Sal taking fifteen minutes to make his entrance.

"You doin' your hair all this time? Jee-sus Christ, it's takin' longer and longer to make yourself pretty." He shook his head in mock disgust as Sal slammed the door.

"Nah, first I had to change Mikey's diaper. Damn, that kid can poop." He raised the volume to better hear Howard. "Then Angie springs a honey-do bullshit list on me. So I had'a scramble to fold clothes and make the bed as she fed him some of that mothers' milk. She pulls this last-minute crap on me all the time when we go to Foxwoods. I swear I love her, but sometimes ..."

"Yeah, yeah, I know. Sometimes a bag of lime, a shovel, and a long drive to the country's the best marriage counseling."

Before they drove off, Sal looked up to his wife on the second floor. Mikey was propped up and waving good-bye to his daddy from the bedroom window. "I think I'll keep her. She never stays mad too long anyway." He finished the good-bye by mouthing "I love you" and blowing her a kiss.

Around the time he had gotten married fifteen months earlier, Sal had been presented with a very attractive offer by one of his regulars. He had jumped at the chance to live in a condominium in the secluded section of town for a 60 percent discount on the going rate of $1,000 a month. His new landlord had the misfortune of believing that after winning the first three games of the football season, the Giants would win at least one of the next seven. They did not, and more importantly, they also did not cover the point spread. On the hook for $8,800, the landlord worked out a deal where Sal could live in the one-bedroom, one-bath unit for as long as he pleased.

The four-building complex sat nestled along the Bronx River, adjacent to the Parkway Oval field, where they had played ball as kids. It was now completely covered in a blanket of snow. As they passed, he fondly reflected about the countless hours they had spent playing sports and hanging out on the bleachers with their good buddy Chris.

The three lifelong friends had spent almost every second together on and off the field. While their blood brother was now working for some financial firm in Texas, Sal and Tony never thought twice about leaving their place of birth.

Tony made a quick right and then a left turn out to the main business district before crossing over Columbus Avenue. "I hav'ta stop at your restaurant first. Pops wants to come with us."

After Tony's *nonna* had passed away, his seventy-seven-year-old grandfather had moved back from a retirement village in Port St. Lucie. Now, he spent most of his days playing *briscola* and drinking black coffee in Ressini's with his dwindling number of geriatric friends. Still spry for his age, many nights were also spent playing poker in the private room of the establishment.

Even at his advanced age, he was considered one the best card players in town. In the short time since he had been back, his eyes always lit up whenever he got wind of his grandson venturing to the casino. These legal gambling excursions located so close to home had not been an option before he and Teresa retired and moved to the Sunshine State.

As soon as he recognized his grandson's truck at the traffic light, he was out the door. Before they had even pulled to a stop, he was outside waiting, wearing a gray-checkered fedora hat with a matching overcoat. Tony was amazed by the old man's mobility and senses. Pops still had it, and he would know. As a child, with his father and mother working endless hours to make ends meet, he and his sister spent most of their formative years with their grandparents.

Whenever he looked at the old black-and-white Kodak Brownie pictures from when he was younger, Tony could not believe how much he looked and acted like his grandfather. They stood the same way, smiled identically, and commanded the same respect and attention. While he was now stooped over a bit, it was obvious that Pops had been a dominant presence back in the day. By simply shaking his thick, beefy hand, you could tell this man had lived an interesting life.

"You can't wait, can you?" The younger men laughed as Pops shut the door securely and buckled his seatbelt before answering.

"Well, you going to drive or what, Anthony? Turn that crap off and put on the news!" Then he closed his eyes and napped for the next two hours. They waited the five customary minutes before turning it back to the "King of All Media."

While the two wiseguys had both gambled large amounts in the past, they now had families to support. Tony and his wife, Victoria, were expecting their second baby in June, and Sal and Angela were gearing up to have another kid. With a portion of their snow plow profits, they gave them both $5,000 to pay household expenses for the month.

With $2,000 or so, they would gamble and then have a hearty meal with the old man. The remaining seven grand would be invested. Not the way their buddy Chris did at that investment company. Sal and Tony had a much better way to generate above-average returns. Prior to the trip, they had spread the word that they were liquid and would be available to help change the luck of anyone who happened to be at Foxwoods that day. If these degenerate gamblers paid the loan back before leaving the casino, there would be only a minimal fee. However, if the odds got the better of them, then another $2,000 of additional profit was expected to be generated if not repaid by the end of the following week.

It ended up being a very profitable day. Pops took advantage of sucker after sucker who believed he could outplay him in Texas Hold 'em. Early in the evening, Tony stopped by his poker table to see how he was faring and stood in silence, viewing a hand in play. Minutes later a surge of energy went through his veins as Pops raked in an armful of red five-dollar and green twenty-five-dollar chips. His diamond-suited flush had out-dueled a straight to the king.

The young man, who obviously had had too much to drink, sarcastically yelled out a compliment: "Old man, you're kicking my ass."

Never one to miss having the last word, Pops looked up as he stacked his chips. "Son, I haven't even started kicking your ass yet."

Tony let out a huge belly laugh and kissed him on top of his head before returning to the craps table to meet up with his partner. Besides Pops' good fortune, Sal worked the dice like a maestro and had doubled his initial investment. While Tony also wanted to play the tables, he was too busy approving loans to "friends" and then lending more and more throughout the early evening.

With things going their way and yet another snowstorm bearing up the coast, they decided the prudent move would be to spend the night in safety.

Their wives were not happy with this decision, but they had to look out for the old man. *"Hey, do you expect us to drive Pops home in this treacherous weather?"* Before they had left that morning, they had seen the advanced weather report. This precaution had been their plan all along.

Plan A was that if things were going well (which they were), they would enjoy a hearty steak and fine bottle of cabernet with their favorite person in the world and spend the night at Foxwoods. Plan B was to rush through a meal and not get home till well after midnight. Rest assured, they were sure to get woken up at dawn by the baby crying. Plan A seemed the better course of action.

In between, Sal lamented about how he could cook circles around the chef in this place, and both retold gambling adventures, proudly bragged about their baby boys, and then halfheartedly bitched about their supposedly hard-ass wives whom they loved so much. By the time the salads arrived, the floor had been turned over to Pops. He had captivated them since they were kids, and they never tired of his ability to give a life lesson. It seemed like he had been around forever, and he was the best source for stories of the good old days.

The truth of the matter was that Salvatore Esposito, Anthony Albanese, and Christopher Cameron—the Columbus Avenue Boys—were somewhat related, as they shared lineage back to before the turn of century. While their Italian blood had been diced and sliced over the past hundred years, they each laid claim to sharing relatives from Italy before their ancestors immigrated to America in the late 1800s. Because of this bond, they were proud of their self-anointed blue-blood, blue-collar heritage. Pops was one of the last of Tuckahoe's old breed. He had outlived most others from his generation, and they relished every moment spent with him.

2

THAT MCGOVERN'S A TERROR

April 8, 1892

Concetta Scalamarri looked up in amazement as her nearly month-long journey was almost over. The SS *Cachemire* was slowly making its way into New York Bay through the Verrazano Narrows. Separated by Staten Island and the borough of Brooklyn, the vessel steamed closer to her final destination.

In the distance, Concetta could see the right arm of the Statue of Liberty raised high in the morning sky, welcoming them to the New World. Slowly passing the breathtaking structure, she wept as she bent down and embraced her two children. It would not be long before they would see their father and her husband again. He would be very proud of how his children had grown in the two long years since he had seen them last.

The last letter she had mailed back to her beloved Antonio had ended with *Al mio carissimo sposo, ti voglio tanto bene. Tuo figlio Pasquale e tua figlia Maria non vedono l'ora di abbraciarti.* (My beautiful husband, I love you dearly. Your son, Pasquale, and daughter, Maria, cannot wait to see you again.)

Concetta was an attractive woman. Not yet thirty, standing five feet four inches, she was strongly built from working in the hilly farmlands of southern Italy. She wore a long light blue dress that was soiled and grimy after the twenty-nine-day voyage, and her shoulder-length dark brown hair was pulled back in a bun.

Antonio had sent his *bella mia* numerous letters enclosed with American dollars and wonderful stories about their soon-to-be life. He had worked hard, toiling as a laborer at a marble quarry and as a landscaper at a golf course. As always, he kept his promise and sent for them as quickly as he could.

The last joyous letter she had received in February included three steerage-compartment tickets on the *Cachemire* along with details for the forthcoming journey. Antonio had spoken with recently arrived *paesani* about their experience at Ellis Island. Concetta's husband of ten years had braced her for the hardship of the voyage and briefed her on what to be prepared for when they disembarked, whom to steer clear of, and whom to look for.

This new federal facility had recently opened to accommodate the influx of mass immigration from Europe. When Antonio came to America, he was processed through the much smaller facility across Hudson Bay at the Castle Garden immigration depot in Lower Manhattan.

The preparation came in very handy. Many of the *Cachemire*'s 833 passengers were detained due to sickness acquired on the transatlantic voyage. The Scalamarri family had survived by packing an ample amount of warm blankets, dried meats, and cheese.

Maria had dark brown eyes and even darker brown hair. She was a tall and gangly nine-year-old, but she was also alert and in good spirits. Pasquale, getting ready to turn seven, was the spitting image of his father. With thick dark brown hair and eyebrows, his face had a self-determined look. While standing only four feet tall, he maintained a stocky, self-assured build.

On April 10 their health was approved by the public service physician. Social, moral, and economic fitness was then established. Concetta was asked many questions, including name (on Antonio's arrival his lazy processor had shortened *Scalamarri* to *Scala*), occupation (*farmer*), and amount of money in her possession (while she hid eleven dollars in her undergarments, she disclosed four). The fact that her husband was gainfully employed and they had a place to live also quickened the processing.

Antonio arrived early and waited for close to sixteen hours. Upon noticing his beautiful bride looking for him outside the registry room, he rushed over and cried. Then he hugged and kissed her deeply. This was confirmation enough for the immigration inspector to release her and the children to his custody.

The Very Early Years

ANTONIO WAS THE SIXTH of nine children born to Vito and Isabella Scalamarri in Mileto, a small farming village in the province of Reggio Calabria in southern Italy. This mountainous community was the country's southernmost city, occupying a hilly area descending toward the Ionian Sea.

His four older brothers had all ventured off to America between the years 1885 and 1887 to make a better life. In 1887 their father, Vito, had fallen ill and soon passed; he was sixty-seven. The family decided that as the youngest man in the family, Antonio would remain to tend to the farm. Besides his wife and children, he was also tasked to take care of their aging mother and three younger sisters until they wed.

By 1890, the Scalamarri sisters had all married and vowed to remain in Italy and take care of their mother. In America, Antonio's older brothers had all found work and had established roots in New York. There were many transportation projects underway across the entire region that needed hardworking immigrants to help with the construction. Three brothers—Rocco, Vito, and Giuseppe—were hired as laborers on the massive expansion of the subway line and worked for the rapid transit companies in Brooklyn and in the Bronx. One brother, Pasquale, had settled just north of the city. He found employment in the Tuckahoe Marble Quarry within the farming town of Eastchester in Westchester County. Pasquale had been the last to write Antonio about coming to America, so he decided to go to Eastchester upon his arrival.

The tall, rugged Antonio labored in the marble quarry alongside his brother. He also worked as a groundskeeper at the newly opened Saint Andrews Golf Club. After backbreaking work during the day, he would hitch a buggy ride or if need be, walk the seven miles. He helped construct the clubhouse and then assisted in manicuring the greens and fairways of the converted hilly pasture along the Hudson River. He slept when he could, but for those two years he was determined to save enough to send for his family. When Concetta finally arrived, they lived in a small tenement on Maynard Street, which was in close proximity to the quarry.

By 1895 the children had begun to work to help their parents. Maria assisted her mother by cleaning clothes and serving meals to the quarry workers, while young Pasquale spent his time at the golf course with his father. As a ten-year-old, he was an eager ball retriever for the small cadre of the original Saint Andrews Apple Tree Gang.

Seven years earlier, these Scottish sportsmen had taken an armful of clubs, some *gutta percha* balls, and hearts full of enthusiasm to a pasture in Yonkers for a friendly round of *gowf*. There in front of a gallery of bemused cows, these golfing pioneers knocked the balls around a three-hole course. Called "Patsy" by the Scottish gents, Pasquale had grown into a handsome teenager. He was attentive, and he absorbed many conversations of the businessmen who frequented the club.

Due to his knowledge of the challenging hills and undulations, he was chosen to caddie regularly. In the spring of 1899, while looping for a guest of John Reid, the president of Saint Andrews, he overheard a discussion of a boxing match that was to be held in an open field adjacent to the Bronx River. The guest was William Landau, the head of the Westchester Boxing Club.

A ferocious bantamweight from Brooklyn, "Terrible" Terry McGovern, was scheduled to defend his title against Chicago's Johnny Ritchie. In a first of its kind, the contest would be held outdoors on an afternoon in July. While the 36–0 McGovern was a three-to-one underdog, Pasquale's ears perked. Landau had confidently stated that Ritchie had zero chance.

"That McGovern's a terror. I'd bet heavy on that hungry lion if I could." Landau expected McGovern to stay low and wreck Ritchie like he had done to all of his previous opponents.

Landau then turned from Reid and grabbed his putter from the immigrant teen. As he was lining up his shot in the tightly contested match, Pasquale stopped him and whispered into his ear, "The green's breaking very hard to the right. You'll want to slow your swing down. It hasn't been watered in days, sir."

The boxing executive stepped back to recalibrate his motion. Then he proceeded to sink the eighteen footer and best the club champ. He was so happy that in appreciation he offered a one-dollar tip to the boy. Pasquale's eyes went wide at such a large sum, but rather than simply accept it, which he did, he seized the moment.

"Thanks for the tip, mister, but I'd love it if I could have a job helping at that match. I live right by that field."

Patsy was hired to help with the construction of the boxing ring and attendance seating. After its completion, he noticed that it would be easily viewed from their rooftop on Maynard Street. The young entrepreneur huddled with his father.

"Papa, we can charge ten cents to view the match. I'm sure we could fit twenty of your fellow workers up on the roof. Momma could feed them, too." His father agreed it was a good plan. They would easily make two or three dollars.

"Papa, I heard McGovern can't lose, and he's a big underdog. We should accept wagers. Everyone'll surely wanta bet the big favorite from Chicago." While Antonio was not a gambling man, his son was. There were many times when Antonio caught the boy behind the caddie station playing cards with his earnings. There were days when he handed over only a few coins.

Antonio agreed with the plan and spread the word. He also touted the favorite. On the hot July afternoon, the gamble paid off. At the start of the third round, McGovern landed a blistering combination: right to the jaw, left to the eye, right to the jaw. The fight was over. Pasquale and his father embraced. They had made five dollars for food, wine, and admission. More importantly, they also won twenty-seven dollars on the boxing match. This amount was more than Antonio's entire monthly pay at the quarry and made him think hard about this quick way to earn extra income.

The next McGovern fight, against Great Britain's Pedlar Palmer, proved to be even more lucrative. Two months later, the match was held at the same locale but was delayed by a day due to rain. Because of the postponement, a second weigh-in wasn't necessary. When Pasquale saw Mr. Landau strolling around town the night before the fight, he boldly stopped the man. "Whata you think of Terrible Terry for tomorrow, sir?"

"My boy, look!" He pointed inside a restaurant window. "Terry hasn't stopped eating since he found out they're not having another weigh-in. He's gonna murder him." Landau rubbed the top of the boy's head and walked away.

That's all Pasquale needed to hear. His father offered generous odds on the Englishman. They did not make much on the refreshments but didn't mind, as McGovern overwhelmed Palmer and registered a first-round technical knockout.

The Scalamarris were in the right place at the right time and with the right service. They took advantage of the rapid growth in the region. As the marble quarry was being depleted, the construction of the New York and Harlem Railroad stations ushered an influx of people and businesses.

Tuckahoe incorporated as a village in 1902 after its population passed one thousand.

The Scalamarri crew grew and, by 1907, had expanded to include relatives from the entire New York City area. Family members from Brooklyn, from Lower Manhattan, and from the Bronx partnered with the Tuckahoe and Eastchester factions. In addition to boxing matches, the growing popularity of baseball led to wagering on the New York Highlanders and Giants. Their base of customers expanded as the construction of the Tuckahoe and Crestwood train stations led to a growing number of hardworking and hard-drinking men in the area.

That year, the family also laid the foundation for their greatest opportunity yet. Now twenty-two, Pasquale had remained employed at Saint Andrews, and he believed the private club presented invaluable information for potential ventures. While bartending in the dining room, he overheard a boisterous discussion by the inebriated new Bronx River Parkway commissioner.

"My good man, things are changing up here in the country. The automobiles made us rethink our projects." He motioned to the silent Italian for another Scotch.

"I just reviewed plans for a roadway that'll be built parallel to the railroad," he shouted to Mr. Reid and slapped his back in excitement. "It's gonna be revolutionary!"

Planning for the Bronx River Parkway started in 1907, but construction of the Westchester section did not begin until 1917. To meet the stringent construction demands set forth by the Bronx River Parkway commissioner, contractors deployed new machines to move earth, grade the roadbed, lay pavement, and erect bridges. When fully completed in 1925, the roadway became the first modern multilane, limited-access parkway in North America.

Pasquale had overheard many conversations about the massive project. While the family had no desire to get involved in construction, he gained valuable insight as to where supply and machine yards would be located. By 1910, they had opened three dining cars strategically placed along the planned construction route. These establishments were quiet for the first year, but as the project ramped up, they quickly made a return on their investment. They fed the laborers during the day, quenched their thirst at night, and provided a much-needed outlet to let off steam by hosting card games and an easy access for sports wagering.

By the end of the first decade of the twentieth century, the Scalamarris had become the wealthiest family in the small village. They even purchased a Lambert model 48-C touring sedan and a large home on top of the hill. The house had a wrap-around porch and two fireplaces. It was landscaped with beautiful trees and an apple orchard out back toward the new Siwanoy Golf Club property line.

The Scalamarris then built a new establishment to meet the needs of the changing demographics. In 1917, they tore down the first boxcar luncheonette. It had been located adjacent to the Tuckahoe entry of the Bronx River Parkway. In its place, an elaborate banquet hall was constructed.

The River House served food and alcohol, but most importantly, it also hosted illegal ways to make even more money. While gambling activities had been banned for over a quarter of a century, the Scalamarris operated openly by paying hush money to local law enforcement authorities.

A new set of challenges would soon be faced in 1920 with the passage of the Eighteenth Amendment to the Constitution. Vetoed by President Woodrow Wilson but enacted by the Sixty-Sixth Congress, the Volstead Act outlawed the sale of alcohol. Prohibition was undertaken to reduce crime and corruption while attempting to improve the country's health and social well-being.

Always forward thinkers, the Scalamarris purchased a mass inventory of alcohol during the one-year period between when the law was passed and when it would go into effect. The River House also had many unique structural features that were enhanced and reinforced that year.

When the land was excavated four years earlier, the engineers had a difficult time locating a solid foundation. There were many natural caves and tunnels under the property. While a secure area to pour the concrete was eventually found, the family asked that access to the many arteries leading outward from the property be fortified and built into a sub-basement. The end result was a catacomb of hidden tunnels. This provided ideal storage compartments for their soon-to-be-illegal refreshments as well as escape routes if and when law enforcement officials came their way.

3

LOUISIANA SUPERDOME

January, 11 1996

JAMES "JIMMY TREE" TRACINO had embraced the life of a mobster for as long as anyone could remember. While his older brother, Dominic, had shunned the life and moved out of the state, Jimmy had one goal: to emulate his father.

Born and bred in the Bensonhurst section of Brooklyn, Santo "Tentacles" Tracino was a made member of the Gambino Crime Family. He earned his nickname because he always seemed to have his hands in any number of schemes. His claim to wiseguy fame came after he had moved up to Westchester and opened the infamous Sandy Beach Theater in New Rochelle.

Set along the Long Island Sound, the Sandy Beach scam came to fruition in 1970. After getting a stockbroker to front the deal, Santo and his associates started an urban renewal operation on sixteen acres of abandoned waterfront property. Local politicians were paid off, and the project was brazenly sold to revitalize an area that had once been bustling but was now a trash dump. The end result was the construction of a beautiful theater for live performances that drew major entertainment talent. The place thrived.

Tentacles bilked the place from the start. Duplicate tickets to sold-out events were scalped, cases of premium liquor and high-end meats were stolen, and he received weekly cash stipends from vendors. His construction company even submitted fictitious invoices for enhancements to the facility. When city officials had originally approved the project, it was granted federal and state assistance to revitalize the area. The majority of this "free money" was never reinvested back into Sandy Beach, but rather went directly into Tracino's pockets. He earned respect as a major earner, and his star shone bright. Even when the FBI finally caught up and had Sandy Beach shut down, Tracino did his seven years in silence.

In his absence, his son filled the void. Jimmy Tracino became a major confidant to John Gotti Jr., whose father was the acting head of the Gambinos. Even with the "Dapper Don," Gotti Sr., serving a life sentence in a federal prison, he still led the family up until his conviction. Then, in 1992, the younger Gotti took more control with his father's backing.

As a captain in Junior's crew, Jimmy Tree was in charge of all operations in lower Westchester. Based out of Yonkers, he feasted on a multitude of opportunities to skim money in the construction trade and through all aspects of illegal gambling. He capitalized on extracurricular activities spawned from his two strip clubs and extorted restaurant and other small business owners for protection insurance.

He had made a trip up to Foxwoods to discuss a "thing" with two of his most-trusted guys. The "thing" was an opportunity to work with an NCAA referee who was on the take. Tom Delvin's career as a college basketball official began in 1991 after he had spent four years working Mississippi high school games. A graduate of Fordham Prep and Tulane University, the Yonkers native was a childhood friend of Dom Tracino. Delvin was also a compulsive gambler who had lost tens of thousands of dollars in bets on NBA games played during the 1993/94 and 1994/95 seasons. This unfortunate string of bad luck made its way onto the book of a Gambino associate. Jimmy Tree then approached the unlucky referee to make up his obligation by swaying games he officiated in.

Jimmy Tree and his associates had successfully worked the point spreads and made close to $180,000 dollars on the outcomes of ten games in which Delvin had officiated during that past winter. In four of the games, they had wagered so much that they were able to "play the middle" and ended up winning both sides as the point spread had moved close to two points before tip-off.

"Hey, Sonny, this is Click. What's the spread on the Georgia–Clemson game? Georgia plus four … Okay, give me Georgia two hundred times."

"Yo, Hollywood, this is Clack. What's Clemson–Georgia at now? Wow, spread's down to minus two, give me Clemson two hundred times."

The Clemson Tigers won the early January game against the Georgia Bulldogs 76–73. Jimmy Tree sat smiling on his living room couch, watching players go to the foul line during the final three minutes as Delvin worked his magic to keep the game close.

With the SEC Championship on tap for early March at the Louisiana Superdome, the Gambinos wanted to maximize the final opportunity of the year. Suspicion was sure to be raised if large amounts were bet on a Southern tournament from the Northeast, but Jimmy Tree had an idea. Since he knew Sal and Tony had rare connections in the South, he was certain they could stealthily work his plan through the Cajun underworld. This would be just another way for his valuable associates to make lemonade out of lemons like they had always found a way to do.

Two muscle-bound thugs adorned in gray satin suits and skinny red ties entered Figgaro's Steakhouse. They took in the room, moving their gaze until eventually locating Sal and Tony, who were with an older man, seated in a brown leather booth between two mahogany pillars toward the back. The bruisers left and came back five minutes later with the boss.

Jimmy Tree swaggered into Figgaro's lounge and ordered a Scotch neat. He then called the bartender over and whispered into his ear. After a brief exchange, the message was relayed to a waitress.

"I see you gentlemen enjoyed your meal." The beautiful blonde smiled from ear to ear. She had interrupted Pops as he was finishing up a story.

"You tell the chef he did a great job with my rib eye, perfectly cooked." Sal did not give compliments easily. He was a food snob who would, if a gun were pointed at his head, choose cooking over any other type of career.

"Mine was good, too. I just wish the portions were bigger." Tony proudly opened up both palms of his hands. A half hour earlier, there had been a forty-eight-ounce porterhouse with a mammoth baked potato next to it on the barren plate. Amber, the cute waitress, tried to control her forced laughter as she cleared the table and walked away.

"Anthony, my boy, you are so much like your great-grandfather." Pops's face beamed as he rubbed the top of his grandson's right hand.

"I thought I looked like you?" His grandson was heartbroken.

"Who the hell do you think I got it from? Our side of the family always had an easy time getting the ladies' attention." The old man was really fun to be around.

"Your great-grandfather and even your grandfather had their moments, too, Salvatore. I was only a teenager, but the things I witnessed ..." His words trailed off as his eyes clearly showed a man reminiscing about the good old days.

"Pops, I always get confused by this. Now, Tony, me, and Chris are related by some great-great-great-great-great-grandfather back in Italy in the friggin' early 1800s?"

"Nah, I think it's a great-great-great-great-great-uncle's friend." Sal laughed heartily.

Before Pops could begin to decode the family tree, Amber returned. "There's a gentleman who would like to buy all of you handsome men a drink. I can recommend a good dessert brandy, or I can get another bottle of the cabernet you seemed to enjoy?"

Sal moved his gaze to the front of the establishment. He recognized the source and nodded his appreciation. After Sal sat back down, Tony mirrored his actions. They then deferred to Pops to make the after-dinner selection. After a few moments of silence, he chose the Baron de Sigognac VSOP.

When the snifters arrived, the three toasted *"Salute"* and took a taste.

"Excellent, very smooth. Hey, Pops, will you excuse us? Tony and I have to go say thank you. Be back in a minute." They both walked over to the bar.

Back In The Day
THE EASTCHESTER BLUE DEVILS were the premier youth football club in southern New York. The Pop Warner program, to which the Blue Devils belonged, was founded in 1929 and served as the only youth football organization that required its players to maintain academic standards in order to participate. This commitment separated it from other sports programs around the world.

Formed in 1967, the Blue Devils now fielded teams at every level of play. There were three Junior Peewee teams (for eight- to ten-year-olds) and one team each at the Peewee (for eleven-year-olds), Junior Midget (for twelve-year-olds), and Midget (for thirteen-year-olds) levels.

Besides good school grades, fairness of competition was stressed. If players failed to stay in the appropriate weight range, they were required to move up to a higher level in order to participate. The dedication of players, coaches, and community was clearly shown. Not only did teams compete at a high level, but because of the professionalism of the organization, there were many children from outside of Eastchester and Tuckahoe who strived to play for the Blue Devils.

Since they were toddlers, accompanying their parents to the many games played by Sal's two older brothers, the Columbus Avenue Boys dreamed of donning the pads for the blue and gold. They were told that when they were big enough, they would get to wear the Holy Grail—a Blue Devil jacket complete with position and number embossed on the upper sleeves. When the time finally did come, the trio embraced the challenge. Chris had an easy time with the academic side, and for these three months of the season, Sal and Tony also buckled down and diligently did their homework.

By the time they were ten years old, when they began to sprout through puberty, their mothers' famous cooking had caught up with each of them. They all blew past weight limits and were required to compete at the higher levels with the older kids. It did not faze them in the least, as they flourished at their respective offensive and defensive positions. Chris was a standout running back and linebacker, while Sal and Tony were starting offensive and defensive linemen.

When they moved up to the Junior Midgets as eleven-year-olds playing with twelve-year-olds, they became friendly with a skinny kid with a great sense of humor who also happened to bring with him a bag of candy to every practice.

"Fuck this, fuck that"—shocking language for preteens to hear. However, it was not shocking for their new friend, "Crazy" Jimmy Tracino. When they traveled to the annual bowl game in Georgia, it was also the Columbus Avenue Boys' first introduction to Jimmy's father. The initial impression was that he was the coolest guy in the world. Jimmy swaggered over to him at the hotel lobby bar, demanding quarters to play the video games. Santo took a sip of his drink, reached into his pocket, and took out a four-inch-thick roll of bills. He peeled off a twenty and handed it to his son.

"Make sure you give some to your friends. Come back for more if you run out."

The following year, after sweltering summer practices were over, Jimmy would invite the boys to his mansion to swim in his built-in pool. This was a life they had never even dreamed of.

Unfortunately, all good things come to an end. Jimmy outgrew the Blue Devils, and he never showed his face again. His school was in Yonkers.

That was also when Santo began to feel the pinch of the Sandy Beach scandal. Sal, Tony, and Chris never saw him again and were too involved in their own lives to think much about it.

After high school, with Chris off to college in Texas, Sal and Tony spent most of their free time lifting weights. The place to get huge back in the eighties was East Coast Fitness Center in Yonkers. As with the Blue Devils, East Coast had a powerful marketing campaign. They had the coolest sweat suits and shirts worn by the steroided-out Italian muscle head members. This was all Sal and Tony needed to get hooked. The summer after graduation, Sal's father surprised him with a used blue 1974 Cadillac. They finally had their wheels to take them to the best gym in the area.

They had both grown to be "big boys," standing over six feet four and weighing well over 230 pounds. Even so, those first few months at the gym were an intimidating and humbling experience. They soon found their groove, and their natural strength was enhanced with a lot of hard work. In less than six months they had filled their frames out and now presented very impressive appearances. Both were now over 260 pounds. Their muscles were bulging from everywhere, and many were in awe of their hulk-like transformations.

While primarily training before work each morning, one night they decided to hit the gym before going out on the town.

"Need to get my guns ripped before the club tonight," Tony said as he completed one last set of preacher curls with two forty-five-pound plates.

Sal called over to see what type of protein drink he wanted. While always meticulous, Tony had not had a chance to return the iron plates to the storage rack.

"Just order me a mango strawberry with protein powder. I'll be there in a sec." He yelled this comment back through the mirror as he stopped to admire his throbbing guns. Then he went back to clean his workout area.

Tony apparently was not quick enough for the gym's king muscle head. Felix Bannos was a monster of a man who had given Lou Ferrigno a run for his money at many bodybuilding competitions.

"Hey, new guy, clean your goddamn mess." Bannos pointed at the curling bar and disgustedly shook his head. Then he called to the floor manager, "Henry, make an announcement. These assholes need to clean up their crap."

"Felix, sorry, man, I was coming right back." Tony had made many friends in the gym. With a phenomenal gift of gab, he thought he could easily smooth this over with Mister Muscle.

"I don't give a damn what you were doing, kid." Bannos flexed his shredded triceps in the mirror and then walked past, bumping Tony in the process.

From the direction of the juice bar, Sal's eyes seared through the back of Bannos's head. Tony made eye contact with his blood brother and then slowly walked over. His head was down, and he was shaking it slowly from side to side.

"Not in the mood for my drink right now, my friend. Let's go outside." His eyes were those of a psychopath.

Not another word was said. They sat on the hood of the Cadillac in silence. Sal breathed heavily while Tony mumbled curse words to himself, cracking his knuckles incessantly. Ten minutes later, they got what they had hoped for. Bannos and three friends opened the exit door, laughing boisterously. They had weight belts slung over their shoulders and were waving their arms awkwardly from side to side like robots while slowly walking with inflated chests.

Sal and Tony hopped off and bolted toward the four bodybuilders. With a car key poking out of his right clenched fist, Tony moved faster until he was directly in front of his instigator. Bannos may have had a formidable reputation as a tough guy and was a bouncer at a hot night club in the area, but suddenly he felt uncomfortable.

Sal surged past Bannos, cold cocking the biggest of his three friends. Muscle head number one crumbled to the ground. The two smaller guys backpedaled with hands up in surrender fashion. Sal shooed them away from the heavyweight bout.

Tony slammed the inside of his fist into Bannos's temple. The dull point of the key found its mark and punctured his eye socket. The hulking figure staggered backward, yelping as he attempted to find his bearings. Tony did not let up; he thrust forward and gave a two-hand shiver, exploding into Bannos's chest. *Coach D'Arco of Tuckahoe High would be very proud.* The former tough guy fell to the pavement, rolling onto his side and covering his face with bloody hands. Reaching down, Tony grabbed the back of his neck and slammed the mangled face, smashing it down forcefully against the pavement. He followed it up by kicking him underneath the chin. Bannos's mouth exploded as his bottom teeth were forced through his upper lip.

The crowd that was now building around the uneven bare-knuckle brawl was not disappointed. Tony continued to pummel the larger man, crashing his head against the side of a car. Kick to the ribs—*crack*. He took no mercy.

"Yo, Albanese! Let him go … Enough!" A commanding, familiar voice brought Tony back to reality. He looked over his shoulder and recognized a smiling Jimmy Tracino walking toward him with arms wide.

"He-he! What's up, Jim? Been a while." Tony was now breathing heavily, and his face showed a devilish smile. He gave Bannos one last kick to the head, and then he went over and gave a warm hug to his old friend. Sal also made his way over and did the same. Jimmy had restored calm, and after a short while most of the crowd dispersed.

Bannos remained on the ground, writhing in pain. Jimmy Tree walked over. "These guys are my friends, numb nut. Go clean yourself up."

That occurrence set off a new relationship with their old Blue Devil buddy. Sal and Tony were indoctrinated into Jimmy Tree's crew, and they quickly embraced the life. While previously they had only thought of the prospects of taking steroids, they now went full force on the juice. Deca-Durabolin, Danabol, and Winstrol were regularly cycled into their system, and they became gargantuan and feared throughout the area.

Jimmy assigned them to his crew in northern Westchester locations, but they pleaded with him to develop opportunities in their backyard. As his father had also been connected and ran scams through the restaurant, Sal wanted to capitalize on the expansive upstairs dining room of the establishment. He received approval to host card games and to develop a loan sharking and sports book. It succeeded beyond his wildest dreams.

Besides the singles and doubles hit by collecting the vig and fees for the hundreds of hands of card play each night, triples and homeruns were hit by feasting on degenerate gamblers who got in over their heads. When this happened, say if the owner of a carpet store lost thirty grand during the football season, then a smooth transfer of ownership would occur. Not 100 percent, but just enough for the guys to have their toes dipped into many cash-rich businesses that could then be leveraged to launder money for other Gambino enterprises.

Sal and Tony lived fast and partied very hard. Their twenties were wild times, but luckily they always seemed to skirt the law. By holding card games in town, they knew all the law enforcement officials and made it worth their while to look the other way. No violence was ever committed, and if they ever had to collect with force, the transaction was executed professionally or done quietly and in other jurisdictions.

The reputations they commanded from their bone-breaking early days carried with them into the new decade. They graduated from enforcers to earners. Never destined to get their buttons, they were almost-there wiseguys and forever relegated to associate status. They had limits—almost beating Felix Bannos to death was justified, but they simply could not kill a man they had no emotional connection to. But they were considered stand-up guys, not like the unreliable Young Turks who seemed to be forever seeking recognition to advance. Since Sal and Tony generated so much cash, Jimmy had many other lower-ranking *cugines* with their gold chains and slicked-back hair looking to get made to do his dirty work.

Jimmy Tree got Tony a sweet deal with the teamsters; he became a crane operator, in name only, to show earned income. Tony maximized the environment and realized the construction trade enjoyed spending overtime dollars on gambling activities. He leveraged his power and was elected business agent to represent his local union in contract negotiations.

4

A BEAUTIFUL DAY TO GET MARRIED

January 12, 1935

PASQUALE GLANCED AT HIS pocket watch and then placed it back into the front pocket of his trousers. It was 12:17 p.m. The Harlem line train was eighteen minutes late. These new, heralded electric cars that had been in service for over a year now still ran very inconsistently, especially when the temperature dipped below freezing. He fastened the top button of his overcoat, readjusted his leather gloves, and then leaned over to view the tracks curving from Crestwood Station, located a mile north of Tuckahoe Station. His line of sight was blocked by the broad shoulders of his son, so he had to adjust his stance to see clearly. Vincent was too busy admiring an attractive young woman standing a few feet away, and he appeared oblivious to the cold weather. *Ahh, to be a virile sixteen-year-old and not a broken-down middle-aged man with much on his mind,* Pasquale thought.

Their small empire had been family-owned since the turn of century, but because of the crackdown during prohibition times, Pasquale needed a strong business partner. The local cops were not the problem, but the feds had been a major hindrance to their ability to serve alcohol at one of the most popular restaurant and dance clubs outside of the city.

Pasquale saw the train approaching in the distance. He tapped Vincent to get his attention. They still had ample time to make it to Manhattan for his 2:00 p.m. sit-down with the boss. His son had agreed to come, even though he would not be allowed in the meeting. In the middle of his junior year of high school, Vincent was a good student but still gravitated to the club for most of his free time, and he embraced his apprenticeship at the feet of his father. Pasquale though, still had dreams of his son being the first in the family to attend college.

While they had a lunch reservation at the 21 Club, Pasquale did not expect his discussion to take much longer than a few minutes. Lucky Luciano was always direct and to the point. Born Salvatore Lucania in Sicily in 1897, the lifelong mobster had recently cemented himself at the top of organized crime.

Having grown up on the Lower East Side of Manhattan, he and his longtime associate, a Jewish immigrant named Meyer Lansky, had established themselves as creative criminals. Luciano's notorious reputation led to him working his way up the hierarchy to become a top aide to Giuseppe "Joe the Boss" Masseria. During the 1920s, a turf battle labeled the Castellammarese War ensued between Masseria and rival crime boss Salvatore Maranzano. Masseria ended up losing much of his power, and by 1931 Maranzano's crew began hijacking truckloads of liquor and taking over speakeasies that had previously been under Masseria's control. These underground establishments had flourished throughout prohibition, as the country would not be deterred from their libations and nighttime fun. Much of this liquor found its way to the Scalamarris' banquet hall, as the family had the foresight to change allegiances from Masseria to Maranzano in 1927.

While continuing to expand his bootlegging empire, Maranzano had also built a legitimate business as a land broker in Brooklyn. Vito Scalamarri from the Brooklyn faction had introduced Maranzano to the real estate potential of the growing suburban countryside of Westchester. While on trips north to view properties, he would also stop at the River House. These appearances increased during the height of the Castellammarese War. The locale was away from the heat in Brooklyn and, with its catacomb of tunnels and escape routes, provided an ideal safe house.

Even though Maranzano was gaining the upper hand in the Castellammarese War, Lucky Luciano ended any chance of him becoming the boss of all bosses. First, he orchestrated the murder of Masseria to effectively end the conflict. Then, shortly after Maranzano had called together several hundred Mafiosi to lay out his vision of a new gangland, Luciano had him murdered as well.

Maranzano's vision had been to organize the mafia into five families with Luciano acting as second in command. He also detailed rules for a

Mafia Commission. To signal his dominance, he called the meeting, which was held in a secluded location in Wappingers Falls, to tell influential nationwide figures that he was now the leader of all New York underworld operations.

Maranzano's scheming and arrogant treatment of subordinates as well as his fondness for comparing his organization to the Roman Empire did not sit well with Luciano and other leaders, like Vito Genovese and Frank Costello. Luciano believed Maranzano to be more power-hungry than Masseria, and despite his advocacy for modern methods of organization, many younger Mafiosi resented him. He was considered by many to be a Mustache Pete, and too steeped in the Old World.

Luciano hatched a plan to get rid of the acting boss, but Maranzano found out about this and wanted to eliminate Luciano, Genovese, Costello, and many others. He did not act quickly enough. On September 10, 1931, four of Luciano's henchmen entered Maranzano's office in the Helmsley Building, posing as police detectives. Once inside, they disarmed his bodyguards and then shot and stabbed him to death. Luciano reorganized the Five Families and abolished the position of *capo di tutti capi* (boss of all bosses).

The Scalamarris all reported to Luciano through Bugsy Siegel. Siegel had strong ties to Luciano, Meyer Lansky, and Frank Costello, and he was one of the gunmen who had murdered Joe Masseria. He was also co-head of Murder Incorporated with Meyer Lansky. This group of thugs was established as enforcers for organized crime. These killers were paid a regular salary as a retainer, as well as a fee for each killing. If caught, the mob would hire the best lawyers for their defense.

Siegel had recently moved from Manhattan to nearby Scarsdale in Westchester County. He also had a fondness for hanging around at the River House. With this fondness, he grew from being collector of monthly payments to being a brazen extorter of money and inventory. When prohibition ended, he squeezed even more. In the three years Siegel oversaw operations at the River House, the Scalamarris' profits had been cut in half.

The meeting Pasquale had scheduled for this cold winter day was precipitated by the request of the entire family. They had recently met to discuss their financial future. Pasquale, Antonio, Giuseppe, and Rocco agreed that they must voice their concern to Luciano and let him know that their business was now in serious jeopardy of going under. They were perfectly fine with upping the monthly payment to Siegel; they would even double the amount. In return, they needed reassurance that Siegel would not continue to take advantage of their operations.

May 5, 1935

ON A BEAUTIFUL SUNDAY afternoon, Julia Scalle took the hand of Joseph Cavazzi to be his wife. Limited to family and friends, the River House still overflowed with over two hundred people from across the area dancing, laughing and having a wonderful time.

As was common with immigrant families with many letters in their last names, officials at Ellis Island and its predecessors, Castle Garden, had been very liberal during the documentation process. As a result, the extended Scalamarri family who had immigrated at the turn of the twentieth century all had similar but different names.

The Scalamarris, originating with Vito, lived in the Bensonhurst section of Brooklyn. The Scallaros of Morris Park in the Bronx descended from Rocco. Giuseppe Scalle and his family took root in Manhattan on Mott Street in Little Italy. Pasquale Scalo and Antonio Scala both settled in the town of Eastchester. Antonio lived in a section of the town that eventually became the incorporated village of Tuckahoe.

The River House was the de facto location for all family events with no less than eleven family members having celebrated their nuptials at the establishment. Nineteen-year-old Julia was the daughter of Frank and Isabella Scalle. Her grandfather was Giuseppe Scalle. The five original Scalamarri brothers had passed on, but they had all died proud of the way the family had built a life in America. Four of the sons, headed by fifty-one-year-old Pasquale, ran the operations. He was supported by a multitude of extended family members to carry out their underworld activities.

Since funerals and weddings were the few times the entire contingent seemed to be together in one place, Pasquale decided to call a meeting after the wedding reception. It had now been almost four months since his Luciano sit-down. The boss had said very little during his lamenting about Siegel's extortion activities.

"I'll take it under advisement. Give my best to your family." This was Pasquale's hint from Luciano that the meeting had ended.

To his surprise, over the next few months, Siegel lessened his slippery hand while also spending far less time in the establishment. He sent surrogates to collect the agreed-upon inflated payment, and when he did come he showed no ill will.

The family discussed this good turn of events in the basement office of the River House. Besides Pasquale, Antonio, Giuseppe, and Rocco, there were eight other family members who were interested in hearing the update. In addition to Pasquale's encouraging news, others reported similar favorable changes. It appeared Siegel was loosening his grip at the direction of Luciano.

5

THE GREEN HORNET

February 29, 1996

ON BOARD DELTA FLIGHT 1499 from LaGuardia to Dallas–Fort Worth, Sal and Tony's demeanor was much different from the last time they had flown. During that trip to Puerto Vallarta with their wives, sans kids, they drank eight mini-bottles of vodka while thoroughly entertaining the other first-class passengers with lively stories to kick-start a free vacation at the CasaMagna Marriott Resort & Spa. That type of vacation should have cost over seven grand, but it did not cost them a dime. The two business partners had accepted the gift in lieu of extending payment terms to a steady customer.

Billy Bones was a Wall Street guy who tended to do everything to excess. He worked extremely hard, making four hundred grand as a salesman for First Boston Securities, but he also seemed to work equally hard pissing it away at poker clubs three nights a week and God knows where the other four. Each month he would be on the hook for five thou, but he never failed to pay it back. So when he was late by three months, Tony had to have a good heart-to-heart with him. Billy Bones filled him in on his situation.

"Sorry, Big Tony, I'm not runnin' or nuthin'. Just lost my job. Friggin' managing director left to go to Morgan Stanley, and he didn't bring me with him. They fired the rest of us 'cause they thought they couldn't trust us anymore."

Tony put his big hand on Billy's shoulder and whispered in his ear. "Three months is a long time." He squeezed down, and Bones felt the nudge.

"No worries, big guy. I'm interviewing like mad and guarantee I'll be back making the big bucks real soon."

"That don't put diapers on my little guy, know what I mean?"

"Perfectly understood." Billy smiled nervously.

"My friend, don't you belong to any frequent flyer program or something? Damn me, I don't. Love to, though, could use a nice vaca' every once in a while."

"Actually, I traveled a lot. They had me running around the country nonstop … Never had time to cash in, though … Hey, I got an idea!" Bones breathed out and forced a smile on his face.

Tony agreed to extend terms to his long-standing customer. From the goodness of his heart, Billy transferred over 200,000 Delta frequent flyer points and 350,000 Marriott rewards points so Tony and Sal could take their wives on a much needed rest.

Sal and Tony always tried to maximize lines of business. They realized early on that knowing the customer was an important part of keeping the cash flowing. Immediately after Chris went to work at the investment firm, he gave them the heads-up that there was a huge untapped opportunity that could be exploited. In his role as an analyst, Chris was excessively wined and dined. Brokerage salesmen and analysts would come to Dallas to smooze him so that he would direct more of Conway Wealth's commission dollars through their trade desks. Over the course of getting to know these bankers better, Chris took note. They bragged about how much they traveled and how many free trips they went on because of the vast amount of points accumulated. Since many regular players at Sal and Tony's game also worked on Wall Street, he enlightened his buddies to gather this type of customer information. They took heed, and while they had always required a driver's license so they could track where their investments were, they now asked the type of work and if there were other business-world perks that could be exploited.

It became quite lucrative. Besides the frequent traveler perks, they were also benefactors of the best seats at major sporting events and found their names on the guest lists at the hottest nightclubs. They also received a multitude of the corporate swag, such as polo shirts, gym bags, fleece jackets, and baseball hats.

Jimmy Tree was also given a taste of these perks, but they were now not very inclined to share much of anything with their captain. As they walked through the terminal, people parted like the Red Sea. Normally smiling and upbeat, the bruisers had been uncharacteristically surly for over a month now, and it showed on their facial expressions.

That night at Foxwoods, Pops divulged the unimaginable. Sixty years earlier, most of their family had been murdered at the hands of Bugsy Siegel. Pops despised the Mafia. When Sal and Tony were told this by the person whom they respected most in the world, they were in an utter state of shock. Since Sal's father ran numbers and underground casinos out of Ressini's, they had naively believed that since Pops had managed Ressini's that he had also been actively involved. They were just stupid kids and never privy to the illegal business side of Sal's dad's operations. Then, just as they hooked up with Jimmy Tree, Pops and *Nonna* Teresa retired to Florida. Pops had never been aware of his grandson's livelihood.

When Sal and Tony came back to the table at Figgaro's after the meeting with Jimmy Tree, they were curious as to why Pops demanded to go home immediately.

"Let's get the hell out'a here. Just lost my enthusiasm."

"What's wrong, Pops? You feelin' okay?"

"Feelin' fine, Anthony. Just get the car. I need to speak with you two!"

They got settled for the drive and headed south on 95 as flurries began to fall.

"You boys are better than to hold up with a two-bit, wannabe gangster!" Pops chastised them, and suddenly they felt like they were eleven years old again.

Later That Night

CHRIS CAMERON HAD BEEN sitting in the driver's seat of his forest-green-colored Dodge Shadow with the new Motorola StarTAC mobile phone pressed to his ear. He was checking voice mails and waiting patiently for his buddies to make their way out of the terminal. Sal and Tony still refused to buy into the new mobile phone craze, so he had left them specific details on when and where he would be waiting for them.

It was 10:15 p.m. when he finally spotted their enormous frames emerging from the revolving doors. Both had gym bags slung over their shoulders and were looking around intently. Sal wore a black Metallica concert sweatshirt and formfitting blue jeans. Tony was wearing a pair of olive-green cargo pants and a gray teamster sweatshirt. Of course, he had customized it by cutting off most of the sleeves below the elbow. He never missed an opportunity to showcase his eighteen-inch guns.

Chris snapped the phone shut and flashed his high beams a few times. They noticed, waved, and walked toward the car.

"All the friggin' money you make, and you won't buy a new set of wheels. You are one cheap bastard, Cee," Tony amusingly greeted his friend as he opened the front-passenger-side door.

When Chris had ventured off to Texas again two years earlier, his mother gave him her car as a gift. He pleaded that he could manage on his own, but she knew he had no money and it was far easier for her to walk back and forth to the family store rather than him trying to maneuver a big city like Dallas on foot. He did not have it in his heart to tell her that a six-foot-one, two-hundred-pound man really should not be driving a six-year-old domestic compact car. The vehicle was sentimental, as his father had surprised his mother with it on her birthday two years earlier. This gift was presented right before his father was diagnosed with incurable pancreatic cancer. This was also the first Chrysler Mike Cameron had ever owned. After the Chevrolet plant in Tarrytown had closed down, the longtime General Motors employee took a job at a Chrysler dealership and used the employee discount for the purchase.

Sal lowered the passenger-side seat, tossed the luggage in, and then squeezed into the back. "My friend, I think it's time you returned this vehicle to your mother and get a car without a vagina. How can you drive this in a city with a million pickup trucks?"

"Fuck you, guys. Megyn actually likes it." Chris paused for effect before continuing with the self-deprecating humor. "She said it reminds her of her grandfather. He's got the same one, only in red." They all laughed at his expense.

Chris pulled away from the curb to begin their eight-hour drive. With Sal and Tony jammed in, the "Green Hornet" now looked comically like a clown car, with heads seemingly pressed against the roof and with very little room to maneuver.

The final destination was not Dallas. It was five hundred miles away. In preparation for the SEC Championship at the Superdome, Jimmy Tree had tasked Sal and Tony to find willing bookies on Bourbon Street to spread action around without raising suspicion. Chris had many former teammates throughout the South from his days of playing defensive back for the Texas Longhorns, and he had been a valuable resource to tap into whenever things needed to get done outside the New York area. He let them know there would be no problem laying action through a few old friends who had remained heavy gamblers after their college football days came to a close.

Chris had also rekindled friendships with a number of old teammates in his new role as a research analyst. He had bought into his firm's philosophy that the best source of information on a potential investment was not through the brokerage analyst pitching his work but by visiting the operations of a company to see if it all made sense. He had taken a strong interest to the energy sector. With friends working for companies drilling for oil and gas from the Texas panhandle all the way down to the Gulf of Mexico, he was able to gather a tremendous amount of industry insight. He frequented New Orleans a great deal and conveniently scheduled many meetings on Fridays so he and his fiancée could parlay the time into romantic, long weekends.

Romance was the last thing on any of their minds at the moment. After the jocular greeting at the airport had waned, Sal and Tony filled Chris in on the details Pops had confessed to them. During the first part of the all-night journey, as they sped east along I-20, Tony spent the majority of the time emotionally talking about how his beloved grandfather had witnessed the gruesome murder. The guys thought back to how their grandparents and parents had told many stories of the old days but always seemed to omit references to any turn-of-the-century relative. Though it was always known that there was Scalamarri blood flowing through their veins, there was never an impetus to go through a detailed explanation of the lineage.

They now knew the whole tragic account. It was a devastating story that took them from being rich to just scraping along. Besides the death of most of the men in the family, the business was lost and most surviving relatives were forced to sell their homes or move away.

On the second phase of the road trip, during the four-hour stretch south from Shreveport on I-49, the conversation became more philosophical. Sal simply could not believe his father had willingly allowed him to enter and, more importantly, embrace the life of a gangster. With the Esposito family originally from Brooklyn, he reluctantly concluded that his old man had known very little about the tragic history of the original Scalamarris. The life of a wiseguy was the only one he ever knew, and Sal believed his father would never change his ways. Besides, he died soon after Sal graduated from high school, so there really was never much time to bond on this type of issue anyway.

In his heart, Tony always knew that his father was never connected. His butcher shop on Columbus Avenue had been the family's sole source of income since the 1940s, and "Big Al" attended church regularly. He was a very hardworking man who took the reins of Albanese's Butcher Shop at a very early age. Tony's parents never had much money, and they spent countless hours working at the store. They relied heavily on Poppa Vince and *Nonna* Teresa as well as Maria Cameron to help out during the preteen years of Tony and his sister, Joanne.

In regards to Chris, he also knew his father was not connected. He had worked so many hours at the General Motors plant and the family store, and they still barely had enough money to survive. Chris even left the underworld life for good after a brief and bitter taste of it when he completed his military service. While he initially embraced the adrenaline rush of assisting Sal and Tony with collecting money from deadbeat gamblers and helping run casino and poker nights, his heart was not in it. After his father's dying wish that he end all the illegal nonsense and make something of himself, he pulled away and landed upon a great opportunity in the investment world of Dallas.

With dawn approaching, so was the final leg of their journey. The aftereffects of 7-Eleven burritos and sticks of beef jerky began to take full effect—and in brutal fashion. The Dodge Shadow, with all of the windows rolled down, was not the place an outsider wanted to be. With two hours still to go before they reached New Orleans, they chugged along moving east on I-10. Sal interrupted a half hour of silence.

"I'm done, man. Fuck this shit. Jimmy Tree can try and kick my ass if he likes. He complains that we don't kick up enough, even after surprising him with the blizzard windfall and I guarantee he's gonna think we're holding back on him with this thing in Cajunland. Since his mom's had the stroke, him and Santo have pressed way too much on everyone. All the crews are getting fed up with this bull shit."

He reached down to the Styrofoam cooler behind the driver's side seat and pulled out a Starbucks Frappuccino. He shook it, popped the bottom a few times, and then snapped open the top. He took a huge gulp.

"Seriously, I just don't wanta do it anymore. Cee, put in a good word for me with your boss. I think I'll be a stock analyst, too." He grabbed Chris's shoulder from behind and shook it playfully.

Tony turned to face Sal in the backseat. "We can't just leave, my friend. It's not that easy. Jimmy Tree gave us a hundred grand, and he's not gonna just accept our resignation and two weeks' notice. We have to at least do this one last thing. My heart just isn't in it anymore either after what they did to our blood."

Sanctioned by Lucky Luciano, what Bugsy Siegel and his crew did was commit mass murder. In what was known as the Sunday Night Massacre, twelve family members were burned to death in a five-alarm fire. After the blaze was extinguished, the charred corpses were unrecognizable and interwoven with their limbs bound.

The remains were Tony's great-grandfather Pasquale Scala, Sal's Great-grandfather Vito Scalamarri, Sal's grandfather Benny Scalamarri, and Chris's great-grandfather Frank Scalle. Great-uncles Tino Scalamarri, Santo Scalamarri, Roberto Scalle, Frank Scalle Jr., Rocco Scallaro, Frank Scallaro, Al Scallaro, and Victor Scalo also perished.

Of the extended family members left to mourn were three teenage daughters of Victor Scalo and nine teen and preteen children of the Scallaro widows. Chris's extended family was survived by his great-grandmother Sabina Scalle who raised his great-aunt (*Zia* Fortuna) by herself. His grandmother (*Nonna* Julia) had recently married. Sal's grandmother Mary Ressini became a widow at age thirty and was left alone in Brooklyn to raise three small children alone—her two sons (Marco and Angelo) and her daughter (Dina, who grew to be Sal's mother). Tony's great-grandmother Julianna Scala was widowed and left to raise two daughters (Amelia and Sophia) as well as a teenage son. The son was Vincent, and he was supposed to be side-by-side his father that tragic night.

The Green Hornet made good time. It was not yet 8:00 a.m. when they passed through the historic French Quarter and pulled into the heart of New Orleans' central business district. Chris stopped in front of the Comfort Inn on Barrone Street and let Sal and Tony out to check in. Before he pulled away to the visitor's garage, he lightly tooted the horn. They turned, and Chris leaned over and rolled down the passenger window.

"Guys, I've been thinking this through. Don't stop what you're doing for Jimmy Tree. In fact, you should give the appearance you want to do even more, okay."

"You got a plan or what, Cee?" While he was very groggy and needed a proper nap before going about their business later that day, Sal showed a large, toothy smile as Chris teased them with the introduction of his idea.

"Yeah, I have a plan. If this works, not only will we take out Jimmy Tree, but our relatives will be smiling down on us from heaven if we can pull it all off."

David Carraturo

Scala Family
1860 - 1935

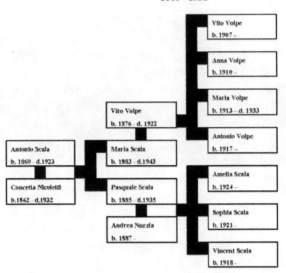

Scalle Family
1856 - 1935

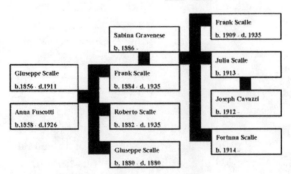

Scalamarri Family
1852 - 1935

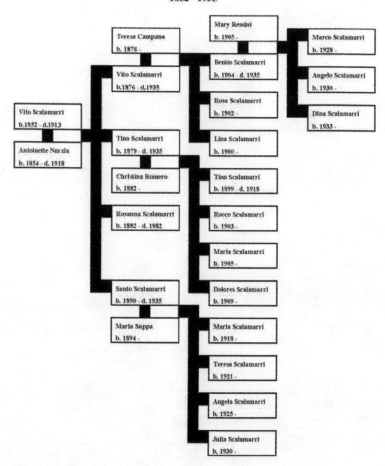

Mary Ressbi
b. 1905 -

Teresa Campane
b. 1878 -

Marco Scalamarri
b. 1928 -

Benito Scalamarri
b. 1904 - d. 1935

Vito Scalamarri
b.1876 - d.1935

Angelo Scalamarri
b. 1930 -

Rosa Scalamarri
b. 1902 -

Dina Scalamarri
b. 1933 -

Vito Scalamarri
b.1852 - d.1913

Lina Scalamarri
b. 1900 -

Antoinette Nurzia
b. 1854 - d. 1918

Tino Scalamarri
b. 1879 - d. 1935

Tino Scalamarri
b. 1899 - d. 1918

Christina Romero
b. 1882 -

Rocco Scalamarri
b. 1903 -

Rosanna Scalamarri
b. 1882 - d. 1882

Maria Scalamarri
b. 1905 -

Santo Scalamarri
b. 1890 - d. 1935

Dolores Scalamarri
b. 1909 -

Maria Suppa
b. 1894 -

Maria Scalamarri
b. 1918 -

Teresa Scalamarri
b. 1921 -

Angela Scalamarri
b. 1925 -

Julia Scalamarri
b. 1930 -

Scalo Family
1853 - 1935

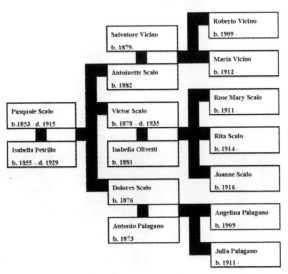

Pasquale Scalo
b.1853 - d. 1915

Isabella Petrillo
b. 1855 - d. 1929

Salvatore Vicino
b. 1879 -

Antoinette Scalo
b. 1882 -

Victor Scalo
b. 1878 - d. 1935

Isabella Olivetti
b. 1881 -

Dolores Scalo
b. 1876 -

Antonio Palagano
b. 1873 -

Roberto Vicino
b. 1909 -

Maria Vicino
b. 1912 -

Rose Mary Scalo
b. 1911 -

Rita Scalo
b. 1914 -

Joanne Scalo
b. 1916 -

Angelina Palagano
b. 1909 -

Julia Palagano
b. 1911 -

Scallaro Family
1858 - 1935

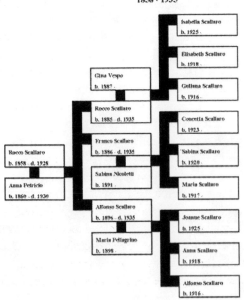

Rocco Scallaro
b. 1858 - d. 1928

Anna Petricio
b. 1860 - d. 1930

Gina Vespo
b. 1887 -

Rocco Scallaro
b. 1885 - d. 1935

Franco Scallaro
b. 1886 - d. 1935

Sabina Nicoletti
b. 1891 -

Alfonso Scallaro
b. 1896 - d. 1935

Maria Pellagrino
b. 1898 -

Isabella Scallaro
b. 1925 -

Elisabeth Scallaro
b. 1918 -

Guliana Scallaro
b. 1916 -

Concetta Scallaro
b. 1923 -

Sabina Scallaro
b. 1920 -

Maria Scallaro
b. 1917 -

Joanne Scallaro
b. 1925 -

Anna Scallaro
b. 1918 -

Alfonso Scallaro
b. 1916 -

6

ENGULFED IN FLAMES

May 5, 1935

EVER THE GENTLEMAN, VINCENT removed his Brooks Brothers suit jacket, reached around, and covered Teresa's shoulders with his oversized garment. The sun was setting quickly on this beautiful spring day, and the temperature had dropped at least ten degrees over the past hour. From his viewpoint, she certainly appeared to be having a nice time. As they walked and talked, he noticed her clasping her arms around her torso, so he rightly decided the chivalrous act was to provide her with warmth.

Teresa was the only daughter of Angelo and Maria Carpinello. Angelo and Pasquale Scala were *paesani*, having known each other since the early days working the grounds at Saint Andrews. His small produce company supplied the River House with fresh fruits and vegetables, and it had been a successful family business for the past twenty-two years. Vincent had met Teresa only once, but that was at least two or three years ago and well before her blossoming into a beautiful teenage girl.

From afar, they appeared to be the perfect couple; strolling and teasing each other as they completed the circular path around the Bronx River Park. This had already been their third loop on what was now a brisk early Sunday evening. On each stop over the wooden bridges, they would look at the mini-waterfalls, stare into reflections in the river, steer clear of the ever-present geese and feed the orange carp swimming below.

While she was one year his junior and he towered over her by at least a foot, it still took the confident and handsome Vincent almost the entire afternoon at his cousin's wedding to ask Teresa to go for the walk. He had first assured her parents that he would drive their daughter home safely and promised that it would be well before it got too dark. The Scalas had recently purchased the Plymouth Deluxe PE, and since Pasquale was currently hosting a meeting, Vincent was sure the car would not be missed.

With the sun setting quickly, they reluctantly decided to head back. Vincent was actually looking forward to this, as he wanted to further impress Teresa with the new expensive car. He planned to walk her to the front door holding her hand, and if lucky he would kiss her good night. Then he would ask her on an official date.

Once off the path, they headed back to the banquet hall and to where the sedan was parked. Only a few hours earlier the largest and grandest structure in the small village had been completely packed, but now there were only five cars remaining.

Vincent felt the need to show off. "Teresa, would you like to see one of our family secrets?"

Her beautiful hazel eyes sparkled. "Oooh, yes. I love surprises."

"All right, but you havta' close your eyes and take my hand." She did so, and his body surged with excitement. Her hand being soft and smooth, he could not imagine any other hand feeling more wonderful than that of his new friend.

He guided her around back, past a row of overgrown bushes and then down a short flight of cement steps. "Careful, watch your head here," he teased her.

He gently touched the back of her flowing auburn-brown hair, which was long and loose now, contrary to earlier in the day when it had been curled up in a bun. As he lowered her head, he thought to himself, *This girl is so beautiful.*

"*Dove mi porti Vincenzo?*" Teresa pressed him in Italian dialect, eager to find out where they were going.

"Careful, it's just another few steps." He guided her below the berm of overgrown weeds and bushes. Now ten feet below ground level, they carefully shuffled up a slightly graded cement walkway constructed adjacent to the Bronx River, away from the River House. They could hear water flowing. Vincent removed a key from his pocket, and then unlocked a steel door. He grabbed the knob and yanked. It creaked with a sound indicating it had not been opened for a quite a while.

"*Per favore Vincenzo*, where have you taken me?" Teresa frustratingly opened her eyes and looked around.

He grabbed her hands and whispered into her ear, "This was a *segreto* entrance. Not many people know about it. I trust you, Teresa." He gently grabbed her right index finger and placed it over her lips in a "shush" gesture.

"*Dove?* Take me to this secret place!" She was excited and ready for an adventure.

"There's a few more of these doors. It's like a maze, and you can get lost if you don't know where you're going. All of them lead to a subbasement. These escape routes were used a lot when drinkin' was illegal, when the feds came to raid the place. Since prohibition ended, they're barely used now. Bet it's all dusty in there."

"I'd love to see where this one leads. Do you know your way around?"

"Been running around this place since I was a kid. I know it better than anyone." He boasted, leveling his hand to his waist indicating half of his six-foot-four-inch height from ten years earlier.

"*Vieni*! Follow me!" He took her hand and escorted her into the darkness. After a few feet, they made a right turn and walked up three concrete steps. Then, after a few more feet, they turned right again, this time walking up a set of six wooden planks.

"The steps below hafta be concrete so they won't rot. Once we get …" He stopped the explanation, hearing unfamiliar voices beaming from the floorboards above.

The young couple froze and stood silently, now listening to an array of deep baritone commands. "Get on the floor! … Back against the wall! … Don't even try it!" This was followed by the scraping of tables and chairs being forcefully turned over and crashing to the ground.

Vincent motioned to Teresa to remain still as he took off his wingtips to mute his movement. He slowly inched closer to better hear and hopefully see the commotion. He reached an area where light was seeping down from a broken floorboard. Bugsy Siegel was standing over his father who was bloodied and sat bound to a wooden chair. The side of Pasquale's face was mangled. It had apparently been slammed with the butt of a Colt Monitor, which the gangster was holding cocked in his right hand.

Bugsy had brought with him a ruthless gang from Murder Inc., which had overwhelmed the surprised contingent of Scalamarri's. Other family members were standing with their hands clasped over their heads, facing the far back wall. One by one they were led out to the hallway.

"Where's the damn safe!" Pasquale shook his head defiantly. He attempted to spit blood, but it *spittled* and smeared on his lower chin.

"No, Bugs. It's our family money. You've gotten your fair share. We can't give you more." Tears flowed down the side of his face, but he held his ground.

"No one calls me Bugs!" He took the butt of his Monitor and slammed the other cheek. Then he grabbed a mat of hair and threw him to the ground. Pasquale hit the floor with a thump. Bugsy stood above him, kicking his ribs as he held a handful of his salt-and-pepper hair. Lying on his side, helpless, Pasquale screamed in pain with his bound body constricted by the ropes tied around his arms and legs.

Vincent's eyes welled, and he clenched his fist, viewing the nightmare. He was standing less than three feet from his father but could do nothing to help. Two of the henchmen located the drop safe on the other side of the room. It was hidden in the floor of a closet behind the desk. They dragged Pasquale over.

Siegel bent down. "One last time. Scala … Give me the goddamn combination, and everyone'll live," he whispered menacingly into the broken-down man's ear.

Pasquale finally relented, gave the code, and then closed his eyes. Siegel's men quickly opened the safe and began taking a bevy of cash, gold bars, and jewelry. They left nothing of value behind.

After the robbery was completed, the other family members were thrown back into the small confines of the office. They lay in a large pile on the floor. All of them were hog-tied and beaten badly. Silence enveloped the room, but after a few moments, it was quickly replaced with groans and sobs. Vincent exhaled and bent down to put on his shoes, hoping the torture was finally complete.

He was wrong. As he turned to face Teresa, she witnessed his crying eyes illuminate in the darkness. Upon their retreat, Siegel's men had thrown two glass bottles into the small confines. Filled with kerosene and lit rags, the projectiles shattered and exploded on the back wall. The room was quickly engulfed in flames. The henchmen tossed a dozen more flaming bottles throughout the banquet hall and then hurried out of the building.

Vincent ran toward Teresa and guided her to their original point of entry. Then he spun around and ran back toward the fire. He made a left turn up a flight of stairs to a now-raging inferno. It had rapidly expanded up to the main floor, and the wooden beams and boards began to creak.

The intensity of the heat was unbearable as the teen maneuvered the few feet through the narrow walkway toward the office door. He knew it was too late to save them, but he also did not want his father and other family members to die like this. After another step, he felt the rumble and subsequent eruption of the office floor imploding into the subbasement level. He hoped Teresa had reached safety.

Vincent screamed uncontrollably, covering his face with his shirt. A searing ember from a ceiling beam crashed a few feet away and brought him back to his senses. He realized his mission was futile and he must now try to save himself. He turned, ran down the lightless hallway, and slammed into a concrete wall. Then he pivoted and made his way left and up a flight of stairs to the main ballroom. The walls were now ablaze, and the intensity of the heat was growing by the second. He sprinted toward the west side of the building, running as fast as he could, and then dove on his chest for the last ten feet into the safety of the kitchen. He leaped up and moved a metal table situated in front of a wooden door in the back of the room. Throwing it open, he grabbed hold of a fireman's pole and slid down two stories below. He slammed against the concrete subbasement floor, leaped up, and headed toward the northwest exit of the tunnel. He staggered down the hallway, unlatched three deadbolts, and forced the steel door open with his left shoulder. A blast of fresh air greeted him. Sirens were wailing in the distance as he took a knee, coughed out smoke, and tried to catch his breath.

Now in a trance, he staggered around to the front of the building and walked toward the parking lot and then into the idle Plymouth. He drove off seconds before the fire engine arrived and minutes before the River House disintegrated into the ground below.

A Few Minutes Later
VINCENT WIPED HIS EYES as he drove away from the fire pit. Beginning a hilly climb away from town, he abruptly stopped short.

"Teresa!" She was holding her shoes in one hand, walking slowly away from town and up Tuckahoe Road. She stopped upon hearing Vincent call out her name and ran over.

"Vincent, are you okay?" They embraced and cried. He kissed her cheek, closed the door, and then drove off.

It was not safe to go back home. While he believed Siegel would not kill women or small children, Vincent knew that as a teenager, he would be sought after. Bugsy was known to close loose ends, and since he had been present many times when the gangster met with his father, he knew they would be out to find him.

At the Carpinello home, Vincent broke down retelling the horrific details. Teresa's mother gave him a shot of whisky, a new shirt, and a pair of pants. He then washed the soot and ash off his face and body. They packed a small satchel of food and a suitcase of clean clothes. Mr. Carpinello also handed him all the money he had on his possession, twenty-three dollars, for his travels.

It was almost eleven in the evening when Vincent began his journey. He entered the Bronx River Parkway heading south and, after ten minutes, took the westbound exit onto Route 1, which brought him over the George Washington Bridge and into New Jersey. He drove south for approximately four hours before reaching Thirtieth Street Station in Philadelphia. He parked the sedan a block away on Market Street. Mr. Carpinello would retrieve the vehicle later that day, return it to Vincent's grieving mother, and relay word that he was safe.

With a suitcase in his hand and a food satchel slung over his shoulder, Vincent walked north on the deserted street, toward the rail yard below. He snaked through an opening in a fence and made his way down an embankment. He was not alone, just one of what seemed like hundreds of young men waiting to jump on a box car and head away from it all. At the height of the Great Depression, almost a quarter of a million teenagers were roaming the country. These hobos hopped the rails for a myriad of reasons. Many were unemployed, lived in poverty, or came from shattered homes.

Vincent approached a group of teens who looked to be of Italian descent.

"*Amici, sediamaci e mangiamo un po?*" He offered some dried salami, and they all sat to eat. He towered over all of them in height, so they accepted the gift and welcomed him to their cluster.

"Sure thing. Thanks fella', mighty swell of ya'. Been a while since I've eaten." Most of these boys were undernourished and readily ate the small morsels he shared.

Teresa's parents had made sure to provide Vincent with ample food stock, as he had no idea how long his journey would be. In his satchel was a supply of fresh apples, dried cheese, and salami as well as a few loaves of bread. Even after he shared with the gang, he still had plenty to last him for the next day or so.

"We're getting ready to go. You're welcome to join us. Headin' west!"

Dawn approached, and the scraggly bunch made their way to a freighter that had started to lurch forward. Vincent led the pack, racing to hop onto the slowly moving train. He reached an open car, flung his belongings on board, and held a metal pole to help two others up. As he finished assisting the last one, he felt a tug on his fingers.

"Knock him off! Rip his fingers apart!" He saw two teens attempting to pry his grip. Behind them, he glanced at another beginning to pillage his belongings.

With his free hand, he instinctively grabbed the torn shirt of the attacker and easily tossed him over the side. The youth fell to the gravel below and rolled away from the tracks where he was engulfed by the weeds along the edge.

The train picked up speed. Vincent regained his footing. He let go of the pole and slammed his hands together against a shorter boy's head, boxing his ears forcefully. Writhing, the kid grabbed his head and crouched forward. Vincent thrust his right knee into the bent-over face. The youth's nose exploded as his head snapped backward. This boy's journey ended as a writhing mad Vincent snatched his arm and flung him out of the now fast-moving train. His faint scream was barely heard as they sped forward along the tracks.

The three remaining hobos looked on in a mix of fear and shock before quickly scurrying away from his belongings. He pressed on and kicked one in the chest. The weakened boy flew backward, crashing into a wooden crate. Another tried to get away by crawling behind a pallet of boxes. Vincent would not let up as he corralled him.

"Dead end, my friend." He kicked and slammed his head into the exposed wall.

Vincent turned away and returned to the open area to look for the final youth. While still ready to fight, Vincent put his arms down in relief when he located the boy who was cowering in a corner and crying uncontrollably.

"Pa ... pa ... pa ... lease, sir ... I won't bother you anymore."

It had been a very emotional twelve hours. Vincent quietly repacked his belongings and then put his head down on his suitcase where he silently cried himself to sleep.

He kept to himself during the train ride and did not speak with the three defeated boys again. They did not bother him, and he amusingly watched them huddled in the shadows as he chomped on an apple or tore off a piece of bread. In the daylight hours Vincent took in the fresh air and sunshine while attempting to figure which state they were passing through; *Pennsylvania or Ohio*? When nighttime came, he gave up on his landmark game. He fell asleep as they cut across Indiana and into Illinois. By 3:00 a.m., the freightliner came to a stop.

He gathered his belongings, hopped off, and began walking through the massive Chicago Clearing Yard, heading east in the direction of the rising morning sun. This facility was one of the largest hump classification locations in the country. Just west of the city, the railroad yard was used to separate cars onto tracks in preparation for their final destinations across the country.

Accompanied by a group of sullen travelers, Vincent found his way onto Marquette Road, and began a long, arduous walk. He completed the sixteen-mile journey in less than six hours. Starving and exhausted, he staggered to the center of the city. He stepped into the Clark Street Diner for a proper meal and to collect his thoughts.

He heard the bells denoting his arrival and then cast a faint smile. The layout incorporated a familiar railroad car look with a long white counter and rotating stools to sit on. Six booths hugged the outer wall, which provided seating for larger parties. It was very similar to the dining cars his family had owned and that he remembered from the now long-gone days of his youth. He staggered back toward the corner and sat in an empty booth. When the waitress came by, he ordered a roast beef sandwich and a cup of coffee. She walked away, and he sat in silence. Not being able to hold back any longer, he placed his hands over his face and sobbed uncontrollably. The dirt on his hands mixed with tears to further mess his disheveled appearance.

The bells clanked again, and he soon felt the presence of another person. Regaining his composure, he opened his eyes. As he looked across the table, he expected to see the waitress with his coffee and sandwich. Sitting directly in front of him was a man equal to him in size, but with a buzz cut of red hair. The gentleman was wearing a sharply tailored khaki, short sleeve shirt of the United States Marines.

7

BLOOD ON HIS HANDS

March 21, 1996

MITCH BASSETT SMILED AS he hung up the phone and drained the last drop of cold coffee from his SMU Mustangs mug. He had just finished an impromptu ten-minute conversation with one of the men he had served with as an Army Ranger. If it had been up to him, the chat would have gone on for another hour. He always enjoyed reminiscing with the brethren he had fought, trained and socialized with from Bravo Company.

Specialist Mitchell Kelvin Bassett had been honorably discharged from the US Army in May of 1990. His return to civilian life transpired shortly before Saddam Hussein invaded and annexed Kuwait. Over the ensuing six months, Mitch frustratingly watched Operation Desert Storm unfold on CNN while he sat helplessly in his cubicle wearing a suit and tie crunching numbers as an accountant in Exxon's acquisition group.

The man whom he had just spoken with had been awarded the Silver Star for his valiant action during the early days of Desert Storm. His medal citation read that while taking part in a late-night extraction, he maintained an exposed position in order to engage the attacking enemy force. Wounded in the battle, he provided a steady stream of cover fire and killed four enemy fighters. His seven patrol members made their way safely to a Chinook helicopter and then provided cover fire for him. One of those men who made it back happened to be the best man at Mitch's wedding.

Specialist Bassett was a veteran of Operation Earnest Will. With Bravo Company in 1987–88 he supported both the Navy SEALs Special Boat and the 160th Special Operations Aviation teams in protecting Kuwaiti-owned oil tankers from Iranian attack during the Iran–Iraq War. With hands-on experience in that part of the world, he thought long and hard about reenlisting. If the combat phase of the war had lasted longer than six weeks, then he probably would have.

Those military events did lead him to rethink his current career choice. As he looked around his cubicle, he realized that he really was not an accountant. So in the immediate aftermath of the Gulf War, he submitted an application with the Federal Bureau of Investigations. When he received his acceptance letter six months later, he resigned from the oil company without looking back.

The FBI was made up of tens of thousands of men and women similar to Mitch. He was the youngest of five children. His mother was an elementary school teacher while his father was a decorated Korean War veteran and a thirty-year Texas state trooper. Mitch excelled in both academics and sports at Vines High in Plano before attending nearby Southern Methodist University on a football scholarship. As a fullback, "Bam-Bam Bassett" utilized his six foot, 235-pound frame to blow open holes for the Pony Express combination of the great Eric Dickerson and Craig James during the heyday of SMU football. He graduated with honors from the Cox School of Business with a degree in public accounting before hearing the call to serve.

His intelligence-gathering and corporate world experience came into play early on in his FBI career. While working undercover for the Dallas field office, he took part in a twenty-month sting operation, posing as an official selling a compact ultrasound device used to dissolve kidney stones. The target was a small NASA contractor based out of League City that would later be convicted of federal kickback and bribery charges.

Now in between assignments, he welcomed the call from his fellow Ranger. They had agreed to meet for dinner at Bob's Steakhouse. The Lemmon Avenue eatery was probably the best in Dallas. His old friend worked as an investment analyst, and he was researching whether to take an equity stake in a military contractor. He wanted insight into the potential liability the company could have related to a pending lawsuit that was buried among the footnotes in their 10K SEC report.

Mr. Bassett called his wife of two years and told her that he would not be home for dinner and would probably be back very late. If former

Fire Support Specialist Cameron was the same guy whom he remembered him to be then, Mitch was sure that besides the investment discussion, he and Chris would find time to tear it up a bit at the bar to help digest their steaks.

Later That Night

THANKFULLY THE DRIVE FROM the Crescent Court to Lemmon Avenue was only fifteen minutes, even on a heavily trafficked night. Chris hated to be late for anything but especially for a dinner appointment that he had initiated with an old army friend he had not seen in almost six years. It was 6:45 p.m., and he had spent the past three hours listening to four quarterly conference calls of companies his firm owned large equity stakes in. By 6:30 p.m., he was confident that all of these oil drillers would continue to meet their earnings guidance. By early next morning he was also sure to receive at least a hundred e-mails and voice mails from almost every energy analyst on Wall Street reiterating their opinions in the hope he would steer equity trades to their firm.

I really have the best job in the world. Not only did Chris admire the man he worked for, he was also enthralled by the whole process of dissecting balance sheets and income statements to uncover hidden gems. It was a great test to his intelligence every time he found an undervalued investment to commit millions of dollars toward.

The income was good, too. He had started work at Conway Wealth in 1994, making $60,000 in salary and a $40,000 bonus. That had been twice the amount he had ever made in his entire lifetime. Last year his salary was raised to $80,000 with a bonus of $100,000. Because of his stock-picking prowess, he was recently promoted and his base salary was raised to $250,000. He was expecting at least a $500,000 performance bonus this year alone. This was perfect timing, as he and Megyn were getting married on April 27 and they needed every penny to make it work.

Monroe Conway had treated him exceptionally well from the start. He and his wife, Celia, welcomed him into their home. He had needed the time to adjust to the city while he found a reasonable place to live, which ended up taking three months. From that first night sleeping in the Conways' spare bedroom, Chris vowed to work his butt off and not let him down. So as not to impose, he spent countless hours at the office or out conducting grassroots analysis on potential investments. The fifteen-person firm worked cohesively together, and they all reaped the rewards of clients confidently allowing Conway Wealth to invest millions of dollars of their hard-earned savings.

Chris's life in New York had been significantly different than his time so far in Dallas. He grew up in a lower-middle-class family in close proximity to his two oldest friends. His father was "off-the-boat Irish," and his mother was a second-generation Italian. They never had luxuries or extravagances. His and his friends' mothers were distant cousins, and for all intents and purposes, they were brothers. They had lived as one family, with parents and siblings acting as de facto surrogates for one another. Chris would laugh as full-breed Italians, like Sal and Tony, emulated his father's brogue by attempting to copy his dialect from his youth in County Wexford. If you had had your head turned and heard Sal copying his uncle "Irish Mike," you would have thought he had red hair and freckles and not thick brown hair and an olive complexion.

They worked endlessly at their small, family-owned businesses, and Chris rarely remembered seeing both parents at the same time for more than a day out of the week. They owned a homemade macaroni store, and his father also worked as a foreman for the General Motors auto assembly plant in Tarrytown. Tony's family owned a butcher shop. Sal's family owned Ressini's Restaurant. Unfortunately, due to his illegal activities, his father also spent a considerable amount of time in jail while Sal was young.

Chris's father had encouraged him to expand his boundaries in all he did. Whether it was reading a book, solving a math problem, having a discussion, or working a puzzle, Michael Cameron pressed his son to be the best. He encouraged him to leave home (as he did at a young age) to attend the University of Texas, and he was proud when he served his country. As Michael lay on his death bed, he praised Chris's efforts to succeed and knew his son could be the best in anything he did.

"Make me and your mum proud, Christopher. I've never taken a breath where I was not honored to be your father." This was one of his last words to his son. Chris was driven from that moment to not be a failure in life.

He was gifted, and in a lot of ways. He excelled in sports to the point where a top college football recruiter noticed his abilities while scouting a player on another team who was the supposed best running back in the state. Chris chased him down not once but twice. He forced a fumble on a jarring hit and ran an interception back fifty-five yards for a touchdown.

Just in case the scout had not noticed up to that point, he ran an off-tackle play forty-six yards on the last play of the game.

In the classroom, his teachers were taken aback by his grasp of history and mathematics, and he graduated second in his class. There were times when he would get visibly excited debating current events. He was well up to speed on many issues, as he had worked diligently with his father while he studied to become a United States citizen. He also tutored Sal and Tony frequently. As added fodder, his beliefs were the exact opposite of his sister, who was as liberal as they came. Chris always had to be well-armed to debate Sabina, and they had many a discussion on history, politics, and social values. Both siblings had the dominant traits of their parents. His father had a fantastic memory and always worked a task until completion, never admitting defeat and always being a good friend. Their mother was the general of the family, and she demanded they treat all with respect. His parents also adored each other, and they would embarrassingly show this affection at all times. She was by far the best cook in town.

After his father passed, and with his subsequent move to Dallas, Chris vowed never to go back to the way of life that was embraced by his friends. Very close to having "arrived" in the world, he could never imagine living as a thug again.

Like Sal and Tony, though, he did have blood on his hands. But he was very content for having it there. Sal was the youngest of three brothers, and John and Robert toughened him up (sometimes too much) and also protected him throughout his youth. Tony's sister was five years younger, and he protected and watched over his Joanne at all times. Sabina was one year older than Chris, and he had much guilt about not watching over her better. Unbeknownst to the family, as a child she had been tragically molested by an uncle. She was severely traumatized by the events and by her early twenties had begun to drink heavily. Sabina had done this to help deal with the pain and anguish. At this lowest point in her life, she had confessed all of the horrific details to her brother.

While this piece-of-shit uncle had moved away to Florida years earlier, Sabina saw him once again at their father's funeral. This encounter triggered nightmarish memories and brought them to the forefront. After hitting bottom, she began a program of alcohol and psychological treatment to address her problems. Chris, though, still felt a need for vindication and closure for this monster's actions. So, besides mulling over financial reports, he also spent many late hours plotting a way to torture uncle molester.

It all came together while analyzing a luxury-yacht maker. The economy had begun to grow, and Chris believed luxury good purchases were poised to rebound. In the course of his due diligence, he visited the manufacturing facility of Platinum Marine and Engine Works in Miami. At the facility he had an epiphany: he realized how to commit the perfect crime. He thought that among the Sunshine State's illegal immigrant population, there must be some willing and able hombres eager to earn extra money. If they could get the body on a boat, once out in the ocean, vengeance could be fully exerted.

As a result, the Columbus Avenue Boys formed a plan that flawlessly came to fruition two days before the New Year. It consisted of Sal and Tony (with the assistance of Cuban kidnappers) taking the bound body of Uncle Pat out to the Atlantic. They used Tony's meat-cutting skills to brutally torture and dismember the pathetic old man. Then they tossed the useless body parts over the side to send him to hell the only appropriate way. This course of action was also an added measure for Sabina to receive closure. Sal and Tony had casually presented the plan to her throughout the year. This method of persuasion led her to sanction the execution. She fully believed it was the right thing to do to gain closure and to be able to move on and get stronger. While Sabina had the heart of an angel, the pain she had endured from this animal led her to want to accompany Sal and Tony on the boat. She was there to witness the gruesome ending. They had even borrowed the boat of her boyfriend's parents to carry out the deed.

Sal and Tony decided from the start to disassociate Chris from the plot as much as they could. They were even able to convince Sabina that her brother was unaware of the plan. Chris did provide the financial commitment with his first bonus from Conway Wealth being primarily allocated toward the $20,000 for the Cubans' assistance, but his two gangster friends did not wish to include him in the festivities. He had far too much to lose professionally if things went wrong along the way.

As was always the case when Sal and Tony conducted business, the entire operation was handled flawlessly. There had not even been a missing person report filed for the deceased in the three months since his unfortunate departure from this world. He appeared to be the only person broken up about it.

In Chris's mind and heart, unfinished business had finally been finished. He was content with the consequences for this horrible old man and slept very comfortably beside Megyn every night, knowing Uncle Pat would never be able to harm another innocent soul. However, even before the Louisiana trip, he had begun to think about how to pull Sal and Tony out of the underworld life. To their core, they were good men. They had simply gotten involved, while at a young age, with the very wrong people.

The dilemma was that they both needed to survive physically and financially. Counterbalancing this was that they did not have it in their heart to continue this way of life anymore. Since you simply could not resign and move on from the Gambino Crime Family, Chris wanted to discuss an alternative route with his old Ranger buddy.

Chris arrived at the overflowing eatery at precisely 7:00 p.m. and was lucky enough to find a parking space a block away. He laughed to himself on the two-minute walk from Rollins Avenue, thinking that Sal and Tony were right. He would have to step up and buy a new car. He could not keep parking his mother's jalopy blocks away instead of being embarrassed to pull up to the valet. Besides, he was making good money now and a new car was definitely warranted. Maybe he would even buy his mom one, too.

Before he had a chance to ask the hostess if the other member of his dinner party had arrived, he felt a tap on his shoulder. He and Mitch gave each other a proper man hug. Then they were led through the maze of small rooms to the table for two. Chomping on marinated pickles and sweet peppers in the center of the table, they began the conversation with small talk about family and friends. Mitch's wife was five months pregnant with their second son, and Chris was looking forward to tying the knot.

By the time the appetizers had arrived and they began to feast on the scrumptious shrimp platter, a good opportunity had come to segue to the topic of the evening.

"So you need my help one more time, huh, C. J.?" After Mitch made the comment, Chris thought back to the time when he and Specialist Bassett had served together. He remembered initially having a hard time recognizing the sounds of different types of ordnance, and pressing Mitch to help him get better at it. It didn't take long for him to figure it out, and he repaid the gesture to Mitch on more than one occasion.

"Yeah, buddy. I know I said this was work-related, but it's not; it's personal. It's about a dicey problem two buddies of mine have gotten themselves into." Chris swiped the last shrimp through the remnants of the rémoulade and swallowed it whole.

"I gather it's something my current employer would be interested in discussing?" The federal agent looked like he also wanted the last shrimp. They were so good and a great appetizer before his pending eighteen-ounce bone-in Kansas City.

"You could say that. Maybe not here in Dallas but definitely in the Northeast." Chris phrased the comment without giving away too much meat to the story. "You may remember me mentioning from time to time that I had some crazy friends back in the neighborhood where I grew up, right?"

"Yes, sir, I actually do recall that a bit. You tried to make fun of my cow-tipping escapades compared to you hanging out with Gotti's son. That big-city shit may be a bit more intense than life in rural Texas, but watching a cow flailing in a pasture is quite hysterical." Mitch gave a soft chuckle as he eyed the waitress placing a twelve-ounce filet mignon and massive baked potato down in front of Chris. Then he slightly tilted backward so she could place his steak and a huge broiled glazed carrot in front of him.

As they started on their main courses, Chris told more. "My buddies are really gentle giants, but the mob life is all they know. They took to it like fish to water, but now they just don't have it in their heart to continue."

Like a potential investment, he then described major assets in Sal and Tony's portfolio, potential liabilities, competition to their business model, and importantly, the internal politics of possibly pissing off ruthless killers.

"These guys run one of the of the most trafficked card games in the New York metro area. Heck, I remember a night when I played in a hand against this wiseguy named Frankie Scars. I almost shit my pants as this guy cursed me out 'cause I re-raised on a bluff, then sucked out on him. As I scooped up the chips, Sal intervened and calmed him down. The guy was embarrassed because his brother 'Nicky Little Neck,' who was also playing, teased the shit out of him about being taken to the cleaners by some fresh-faced kid." He had a lot more information on this wiseguy who also ran a Wall Street pump-and-dump scam out of a bakery warehouse in Staten Island.

Chris laughed as he told the story. With years of Special Forces training to fall back on, he could have easily taken care of the situation on his own. Regardless, he thanked God that his buddy was there to restore order. He always downplayed his appearance when playing cards and hid his muscular frame in baggy sweats. Most wiseguys knew him as the guy who was a friend of Sal and Tony, not their blood brother and a decorated war veteran and trained killer.

"They have some funny-ass nicknames?" Mitch looked interested to hear more.

"You think Donny Nose, The Chin, Italian Dom, and Crazy Johnny are strange names, huh?" Chris amusingly shook his head and then looked into Mitch's eyes very seriously. "Heck, I just wanta get these guys out and into respectable ways to earn a living. They have way too much to live for to go on like this."

"I know you wouldn't just dust off an old friendship and call in a favor if this were not serious. What you just divulged about these two guys intermingling and being well respected by the Mafia higher echelon seems definitely worth hearing more about." Mitch took a sip of his beer.

"We need this to work on so many levels. They want to take down those bastards." Chris drained his beer and signaled the waitress for another round.

"Tell me more. What else have they done that could blow up if I go to bat for you here? Of course I can give you a stellar endorsement ... but I don't know them from shit." Mitch whispered across the table, "Are they killers, extortionists? Heck, dude, why should we trust them?"

Chris politely answered by nodding his head forward a few times and smiling slightly, but never confirming verbally that his buddies were the ruthless thugs who earned respect by simply being ruthless. Besides, fresh off the ceremonial execution of poor old Uncle Pat, he did not want to divulge any more information than he had already.

"Mitch, I will tell you that these guys are the most loyal, stand-up men I know. Whatever they did they did to survive ... No excuses ... I know if we can come to an agreement, then what they can do for you is open up Pandora's box, give you the keys to the Emerald City, strike oil. Use whatever metaphor you like. All I'm saying is that the wealth of information they have under their dirty fingernails is more than enough for you guys to stay busy for a heck of a long time."

Chris wanted to treat for dinner, but rules were rules, so they split the check down the middle. They also decided that to further the evening was probably not the proper course of action. Special Agent Bassett said he would be in touch in very short order.

8

ONE SPECIAL PERSON

July 17, 1941

ON A SUNNY AFTERNOON in Cleveland, Joe DiMaggio's two hard-hit shots were countered by great plays by the Indian third baseman, Ken Kelter, and that was it. The fifty-six-game hitting streak had come to an end. *Time to start a new one, I guess?* The odds had been stacked against the Yankee Clipper from keeping it going much longer anyway, but it was still an amazing accomplishment. Vincent read about these daily exploits of his fellow Italian-American and was enthralled throughout the entire streak. It was the perfect way to keep his New York blood flowing during his rest and relaxation in the Southern California sun before he would join up with his new division.

Since coming back stateside, he had maintained a strict daily routine. A morning run on the beach was followed by calisthenics. Then he headed into the San Diego surf for a brisk swim. By noon he would pick up the *Union-Tribune*, stroll back to his apartment, and check for mail. More important than reading the sports section was the anticipation of receiving a letter from Teresa Carpinello. It had been six years since he had seen her, and these notes contained the words that kept his heart pumping.

He perused the horse race lines from Del Mar, and checked baseball scores. While reading articles and box scores, he would fondly think back to the friendly banter about who was the better New York baseball team— the Yankees, Giants, or Dodgers. With his relatives scattered throughout the New York City area, the fan allegiance had been evenly split. If his cousins or uncles had still been alive today, they would have witnessed his Yankees win four World Series in a row including two against the Giants. This year there was a good possibility the Dodgers would finally get their chance while the Yanks and Joe D still had to get through the Red Sox and Ted Williams.

Vincent missed the days when he would skip school and sneak off to watch his favorite Lou Gehrig play. But as the Scalamarris' lives were forever changed, the Iron Horse was also dealt a fatal blow and was forced to retire from baseball in 1939 after being diagnosed with an incurable illness. Gehrig had played in 2,130 consecutive games, which began from the time Vincent was seven and lasted till was twenty-one, a remarkable fourteen straight years.

Regardless of the great Yankee accomplishments, his only real idol in life was his father. Pasquale had been fully aware of his only son's admiration of the first baseman and had surprised Vincent on his tenth birthday. Besides tickets to the 1928 opening day game, he had arranged a private dinner for his son with the two Yankee greats—Gehrig and Babe Ruth—the night before the start of the season.

The Babe was a member of Leewood Golf Course in Eastchester. He had been a frequent visitor to the River House, and the Bambino owed Pasquale a huge favor. Pasquale had leveraged connections with the Bronx River Parkway commissioner to approve construction of an underpass near the entrance to the golf course. After playing eighteen holes, he needed a quick exit to get to the ballpark for an afternoon game. Vincent fondly remembered sitting near the two greats during that special dinner. He thought that they were the lucky ones, sitting with the best dad in the world.

Vincent missed so much: his family and friends, the comfort of the neighborhood, the delicious food, talking baseball, and one special person most of all. So after he finished reading the sports news, he neatly placed the paper on the corner of the kitchen table and for the third time that afternoon reread his most recent letter from Teresa.

My Dearest Vincent,

I received your last letter and the three pictures of you. Thank you for the silk scarf from the Orient. It is beautiful. I love the floral print. The pictures are wonderful, and you appear so tanned and healthy. The beaches in California look nice. I hope you still miss me as much as I you. I truly wish I could come be with you in San Diego. Since you will now be stationed there, I would have loved to visit you.

Regrettably, I cannot make it at this time but plan to come out to visit you after Christmas. My father has taken a turn for the worst, and we do not think he will last much longer. As you know, he has been sick for two years now, and by the time you receive this letter he may be gone. I simply cannot leave Momma at this time.

We have lost the business, and my brothers have gone off to work at a submarine plant in Connecticut. They send her as much money as they can. I have just gotten a job as a telephone operator, and that should help support the family so we do not lose the house. Hopefully, the economy will get better.

Lovingly yours,

Teresa

He carefully folded and placed the note in the El Producto cigar box situated in the top drawer of his dresser with the fifty or so others he had accumulated over the past six years. He then went to the icebox for a can of Schaefer, snapped open the top, and took a healthy swig.

While he and Teresa had only known each other for a brief moment, she was his reason for breathing every day. Because of the prolonged length of the depression, the thought of leaving the military simply was not an option. The money he earned in the Marines had been good, and he regularly sent his mother much of his pay. Luckily, he was able to capitalize on his skills as a well-above-average poker player for extra cash.

His original Fourth Marine Division mates learned soon after basic training at Camp Holcomb not to play against him in a serious card game. Then, while stationed in Beijing as part of the Embassy Guard detachment, he found new pigeons to pluck at the expense of the hundreds of unsuspected British, French, and Italian troops also assigned to the Chinese city. When he was withdrawn to the Philippines in 1939 after the Japanese and Chinese fighting had intensified, his Filipino opponents fared even worse.

As he looked out from his kitchen window at the waves breaking along the Southern California surf, he remembered back to that tragic night. He thought about his father frequently, as he had always been by his side at every turn. His goal in life was to be half the man his father was and to strengthen the family once again.

For now, it was all gone. From status updates he received from Teresa and his mother regarding the tragedy, he had committed himself to send as much money home as he possibly could. They had lost their beautiful house on top of the hill. His mother along with his two young sisters had moved in with his Aunt Rose Mary. *Zia* Ro had also been forced to move out of her house, and they were all crammed into a tenement apartment in town. The massacre had remained unsolved. Siegel disappeared from the area, and he and his crew had not been seen or heard from since. The gangster stole all of their life savings, destroyed their place of business, and devastated the entire family.

The Few Years Prior

SOMETIMES WHEN YOU ARE at your lowest point, you can pinpoint the precise second when your life was saved. Vincent believed his life was saved while sitting with First Sergeant William Conley of Tidewater, Virginia, and occurred moments after he had lost his composure and was on the verge of a breakdown.

First Sergeant Conley may have been only twenty-four, but he looked at least ten years older. A six-year veteran of the United States Marines, he had served in combat during the Banana Wars. These interventions throughout Latin America in the 1920s and early 1930s were undertaken by the US government to help preserve commercial interests, advance the US political agenda, and maintain a sphere of influence in the region.

In 1930 then Lance Corporal Conley had been sent to assist in suppressing a peasant uprising at the Haitian port town of Les Cayes. President Hoover appointed two commissions to study the situation, and he subsequently ordered a withdrawal from the Caribbean country. President Roosevelt reaffirmed this disengagement agreement when he was elected, and the last contingent of US Marines was withdrawn in 1934.

Essere sempre fedeli was the Latin origin of the Marine motto "Semper Fi" or "always be faithful." This was the code by which Vincent Scala lived his life. From the start, he became more than simply a jarhead. He had the esprit de corps and became totally devoted to its history and embraced this branch of the military's traditions and honor. Ooohh Raaah!

He had just turned seventeen years old and lied about his age in order to enlist. Then, while stationed in the Philippines after his first tour came to an end, he immediately reenlisted. California, Hawaii, China, New Zealand, Australia, and the Philippines were places he had never dreamed of visiting. Now, by the age of twenty-three and in the middle of his second tour of duty, he had already served in all of these locales.

With storm clouds of war growing, he was now assigned to the officially formed Second Marine's which was created through a redesignation of the Second Marine Brigade. The division had been relocated from North Carolina to San Diego earlier in the year. Now part of the "old-breed" Staff Sergeant Scala was recruited to whip the expected flood of new recruits into fighting shape. He was ready to fight. *If the country is good enough to live in, then it's good enough to die for.*

Earlier in the year, the US had shed its isolationist facade for good with the passage of the Lend-Lease Act. To assist allied nations who were fighting the Axis powers, President Roosevelt authorized the supply of weapons, food, and equipment to any country needing assistance. The March 1941 act built upon previous actions taken by the Roosevelt administration. In mid-1940, large amounts of weapons and ammunition had been declared to be surplus and were authorized to be shipped to Britain. FDR also entered into negotiations with Winston Churchill to secure leases for naval bases in British possessions across the Caribbean and the Atlantic coast of Canada.

While Vincent wanted to see Teresa again, he realized that they would have to continue to be patient. As he sat down to reply to her most recent letter, he needed to give his condolences regarding the presumed death of her father. Vincent owed Mr. Carpinello so much and would have been honored to ask the man for his daughter's hand in marriage. That would not be possible now, but hopefully the time would come when he finally would be with Teresa again.

9

VENETIAN TABLE

April 27, 1996

IT HAD ALL THE ambiance of a villa on the Italian Riviera. But instead of views of the Ligurian Sea and Apennine Mountains, guests cast their eyes on the Throgs Neck and Whitestone bridges arcing over Long Island Sound with the Manhattan skyline in the distance.

Three hours had passed since Megyn Erin Kelly took the hand of Christopher Joseph Cameron in holy matrimony at St. Thomas the Apostle Church in Woodhaven. Now it was time to party at the Marina Del Rey, one of the most picturesque locations in the entire metropolitan area.

The venue was conveniently located on the northern shores of the Bronx, halfway between Megyn's predominantly Irish family and friends from Queens and Chris's family and friends from Westchester, who, even though Chris had quite a bit of Irish blood himself, were of Italian descent. Set to be introduced for the first time as man and wife to over three hundred awaiting guests fueled by a half-hour-too-long cocktail hour on an unseasonably warm spring night, the new couple had averted disaster and turned lemons into lemonade. What could have been a complete disaster ended up being the most memorable day of their lives.

They had the assistance of Sal and Tony to squeeze this sour fruit into something refreshing to drink. Four months prior to their expected nuptial date, Megyn had received a call from the owner of the Water Club in New Rochelle. Also situated along Long Island Sound, this banquet hall had been in the midst of major renovations and the Kelly–Cameron affair was to be the first event to christen the new and improved locale.

The young couple had been enticed with a discounted eighty-dollars-per-head fee to partake in a gaudy twenty-selection cocktail hour followed by a four-course dinner and, to cap off the evening, a breathtaking Venetian Table dessert extravaganza. After being blown away with the too-good-to-be-true offer, Chris and Megyn flew up from Dallas in October and sealed the deal. The Water Club's owner, a short, squat man named Lou Passeri, even assured them that the construction was going along smoothly and would be completed well before their nuptial date.

The pre-Christmas call Megyn received told a much different story. Renovations hit a snag, and Lou asked if it were possible to push out the date by a month or so. Chris raced over to visit the construction site on Christmas Eve morning and stood with his mouth a gasp. It was highly unlikely the large crater with mounds of dirt piled high all around would magically transform into a grandiose banquet hall in four months. It looked like it would not even be ready the next time Santa Claus came down the chimney.

So, with Sal and Tony by his side, Chris knocked on the door and entered the makeshift rectangular trailer located a few feet behind the massive hole in the ground. Chris extended Mr. Passeri a bottle of holiday cheer, shook his hand, and proceeded to discuss the dilemma of how he would be able to assure his beloved that her day of all days would be even more wonderful than she could ever imagine.

After an hour of tough negotiations, a solution was agreed upon. Chris did not participate in the granular details, as he had to take a call and stepped into the blustery morning air to console Megyn yet again shortly after the meeting had begun. As he clicked off the phone forty-five minutes later, his two buddies had emerged from the narrow wooden entrance way of the temporary office arm in arm with their new best friend. They were smiling broadly, making jokes, and eager to tell Chris the great news.

"Chris, err, Mr. Cameron, I, I mean, we at the Water Club just feel horrible about the inconvenience we caused you and your beautiful future wife." Passeri had both of his hands grasped tight as he spoke.

"And?" Chris stood there looking amusingly at Sal and Tony standing behind their new "bestest" buddy with arms folded.

"And we are gonna do everything in our power to make things right." Passeri then went on to say that he had just got off the phone with the manager of the Marina Del Rey and the two had worked out an arrangement where the Water Club would pay for the extra person charge of fifty dollars a head at the higher-priced venue.

"Tell him the best part." Sal rubbed Passeri's shoulders from behind.

"For the inconvenience, we would personally like to include a complimentary raw seafood bar, upgrade the entrée selections from a choice of chicken or stuffed flounder to a much broader selection of chateaubriand, lobster tails, or sword fish." He looked back at the broad-shouldered masseuse, seeking approval.

Passeri then added further. "As a wedding gift from the Water Club, we would also like to pick up the cost of the transportation from the church to the Marina Del Rey."

"You really don't have to do that. Megyn wants a stretch limousine for the wedding party, and she had her heart set on a 1966 Rolls-Royce Phantom for us," Chris responded.

"Cee, he said they insist for Christ's sake. You don't want him to get upset, do you?" Tony wanted in on the fun, too.

"I guess you're right. It's like eight miles from Queens to the Bronx, so we should get there in style." Chris shook Passeri's hand to seal the deal.

The averted tragedy was now long forgotten. Little Joey Duggen, the lead singer of the Shamrock Elegants, Megyn's carefully chosen band for the evening's festivities, called for the fully packed room to be silent. The newly minted Mrs. Cameron was an avid Irish step dancer, and the diminutive baritone's silvery brogue had been a staple at many a Kelly family celebration. She and Chris were in agreement that Irish heritage would be the musical theme in honor of the deceased whom were close to their hearts—his father from Wexford and her grandmother from Belfast. The food of course would be Italian.

"Will Salvatore Esposito and Anthony Albanese please come to the dance floor to give the toast to the bride and groom." The announcement was made by Little Joey Dugan as the guests hurried to get settled into their seats around the large oval tables in the grand ballroom.

Bouncy Irish background music played as the two dapper-looking men dressed in black tuxedos with matching bow ties and cummerbunds stood up, downed the remnants of their beer bottles, and cockily made their way side-by-side to the center of the room. With the house lights dimmed low, the spotlight was on the pair of best men to give well-wishes, tell an amusing story or two, bring the room to its feet, and punctuate the specialness of their friendship.

Little Joey had received his nickname due to his five-foot-six-inch stature, and he comically looked up at Tony and then Sal. The room roared with laughter. The little redhead could have passed for a leprechaun standing in between the two Conan the Barbarian look-alikes. He gave Tony the microphone while a waitress came over and handed them both a flute of sparkling champagne.

Tony smiled from ear to ear as he reached into his jacket pocket for a stack of index cards. His cheeks reddened as he composed himself, cleared his throat, and looked at Chris and Megyn sitting ten feet away. They were both beaming with anticipation from the center of the dais.

The big man cleared his throat yet again and then awkwardly looked for a comfortable way to hold the microphone, champagne glass, and index cards all at the same time. Finally, he bent down, placed the libation on the wood floor, stood up, and breathed out. Sal stood next to him, amusingly watching the nervous delaying tactic.

"Whew. Sorry, about that. Um, well first I, I have to tank … Heh, Heh, I mean thank Megyn and Chris. You two are so special to me and my wife, Vicky, and eeerrrr, ummm …" He froze and turned silent. Tears welled up in his eyes. The burly brute could not continue. Sal extended his hand and took the microphone. Tony turned away and wiped his face with his sleeve. He gingerly took a few steps backward.

"Now for the real speech!" The room erupted with laughter as Sal glanced back and gave a *"you gotta be kidding me"* gesture. Tony threw his hands in the air in a surrender fashion. Chris had bet his bride that Tony would not be able to make it through his toast. While he was a rough, tough guy, if you put a spotlight on him during an emotional moment, he would transform into a very big baby right before your eyes.

"I think I can speak for the guy blubbering behind me and say that we are so honored to be part of Chris and Megyn's special day. Clearly the extended cocktail hour has gotten the best of Baby Tony here, but you also have to realize that Cee has been the glue that keeps us together and our friendship's one of a kind. Just a quick story for you people, growing up we always joked with Chris that he never spoke about his women friends. He always said that his love life was secondary to getting his shi … I mean stuff in order and that no one even came close to making him feel that way. Now since Cee is a neat freak and an in-shape, good-looking guy, we began to have our doubts about him." The audience roared as Sal raised his left hand and twinked his pinky finger signifying the stereotypical expression that someone may be *finocch*.

Chris and Megyn shouted the classic *Seinfeld* line back in unison, "Hey, not that there's anything wrong with it!" The room erupted again.

When the rumbling died down, Sal continued, "Where was I, oh yeah. Well, then Chris goes back to Texas again, and boom, about a year ago, all we began hearing about was Megyn this, Megyn that. I bet he even drew hearts with their initials on his notebooks at work. He goes from never mentioning a girl's name before to gushing about this one specific chick … I mean classy woman." He smiled at Megyn, winked, and continued. "So we finally meet her, and I swear if I wasn't in love with my beautiful wife, Angela, I would have felt the same as he did. Meg, you really are something special, and I know you two lovebirds will do great."

Sal went on for a few minutes with adoration for the new couple. As he always did, he kept the room entertained along the way. Finally, he ended with a toast and a promise to sing Elvis Presley's *The Wonder of You* later in the evening. Then the now-composed Tony finally rejoined him as they went over to Chris and Megyn to hug and kiss them both.

Three Hours Later

DRENCHED IN SWEAT AND long since having removed his bowtie and cummerbund, his head bopping to the music, Tony sauntered his way over to stand between Chris and Megyn. He wrapped his thick arms around them and then proceeded to slobber kisses for the hundredth time of the night while Vicky and Angela took more very memorable pictures.

"Sorry about what happened before, Cee. I think some dust blew into my eyes and it got all teary." They all laughed boisterously. "I'll show you what I had written down to say; it was beautiful. Much better that Sally Nuts over there." While Tony shuffled the index cards, he pointed at the other big man who was currently by the Venetian Table.

A seven months pregnant, Vicky piled more on her husband of two years. "Meg, you should'a seen this big teddy bear crying uncontrollably when Tony Junior was born. And if you think he's bad, my God, his father, Big Al, is ten times worse. Every time his old man sees that boy, he gets all choked up. I just can't imagine how he'll be after the new baby is born."

"Did you find out yet if it's a boy or girl?" Megyn asked excitedly.

"Na, we wanta be surprised, but I'm carrying different than with Junior, so I think we're havin' a girl this time." Vicky rubbed her stomach in a maternal manner.

They all looked across the room. Big Al had just sat down after partaking in Venetian Table sweets. One of his mini-plates held four cannoles; another had a mountain-high stack of cookies, and a third was his favorite, a big piece of lemon cake. Sal had been following his self-anointed uncle and acting as an extra set of hands. He gave Big Al his espresso and then walked over to join the group.

"I swear to Christ, Sal. You look like a slob," Angela scolded her husband when he came closer. She found a linen napkin on a table, dabbed it in a glass of cold water, and proceeded to rub a chocolate stain out of his shirt collar.

Angela Esposito may have stood only five-two, but make no mistake about it; she was the general of the Esposito household. For Sal, it had been love at first sight. Six years earlier, he was out drinking with friends and playing darts at an Irish pub in Bronxville. For some reason, Tony was not there, and as he would later tell the story, "Angela would have never even looked in Sal's direction if his better-looking friend were also in the room." Anyway, Sal needed a partner for darts.

The then Angela Messina was sitting at the bar surrounded by three *chooches* trying to chat her up. She looked uninterested, so he decided to rescue her by squeezing between the fellas. He smiled and asked her if she would like to kick some butt in darts. Even though they lost the match to two of Sal's friends, she thought he was a nice enough boy to go on a formal date with, and besides, she really did want to see Patrick Swayze in *Ghost*.

Sal did not impress on the date; he fell asleep in the flick, and Angela thought he was way too cocky and laughed far too much at his "you had to be there" jokes. But over time he wore her down, cooked many a romantic meal, and showed courtesy and respect to her family. Soon after that encounter as his courting phase was in full swing, he began to devote more time to the legitimate activities in Ressini's and also steer clear of the ruthless end of Jimmy Tree's operations. He convinced his capo that he was much more valuable focusing on money-making opportunities as opposed to the enforcer role he took on in his younger days.

Tony and Vicky had taken a different route to wedded bliss. Back in the day, Victoria Enrico had sat next to little Anthony Albanese when they were kindergarteners in Ms. Pellner's class. Toward the end of that first school year, the future elementary school teacher taught her future husband how to tie his shoelaces. He was a smitten six-year-old but was soon heartbroken. Over that summer, Victoria and her family moved seven miles away to White Plains.

Fifteen years later, in between games of a weekend softball tournament, Tony walked into a deli in White Plains to pick up some sandwiches. When the cute, tall, brown-eyed brunette behind the counter read the back of his jersey with Albanese spelled out, she flirted with him and asked if he was little Anthony from Tuckahoe. He blushed and could not believe his good fortune to reunite with his prepubescent crush.

The next night during a Billy Joel concert at the Meadowlands, they sang all the legendary pianist's greatest hits together. It would not be all fun and games. Their early years as a couple were wrought with drama as they fought, argued, cried of course, broke up monthly, but always managed to find their way back into each other's arms. It was not until Sal found his true love with Angela that Tony also began to tone down his ruthless activities for Jimmy Tree, convincing him that he and Sal worked as a team. While they would still squeeze every nickel out of a customer who owed, they could not be counted on to get blood under their fingernails for other family business.

"Tony, you gotta try the tiramisu. Your dad and I shared a plate while we were waiting for our espresso," Sal said, waiting patiently for his wife to finish cleaning his rented white shirt. "Angela, please, you're embarrassing me in front of my friends." Now directing his comments to Megyn, Sal lamented some more. "Meg, please don't do this to Cee. I swear my wife really believed I couldn't wipe my ass before I met her." Sal quickly followed this remark by kissing his wife on the lips and giving her a hug.

"Check it out guys: a showdown between Big Al and Pops," Chris said. This caused all to look across the room where they amusingly watched Tony's father trying to play keep-away with his plate of cookies so Tony's grandfather could not get to them.

"My dad takes his cookies very seriously. He also knows Pops can't have too many sweets anymore. Poor guy's breaking down ... so ... much ..." Tony's voice trailed off.

"Hey, ladies, would you mind getting Pops a few cookies? Can't you see he's gonna explode. I just wanna talk to the guys alone for a minute too." Chris kissed his wife and whispered into her ear, "Let's share a bowl of chocolate ice cream. I'll be over in a second ... Okay!"

After the three wives club departed to the dessert room, Chris reached into his jacket pocket and handed Sal and Tony each a white envelope. "Here, guys ... Looking over at Pops reminded me that I had something to give you two. Don't open it yet. From that thing we discussed in the Green Hornet. Just follow what's in there."

They both folded the envelopes and put them into their front pants pockets. Sal and Tony had actually not thought much about the supposed plan Chris had briefly mentioned to them before the successful fix of the basketball tournament in March. They had reluctantly handed over $63,000 of profit to Jimmy Tree as the three games, which had been fixed, all covered the point spread. The four acquaintances Chris had introduced Sal and Tony to in the bayou had flawlessly spread their wagers among sixteen unsuspecting bookies. Chris didn't participate, but Sal and Tony made about ten grand each for their hard work.

With the winnings in their pockets, they waited patiently. Their prey was outside in the lobby at an investor conference at the Sheraton on Fifty-Sixth Street in Manhattan. They stalked and then finally pounced, throwing a pillow case over his head and carrying him to an awaiting car. First, though, they kissed Megyn good-bye and assured her that they would take excellent care of her fiancé for his bachelor party weekend.

That was in March. During the raucous two days they were celebrating his last precious time of being a free man in Atlantic City with six other friends, they did not bring up their dilemma. It would have been awkward anyway, as Jimmy Tree was one of the others in attendance. He helped arrange for the party suite at Caesar's as an act of gratitude for Chris's assistance in New Orleans.

10

NOT MUCH LIKE OKLAHOMA

December 1941–June 1942

THE US LOSS WAS devastating when Japanese torpedo and bomber planes launched a surprise attack on the Pearl Harbor Naval Base on the morning of December 7, 1941. This had been the integral part of the Japanese military's master plan to shatter the American will to fight. The second phase, which was implemented over the next few months, was designed to lure out and destroy the remainder of the depleted US Navy. Japan's ultimate goal was for a quick surrender so they could continue to pillage the natural resources of the Pacific Rim without retribution and to be regarded as a world power.

The initial Japanese attack may have been overwhelming, but it was not complete. They failed to damage any aircraft carriers, which by a stroke of luck had all been absent from the harbor during the raid. American technological skills quickly led to the immediate repairs to all but three of the ships sunk or damaged that day. Most importantly, the shock and anger caused by events from the "date that would live in infamy" united a divided nation to a wholehearted commitment to victory.

While the US military was regrouping, the Japanese extended a defensive perimeter from the Philippines to the Indian Ocean. Then, on May 7, 1942, the US carriers *Lexington* and *Yorktown* were patrolling in the Coral Sea and were alerted that the Japanese had moved outward from their main base in New Britain.

What followed was the first true carrier-versus-carrier battle. Neither of the task forces came within sight of each other, and the battle was decided entirely by aircraft. The Japanese Navy won the tactical victory by sinking three ships, including the *Lexington* and also damaging the *Yorktown*. The US achieved its first substantial warship kill by sinking the light carrier *Shoho* and severely damaging the big carrier *Shokaku*. They were also able to secure vital supply lines running to Australia.

The loss of *Shoho* and *Shokaku* occurred weeks before what became the Japanese strategic high-water mark. The Battle of Midway was fought during the first week of June and resulted in the US decimating the Nippon carrier fleet. Up to that point, Japan had possessed naval superiority and could choose where and when to attack. After that battle, the two powers were essentially equal. With trade routes now fully secured, the production of new vessels, munitions, and equipment could be delivered safely, and the US began to take offensive actions.

With a more favorable tactical situation, the US Joint Chiefs of Staff proposed a two-pronged assault on Japanese positions. The first was in a northwesterly direction up through the Solomon Islands. The other was from Port Moresby on the southern coast of New Guinea.

Of all enemy strong points, the islands of Guadalcanal in the Solomons appeared the most threatening. By mid-June, word came of a major threat developing. At the Lunga plantation, an airfield was being built, and over three thousand Japanese soldiers were now stationed on the island.

August 7, 1942
CODE-NAMED OPERATION WATCHTOWER, THE first US offensive land raid in the Pacific was ordered. On D-day, Staff Sergeant Vincent Scala and the amphibious landing force of the Second Marines made an unopposed landing at 7:40 a.m. on Tulagi's western shore in support of the First Marines Raider Battalion. This narrow, two-mile-long atoll was approximately halfway between the two ends of Guadalcanal's oblong-shaped archipelago.

The Japanese forces of the Yokohama Air Group had fled to the southeastern end of the island where they set up a heavily fortified perimeter. By the afternoon of D+1, the enemy had repositioned on top of a hill overlooking a nearby ravine. Excellent at camouflage, the well-organized and highly trained Japanese troops had dug dozens of caves and set up sandbag-protected machine-gun pills to defend their positions.

Against no opposition, marines secured the village of Haleta and then quickly pressed on and sealed the western flank. The Second Marines linked up with the First Marines Raider Battalion for an advance into the dense tropical rain forest to break the defense.

"Not much like Oklahoma, hey Lieutenant?" Sgt. Scala said in a joking manner but with an edge of nervousness. They had reached their current position before dusk and were hunkered down in the darkness of the jungle, bracing for an imminent attack.

"Never been so thirsty in my life," Sgt. Scala whispered in the other direction to a private crouched down next to him. Tuckahoe would never be confused with a jungle in the South Pacific. "Whatever you do, try and stay awake. These Japs'll come at us in all directions," he further reiterated the order to another enlisted man, who just nodded silently.

The Japanese subscribed to the code of Bushido, preferring death to capture. They had proved this with significant casualties on both sides during two frontal charges on his platoon's flanks. So far unscathed, Sgt. Scala and his men braced for an assault in their direction.

Lt. Bailey leaned over and whispered to his senior NCO, "Scala, listen close ... I can hear them. They're jabbering out there. May be only fifty feet away as near as I can tell!" The twenty-four-year-old native of the Old West Oklahoma town of Pawnee quietly slithered away. A few minutes later he returned. Panting rapidly, he removed his helmet and lay on his back after a quick check of the men and their surroundings.

He leaned close, sweating profusely, and whispered, "I think I saw 'em by Guidone's position. Take a squad, circle to the back, and resupply him. They were hit pretty bad earlier. We'll dig in here." He rotated his hand and gestured for his sergeant to make his way fifty yards to the right.

Sgt. Scala remained low, crawling back out of his position with three riflemen. They were careful to remain camouflaged by the thick cover of the jungle growth.

"Stay five paces apart. We gotta get this ammo to them!" Sgt. Scala ordered as they slung .50-caliber machine-gun rounds over their shoulders and carried boxes of .50-caliber ammo in their hands.

Scala's unit circled thirty feet to the rear and then moved out toward the perimeter. Along the way, they dropped off supplies to the troops and alerted them to where the enemy was positioned.

Before reaching Lt. Guidone's position, small arms fire opened up, followed by the thumps of mortar rounds. Sgt. Scala ordered the men to take cover as machine gun tracers and bullets whizzed overhead. Pinned down, he tried to spot where the lieutenant was positioned.

Guidone had seen the enemy approaching and began lobbing grenades from a fortified position. Without a clear line of sight, they appeared to be landing off-course and exploding wildly. Vincent ducked. Branches above snapped and cracked. Guidone screamed and then fell silent after the unmistakable bump and flash of a grenade exploding. Vincent rolled to his side, then got on all fours, and made his way toward the fire. He saw a soldier writhing on his back, holding his pant leg. He had been hit by a mortar shell fragment.

"Medic! ... Corpsman!" Sgt. Scala yelled out as he applied pressure on the bloody leg of a blond-haired kid no older than nineteen. He took out a serrate of morphine and pressed it into his upper thigh. It calmed him down immediately. He then placed a gauze bandage on the groin area and pressed down. A corpsman tapped him on the shoulder.

"I've got it from here."

"Thanks, Doc." Vincent got up from his knee and galloped forward, holding his M-1 with both hands. He dove for the protection of a tree as the air above him continued to crack and pop. Breathing heavily, he leveled his rife on an approaching intruder. Two bursts and his victim fell to the ground. He gasped for air; the heat and humidity were unbearable.

The ground shook as an artillery round exploded nearby. Flairs burst high above, and with that he was able to view the tropical surroundings. Through the smoky, murky air, he recognized the bloody face of his first lieutenant standing and facing him a few yards away.

"Cover me!" Bailey yelled as an enemy fighter charged toward him. The Jap surged forward with only a bayonet grasped in his hand.

Sgt. Scala provided cover fire into the brush. He heard screams and then silence. As he continued to shoot targeted bursts into the darkness, he also witnessed the most heroic act of his life. Thomas Bailey drew out three assaulters over a fifteen-minute period. Each time a Jap bolted out, they exposed positions of reserves hidden and waiting for an eventual attack. Sgt. Scala and other dug-in Marines hurled grenades and lit up the bush with machine-gun and M-1 fire. The courageous lieutenant proceeded to disable the first two enemies but was cut up badly in the exchanges. With an indomitable fighting spirit to his troops, he held up for as long as he could before the final assailant got the better of him and thrust a bayonet into his abdomen. For his actions that night, he would earn the Medal of Honor.

Sgt. Scala leveled a shot and blew the Jap's head apart. The enemy had been crouched on top of Lt. Bailey's limp torso and was set to continue to mutilate the body of Sgt. Scala's brave leader with the bloody bayonet. Sgt. Scala then stood and hurled two grenades into the brush. An attacker charged him. He sidestepped and then shot the enemy in the back. Seconds later, the concussion of an artillery round knocked him off of his feet.

Vincent groggily opened his eyes to bright sunlight. It had been eight hours since the fight and he was being carried to the back of the lines by two comrades in a makeshift stretcher. The last thing he remembered was moments after the final kill as he grabbed at his helmet and fell on his stomach. An enemy shell had exploded, tearing off part of the tree above. The concussion of the blast combined with the heavy branches that glanced off of his head knocked him unconscious.

He had a severe head wound, and his leg and shoulder were ripped up pretty bad. Relieved of action, Vincent was evacuated for treatment on board the USS *Nashville*. A week later he was brought ashore to recuperate at a naval hospital in Melbourne.

On December 1, 1942, Sgt. Scala rejoined his comrades on Guadalcanal where he assisted in operations to secure the island. The Second Marines and the other elements that had landed back in August were finally pulled off the island on January 31, 1943. Mop-up continued and Guadalcanal was declared secure on February 9, 1943.

From start to finish, the Second Marines had fought gallantly and their actions had not gone unnoticed. President Roosevelt awarded the unit the Presidential Unit Citation for their actions during the capture and defense in the Guadalcanal operation.

July 1943

THE BACK ROOM OF Wool's Pub was more boisterous than it usually had been since Vincent began to frequent the ratty establishment four months earlier, and that was saying a lot. On a slow night, the rectangular-shaped, hundred-by-thirty-foot-long pub located on Worcester Street was usually packed with an assortment of dogface marines, army grunts, and swab jockeys. Now, the place was overflowing with troops of all kinds from at least four different countries who were squeezing in their last precious moments of freedom. It was almost time to be shipped off to ungodly places to experience and perform ungodly tasks to help end this godforsaken war as quickly as possible.

After the well-deserved rest, the Second Marines were now vigorously training for their next operation. They had been practicing amphibious landings and tactical maneuvers off the coast of Christchurch and the beaches of New Zealand's South Island. Vincent had recently been promoted to Master Gunnery Sergeant, and he was decorated for his bravery on the battlefield. For the past five weeks, he had been tasked with making sure replacement troops, many of which were just shipped in from the states, were trained endlessly and relentlessly. These kids came from cities and farms, and he did not want to risk his life and the life of other marines if they froze up on a beachhead or in a jungle. "Keep moving forward … listen to your NCO … stay the fuck down … stop crying and move," he would shout at them.

He prepared them for the worst, as the worst was what they would surely get. If they lived to tell about it, they would probably experience even worse. The Japs were brutal, tenacious, and well trained. They would fight fanatically to the death for their emperor. He stressed to the newbies that nighttime would be the worst. "Stay alert and never get captured, 'cause you'll never come back alive," he cautioned one scared kid from Ardmore, Pennsylvania.

"Private, get that smile off your face. The enemy's not bucktoothed cartoon figures. They're seasoned veterans and hidden everywhere. They'll carve out your liver and eat you for dinner." The private as well as his fellow marines never joked again during a training exercise.

That was in the future. This night was for the present. Gy. Sgt. Scala had formed close bonds with a few NCOs, and in this smoke-filled card room he was in command. Behind him stood M.Sgt. Don Nailor from Brentwood, Tennessee, while next to him stood Sgt. Maj. Bill Neill of Newton, Massachusetts. These two large men were currently blocking any attempt by onlookers to view the hand in play.

Over two hundred American dollars were piled in the center of a small wooden table as a straggly Aussie with a confused expression on his face contemplated whether to call a seventy-dollar raise from the New Yorker.

Five-card draw had continued to be a profitable past-time. Just that morning, Vincent had sent $250 to his mother along with a letter asking how things were faring back home. Since Teresa had not written him in over six months, he came to the conclusion that she had moved on. She probably did not wish to upset him with a Dear John letter. She was only twenty-three. As beautiful as she was, she most likely met some Four-F factory worker and had already forgotten about him.

After an initial burst of wild nights with friendly New Zealand females, he had decided to refocus. Coinciding with his promotion, he had absorbed himself in poker rather than getting drunk and carousing. He relegated his life to train his men until it was time to ship off and most likely get his head blown off for his country.

"I think ya got me mate," the Aussie said as he tossed his two pairs, fours and deuces face up into the muck.

Vincent exhaled, "Should'a called my friend … Bluffing all the way." He smiled and fanned his five cards for all in the tiny room to see. A busted straight to the jack.

He had rightly believed that an intimidating bluff was the appropriate gambit. With a wad of cash already in his pocket, he was now ready to have a drink with his buddies, so he decided to end the game in a blaze or in glory. The room erupted with laughter and catcalls. As was the norm, Nailor and Neill scooped up the winnings and safely secured the pile of bills.

"No disrespect, Walter. I've enjoyed competing against you over these past few months." Vince shook his Australian counterpart's hand and bought him a scotch and they walked out of the room.

Donny Nails and Billy Barrel slapped him on the back in congratulations as they made their way weaving through the crowded revelers. Bill yelled out for three beers, his huge chest clearing his way to the front. He paid the bartender, grabbed three frothy mugs, and then made his way over to the table where Vince and Don were sitting.

"Cheers." All three NCOs clinked and then drained half their beer in one motion.

"Whew! Another day, another dollar. What was the take tonight, Don?" Vincent said as his buddy handed over the now-organized mound of bills with an approving nod.

"I'd say you took 'em for two eighty in that last hand, and based on what I saw earlier, you probably won five hundred total." With his eyes closed, Donny calculated the math in his head. When he opened them, Vincent had changed positions and was now standing and looking intently across the room by the entrance.

"What's happening over there, buddy?" Billy had noticed his abrupt change. He stood up and looked over in the same direction. "Very pretty ladies they are … You take the blonde; I'm gonna charm that cute brunette … Hey, Nails, there's even one for you."

"Look out, WAAC's in the house. Let me at 'em." Don was now standing, but while he and Bill were laughing and ogling the three Women's Army Corps beauties, Vincent remained silent.

"Oh my, God, it's her." He moved quickly across the room, bumping into swarms of people along the way. He tapped the brunette on the shoulder, and she turned.

"Vincent!" Her eyes lit up as she smiled and hugged him around the neck. He carried her outside, oblivious to all around him.

Cupping her face with his hands, he kissed her on the lips. Tears welled in his eyes as he buried his face into her shoulder and cried uncontrollably. "Teresa, I can't believe it's you. I've missed you so much."

August 23, 1943

To FREE A MAN for combat, this was the rallying cry of the Women's Army Auxiliary Corps. In the months after President Roosevelt signed the bill into law, tens of thousands of able-bodied young ladies enlisted in droves to serve their country. Secretary of War Henry Stimson even authorized an increase to 150,000 recruits for 1943 after the first-year goal of 25,000 was smashed. The WAAC was established to work with the army to make available to the national defense the knowledge, skill, and special training of the women of the nation.

After Teresa's father had died in 1939 and then after the sudden loss of her mother two years later, she and her two brothers sold their small home in Yonkers. She partook in the war effort and got a job at the Burroughs-Wellcome pharmaceutical plant in Tuckahoe. As a quality control inspector of the millions of vitamin B_1 capsules coming off of the assembly line, she still believed she could do more for the war effort.

Her brothers had both enlisted after the Pearl Harbor attacks. Carmine was serving in the army in North Africa. Teresa had not heard from him since he had shipped out in May. Paul, her oldest brother, had joined the navy but, regrettably, was killed in action off the coast of New Britain after his destroyer was sunk by a Jap submarine.

With word of her brother's death, Teresa heard the calling herself. She applied and was accepted to the WAAC and then went proudly off to Fort Des Moines for basic training. Trained as a filter board operator, her job was to plot and trace the paths of aircraft in a station area. New Zealand had been her first stop, and she was set to leave in less than two weeks for her assignment. With the Henderson airfield secured, she would be serving her country on Guadalcanal.

Poker games and carousing with friends ended the moment Vincent held Teresa in his arms. He spent every spare second he had with her prior to her departure. Their few weeks together were the happiest times he could remember in a very long time.

The day before she was set to leave, he bent down on his knee and asked her to be his wife. He did not know what the future would bring for him and her for that matter, but he was sure that kismet had brought them together for a reason. Later that day, Teresa Carpinello took the hand of Vincent Scala. They spent their first night together as one and then said good-bye. He now had a reason to fight on and come back to her after this hell of a war was finally over.

Part 2

Infiltrate

11

HELLO, MR. ESPOSITO; GOOD EVENING, MR. ALBANESE

May 10, 1996

HIS WIFE OF FIFTEEN days did not know it, but she was making it extremely hard to enjoy the excitement of the moment. Over the last two weeks, though, in and around their overwater bungalow on the secluded island of Bora Bora, Chris had thoroughly enjoyed her company at least twenty-two times, as he and Megyn christened their first few days as man and wife.

However, after consuming three beers in half an hour while his wife controlled the dice and rolled them like a magician, the only thing on his mind was a well-deserved bathroom break. Well, that and counting the red, green, and black chips packed into the wooden craps table tray.

"Seven Out!" the stickman expressionlessly called. He raked the dice to the center and waited for the felt to be cleared. There had been a massive amount of action in play over the last eight rolls as the hot blonde with the rock on her finger had a great run rolling those bones.

When the dice had landed with Six-One displayed, the table participants collectively sighed and then gave Megyn her well-deserved kudos for a very profitable roll as shooter. The three before her had all immediately crapped out, and a few gamblers had even left the table in frustration. By the end of her hitting the first point in style with a Hard Four (Two-Two), the vacant slots were filled and all those surrounding the jam-packed green oval pit proceeded to hoot and holler in excitement.

As the newlyweds organized their winnings, she and Chris were giddy with excitement. So far so good. This had been a great way to end their honeymoon—twelve days in the South Pacific followed by three days in Vegas. Only two days remained before they would be back to the real world of spreadsheet analysis, take-out Chinese food, and movie rentals.

After the chips were secured into the rack, Chris gazed into her eyes, leaned over to kiss her neck, and then whispered romantically into her ear, "I've gotta pee like a racehorse! Back in a sec." He bolted from the table.

She shook her head in mock disgust and then placed two red five-dollar chips on the pass line. Hopefully, the other end of the table would keep the magic going.

"A pretty little thing like you shouldn't be standing here alone." A voice from behind got her attention, but Megyn did not turn around.

A different, deep baritone voice followed. "Where'd that pip-squeak you were just with run off to? He shouldn't leave a classy lady like you alone this long."

They moved in close as the box man and pit boss took notice. Megyn slowly turned around and proceeded to give Sal a poke in the stomach with her elbow. She then reached up and jabbed Tony on his chest with her petite clenched fist.

"You guys just missed the roll of a lifetime. Had the dice for a half an hour. My sweetie pie was about to whip it out and go in an empty bottle 'cause I rolled so long."

Chris returned moment's later, feeling like a new man.

"Pheewww ... Hey, you guys just get here?" He greeted them with strong man hugs and kisses on the cheek.

"Yeah ... Landed an hour ago, we were on our way up to the room when we saw you sprinting across the floor. Then we saw Meg standing ova here ... Wow, this place is real nice," Tony said as he looked around admiring the Mirage's casino floor.

"Never stayed here before; usually get comped at MGM," Sal approvingly added.

"If I'm gonna treat you guys to a free trip, I want you to travel in style. Go up and drop your bags off ... Actually, to tell you the truth ... I probably won't see you the rest of the night." Chris rubbed his wife's ass cheeks over her tight fitting red dress before kissing her on the lips. "Let's catch up in the morning ... Enjoy!"

Sal and Tony said their good-byes and then walked away within the rainforest-themed environs to the elevator bank. Tony pressed the up-arrow button. Then they walked into an open car. "Oh, good. The eleventh floor's pressed already," Sal smiled.

A matronly looking mother with two preteen sons looked up in fright seconds before she grabbed the boy's arms and whisked them out to wait for another way to get to their final destination. After the doors closed, the two men looked at each other expressionlessly and then burst out laughing.

When the door opened, they got their bearings and headed left down the long corridor. "Room 1148, all the way at the goddamn end. This is the last time I take a free trip from Cee." Tony pretended to be upset.

After they had returned home from Chris and Megyn's wedding reception, both men read the contents of their envelope. Inside were tickets to Las Vegas on Delta Airlines, *three friggin' connections*, with Mirage!!! written neatly on top. Angela and Victoria gave them hell, but hey, *who'll watch the kids if they were to go, too?* It was nice for Chris to think of them, and besides, they both knew he would definitely need a break to male-bond after being with his beloved for two straight weeks.

At the end of the hallway, Tony took out the plastic card and slid it into the door reader. It chirped, turning from red to green. He turned the handle. The door slammed shut behind them. In confusion, they looked at a sultry redhead sitting at the circular table located against the picture window overlooking the strip. Next to her stood a middle-aged man with a gray salt-and-pepper buzz cut. They both had blank expressions. In unison, they lifted their right hands to show shiny badges. The redhead stood up.

"Hello, Mr. Esposito; good evening, Mr. Albanese. I am Special Agent Dawn Nicholas of the Federal Bureau of Investigations. This is Agent Ronald Sikes."

Two thirds of the Columbus Avenue Boys dropped their gym bags on the queen-sized bed closest to where the agents were standing. The pair was both panting and noticeably nervous.

"Chris Cameron arranged for this meeting. He gave us the key to the room. You don't mind if we have this discussion in private, do you? I'd hate if friends of yours found out we were speaking," Agent Sikes finally spoke.

The "friends" comment was in reference to the code phrase wiseguys used to introduce others for the first time. A "friend of mine" denoted an introduction by a made member of a guy who was not a member of the family but could be vouched for. A "friend of ours" was an introduction of one made member to another. A made member was someone who was officially inducted into Cosa Nostra. Once they "got their button," a made member was then granted certain privileges, became officially part of the Mafia hierarchy, and was off-limits to retribution by soldiers below them on the food chain.

"There ain't no friends of anyone here, pal," Sal deadpanned. He calmed down. Both he and Tony were not yet vouched for, and because of their current attitude change to the Gambinos, they were not heartbroken by it.

"Yes, we're quite aware of that. To tell you the truth, you two gorillas are not even on our radar screen. But there's someone you know quite well who is." Agent Nicholas sat back down.

"What can you tell us about James Tracino?" Agent Sikes opened a folder to display a black-and-white picture of Jimmy Tree having a discussion with some older-looking Italian guy on a street corner. Sikes turned and sat on the opposite chair of the table across from his female counterpart.

Sal held the photo with one hand, studying it as he plopped down on the bed. Tony sat next to him. A few moments of silence followed.

"These guys look like real bad news, my friend. I'd hate to cross them. If I didn't know any better, it looks like if they ever found out you were stabbing them in the back, they'd probably cut you up into a lot of little pieces." Sal made the comment then turned his head slowly to face Tony. They both couldn't help but smile at the ironic comment. This was exactly how dear old Uncle Pat had perished.

"Look, you guys are not in any trouble. Quite frankly, after this meeting, you could simply take this as a stern warning, walk away, and close up your little gambling operation. We'd never be able to convict you."

"And I might add if you do that, then Jimmy Tree and the garbage he works for would just go on." Sikes showed the men additional photos of gruesome murder scenes and news stories of an assortment of crimes. The last clipping was an old yellowed *New York Times* article. He handed it directly to Tony.

"I know this current group of young guns had nothing to do with this. I just wanted you to see some of the proud history behind the glamorous mob life."

Tony immediately tossed it to the floor. Sal looked down and read the bolded headline. "Tuckahoe Inferno ... Twelve Dead ... Cause Unknown ... Police Suspect Foul Play."

"Yeah, we heard there was a really bad fire back in the day," Tony responded unemotionally and then folded his massive arms.

"I can see you two are a little apprehensive. Look, I'll make this very easy for you. We don't want you guys. Don't be offended, but you're small fish. We just want access to your club and what's inside your heads. You don't even have to stand up for our undercover agents or give any introductions. We need you two to give us a blueprint. Lead us to weak links that we can crack. If we need more, we'll let you know." Agent Nicholas leaned over to pick up the newspaper article.

Sal and Tony giggled like teenagers, admiring the special agent's trim fit figure. One thing about them, even in a hot situation, was they always found a way to release stress through humor. Agent Sikes remained seated. He was not amused by the pair's antics and it was apparent by the tone of his voice when he spoke.

"Gentlemen, this is serious. You're not the only place we're looking to infiltrate. We need to gather an overwhelming amount of evidence against as many families and high-ranking members as possible. We may not do anything for years, so when all is said and done, hopefully you'll have passed the reins to another mule."

The FBI was in the early stages of a wide-scale investigation targeting organized crime. The frustration from earlier years when they had futilely focused on a few high-profile leaders led to great media coverage but very little in quantifiable results. Show trials, rampant juror tampering, and unreliable or disappearing witnesses had forced them to change tactics.

The new game plan was to gather reams of evidence on hundreds of associates over long periods. Then, when the time was right, they would systematically swoop in and conduct a massive arrest up and down the food chain. By corralling so many at once, investigators would be more likely to get individuals to cooperate. Even a single turncoat could do a lot of damage, and the probability of finding this diamond in the rough would increase tremendously. The chain reaction of a mass bust would ripple through all levels of organized crime. Power vacuums would form as young and inexperienced soldiers make their mark. Violence would surge, and suspicion of who could be trusted would create a highly stressful situation all around. At every step along the way, the FBI would be able to monitor these events and build additional cases for a fresh wave of indictments.

"And what if you screw up? What then?" Tony asked. He knew the government was inefficient, even on straightforward investigations. Imagine the mistakes the prosecutors could have made if they had had fifteen cases open at the same time.

"That's why we're looking for your help and cooperation." Agent Nicholas finally smiled, but just slightly.

Sal decided to open up a bit. "There's a heck of a lot more than what goes on in a gambling club. I've heard stories of other scams that they're into besides the usual local crap, like sports books and construction scams. This shit's global. The Internet's huge for every racket. Lotta' guys talking smack about new technology and whatnot and how they're killing it. Porn and theft have gotten off the street corners, know what I mean?"

"Yes. We're aware of this. The local activity's just the tip of the iceberg. These bosses don't have colossal mansions and millions socked away for nothing. They may be old school in many ways, but there's no doubt that they always tend to be on the cutting edge of technology innovation."

"Hey, you know why the Betamax never took off ... Cause they didn't support triple X flicks. VHS ate their lunch ... Sal, remember when we had to make those bootleg copies of *Debbie Does Dallas*," Tony added. He loved this bit of trivia he knew about. "Chris always says to look for porn to set the tone for technological advancements."

"You just can't get enough of telling that story, can you my friend?" Sal smirked.

"Gentlemen, can we please focus here ... We'd love for you guys to point us in the right direction. Make it easier to get to the source. We know it's a multibillion-dollar epidemic." Agent Nicholas had made her case.

"Look, take some time to think it over. We want to help distance you as much as we can. We'll be in touch." Agent Sikes and his partner left the room without saying good-bye.

Sal and Tony sat silent for a few minutes.

"Well, if we're gonna do it, I say we do it big." Tony stood up and looked at his reflection in the mirror.

"I say we keep up appearances, starting now. Whata' ya say, craps or blackjack?"

"How 'bout both? First, though, I need a few beers."

"Heck, I was thinkin' a lot stronger than that. Say good night, Jimmy Tree."

Sal put his arm around Tony's shoulder, and they both nodded in agreement.

"Jimmy Tree and the whole gang of rats, my friend. Let's go, Sally. I'm thirsty."

The Next Morning

JET LAG FROM THE six-hour cross-country flight through three time zones, combined with an unexpected 10:00 a.m. wake-up call, left Sal and Tony no chance of falling back to sleep. The night before, they had left the room at almost midnight. They did not return till sevenish, with the morning sun beaming through the partially closed curtains. An hour of "appetizer beers" while toiling with the video poker machines was followed by two straight hours of craps and vodka on the rocks. The night was concluded with almost four hours of blackjack as they sat sipping sambuca shooters.

Sal went to the bathroom, then came out, and reached into his duffel bag. He pulled out three yellow chips. "Hey, wouldn't you know it. Three grand. I think I made a little profit last night." His voice was cracking, and he was still a bit tipsy.

"I checked my stack, too. Think I broke even. Came downstairs with two grand and got about nineteen fifty over there on the table." Tony pointed to where the FBI agents had been sitting. "I need a big gulp of coffee, my friend. Let's go see the man."

They both haphazardly got dressed. Sal left the room in orange sweatpants, a white wife-beater T-shirt, and black flip-flops. Tony wore black sweatpants, a plain orange T-shirt with the sleeves cut off, and black flip-flops. When they reached the elevator, Tony checked his reflection in a wall mirror as they waited.

"Even hungover, I am a handsome man." He ran his fingers through his "morning hair." Then they both entered the crowded car.

At the lobby level, they turned down the causeway and past a coffee kiosk. It had a long line of people waiting, so reluctantly they kept walking. When they reached the glass doors of the Mirage Spa, they opened them and walked in.

"Two day passes, please." Tony flirted with the attractive Chinese attendant behind the counter.

They signed, took the receipt, and then walked toward the men's locker room.

"Love Asian chicks, Damn, if I weren't married." Tony looked back for another look at the cutie.

"Ha. Vicky probably made you leave your dick home before you left anyway." Sal shook Tony's shoulder playfully.

"You got that right, my friend. She'd waste a good knife, though. For me, it just ain't worth the trouble."

They stripped and walked bare-assed. Opening the glass locker room door, they passed the whirlpool and sauna and went directly to the steam room. The hot, moist mist blew fiercely, and they could barely see in front of them. One person was in the room, lying naked on a towel above the white marble tiles on the top ledge in the back.

"Morning, fellas', damn, I can smell the alcohol from here." Chris sat up and teased his friends. "I've been here for two hours. Ran, lifted, whirlpool and now been in here for fifteen minutes."

"Bully for you, my friend! I doubt you got in at seven and had sambuca instead of orange juice for breakfast." Sal let out a loud fart and sighed heavily.

"I'll be quick. I know you need to get back to sleep, and Meg should be done with her salon appointment in another half hour."

"She's really something. Good luck." Tony gave Chris a sincere compliment.

"Thanks. Hey, Meg, and I are super crazy with work. Getting our life together in Dallas is gonna consume a lot of time now. I really don't know when we're gonna be able to hang out again, at least for the foreseeable future … It's setting up to be a fun ride. I could make seven figures this year. I'm killing it and want to dedicate my all to being the best portfolio manager I can be."

"Speaking of fun rides … What da' you make of last night? … So that's your master plan?" Tony asked as he wiped perspiration from his face.

"Guys, I've had five separate discussions with New York field agents through the Dallas office. I didn't give your names till I was certain they wouldn't be focusing on you. I did drop a few of Jimmy Tree's friends' names, and that got them going. They got back with an interesting proposition." Chris looked at both of his friends very seriously. "You have to get out. This is the only way to break their back and step away clean. The hierarchy will be in disarray."

"Lot of downside if it gets all fucked up." Sal wiped perspiration from his face.

Chris took a sip of ice water from a plastic cup. "I know, Sally. I got a plan, though. We can keep you guys scrubbed clean the entire time. Go in as confidential informants. You set the rules, and they are bound by law to never divulge your names. You never even have to testify if you don't want."

"We don't want!" both Sal and Tony emphatically said at the same time.

"After it's all over, for good … As I was just saying about my job, if things work out and I make seven figures, I'll fund legit businesses for you guys."

"How 'bout a restaurant?" Sal asked as he cupped his hands together, looking like he was asking for a donation.

"Yeah, that could definitely be in the picture. I'll need somewhere to eat when I'm with my new and more better Wall Street buddies."

"'More better' my ass. I'll rip you out of your two-thousand-dollar Barneys suit and make you do dishes in front of those bankers." They all laughed.

"I won't forget. Hell, remember when you made your first specialty dish?"

"Slam sandwiches," they all said this in unison, remembering back to the poor old days when they had to improvise with two pieces of bread slammed together with nothing in between.

"Yeah, we must'a been like five or six. Who'da thunk you actually could cook—and with flair," Tony proudly complimented Sal. Then he turned to Chris.

"Cee, you don't have to sell us. We made up our mind. You're right, the Fibbies are right. We gotta end this, but I just don't wanna get thrown into witness protection. I want my kids to grow up right where I did and not live a lie. I can't look over my shoulder all the time." Tony's voice began to crack. He was getting emotional again.

"Phase one's complete, I guess. Tell them we're in, and we'll be ready and waiting," Sal confirmed their commitment.

Later that night, they joined Chris and Megyn for dinner. A raucous time was had by all, and they laughed telling tales of the good old days. After midnight they said their good-byes. Chris hugged each of them tight and came to the conclusion that things may never be the same.

Chaos theory stated that even minor changes in initial conditions yielded widely diverging outcomes. If a butterfly flapping its wings could create tiny changes in the atmosphere that could ultimately alter the path of a tornado, then what was expected to happen if both Sal and Tony changed their way of life and turned from the dark side to assisting with the greater good?

12

THE HOLLYWOOD REPORTER

November 25, 1944

WHEN A SERVICEMAN WAS lucky enough to get the sweepstakes ticket home, there was never a direct route back from the Pacific theater. With an overwhelming amount of troops, fresh supplies, and warships heading in the opposite direction, it simply was not a priority to return a veteran to his mother or to his girlfriend's waiting arms.

As the Japanese high command had feared from the outset, they were now facing a vastly superior strike force. The US had shaken off the initial blow at Pearl Harbor and then capitalized on the huge tactical error at Midway. They were now in a commanding position against the Rising Sun for however long it would take. Battles were expected to continue to be fierce due to the *yamato damashii* of the Japanese soldier, but it would just be a matter of time before Uncle Sam would be knocking at the door of the emperor.

That would now be the responsibility of others. After almost ten years of service to his country, Vincent had been granted his honorable discharged from the United States Marine Corps. The V-12 officer had first tried to convince him to enter Officer Candidate School, but he declined. "I've seen enough to satisfy my curiosity to fight, and while I obeyed orders and risked dying for my country, I simply cannot in my good conscious order a man to possibly die in battle." This was all that the V-12 officer needed to disqualify him for OCS.

When he received the good news in the midst of his third campaign in the Pacific, he was lying on his cot shooting the shit with Billy Barrel on a sweltering afternoon on Saipan. Over the previous three weeks, they had been leading squads to patrol for straggling Jap infantry that had remained hidden in caves and tunnels. The island may have officially fallen on July 9, but the threat of banzai attacks continued to be a major problem, especially under the cover of darkness.

"Why don't they just give up?" Vince and Billy were drinking their ration of one warm beer and smoking stolen cigars as they lamented. "They got no chance, but keep coming. Friggin' slant eyes have ratcheted up their intensity as the situation became even more direr."

Casualty reports from Saipan had been eerily similar to those compiled from other islands and islets captured over the past two years. Close to 3,000 Americans had been killed with 10,000 wounded over the past two months on this island in the Marianas. The Japanese fared much worse. Some 24,000 were reported dead with only 1,700 taken as prisoners. There were always very few Japanese wounded prisoners taken as most decided suicide to be more honorable than falling into the hands of the Americans.

The top priority of the US for all of the Pacific battles was to capture vital airfields. After Midway, the US had launched a series of counteroffensive strikes known as "island-hopping" to establish a line of overlapping bases and to gain control of the air. The idea was to capture key islands, one after another, until Japan's mainland was within range of American bombers.

One American Marine killed on Saipan was their good friend Donny Nails. In the morning hours of June 16, the Army's 165th Infantry along with the Second Marines had overrun the Aslito airfield. After completing this task with only minor casualties, the Second and Fourth Marines linked together with the Twenty-Seventh Army Infantry Division for a broad sweep northward to clear out enemy bunkers. Now grizzled veterans, the men were prepared for very personal hand-to-hand fighting. M.Sgt. Nailor had been leading a unit that included Private First Class Steven Bracety, a nineteen-year-old kid from Prescott, Arizona.

Enemy units were pushed into a small elevated pocket at Marpi Point, on the northern tip of the island. Then at 4:45 a.m., the Jap bugles sounded for a counteroffensive. Thousands armed with rifles, spears, or nothing at all charged, yelling as they came from all directions. The sheer numbers overwhelmed the American front.

They came down the valleys and onto the narrow coastal plain along Harakiri Gulch. Scala's and Neill's units were forced into a pocket just southwest, at Tanapag Village. They were safely evacuated by AMTRAKs. As cover for their retreat, a barrage of howitzer fire by the nearby Second Army stabilized a front west of the ridge in front of Mt. Tapotchau, in close proximity of Hashigoru. The fighting became so intense in this area (which was known as "Hells Pocket" and "Purple Heart Ridge") that army gunners had to literally move around the stacked dead to better their fields of fire.

Isolated and regrouping southeast of Marpi Point, M.Sgt. Nailor's unit braced for another counterattack as they began to evacuate the wounded. Then, at approximately 5:30 a.m., while he was ordering troops into position, they were ambushed. Nailor was bayoneted from behind by a hidden enemy fighter. Pfc. Bracety immediately pulled the crazed Jap off and bludgeoned him to death with the butt of his rifle. With his sergeant lying on the ground, gasping for air, and taking his final breath, the private commandeered an abandoned ambulance jeep. Under heavy fire, he evacuated the mortally wounded body and then proceeded to evacuate even more of the injured. With utter disregard for his own safety and under extremely perilous conditions, Pfc. Bracety single-handedly evacuated eighteen casualties on multiple runs along the eastern coast. At 8:45 a.m., under intense and persistent enemy fire, he ran out of the jeep to aid two wounded marines. On this final run he was killed by a Japanese sniper. Pfc. Bracety's brilliant initiative, great personal valor, and self-sacrificing efforts earned him the Medal of Honor.

Vincent did not look back and had no regrets for leaving his men on this godforsaken island. He had fought and seen enough, far more than a twenty-six-year-old should. He was emaciated, sick, and nursing sores throughout his body. No one who was still alive from his original company from Guadalcanal would have done anything different.

"Good luck, Sarge. Godspeed. Thanks for protecting my ass."

"I hope you're not thinkin' 'bout staying. We got plenty of NCOs to take your place. Get out'a here!"

"Vinny, can you take back a few of these trinkets with ya? I got a bag of Jap goodies that my little brother would love if I don't make it back! No gold teeth, just pistols and such."

Vincent hopped a ride on a mail plane that first took him south to Tinian and then to the Marianas. After a brief stop, he overheard another pilot mention that he was traveling on to Guadalcanal. With only a promise to send the man a hundred dollars to go along with his undying gratitude, he hitched a ride to see his bride.

After surprising her at Henderson Field, Teresa and Vincent spent three days together. This was a very special substitute for their lack of a honeymoon on New Zealand. Teresa had not been able to leave her station, and Vincent had been busy trying to just stay alive, first in the Battle of Tarawa and then on Saipan.

On Tarawa he had been fortunate. His battalion did not participate in the battle until the third day when they were ordered to relieve the first two waves of troops. Operation Galvanic had been undertaken to secure the lines of communication from the US to Australia and New Zealand.

The initial assault had run into trouble during the morning hours of November 20, 1943, when they landed on the three-thousand-yard-long islet of Betio. This was the first major amphibious landing by the Marines, and because the Navy was still in the process of rebuilding the Pacific Fleet, they used older and less capable equipment for support.

Coming in at low tide, the assault boats were forced to disgorge men far from shore. Yards from the beach, wading through waist-deep water over piercing, razor-sharp coral, many were cut down by merciless enemy gunfire. Those who made it ashore huddled in the sand, hemmed in by the sea to one side and the Japanese to the other. The next morning, reinforcements made the same perilous journey but this time with the assistance of tanks and artillery.

By the end of that day, marines were able to break out from the beach to the inland. The fierce combat continued for another two days, but the cost of victory was high. Nearly three thousand American casualties were recorded. The toll was even higher for the Japanese. Of the forty-seven hundred defenders, only a handful survived.

D+3 dawned with Gy. Sgt. Scala's unit hooked up with the remnants of M.Sgt. Nailor's unit, which had just halted a banzai charge. Following an air strike and with the support of Sherman and Stuart tanks, they advanced along the tail of the island. L Company was on the left and I Company patrolled the right. I Company, with the support of a few tanks, cleared pockets of emplacements, trenches, and pillboxes that ran across the width of the island. L Company continued on with only moderate resistance. Marines then reached the far end of Betio by early afternoon. The only sizeable pocket of resistance came from the complex of pillboxes and emplacements by Takarongo Point near the junction of Red Beaches 1 and 2. Marines gradually wore the defenders down, and by 3:00 p.m., this pocket had fallen.

Scala's unit conducted mop-up operations for a few days but at 12:10 p.m. on November 24, 1943, all was deemed secure. Nailor's unit pressed on, hopping from island to island along the rest of Tarawa where they fought a decisive engagement with a smattering of Japanese on Buariki. With no enemy found on the small island of Na'a, the entire Tarawa atoll was deemed secured by the end of November.

December 20, 1944

WITH SIX MONTHS STILL remaining before her WAAC commitment was fulfilled, Teresa and Vincent decided it was best for him to go back to San Diego. He could get settled, and she would reunite with him in the spring. While on Guadalcanal, he got word that a wounded aircraft carrier would be heading back toward San Francisco for repairs. He seized on the opportunity to assist with carrying medical supplies to the ship on a commandeered mail plane. He remained there for rest of the journey to California.

The USS *Intrepid*, known as the "Fighting I," was one of twenty-four Essex-class aircraft carriers built during World War II. Commissioned in 1943, she had already raided islands along the northeastern corner of Kwajalein Atoll during the first few months of 1944. Later in February, the *Intrepid* headed on and sunk two destroyers and two hundred thousand tons of merchant shipping near Truk, a supposed tough Japanese base located in the center of Micronesia. In that battle, an aerial torpedo struck her starboard quarter and damaged the rudder. The crew made temporary repairs and the *Intrepid* was able to reach Pearl Harbor for more extensive work.

Back in fighting trim, she then departed for operations in the Marshalls. In early September 1944, the *Intrepid* struck positions in the Palaus and then steamed west, attacking positions on Mindanao and in the Visayan Sea. The carrier circled back and supported marines overcome by opposition from hillside caves and mangrove swamps on Peleliu. Further striking throughout the Philippines, she pounded Okinawa and Formosa and helped neutralize air threats to Leyte.

After the Battle of Leyte Gulf, the *Intrepid* scored hits on a Japanese fleet carrier and a destroyer in the process of disabling Clark Air Field. A burning kamikaze then crashed into one of her port gun tubs. Ten men were killed but the *Intrepid* continued to hit airfields and shipping. Then on November 25, 1944, a heavy force of Japanese aircraft struck back and two kamikazes crashed onto the deck, killing six officers and five crew.

Vincent spent most of his time below deck during the almost four-week journey back to civilization on the wounded hero ship. He sniffed out many card games and, for the first time, got to know a few of the seamen. He had previously only viewed these swab jockeys from afar during peace time and in conflict. They were interested in his experiences, and Vincent quickly earned their respect. In turn he fully admired the commitment and sacrifice of these brave men.

"I've witnessed banzai attacks first hand. These Japs just won't give up ... Heard those kamikaze attacks are just as horrific." Vincent spoke about his experiences during an engine room poker game with three sailors.

"Yeah, they get your attention in a hurry," Lenny Adams, a gunner from Floral Park, Illinois, responded. "We saw this twin engine attack bomber dropping its cargo out of our field of vision, and I looked at Ernie next to me and said 'Holy shit!'" He started using the playing cards as a prop. "Okay, so this is our carrier, and this is the Jap plane." He added his index finger to visualize his story. Then he included his left hand.

"This bastard was fast, even faster than Marine Corsairs. A squadron of them couldn't even keep up. He's 3,500, maybe 4,000 feet in the air, and then he can't evade anymore, so he decides to go out in a blaze of glory."

"Yeah, just like those fucking banzais. They're pinned down, but out of nowhere, here they come." These images would be hard for Vince to ever forget.

Lenny continued, "He takes a tight 180-degree turn, flies back over the island, then directly toward us. Fucker's nose is down. I'm standing next to a .50-caliber, trying to stay calm. I yell to Ernie to hold his fire till he's in range!"

"Then what?" Vince was locked in on the story.

"The eighteen-year-old kid ignores me. He's firing tracers, which of course are far under the path of the bastard. So I yanked him aside and took over." His visual display moved from the playing cards and his fingers to him with his arms outstretched with tight fists, mimicking how he fired his guns. "Speed wasn't a factor; bastard's coming head on. I elevated the gun and waited. Plane's getting closer and looking larger and larger. A friggin' second's like an hour. Fifteen hundred feet; I haul it, squeeze the trigger for a two-second burst. Time to do or die!" He was now reliving the story intently. "Nothing hit; time's up. My gun overheated and jammed … Fuckin' helpless. Other guns are firing, too. Nothing's hitting this bastard!"

"Holy crap … what'd you do?" Vince asked as Lenny gave a hollow laugh.

"Wasn't my day to die. Pilot pulled up when he got to a hundred feet away … Leveled off … Cleared our mast and a minute later crashed into a much larger Dutch merchant ship. Slid across her main deck in a ball of flames and fell into the sea. Two hours later, we get nailed on our opposite side. I lost four buddies."

Len lit a Winston and left the compartment. Fortune smiled upon people for a reason. Why else would he and Lenny Adams be alive while thousands were not?

They made excellent time heading east and were scheduled to dock in San Francisco Bay a few days before Christmas. The card games dried up and Vincent found new ways to stay entertained. One afternoon he made his way through the galley and noticed a few sailors passing the time talking among themselves or reading. Paperback novels, heartfelt letters from home, the Bible, and a few magazines had all found their way around the long narrow tables.

Vincent looked over the assortment of material. *Hmmm, don't remember the last time I read an entertainment magazine.* A picture of Betty Grable got his attention, so he reached over and picked up the *Hollywood Reporter.* It was dated July and he thought it would be a refreshing change from the sports he normally read. Since he would now be a civilian, he wanted to know what was going on in the world and who the hot starlets were.

He flipped through the first few pages and looked at some pictures of sultry young women. He perused the first half without much interest, but then his eyes grew intense as he bore down on page fifty-two. In a montage of celebrities on the red carpet of some movie premier, positioned in the bottom left corner, was a picture of Virginia Hill, a B-level movie star being escorted by none other than Benjamin "Bugsy" Siegel.

13

TWO GORILLAS

Fall 1996–Fall 1998

As a CRITICAL MEMBER of Friends of the High Line (FHL), Lou Troncone believed he was the best man for the job. For nine years, the thirty-four-year-old had paid his dues toiling in all of the areas of repair work for this nonprofit partner of the Department of Parks & Recreation. He felt more than vindicated when he received his promotion to maintenance technician. Now the senior man on the team, he was dedicated to the ongoing maintenance of Van Cortland Park in the Bronx.

Lou was a hard worker. After his father passed away earlier in the year, he had moved back home to help care for his aging mother. The move was a trade up from his small two-bedroom garden apartment on Tanglewood Park in Yonkers to the sixteen-hundred-square-foot, three-bedroom colonial in Mount Vernon that he had grown up in. Now his wife and two kids (a four-year-old son and a three-year-old daughter) had a little more room, and he was also relieved of the $1,100-a-month rent payment.

Before his promotion, Lou and his wife had many late-night conversations about the strong possibility of him being snubbed over. In July, the director of horticulture and park operations had hired a new manager of park maintenance (MPM) to run the FHL partnership. Then, two weeks later, while Lou was repairing a faulty sprinkler system, a fresh-faced kid showed up to assist him. He was a tall, lanky Irish guy, no older than twenty-five who introduced himself as Brendan Lynch. He had recently moved to the Bronx from Shirley, out in Suffolk County. Outgoing, he freely admitted that his sister's husband, who was the new MPM, had just gotten him the job.

Lou had seen rampant nepotism within FHL in the past as family and friends seemed to be promoted or assigned to the best projects. With the delay in the appointment of the new maintenance technician (it should have been filled by early June), he was convinced it was just a matter of time before Brendan would be leapfrogged over him to be his supervisor.

Thankfully, that was not the case. In fact, Brendan ended up being a good guy. He had an uncle who worked as a grounds keeper at Yankee Stadium. For the playoffs against the Orioles, he even invited Lou to go to game one. From that exciting extra-inning win on, the two die-hard Yankee fans began to spend a lot of time together. They'd hit the bars for happy hour on Thursday and then during a slow Friday they even skipped out early and bolted down to Atlantic City to play blackjack and poker.

They spoke a lot about gambling and card playing. Frustrated, Brendan had complained he could not find a decent poker game. Lou had an easy solution. He regularly went to card rooms that rotated among bars in the area. He played on Tuesdays on McLean Avenue——"won't hurt you too bad "—or the more lively game up in Tuckahoe when he could get out on Friday nights—"definitely bring your wallet."

By June of the following year, Lou began to feel slighted by his new friend. Brendan had quit his position at FHL, but who could blame him? His uncle secured him a job for a few extra dollars working as a groundskeeper at Yankee Stadium. Lou did not hang around with him as much, and he stopped receiving the plumb tickets to games that Brendan flashed around.

Lynch had made quick friends with many regulars who played the high-stakes games, especially at Ressini's. Lou would amusingly see him whisper with Big Tony or Sally Nuts, begging them to extend more credit. He had become an aggressive high-action player and normally reached his $1,000 limit shortly after arriving. He would wander in after the baseball game was over and then, like clockwork, dangle tickets as collateral for more credit. The two big guys were die-hard Mets fans and hated the Yankees, so they viewed the tickets like they would a piece of discarded toilet paper. What normally ended up happening was Brendan would mope around. Then, when Jimmy Tree or one of his associates came to play, he would eagerly present to them the same proposition.

Before any deal was transacted, Sally Nuts always got the last word in. "Jimmy, that big redheaded mick was gonna let me have tickets to the Saturday and Sunday games for five hundo total. Offer him four. Bet he'll take it. You may even get him to put his best lipstick on and give you some action under the table as a sweetener."

"I'll give you three eighty, kid," Jimmy Tree laughed and then the rest of the room erupted as he tossed a stack of twenties on the floor while he pretended to unzip his fly.

Lou totally distanced himself as Brendan socialized more with people living on the edge. Pretty soon Joe Maggia, a friend of Jimmy Tree's, started having late-night whisper conversations with the unlucky Irishman. By the end of the baseball season, the donkey had delivered in a big way. Brendan showed up on the last weekend of September with twenty-four premium tickets to the wildcard games against the Indians. While the Bronx Bombers didn't advance to the second round, Maggia ended up making over twenty-grand scalping the tickets.

Joseph "Magnum" Maggia was the nephew of Vito "Ocean" Panducci, who was a boss in the Jersey-based DeCavalcante crime family. Magnum ran a strip club that leveraged the scantly clad women and flowing alcohol to sell drugs and sexual favors. He even paid Brendan for the tickets with his own money after beating him in a huge pot. The *botchagaloop* called a $900 raise with two pair, threes and fours with an open-ended straight showing on board. Magnum turned over his ace, and Brendan immediately went to plan B, which consisted of the envelope of playoff tickets. Maggia thought ahead and invited Brendan to his strip club anytime to peruse the merchandise. He needed him in his clutches for the next baseball season.

The 1998 season ended up being the year of the Yankees, and Magnum had the hottest connection. They had the beeline to witness 114 regular-season victories to go along with winning both playoff rounds and the World Series. In all, Lynch bartered over eight hundred regular-season tickets and forty-eight lucrative postseason tickets to feed his gambling habit. Maggia thought it was a good trade. He made at least twenty times the amount.

All in all, it had also been an interesting twenty-eight months working undercover for Special Agent Liam Doherty. Based out of Hartford, he had built quite a dossier on Tracino, Maggia, and a few other associates. The FBI's investment in season tickets had been fruitful. They had concealed tiny microphones to record conversations from the seats "Brendan Lynch" had reluctantly lost on those unlucky nights. Even more valuable was the information garnered from the eight agents who occupied the seats next to, behind, and in front of his seat. While some of the tickets were scalped and found their way into innocent bystander hands, a high percentage was also spread around as a show of gratitude to the infrastructure of organized crime. Many of these oversized backsides ended up having lively conversations as their beloved team played while they drank six-dollar beers for three hours.

The best place to have an Italian meal in southern Connecticut was on Showboat Avenue, adjacent to the Greenwich Yacht Club. The five-star reviews of Edmundo's Restaurante trumpeted the signature veal and chicken specialties, not to mention the out-of-this-world red sauce that formed the base for all of the pasta dishes.

Roberto Palma had been the maître d' at Edmundo's for the past five years. It was excellent money, and he only reported half of his $110,000 income to the IRS. The other half was received under the table in the form of tips from valued customers showing their appreciation for position-A seating or being able to squeeze them in at the last minute.

Palma had been in the catering business his entire life. His family had moved to Eastchester from Italy when he was a small child. He served in positions in the trade to help his parents since high school and then to pay for college (for two years he attended Pace University). His ultimate goal was to open his own place, but for now he was more than content with the money he made. The single thirty-one-year-old dated frequently and had plenty of cash.

A new but friendly (great tipper) customer approached him on a busy Saturday night. He thanked Palma for squeezing him in on such short notice (twenty-five dollars was always very generous), and he wanted to know if he could have a donation from the restaurant for a local charity event he was hosting. Steven Schuster was a doctor of oncology at the Albert Einstein College of Medicine in the Bronx and sat on the board of a new foundation that was dedicated to finding the cure for childhood leukemia.

Since Palma's younger sister had died from the disease when she was seven, he immediately took interest in the cause. Besides donating two gift certificates, he received approval from the owner of Edmundo's to cater the festivities. The inaugural event consisted of a charity poker tournament held on November 11, 1996, at the Bronxville Woman's Club in the affluent village in lower Westchester. It ended up being a huge success, and the foundation raised over $24,000.

Palma got to talking with Dr. Schuster and found he was as avid a poker player as he was. To let off steam and anxiety from his days, which now consisted primarily of preparing physicians to excel in the science and art of medicine, he found a lively round of cards to be quite enjoyable. Palma felt the same way, but his excess energy needed to be relieved after frantically running around a crowded eatery. He usually played late on Fridays at a lively game in Tuckahoe and also on Tuesdays on his night off at an Irish pub on McLean Avenue in Yonkers.

The good doctor was an interesting character. He always seemed to have a friend or a friend of a friend who knew something about whatever people were talking about. He also went through boom-and-bust cycles where he won one week and then proceeded to lose it all and even more the following week. After six months of this behavior, Palma had enough of his far-reaching stories, not to mention having to lend money to a supposedly well-respected physician who probably had a lot more excess cash than he did.

By the summer of 1997, Palma pulled aside Big Tony.

"Yo, Tee … Need to ask you a favor."

"What's up, BP? Hey, how are your parents doing? My dad said they're looking to sell the house and move to Florida." Tony took a sip out of his club soda.

"Yeah, he's retiring in a few months. Worked his ass off for thirty years; now looking forward to throwing away all his paint brushes … Hey, you know the good doctor, right? He's been a pain in my wallet … think he can go on the book … guy has a good job, but he's always coming to me for money, putting a dent in my drinking fund." Palma shook his head in frustration.

"Working out nice so far. Damn, with you as his bank, he's filling my wallet real nice." Tony laughed and tapped Palma on the chest. "He's been playing for some time now, so he's probably safe to go on the book. I hear you, BP. No one wants to miss out on a hand Doctor Doom is in, so as long as you say he's cool, that's fine with me."

Tony and Sally Nuts had always extended credit to Palma, and he never failed to pay back in a timely fashion. Actually, Palma never feared for his life. He had known both of the big men from when he was a kid and played on Tony's Little League team. As an appropriate gesture, though, whenever he fell behind by a week or so, he sweetened the return with complimentary meals at the Greenwich restaurant.

Palma worked out an arrangement with Dr. Schuster that from now on Sal and Tony had agreed to provide him credit on his unlucky nights. It was a smooth arrangement for a few months but hit a snag halfway into the football season. Besides poker, it appeared sports gambling was also a good stress release from lecturing medical students. Unfortunately, the combination of four really unlucky weeks of cards combined with one horrific Saturdays of college football betting was more than the medical professional could handle. He was a stand-up guy, though, and never ducked from showing his face. As a show of good faith, he even paid $800 toward his $12,000 balance and, as a kicker, handed Sal a vial of little yellow pills.

"What the fuck is this? OC?" Sal held the plastic cylinder in his hand with disgust and then handed it back.

Dr. Schuster confidently whispered to him, "Street value's at least eight hundred ... Good forty in there."

"No thanks, Doc. Hold on a second ... Let me change this guy out." Sal went over to his bank and collected a stack of chips from a long-standing regular player and exchanged a handful of hundred-dollar bills in return to the man. "Seems like a good night, Johnny ... I deducted the two thousand you had on the book, so we're square."

Johnny remained standing in place, counting his cash while the unlucky doctor and the business proprietor continued their conversation. Moments later, Big Tony walked over and put an end to the discussion once and for all.

"My friend, no oxy here, no coke, no smack of any kind, nothing ... *capisce?* We'd get closed down so fast ... It just ain't worth it ... Besides, it looks like this guy wants to talk with you." Tony pointed to Johnny and walked away to speak with a player who needed a reload.

The aspiring-up and-coming businessman who had just cashed out at the high-limit table was listening intently as he stood and counted his winnings. As a Good Samaritan, Johnny called the doctor over. He gave him two hundred for the entire vial. He then bought him a beer while they continued to whisper about the prospects of supplying him with even more of the little multicolored pills.

Giovanni "Johnny Boy" Cetto was a low-level Lucchese member who was looking to finally get his button. Based out of a meat company in Queens, his operation used the location as a front that filed false invoices for nonexistent deliveries and in return paid kickbacks to restaurant chefs. Along with this, they supplied kitchen workers with pot, coke, and OxyContin to resell throughout the five boroughs. Dr. Schuster assured his new source of cash flow that he had an ample supply of not just the low-dose pinkies but also the medium-dose yellows and most importantly the high-dose green fat-boy pain killers.

Over the next ten months, Special Agent Matthew Weiner, a twenty-three-year veteran of the FBI built a very damaging case against the Lucchese hierarchy. As he continued to supply Cetto with the most expensive drug on the street, they both finally received their wish. Soon after he had struck it rich with his new supplier, Cetto got his button and was now a made member. The young captain was determined to expand this newfound power, and he remained very interested in keeping his uninterrupted supply of OC flowing. The FBI had been extremely happy with the information obtained against the Lucchese's so far, and they were poised to reap even more substantial information against the ruthless crime family now that they had a direct line to a made member.

As the sun set beautifully on the horizon, Bill Reilly steered *Duct Tape* smoothly toward her berth at the Port Jefferson Yacht Club. He had been out all morning alone, hunting for tuna on his twenty-four-foot Altair fishing boat. Reilly had purchased her late last year from the widow of a friend who had dropped dead of a heart attack. Besides the boat purchase, he also leveraged the large amount of equity built up in his home to snap up a two-bedroom cottage in this picturesque town on the northern shores of Long Island. Since his drywall company was doing phenomenal business, he believed the extravagance was totally justified.

The deal offered to him for the three-year-old vessel was too sweet to pass up. For $56,000 he had his own boat, one that he could take his wife and kids on and, more importantly, one that he could go angling on. The family had already taken two trips to Block Island, and their two boys had even gotten a kick out of the cabin with the double bed and mini-television. They kept occupied watching movies and playing video games while he and his wife enjoyed the end-of-day sunset.

Bill loved his wife with all his heart. She was pregnant with their third child. The boys were sprouting up. His oldest, Brian, was the tallest in his first-grade class at Parsons Memorial. His father had hope that he would follow in his footsteps and be a football stud at Harrison High. Kevin, their three-year-old was a tough, rambunctious towhead who was sure to emulate his brother. To top it all off, Smoothrite, his contracting business, had succeeded beyond his wildest dreams.

After five years of struggle, he was lucky enough to have Ken Collins as his parents' new neighbor, who was the executive secretary treasurer of the Westchester Council of Carpenters. Collins had also graduated from Harrison High, but ten years before Reilly. Even though Collins maintained a hard-partying reputation as an alcohol and cocaine abuser, he had advanced to be one of the most powerful people in the carpenters' union. With doling out drywall contracts under his domain, he had presented the struggling Reilly a very enticing offer. Collins had agreed to give the majority of the drywall work for the Westchester Mall to Smoothrite. Then, when that massive project was finally completed, Collins then gave him another huge contract for the condominium complex being erected on Martine Avenue adjacent to the White Plains train station.

The only stipulation for all of these uncontested bids was that Billy had to work with him. Specifically, he was ordered to circumvent the union by hiring illegal workers so that Collins could avoid paying worker benefits. This allowed him to skim hundreds of thousands of dollars off the top of each contract. With his standard of living now rising rapidly and with the added prestige of being elected as the business agent for his local union, Billy laughed, "It was the least I could do."

As he slowly approached the dock, Reilly noticed two gentlemen standing by his berth. They were inappropriately dressed for a late-summer afternoon in a vacation home community. The two dark-haired, serious-looking men wore sunglasses to go along with matching blue suits and black shoes. Reilly idled the engine and tied the boat off. Requesting permission to come aboard, the two set foot without receiving a definitive answer from her captain.

"FBI, Mr. Reilly ... May we have a word with you in private?" Both said this in unison, flashing black bifolds with the shiny government-issued badges attached.

"I guess I have no choice." They walked down the four narrow steps to the cabin below. Reilly nervously looked around and then locked the hatch.

Over the next three hours, the special agents proceeded to extensively grill the contractor. They treated him with contempt and threatened the loving father with an almost certain indictment. Fraud, bribery, and racketeering charges could be filed related to his illegal activity with the Gambinos. They had had the carpenters union under investigation for quite some time and were building a huge case against Kenneth Collins of 28 Sound Meadow Road in Harrison.

The way the FBI saw it, Mr. William Reilly had two options. First, he could come back to the city with them and stand trial for his crimes. Rest assured, they did have enough hard evidence to send the good husband away for at least seven years. He would lose his business, and his family would be disgraced. The other alternative was for him to work as an informant and assist the government for what they believed to be a systemic problem of union scams and corruption throughout the construction industry. If they could build a strong enough case against the coke-snorting leader of the powerful carpenters' union, then they believed he would lead them on a silver platter to Gambino crime head Stephano Pagnotta.

It was now official. After forty-six years of blood, sweat, and plenty of Cavazzi family tears, all of the Bella's Pasta locations had been officially sold on May 18, 1997. The opening of the flagship store was on September 5, 1951, on Columbus Avenue in Tuckahoe. The eighth and final location on Route 6 in Mahopac was opened on March 12, 1986. In between, six other locations were opened in Yonkers, New Rochelle, Merrick, Hoboken, Greenwich, and Nanuet.

The Cavazzi's granddaughter had managed all of the stores, but the day-to-day responsibilities were handled by partners. Sabina Cameron Ragonese was the oldest daughter of Michael and Maria Cameron. Her brother was Chris, and the family business partners were Sal Esposito and Tony Albanese. Since the early days, Sal's dad had permission from Joe Cavazzi to run numbers out of Bella's. He would always reciprocate with ample purchases of fresh pasta, Italian sauces, and other specialties that were the staple of the pastas and antipasto platters at the restaurant. It took thirty-five years, but it had all worked out. The steady flow of all types of customers (gamblers paying their debts) was a great way to drive traffic. All they had to do was look the other way.

After her father passed away in 1994, things got very rough for Sabina. Her drinking problem escalated out of control soon after the funeral. Thankfully, she had committed herself to treatment at the same time that she met her future husband, Dominic, *in the rooms*. He was also in recovery, and as a public defender the lawyer had always been dedicated to the greater good.

This was one of the initial qualities that attracted Saby to Dom. She had also heard the calling for public service very early in life. Even before she took over management of Bella's, she had received a degree from Iona College in social work. She always gave back to the community, whether it was from collecting items for the poor, serving food at soup kitchens, or raising money for a charity, she believed public service was her true calling. The stars must have been aligned at a charity benefit she helped coordinate. Her friend Antoinella Morelli had lost her younger brother to spinal meningitis three years earlier. He was nineteen at the time and his death had devastated the entire family. Antoinella wanted to start a scholarship in his name for graduates of Roosevelt High in Yonkers. Sabina embraced the cause and subsequently found the higher calling during the night of the inaugural benefit, which ended up raising over $7,000 for the Benito Morelli Scholarship Fund.

She felt so compelled to dedicate her life to the greater good that she walked right up to Antoinella's cousin Rocco.

"Hey, Rock … I'll do it."

"You'll do what, Sabe? Hey, you look great tonight." He hugged and gave her a kiss. "Where's Chris … Did he really give two thou'? Friggin'guy's loaded!"

"I'm proud of my Christopher … Seriously, your friend wanted to buy Bella's. Okay, I'll do it. You're his broker; give me an offer … I want to devote my time to things like this … Charity and such … Mom could use the retirement income anyway."

Sabina's ultimate dream was to create a foundation for children who had been abused. The abuse could be physical like a beating, mental from something like persistent verbal lambasting, or sexual like what had happened to her. Enough said.

His client Rico Vallone ended up purchasing all of the eight locations from the Cameron family. The low-down on Rico was that his true intention was to leverage the gambling and money-laundering opportunities that would be so easy to conceal through a business that transacted primarily in cash. He was expected to wait a few months and then sell a couple of the locations to other associates. Rico was one or two big scores away from possibly getting his button, and his father fronted the seven hundred grand for the transaction. Donato Vallone ran a waste management company out of Stamford. He believed his son needed a strong silent partner, especially one who was a slot below the higher echelon of the Gambinos.

It was after 1:00 p.m. before Damien Morris walked into the New York Sports Club in the Vernon Hills Shopping Center in Eastchester. He tapped the reception counter to get the attention of the girl behind the desk. She seemed preoccupied staring at a computer screen. Everyone knew who he was, but he still had to go through the motions to check in before starting his work out. She took the ID and studied it intently.

"Enjoy your work out," she said with a slight Spanish accent.

He took a few steps, then turned back toward her and smiled. "You new here?"

Damien then proceeded to walk away with a cocky grin on his face. Yes, he would be back. *That chick was hot.* If she was Dominican, that would seal the deal. He would take her out for sure.

Damien had tremendous confidence. The thirty-two-year-old was a six-foot-two, 250-pound wrecking machine and an enforcer for one of the Gambino crime bosses, Santo Tracino. He believed he could go wherever he liked and do whatever he wanted, and he was bold and brazen about all of his alleged violent exploits.

"I don't talk about guns; I do this, you know?" He made a shooting motion with his hand during a conversation with a workout partner to designate he was an action guy.

"Yeah … Whatever, my friend, give me a quick spot, okay." Sal was sitting with his back to Damien on the bench press. He lay down below the bar and then proceeded to pump out ten solid reps of 275 pounds of iron.

"Good set, Nuts. How heavy you goin' today?"

"Don't know, maybe only three fifty, feeling a little sluggish. Tony and I didn't finish up till 5:00 a.m. High-stakes game was sick. We just couldn't let it end." Sal stretched his back.

"Hey, did you see that new Latina behind the desk … Smoking hot body." Damien pointed towards the entrance to the health club.

"I'm married, buddy. You know I don't look at other women. Hehe, yeah, I saw her. Where you been? She's been here for like two weeks?" Sal flexed his fifty-two-inch chest in the mirror. Damien thought he seemed disinterested in the conversation.

"I had to do something for a guy downtown. We took the package to the beach after." He put two more 45-pound plates on the bar and proceeded to bang out ten easy reps of 315 pounds. Sal ceremoniously stood behind him to spot, but Damien did not need one for such light weight.

After almost two hours of heavy lifting, Morris showered and changed from his sweaty T-shirt and black sweatpants into blue jeans and a short-sleeved, multicolored bowling shirt. On his way out, he slowed down.

"See you later, sweetie." The new receptionist smiled and said good-bye.

"So where you from, honey? You have an adorable smile." Damien stopped in his tracks.

"Thank you very much ... Damien, right? I'm from Eastchester now ... live down the street ... But I'm Dominican. My name is Elaudys."

Morris walked cockily over and continued to check her out and flirt. She was about five foot four with a kick-ass body. She probably taught an aerobic class there. Her skin was a light shade of brown, and her lips were juicy. She had all of the qualities he found irresistible. He may have been half Italian and Irish, but his tastes were strictly on the spicier side and he was only attracted to black or Latina chicks. Based on years of hands-on research, he came to the conclusion that Dominican ladies were the best, hands down.

"Hey, Elaudys ... We gonna go out or what?" Sal interrupted the playful exchange. He put his arm around Damien's shoulder while also reaching across the counter. He squeezed her hand in a playful manner.

"Sorry, poppy, I don't date married men." She returned her attention to Damien.

"Forget this guy, honey ... I'm a lot better than him," Sal continued on futilely and then after a few seconds gave up. "Take care, Damien ..."
"See ya, Elaudys."

With Sal out of the way, Damien continued with his charm. It did not take much coaxing for the pretty Dominican to agree to go on a date. She told him she liked the beach, and he was more than happy to show off his six-pack and ripped torso in the sand.

This was the genesis of a romance Damien had never experienced before. As a bouncer for the hottest strip club in Manhattan, he had gone through a plethora of all kinds of women, but for some reason this time it just felt different. He even slowed down from the women he took home from the club. However, it did not slow down his other activities.

For years now, he had regularly participated in a scheme to shake down Jiggles, an upscale gentlemen's club frequented by celebrities and sports icons. He took his cut from everything you could imagine: the coat-check concession, folded twenties stuffed in the strippers' garter belts, and protection money extorted from the owner. Recently, he pleased Santo immensely with a $20,000 payment. He had given the owners of the club permission to fire one of their managers. The manager was a member but not a made member of the Gambino family. He had been causing a lot of headaches among the girls.

After objecting to losing his job, the manager threatened to sue Jiggles for proper restitution. The last thing Santo wanted was heat on his operations, so he received permission from the powers above and then ordered Damien to persuade the guy to rethink his legal rights. The package to the beach which he had referenced to Sal was related to Damien and an associate (who played cards regularly at Ressini's) temporarily kidnapping the litigious former manager. They drove him down to the Chesapeake Bay and then beat him bloody with an ax handle. Not surprisingly, no lawsuit was ever filed.

January 3, 1998
SPECIAL AGENT DAWN NICHOLAS closed the "Two Gorillas" file and placed it safely in the cabinet to the right of her desk within her uncomfortably small cubicle. As she locked it up for the night, she felt extremely satisfied with her accomplishments over the past year and a half. The two gentle giants had provided the government with a tremendous amount of information and uncovered reams of new people to follow, which allowed them to infiltrate the Mafia in a way never accomplished successfully before.

Not all of their infiltrations had succeeded. Of the twenty strategically placed undercover agents in mob-related activities, only six had yielded quantifiable results. But these were so far shaping up to be homeruns. Not only had they direct access to new made members, they also had key locations throughout the metro area wiretapped and under constant surveillance. A construction company owner was coaxed to flip, crooked strip club and restaurant supply owners spent more time with undercover agents than with their own *goomas*, and the crown jewel was shaping up to be a Mafia hit man who was madly in love with Special Agent Dominique Tejata. She even believed her make-believe romance would blossom further and was confident that the killer would soon get down on his knee and propose.

14

CAT'S GOT NINE LIVES

April 16, 1947

BEN SIEGEL HAD BEEN flying across the country all day, but he still managed to have a bounce in his step as he walked out of the Los Angeles Airport terminal. After peering around for a few seconds, he saw the familiar driver waiting by the newly waxed 1946 Chrysler Plymouth. The chauffeur hustled across the road, grabbed his luggage, and placed the bags in the trunk.

Siegel grabbed the *Los Angeles Times* folded next to him on the backseat and began reading the sports section.

"You believe this crap. Unbelievable, friggin' Dodgers signed the colored guy. Baseball just won't be the same." Siegel was reading the headline about Jackie Robinson breaking the color barrier and being the first black man to play major-league baseball for the Brooklyn Dodgers.

"He's a real good player, though, sir. Tough as nails as far as I know."

"I'm from Brooklyn, fella. No way a colored-guy should be playing for the bums. Let some other team break barriers."

"Yes, sir, if you say so. But the Dodgers haven't won a World Series as far as I can remember. Last year was gut-wrenching. They should try anything … if you don't mind me saying." This guy had driven Siegel before. He knew what he was talking about regarding baseball.

"Diehards from Brooklyn made the syndicate a lot of money last year when they lost on the showdown with the Cardinals. Stupid fools, bet with their hearts. Glad I'm on this side of the ledger!" Brooklyn had tied for first place in 1946 with the St. Louis Cardinals, Then they lost to the Redbirds in the first-ever playoff series. "Where you from again fella?"

"From back East, but moved around a lot. Can't really say I have a home, not much family either. Figure I'd just do what I'm doin' here now, try and scrape along." The driver merged onto the freeway.

"Yeah, well, I got my own problems; don't need to know your whole life story." Siegel stopped talking and put the newspaper in front of his face. He was done speaking.

They drove the rest of the way in silence, heading north on the freeway.

A half hour later they approached the West Hollywood area, making a right turn off La Cienega onto Sunset Boulevard before stopping at Ciro's Le Disc.

Dressed in a light gray seersucker suit complemented with a maroon-colored tie, Siegel walked past a throng of people queued up to enter the club. He sauntered along the back, listening to the up-and-coming crooner belt out his rendition of *Try a Little Tenderness* from his newly released album. The joint was packed because of this Sinatra kid, and Siegel was eager to get him to sing at his casino. He would speak with him back stage. Until then, he would wait in Billy's office.

Besides Ciro's, Billy Wilkerson owned a few other popular nightclubs in Los Angeles. A decade earlier, the Tennessee native had staked his position in Tinseltown with the success of his film industry trade paper, the *Hollywood Reporter*. He branched out to own clubs and resorts featuring singing, dancing, and illegal backroom casinos. A notorious gambler, he was infamous for losing over $750,000 while playing at several Las Vegas casinos in 1944. A movie producer friend suggested he stop gambling in casinos and build one instead.

He took the advice, drove out to the desert, and looked into it. While a few gambling parlors had been operating in Las Vegas since the thirties, Wilkerson had grander visions. Not interested in catering to the current assortment of cowboy types, he came across a thirty-three-acre site that was perfect for an elaborate resort and casino.

He pulled no stops and planned to have the resort fitted with luxuries like air conditioning and a golf course. It was named the Flamingo Club. But because of postwar shortages and the extravagance of the project, there were many cost overruns during the early phase of construction. This unforeseen development forced him to expand his financing options. He reluctantly accepted an offer from Meyer Lansky to invest $1 million to complete the project. Wilkerson retained a one-third interest in the resort. Within weeks of the deal, Ben Siegel announced he would be representing Lansky and became a new partner in the project.

Las Vegas had also appealed to Siegel. At the direction of Lucky Luciano, he had come out west in the mid-1930s to explore new opportunities. From a California prison cell, Luciano sanctioned his West Coast power to California crime boss, Jack Dragna.

"The syndicate's moving in ... Ben's coming west for the good of his health and the health of all of us."

"And what if I object?" Dragna replied in a defiant tone.

"You can either take part ... or be taken apart." Dragna was no match for Luciano's East Coast muscle.

One of Siegel's first tasks was to get local bookmakers to subscribe to Trans-America, Al Capone's illegal wire, instead of the competing Continental Wire. It was critical for all serious bookmakers to have access to immediate race information. Western Union, the only legal wire service, restricted horse race results until declared official, and this presented an opportunity for unscrupulous bettors to game the system. With many race results delayed due to photo finishes or jockey objections, inside information by "post-betting" and placing a bet before bookmakers got the official finish was a major risk.

Siegel gained Trans-America's first western foothold by setting up operations in Arizona and Nevada. It took him six years to break into California, but when he did, he quickly eliminated the competition by shooting and killing the leader of Continental Wire, Chicago crime boss James Ragan.

Once in California, Siegel formed a partnership with a childhood friend from Brooklyn. George Raft was an actor. He and Siegel then developed illegal gambling operations and worked a racket to gain control of the movie extras union. Siegel used the threat of the extras walking out on movie productions to lean on stars and producers for extortion money. Even though he was stealing from them, these Hollywood types still craved his appearances at their parties.

With a long history of running backroom casinos, Siegel saw the potential of legalized gambling as a way to print money. He viewed Wilkerson's project the perfect way to backdoor into the business.

Without knocking, Ben walked past the guard outside of Wilkerson's office and opened the door. Billy was sitting at a card table surrounded by four gentlemen. One was George Raft. The other three were movie industry friends whom Siegel had met before.

"We had a good month." Wilkerson nervously walked over to greet his partner.

"I know, just flew in. I stopped off to see things on my trip back from Florida." Siegel had been shuttling back and forth from Los Angeles, Las Vegas, and Meyer Lansky's home in Miami to provide constant progress reports.

A year earlier, Siegel had begun to squeeze Wilkerson from the day-to-day operations of the construction at the Flamingo. As Siegel had no contracting experience builders blatantly stole from him and the price of the project sky-rocketed; escalating fourfold to $6 million. All of the increase was absorbed by Luciano, Lansky, and their East Coast associates. To compound matters, even more disturbing news was revealed. At a conference in Havana attended by Lansky, Luciano, Frank Costello, Vito Genovese, and Joey Adonis, it was revealed that Siegel had apparently been skimming money and putting it in numbered Swiss bank accounts.

"There's only one thing to do with a thief who steals from his friends. Benny's got to be hit." With that comment, Meyer sanctioned the execution but still was not ready to give up on his longtime associate. "If the place works out, don't worry we'll find many ways for Benny to pay us back," Lansky recommended that the execution be stayed until after the opening of the Flamingo, set for the day after Christmas.

"I agree," Luciano said. "Benny's been a valuable guy, almost from the beginning. I really don't wanna see him get hit. But if the place flops, that's it for him."

Christmas came and went, and the Flamingo's casino opened for action. Siegel pulled out all the stops. He hired George Jessel as emcee. Rose Marie and Jimmy Durante were the entertainment, with Xavier Cugat's orchestra providing the music. It was a disaster. The weather in both Las Vegas and Los Angeles did not cooperate and the charter flights for his Hollywood friends never made it off the ground due to heavy fog. With no hotel rooms in the still uncompleted resort, guests gambled at the Flamingo and then took their winnings back to the downtown hotels. Most of the celebrities left after the second day, leaving a vacant showroom and empty gaming tables.

"It's a fuckin' flop!" Lansky reluctantly reported back.

"That's it for him ... done ... Kill the bastard!" There was rage among the gangsters assembled in Havana.

"Gentlemen, just a little more time." Meyer had saved him again. "We all know Las Vegas will become profitable. May I suggest a short delay? In the meantime, our lawyers could put the Flamingo in receivership. Our losses would be stopped. Then we could move in and buy them out for pennies on the dollar."

"Meyer, he's on very thin ice." Luciano and the syndicate heads reluctantly agreed, and their old friend was given yet another reprieve.

Siegel ordered the resort closed until the hotel portion could be finished. He devoted all of his waking hours making sure the Flamingo was ready for its grand reopening. Lansky had managed to buy him a few more months, and Ben made sure he didn't waste it. Even though it was still not 100 percent complete, the casino reopened during the first weekend in March.

"I need Sinatra. You tell that kid I gotta speak with him as soon as he gets off stage," Siegel demanded to Wilkerson.

"Sure thing, sure thing. Hey, you see that guy ... He's gonna be there tomorrow with a few heavy hitters." Wilkerson pointed at one of the card players. He also wanted the project to succeed and had been marketing it to all of his acquaintances in Hollywood.

"Good, good ... We need all we can get. After I talk to the crooner, I'm heading back to Beverly Hills for some rest. I'll be in Vegas tomorrow night."

"I'll be there. The word's getting out that it's the place to be. Shoot, I feel good right about now." The Nashville native nervously shook Siegel's hand and opened the door for him. "I'll get Vinny to bring the car back around. He'll be waiting for you after your talk. He'll get you home as soon as possible."

Hollywood, 1945–47
THAT LAST WEEK ON the *Intrepid*, Vincent immersed himself in all types of variety magazines. After viewing the picture of Bugsy Siegel, he had a new focus, and that was to find out as much as he could about the ruthless killer.

While away, he was unaware Bugsy had moved his scams to the Hollywood set. He needed to bone up on all that had transpired with the mobster's life over the past decade. Luckily, there were plenty of old and new issues of the *Hollywood Reporter* and *Variety* on board. He devoted every waking moment to researching his subject.

After docking in San Francisco, Vincent immediately hopped on a bus heading south to Los Angeles. He found a small apartment in West Hollywood and wrote Teresa that their new home would not be in San Diego. Then, bright and early on the first Monday of 1945, he waited in line to audition for a part in the movie *Nob Hill*. As a tall, rugged-looking, and handsome man, he was cast with a minor part as a bar patron. The leads of the Technicolor film were Joan Bennett and George Raft.

Raft was a forty-five-year-old motion picture actor. While he could have been a major star, he held the unenviable distinction of turning down the lead roles in two of the widely viewed movies of the day, *Casablanca* and *Double Indemnity*. His misfortune was probably due to his illiteracy, as he may not have been fully able to comprehend the movie scripts that Clark Gable and Fred MacMurray were eventually cast in.

Vincent knew a lot about Raft. He had performed many times at their banquet hall. A lifelong friend of Bugsy Siegel, Raft left for Hollywood in 1929. Vincent remembered his parents taking him to the theater to view Raft as the coin-flipping Guido Rinaldo in *Scarface*. Always observant, Vincent listened intently as Pasquale discussed the former regular of the club who had now become a fledging movie star.

As part of his Bugsy analysis, Vincent quickly noticed a number of pictures of the gangster palling around with Raft. He devised a plan. While moonlighting as a bartender, he shadowed the acting career of George Raft. Over the next two years, Vincent was able to latch on as an extra in four of Raft's movies. His patience was rewarded in *Mr. Ace*. Over the week they worked together where he played the part of a gangster, Vincent was so convincing as his right-hand man that after a cast party, Raft invited him to one of his and Siegel's backroom casinos.

Vincent became privy to more of Siegel's life, and on more than one occasion his father's killer showed up while he was playing cards. Neither Bugsy nor Raft had recognized the teenage boy who was now a full-grown man, and Vincent absorbed as many conversations as he could.

One associate happened to be Wilkerson and Vincent continued his surveillance by landing a bartending position at Ciro's. Soon striking up a friendship, Vincent entertained his new boss with stories of his hero friend, the late M.Sgt. Nailor. As they played cards till the early morning hours in the back room of the club, Billy could not get enough of his native Tennessean's bravery in the Pacific. By the beginning of 1947, Vincent became Wilkerson's private driver and bodyguard.

Wilkerson was a boisterous individual who always told it like it was. He spent many car rides speaking with business partners, bankers, and even Siegel about the financial difficulties and construction delays at the Flamingo. Vincent took it all in. As he was the son of a mobster, he began to see the writing on the wall.

May 20, 1947

VINCENT AND TERESA SCALA laid sleeping arm in arm, enjoying each other's company. Teresa had returned from Guadalcanal months before the war in the Pacific had finally come to an end. The couple still lived as newlyweds, even though they were now married almost four years. While her husband spent many hours away, she was fully aware of his actions and the plan he was cultivating.

Vincent had kept his personal life private from Raft and Wilkerson. He even used the alias Vinny Mileto for acting auditions and for when he introduced himself to the club owner. Terrie Carpinello was also able to assist with the infiltration by getting a job as a cocktail waitress at Ciro's. After their detective work, she would laugh to her husband as they compared notes.

"Vinny, it's amazing at how much men speak their mind when in the presence of beautiful women. Bugsy's sure worried about the Flamingo succeeding, he was practically begging Sinatra to sing but got turned down cold." Teresa rubbed his bare chest as they continued their pillow talk.

"Luciano had enough of his game. Darling, his days are numbered." Vincent gave a wry smile and kissed her.

Teresa would be leaving her man once again. Vincent would follow her back to Tuckahoe in short order, but he now wanted his wife, who let him know the previous evening that she was two months pregnant, to be in a safe place.

After breakfast, he kissed her good-bye and headed out to pick up Wilkerson. As he pulled up to the Beverly Hills mansion, there were four large suitcases waiting in front of the steps. Vincent placed them in the trunk and opened the door for the fast-moving club owner. They drove off.

"It's over Vinny … Take me to the airport." Billy wiped his perspiring forehead with a handkerchief.

"That's a lot of bags for a weekend in Vegas, Mr. Wilkerson?"

"You didn't hear me, son. It's over. That fucker Siegel screwed me, and his next move will be to kill me." He took a swig out of a silver flask which had been hidden in his inside jacket pocket.

Billy had known Bugsy since the early thirties and knew his modus operandi from the start. Once Siegel showed up as Lansky's surrogate, he knew in his heart that the Flamingo would never end up being his. First he was forced to sign over most of the construction, and since then gradual steps were taken to gain control away from him.

"They made me sell my remaining interest for six hundred grand. My life vision, my dream … gone. I asked for two mil, and they gave me shit." Billy took another deep pull on the flask.

"I thought you two were partners. I always read it was his vision." As he had a way of doing, Vincent prodded him for additional information. This was always easy when Billy had been drinking.

"Are you kidding me! That hoodlum took credit for my idea. I had it named already. Heard him bragging that he called it Flamingo 'cause the fuckin' bird brings him luck. The idiot was even taken to the cleaners by the landscapers. The dumbass even purchased the same palm trees twice. This project has been a circus since he took over."

"So, where you headed?" Vincent inquired some more.

"I told them to send my check to Paris. I'm getting as far away as possible. My general manager called the other night. She was hysterical crying. Her husband just got paroled, and he told her that they ordered him to kill me." Billy nervously tried to start reading the newspaper but reluctantly gave up.

"I thought Mr. Siegel was safe now. Seems the casino's going along swell?" Vincent found that short inquiries were all he needed to pry the lips of his boss.

"No, Vinny, it looks good on the surface, but he's skirted death a few times. Meyer and Lucky saved him more than once, but his greedy ways have caught up; been stealing since this project got under way. This cat's got nine lives, and he's already used up eight of them."

They reached Los Angeles Airport. "Pleasure to have known you my I-talion friend. You're one heck of a card player and a great listener." Billy shook Vincent's hand.

He disappeared into the terminal, and Vincent checked the bags with the skycap. Wilkerson would be on a flight to New York. From there he would board a cruise ship and head to the safety of Paris. Vincent was not surprised by Wilkerson's demise and abrupt departure. He had seen firsthand Bugsy's ruthless ways and had a strong feeling the end was near.

Vincent now believed he had an ample amount of information to go through with his plan to extract revenge on the killer. He had to be fast, as he did not want Meyer Lansky or Lucky Luciano to beat him to the punch. He knew the Mafia would be blamed for the killing, and no one would lose sleep over one less gangster in the world.

Vincent would spend time over the next few weeks planning his mission. He knew where Bugsy was living, his weapon was in perfect working order, and his Teresa would be waiting for him back home.

15

MORE LIKE A YOUNGER SISTER

February 7, 1998

THE AFTERNOON WAS BRISK and windy. Not what you would expect for Paradise Island even during the middle of winter. It didn't really matter, though, as Sal and Tony were both comfortably shielded from the elements. They were inside, sitting on padded folding chairs in a made-over conference room at the Atlantis resort, watching the quarterfinal round bouts of the World of Arm-wrestling Golden Arm Championship.

Chris was also there, and the guys were getting used to having a sugar daddy. He had surprised them once again with a free trip. When Chris and Megyn came to New York for the holidays, his mom had invited almost the whole town over for the traditional Christmas Eve meal. Her first grandchild was born three weeks earlier, and she decided that was reason enough to invite everyone to celebrate with them. In between gorging on the Feast of the Seven Fishes, Chris asked his buddies if they would like to fly with him on Monroe Conway's private jet to attend an investor conference. To seal the deal, they had the audacity to throw the Pops card out there.

"Vicky, Pops has never been to the Bahamas … He'd love a trip … Don't worry, we'll take good care of him." Tony baited his wife with a slight smirky grin and then had the audacity to give her the sad puppy dog eyes expression.

How could their wives refuse? They loved Pops and besides, his brown eyes lit up as soon as he heard they were going to a place with a casino and golf course.

"Hey, Sally boy … Atlantis has a big room, right?"

"Hehe, yeah, Pops, they got like twenty craps tables … no poker, though."

"Victoria, I will watch my grandson like a hawk … Guaranteed." Pops could subdue a grizzly bear.

Vicky reached over and gave Pops a kiss and hugged him. She then proceeded to punch her husband in the arm as she gave him a dirty look. "Ang, you letting him go too? Christ, you're about to have twins." She shook her head in further disgust.

"Are you kidding Vicky? Salvatore will whine and cry more than three babies if I don't let him go. Besides, I think I'll hold out till March. I'm feelin' good." Angela stuck her tongue out at her husband.

"Sign us up, Cee … Thumbs up here … woo yeah!" Sal rubbed Angela's stomach and kissed his soon-to-be baby daughters.

Chris had to sit through company presentations on Saturday while the next day he would be free to rip up the golf course. Pops loved his golf and had been a ten handicap till he was in his early sixties. Living in Florida, he never got enough of playing the senior-friendly courses, and now back in New York he would definitely enjoy his Christmas gift from the boys, an annual membership to the golf club in town.

Chris knew his buddies would also be interested in the arm-wrestling event, which coincidently was being held the same weekend at the massive resort in a room adjacent to the Recreational Vehicle Conference.

Halfway through the preliminary matches, they escorted Pops to his seat and sat down next to him. A few minutes later, they were joined by an attractive woman with a golden tan. There were many empty seats to choose from, but Tony, of course, was not surprised she decided to take a seat directly to his right.

Still not able to get a clear look at her face, Sal practically sprained his neck with the added treat of looking at her backside as she bent down to pick up an event program lying on the floor. He poked Tony in the ribs. His buddy was well ahead of him and produced a humungous shit-eating grin. Arm wrestling was suddenly unimportant.

"Did you two enjoy the treat?" The woman sat up and faced them. They were now embarrassed, but not really too much.

"You have a nice tan. You Italian, Latin or what?" Tony attempted to break the ice. She just looked at him with contempt.

"Damn it, guys. It's me, Elaudys … Damien's girl." Seeing that they still did not have a clue, she moved in close and whispered, "Special Agent Tejata."

"Holy crap … you look different," Tony shockingly responded.

Dominique Tejata looked much different than the last time they had seen her. A few weeks earlier, in the middle of winter, she had been wearing skin-tight black spandex pants, a deep purple-colored belly shirt showcasing her naval ring and flat belly. Her face was made up completely, and her hair was teased high on top of her head. As she sat next to them in the makeshift arena, her hair was tied in a neat ponytail poking through the back of a Paradise Island baseball cap. She wore minimal makeup, and her attire consisted of a pair of white sneakers, tan slacks, and a yellow top.

On the night they were referencing, Damien had brought her to the club. He had suggested to his old friends that she should now be the waitress for the Wednesday night game. Sal immediately declined; their current waitress was an all-around great girl, and they did not want to cut off income to a single mother. He recommended the game on McLean Avenue, and he should speak with Big John. They needed better eye candy, as the current waitress had let herself go. Elaudys would definitely be an upgrade, and since she was Damien's girl, she was sure to clean up with tips.

"Your friend Chris suggested we only meet with you guys far away from your operations. We've been back-channeling with him through the Dallas field office." Special Agent Tejata began with her reason for calling this meeting.

"Yeah, that's a good thing 'cause our main concern is that we don't get found out. When this thing's over, we want to go about life just like it was before." Sal caught himself. "Well, almost like it was before." He let out a soft chuckle and elbowed Tony in the ribs.

"Baaam! You see that my friend. Like a friggin' freight train … Woohoo, nice one, Bertie!" Tony gave praise to the explosive victory by one of the legends of the sport, Bert Whitfield.

"That guy could slam a revolving door shut," Sal chuckled as he leaned over making the comment to Pops.

"Oh, so you guys like arm wrestling, huh?" Dominique asked inquisitively.

"Naah, don't follow it too much, but Whitfield's picture was on the front of the program, so we thought he was gonna be good," Tony amusingly confessed.

"I actually follow the sport, if you can believe it. My big brother loved to compete, so I combined this meeting with a mini-vacation and came here with him to watch. His friend is a top competitor now."

Elaudys-Dominique segued and briefed them on the case the FBI had built and some of the areas they may need help with over the next few months.

"I just wanted you to know that Damien's really opening up ... He just loves to brag about what he does," she said confidently.

"We heard you were really enjoying your work too. Damien brags about a lot of things." Agent Tejata silently nodded her head in agreement to Tony's comment. She had to admit that certain undercover work had its perks.

Dominique would never come right out and say it, but sex with the killer was very stimulating. When she had originally agreed to take the assignment, she was not comfortable with the prospects of being a quasi prostitute. After a few weeks of internal deliberation, she came to the conclusion that it was the only way to gain the complete trust of the suspect. Besides, she had not had a steady boyfriend or sex, for that matter, since her senior year of college. Her job was her life, so she figured it was all good.

Historically in the bureau, the roles would be reversed. Male johns regularly posed undercover and sex was a fairly common occurrence. With the new commitment to infiltrate organized crime, female agents were now needed to be an integral part of any undercover operation. Because of the "Boy's Club" nature of organized-crime, this was the only logical way female agents could effectively infiltrate.

Dominique Maria Tejata was a very young-looking thirty-one-year-old who had been with the bureau since she was twenty-four. A graduate of the University of Miami, the criminal justice major always knew she would be a special agent. She was a tomboy and an All-State, two-sport athlete at Broward High in softball and soccer. Her father was a second-generation Cuban immigrant and a decorated Vietnam War hero. He later went on to be the chief of police in nearby Dania Beach. Her stay-at-home mother was born in the Dominican Republic but had lived in Fort Lauderdale since she was nine. To top it all off, her older brother was a trooper for the Florida Highway Patrol.

She sat discussing her current assignment with the two big men as they continued to watch the arm-wrestling bouts. She made sure to pat them on the back figuratively and literally. The guys had gone over and above. They had done their homework and had come in prepared with a well-thought-out plan. They also added creative ways beyond the government's current expertise to infiltrate the gambling, extortion, drug, and prostitution dens scattered among all walks of life in the New York metro area. You could tell they had devised a master plan to keep sanitized from any chance of being uncovered. All suggestions made about whom the best targets were had been extensively researched. When the puzzle pieces started to fall into place, they felt like proud fathers.

Soon After

VITREORETINAL SURGERY WAS A medical procedure performed to treat a detached retina. The retina could detach gradually when the vitreous fluid was pulled or suddenly if caused by an injury. Postoperative care involved the patient maintaining a strict four-times-daily eye-drop treatment, and it was not recommended that they drive a car, operate machinery, or perform stressful tasks during the recovery period.

This type of surgery was an unexpected event for Felix Bannos. The day before it occurred back in 1985, he was on top of the world, a six-foot-three, 245-pound bodybuilder. The part-time bouncer also provided full-time muscle for an up-and-coming capo for the Gambinos, and he was feared anywhere he went.

Then out of nowhere, two lunatics jumped him from behind. While he was on the ground, they beat him senseless with pipes and bats—that's still the story he was going with. The thrashing was so thorough that three of his ribs cracked, his lung partially collapsed, his jaw was shattered, two teeth had to be replaced, and from the pounding he took to the side of his face, his left retina detached. He ended up spending eight weeks in a hospital bed with his jaw wired shut and for his internal and external organs to fully recover. His doctors banned him from weight lifting for a year, and he ended up losing eighty-five pounds. To top it off, his capo decided that he did not need his services anymore, and the two lunatics who put him in that condition were hired to replace him.

Thoroughly embarrassed, the emaciated Bannos fled the region to start a new life. He moved in with his grandparents in Lauderhill, built his body back to the standard he was accustomed to, and began a new legitimate career as a trooper for the Florida Highway Patrol. He was even recognized as Duty Officer for the Third Quarter of 1990 after pulling a suicidal man off of a highway overpass.

To pass the time, he and his partner began to attend and then compete in arm-wrestling competitions that were held in sports bars throughout the state. This led to his participation at the Florida State Police Olympics in Tallahassee. With very little practice, he easily won the 1991 heavyweight title. He then began to take the sport very serious and hooked up with a coach who saw his true potential.

Joe "The Blaster" Caggiano was the 1981 world champ and had the distinction of training many modern champions. An expert in the "top roll" technique, he trained Bannos to maximize his massive strength and explosive style with a roll of the wrist as he brought the opposing wrist down. Most duels ended in seconds, and Bannos went on to win ten titles—eight from the right side and two from the left.

By 1996, Bannos was ready for serious money tournaments. He went on to win recognition among the 110-kilogram world circuit regulars after he tore the bicep muscle of a highly ranked opponent from Iceland. Set to further show his skills on the global stage, he ventured off the Bahamas to compete in the World of Arm-wrestling Golden Arm 1998 Championship on Paradise Island.

The thirty-eight-year-old had a strong support network. Besides a bevy of groupies, he was joined by his parents and his elderly grandfather along with a few state trooper friends. He could never thank his partner enough for introducing him to the sport at a time when he was at an emotional low and still experiencing many sleepless nights reliving his nightmare ordeal. At the time when he had moved to south Florida, he had no friends besides his grandparents. To make matters worse, his girlfriend had broken off their engagement from his hospital bed.

Manny Tejata ended up being more than a partner. He took Bannos into his home and treated him like a brother. Felix embraced the friendship and became extremely close to the other members of the family, including his younger sister. Early on, it was the dream of Manny and his parents for Felix to date their daughter, Dominique. It was just not meant to be. She was seven years his junior, and he treated her more like a younger sister. He valued the friendship with Manny too much than to risk it by dating her. They remained close, and Felix even wrote a letter of recommendation on her application to become an agent with the FBI.

His entire support network was in place. Dominique even flew in from an assignment and was there to cheer him on. After Bannos disposed of an inferior quarterfinal round opponent, he regained his composure and walked over to get congratulations from Manny and the gang.

"Solid round, Felix. Looking good for the semis!" Manny said with admiration.

"Thanks, Bro." After a kiss to both of his parents and grandfather, he gave a bear hug to Manny and thanked Mr. and Mrs. Tejata. Bannos then bent down to sign an autograph on a program held by young boy.

"Mamma, where did Domi go? She hasn't even seen the future champ yet," Manny inquired, looking around for his sister.

"I saw her earlier, but she said she was going to sit in the back. She may be over there." Manny's mother pointed toward the exit sign in the far-right corner.

"Oh … There she is. Felix, let's go tell her the good news." Manny grabbed Bannos by the shoulder and guided him away from the crowd. Even after all of these years, he still believed that Felix was the best man for his baby sister to marry.

As they drew close, Bannos stopped in his tracks. He stood in disbelief as his self-adopted baby sister was having a discussion with the two men he hated and feared the most in this world.

"Hehe … Felix, how you doing my friend?" Sal recognized the championship competitor. He smiled and then reached out his hand and accepted a lifeless, shocked paw.

"So, this your girl?" Tony innocently commented, pointing at the speechless and confused Agent Tejata. He walked directly to Bannos, coming within an inch of his face. "What you been up to? … Wrestling arms my friend." He made the sarcastic comment with an icy glare. Bannos, the supposed tough guy, suddenly felt like he was an inferior male dog getting sniffed by a pit bull terrier.

"I'm a … I'm a champ here, Big Tony. I don't do that crap anymore." Bannos shrugged his shoulders and backed away a few steps. After all these years, he still feared this guy. "You know these two, Domi?" He asked her meekly.

"No, Felix. They were just trying their best to entertain me. They don't know squat about the sport, though. I guess they didn't realize I was part of your fan club." She smiled proudly, walked over to Felix, and gave him a warm hug.

"Two more till the championship!" Manny proudly exclaimed. They all walked off without looking back.

"You're lucky I'm not entered here, my friend." Bannos heard Tony's deep baritone voice mocking him, but he tried unsuccessfully to ignore him.

Right After That

TONY, SAL, AND POPS walked nonchalantly out of the arena. This was a story they needed to share and in a hurry, but they did not wish to raise suspicions while still in the same room as their "dear old friend."

Across the vast hallway, Chris was leaving a breakout room where he had spent time asking and listening to questions of a Jet Ski manufacturer management team. The CEO had just presented to a group of fifty analysts for the last twenty-five minutes. Chris was chatting with a few others who had been in attendance.

"Yo, Chris!" Sal yelled from across the room, raising both hands to get his attention.

He really didn't need to do that, Chris thought to himself as he waved. He amusingly laughed. The two Ivy Leaguers he was with just stood there in fear.

They both whispered to him, "You know those guys, Cameron?"

"Sort of ... Later guys." He walked over.

"Cee. I think we got some major problems. Let's go up to the suite ... fast."

Fifteen minutes later, they opened the door to the colossal room on the top floor of the Atlantis. Sal and Tony then debriefed Chris on what had just transpired. They played out all types of scenarios. Bannos had been persona non grata to Jimmy Tree and his crew for a very long time, and they were confident he did not have a line to him. It was just pure stupid luck that he had been friends with Agent Tejata. Hopefully, Bannos would believe her quickly worded story that they had simply been flirting and it was all just a coincidence.

Just then the door knocked. Agent Tejata entered the room. "What the fuck just happened back there?"

"You tell us. You should'a seen your face when he walked over. I see you didn't know that your boyfriend used to be a heavy hitter in Jimmy Tree's crew, huh?"

"Holy shit! Sal, I honestly had no clue." She had a worried look on her face. "He's a state trooper now. I hope we're okay here."

"We may have a problem." Chris directed the statement at Agent Tejata. "I don't care if he's now the president. That guy got his ass kicked by Big Tony way back when, and the way they described the meet up here today, that guy had definitely not forgotten. I don't trust him at all."

"I'm going to have to get back to you guys. I can't believe this. Everything was going so well … I have to tell my supervisor." Special Agent Tejata was visibly upset.

After she left the suite, the guys decided that they could not do anything else here to change what had just happened. They shifted gears and focused on where to have dinner. A bottle of Bacardi rum was on the counter, so they mixed a few drinks as Chris phoned up the operator to make a dinner reservation.

"If I ever see that motherfucker again, I swear, I will beat him down even worse than before." Tony looked toward the bathroom door. Pops was standing there. "Oops, sorry, Pops, didn't mean to curse."

"Wash his mouth out, Pops," Sal teased, looking to change the direction of the conversation.

"What happened just now, boys? Everything okay?"

"Sure, Pops. Always an adventure, though. Excitement everywhere." Tony handed Pops a cocktail. "I know you like Bacardi and Coke. Screw the doctor, have one before dinner."

"Well, just one. A little tired, though. After we eat, I think I'll head up early, okay boys?" Pops took a sip and sat down on the chair. "You guys go blow off some steam. It's obvious you need to."

16

PREFERABLY A GRANDMOTHERLY TYPE

The Postwar Years

ON EVERY SUNDAY AND at least three additional times during the week, Vincent Scala would walk across the narrow street from his house to the Church of the Assumption and pray to his Lord Jesus Christ. This had been his common practice for the past eight years. He would pray for a multitude of reasons.

As a grieving son, he sought comfort that his father in Heaven was watching over and guiding him. As a war veteran he needed strength to help him get over the constant nightmares and flashbacks from the battlefield. He had witnessed the unimaginable in the Pacific. Having a growing family, he prayed for their continued health and happiness. Hopefully, with his and Teresa's love, affection, and support, they would pass on strong traits when they ventured off to start families of their own. He also repented for past transgressions even though he believed his actions that evening in Beverly Hills had been totally justified.

When the life of Benjamin Siegel came to an end, there had been very little mourning. The flashy killer was placed in a $5,000 casket and interred in the Beth Olam section of Hollywood Forever Cemetery. Only five family members paid their respects at the service, and it was held before the cemetery opened for the day.

As Vincent had suspected, various theories circulated about who could have murdered Bugsy. Did Virginia Hill throw him under the bus, and was that why she fled to Paris? Had Meyer Lansky and the commission grown tired, and did they place a contract on his head? Was he alone or with another mob associate, and could that man have set him up? Why was Virginia's brother in town, and was he out to kill Siegel, too?

Only Vincent knew the real story. When staking out the location, he saw Siegel, Chick Hill, and Allen Smiley leave the house together earlier that evening. All three men then returned at dusk. Smiley was with Siegel, but he had left the room. That was when Vincent fired the fatal shots. Smiley, who was Siegel's good friend and a fellow mobster had been sitting with Siegel in the room but was very lucky. On his way back, he had lifted his arm to shield his face as the shots were fired. A bullet pierced his jacket, but he was not injured. Chick Hill had gone to bed early and awoke when the shots rang out. Virginia Hill truly loved Siegel. Since his death, she had been in a constant state of mourning and had fled the Hollywood scene for good. While the syndicate at the direction of Lucky Luciano and Meyer Lansky had wanted him dead, Vincent beat them to the punch. He took care of their problem—no charge. For all intents and purposes, Bugsy would have been dead within the week anyway.

Vincent was now called "darling" by his wife and "Vince" by family and friends. After living, surviving, and killing in the widest array of conditions, he was officially retired from violence and did not wish to ever be referred to as "Sarge." He enjoyed his solitary moments in the church that his family had helped build forty years earlier.

The Church of the Assumption was constructed in the Village of Tuckahoe in 1911. The close-knit group of Italian immigrants had felt shunned by the predominantly Irish congregation up the road at the Immaculate Conception Church. With most of the marble suitable for sale already mined, the quarry owners donated the land and also chunks of the remaining marble to the Italian workers, who built the church with their own hands and in their free time. The women helped mix the mortar while the men constructed their own place of worship on Pleasant Avenue. This was just how things were done in the small community of Tuckahoe.

Vincent's sabbatical from Tuckahoe was far too long, but not surprisingly there had been very few changes. The children continued to play and congregate on the corners of Columbus and Maynard. They still considered a wilderness adventure to be an afternoon of fishing or walking through the nearby Bronx River Park. All the tenement buildings and storefronts maintained the same depression-era aura. From third-floor walk-ups, Italian women who would yell out the window at the neighborhood kids that they were supposedly doing something bad appeared to be the same women, only older.

The biggest change he noticed was in the physical and mental appearance of his beloved mother. She had weathered so much since his father's death. He remembered her as the beautiful woman who was married to the most powerful man in town. Now she was a sunken, fragile widow who rarely ventured out of her small apartment and wore black garments all the time. She had lived an almost secluded existence. Vincent's two sisters had married and moved away to New England. While they both had asked her to move with them, she simply did not want to leave her place of birth. She was content to spend her days mourning or attending Mass.

Vince and Teresa reinvigorated his mother's life by giving her a reason to smile again. This all began when her son opened the door and kissed and hugged her for the first of such a long time. It continued in October 1947 when their baby girl Rita was born and then again when their second daughter, Anne Marie, was born in May 1951.

An eager babysitter, preferably a grandmotherly type, was needed after Teresa was rehired by Burroughs-Wellcome. With her WAAC experience, she became the first female quality control manager for the company and the work was full-time. As a returning war veteran, Vincent took advantage of the GI Bill, which provided him with free education and health care. He took a few courses at a local community college, but after he landed a job as a street sweeper for the Village of Tuckahoe's Department of Sanitation, he did not feel the need to continue with higher learning.

An important provision of the GI Bill was low-interest, zero-down payment loans for returning servicemen. In need of larger living arrangement with a bedroom for his mother, Vince purchased the small, three-bedroom home on the corner of Circle Road and Wallace Street. It was conveniently located near the Church of the Assumption.

1956–57

UNDERSTANDABLY, THE ENTIRE SCALAMARRI family was severely fractured and in flux after the tragic day in 1935. In the aftermath, the surviving relatives from the Morris Park section of the Bronx (the Scallaros) all moved to states unknown. The Scalos from Eastchester moved away as well. The last word was that all of the Scalo relatives were living in Suffolk

County on Long Island and had not returned to town since before the war began.

On a positive note, Julia Scallo, Vince's cousin from Mott Street in Lower Manhattan, now resided in the village. While her younger sister had moved to New Jersey, Julia and her husband, a nice guy named Joe Cavazzi, had moved to Tuckahoe in 1946.

Vince had a special place in his heart for Julia. On her infamous wedding day, she was the one who prodded him to ask Teresa to go for their initial walk. By the time Vince had reunited with Julia upon his return, his older cousin was already the mother of three young daughters—Tina, Rosa, and Maria. Joe was a very hard worker, and after toiling in many odd jobs, the Cavazzis had finally scraped enough savings together to open a macaroni shop. Joe loved his wife very much and thought she was the most beautiful girl in the world, so he named the store "Bella's." Vince helped them out whenever he could, and the store became a staple for residents in town to shop.

The Brooklyn contingent had also stayed in contact with Julianna Scala. During the war years, Vince's *Zia* Mary (the widow of Antonio Scalamarri) visited Tuckahoe regularly to see Julianna. Mary Scalamarri would trudge her daughter, Dina, and two sons, Marco and Angelo, up to the country to get fresh air and to check on her cousin, Julianna Scala's well-being. Little Dina had enjoyed accompanying her mother on these trips, and she spent many hours babysitting for the much younger Scala girls. As they became teens, the boys lessened their visits, deciding to spend more time hanging out with friends in Brooklyn.

By 1956, the now twenty-three-year-old Dina Scalamarri had married. Greg Esposito was a thirty-year-old, low-level gangster for the Colombo crime family. Prior to the wedding, Greg's small pizzeria on the corner of Eighty-Sixth Street and Twentieth Avenue in Bensonhurst caught fire. The business was ruined, and he was forced to close. In reality, prior to the accident the Colombos had been siphoning off cash from the establishment since it had opened its doors three years earlier. Greg still desired to be associated with one of the crime families, but he could not continue to operate under the current arrangement and in the same neighborhood.

Foul play was suspected when the small one-story, stand-alone building went up in flames, but a crime was never proven and Greg was able to collect on the $25,000 insurance policy. With the proceeds, the newlyweds opened a new restaurant away from Colombo influence in Tuckahoe. Ressini's (Mary Scalamarri's maiden name) specialty was traditional Italian fare; their signature, thin-crust pizza, was complemented by a staple of pasta, veal, and chicken dishes. The restaurant was located on Main Street, around the corner from Bella's.

Greg Esposito got reacquainted with an associate in the Gambinos. While he was a thick and large man who was the son of a bricklayer, Greg's forte was running rackets and pushing swag, not breaking bones. He ran numbers and backroom casinos in his new eatery, but a line was drawn. He effectively limited the illicit activity away from his restaurant operations, so the food and beverage deliveries remained untainted by mob influence. To help run the legitimate side, he needed the help of a reliable family member.

"Vince, I need a favor. Actually, this will benefit us both." Greg had stopped by the Scala home to visit his *goombah* shortly before Ressini's grand opening.

"Have some of my homemade vino, Gregorio. It's very good." Vince poured two glasses and then placed the four-gallon jug of red wine back on the floor under the small, round kitchen table. "Now, what's the favor?"

"*Grazie, molto buono*, excellent." Greg took a sip and complimented his host. "*Paesano*, I can only trust you. I need your help with the restaurant, bartend, manage the place, and above all, handle all of the cash."

Vincent took two short successive sips and thought through the job offer. "On one condition: I will not in any way get caught up with the other things I suspect you will be doing there." He smiled and raised his glass.

"*Salute.* I won't have it any other way. That's why I want to have someone like you in charge." He placed his glass back on to the table and lifted up both of his arms to mimic a bodybuilder pose. "No one would think of messing with you, and I want to send a clear message that the front of Ressini's has nothing to do with the back room."

"We'll have to work around my schedule with the sanitation department. Saturdays and Sundays should be fine, but during the week I need to wake up very early." Vincent mentally mapped out his new commitment.

For the past six years he had been working forty hours, Monday through Friday with the town starting at 5:00 a.m. He was also pitching in at Bella's on Saturday and Sunday mornings. This new responsibility would add at least thirty hours to his work week. Importantly, though, it could double his weekly income and allow Teresa to quit her job at the factory if she chose.

"You can trust me to do that. You must also give me control over who gets hired and where we get deliveries from. If any of your friends have a gripe about this, just have them come by and talk with me."

"That's why I only came to you. I trust you and your family above all others. I just want to focus on cooking and other things I can work on." Esposito gave a sly grin.

"Just remember my hands will always be clean. The only vice I may contribute to will be playing cards."

October 20, 1963

LIFE WENT ON VERY nicely for the next few years. The Scala, Esposito, and Cavazzi families all worked cohesively at both Bella's and Ressini's. The small businesses fed off each other to provide vital services and entertainment to the community. Not rich by any stretch of the imagination, they simply worked endlessly to support themselves. Since everyone lived a very similar existence in the small town, luxuries and splurges like an ice-cream cone, a house party, or a drive to the country were always greatly appreciated as an extravagance, and they never complained or wanted for more.

For Tuckahoe residents, Sunday and Wednesday dinners were macaroni and antipasto and purchased at Bella's. The big family night out on Friday or Saturday consisted of a pizza at Ressini's. Many local fathers would remain at the restaurant to drink at the bar and play cards while the wives brought the children home to bed. The local police were never a problem, as most enjoyed the benefits of a free dinner or a pound of pasta while also sitting at one of the card games.

A much welcome addition to the clique was the association with Albanese's Butcher Shop. Rocco Albanese was a bear of a man with an equally large heart who ran the shop located across the street from Bella's. It preceded both Bella's and Ressini's and had been in operation since 1945. Vince and Joe formed a strong friendship with the Bronx native, and over time Greg did as well. This bond between the families worked professionally and socially. Bella's and Albanese's had provided much of the quality food for the Ressini menu. In addition, all four men would chip in when needed at any of the three locations. They theoretically ran as one enterprise.

If an extra person was needed, the proprietors would simply put an If You Need Me Come Get Me At ... sign on the door. It was a common occurrence for proprietors to purchase macaroni and chicken cutlets for their family meal while enjoying a beer in Ressini's lounge.

What had begun to transform the families and make them feel proud was the growing number of small children scurrying around the neighborhood. For the older children, love was in the air. By the early sixties, the streets of Tuckahoe had been overtaken by kids of all ages. The Espositos had two toddlers, Robert and John. Joe and Julia's daughter, Tina, had married and had a baby boy named after his father, Leonard. Her sister Rosa was now dating an older guy named Pat Fortuno, and he had finally proposed. Fortuno acted a bit odd at times and made many crude comments in mixed company, but Rosa loved him, so her parents bit their tongues and hoped for the best. The Cavazzis' younger daughter, Maria, had just thrown a curve ball at the family.

She recently began to date a nice young Irish guy, a year or so older than she, and it appeared she was smitten and falling fast. She proudly introduced him to the entire family during a Sunday afternoon dinner.

"Attention ... Hello, everybody! This is Mike, Michael Cameron." The young couple made their way around a long rectangular table of aunts, uncles, cousins, and a few family friends (*le zie, cugini e paesani*). They maneuvered the tight-quartered room extending greetings to all.

Most Sunday afternoon gatherings were well attended, but the day Michael Cameron was introduced happened to be very well attended. It was Rita Scala's sixteenth birthday celebration, and she was beautifully adorned in a white chiffon dress accented with black polka dots. Proudly sitting next to her was her boyfriend of two years, Alfonse Albanese. Rocco's son was three years older than Rita, but they had been inseparable and he treated her like gold.

There were twenty-five people enjoying the traditional Italian feast of macaroni, salad with oil-and-vinegar dressing, fried chicken cutlets, meat balls, a tray of eggplant parmigiana, and a variety of green vegetables. It was always a combined effort. Teresa Scala was accompanied by Julia Cavazzi and Dina Esposito in the kitchen. *Nonna* Julianna had been getting up there in years, but she also helped where she could.

"Good afternoon to ya," Michael said in rapid fashion and with his strong brogue. He shook hands and kissed a few cheeks. "So who made all this food? By God, it smells divine. But are you expecting an army to come for a visit now?" He maintained a broad smile as they got ready to take the seats next to Pat and Rosa.

"So you speak leprechaun?" The gangly Fortuno deadpanned, expecting a laugh from the table. Everyone groaned at his sarcastic comment.

"Why no, fella. This here's a dialect from the northern region of Italy. This would be how us Italians from Florence speak. You havta get better informed." The room burst into laughter as Michael had put Rosa's fiancé in his place.

Cockily sitting at the table in a pair of worn dungarees and white T-shirt, Pat had a pack of cigarettes tucked in his left sleeve. Vince had noticed that Fortuno had not made a very good first impression to Maria's new friend.

"I met some good people from Ireland. You guys are a tough lot; fun to be around too," Vince complimented Michael's heritage. "So do you drink beer, or will some homemade wine do?"

"My good man, I would never turn down a beverage which would make me even happier than I am now." He kissed Maria on her cheek. "I think I'm falling in love. Not just with this lass here but with the whole lot of you." Those around the table all laughed and accepted Mike's gracious but nervous compliment.

"What kind of work you do, pal?" Fortuno continued in his condescending tone.

"I work on the assembly line at the Chevy factory in Tarrytown, up by the Tappan Zee Bridge." Mike pushed in Maria's chair and he sat down in between her and Fortuno.

"I'm thinking of getting a Chevy. Maybe a Galaxie; that girl got some muscle to it." Fortuno lit a cigarette and exhaled proudly to the ceiling.

"I'm afraid there could be a problem with that friend ... It appears you have your car companies confused a bit. Ford makes the car you be speaking about. Maybe you're thinking about the Nova. That appears to be more your speed now." Michael winked and looked across the table. Vince caught his eye and laughed.

Vince called from across the table. "Hey, Patty boy, why don't you have some string beans and lay off the smokes. It's clouding your brain ... You hungry, Mike?"

"Why yes, I am. A plate of this fine food would be wonderful." Mike held out his plate and Maria spooned a large square of eggplant parmigiana on it.

Toward the end of the afternoon, the room had cleared out a bit and Vince was approached by Alfonse Albanese. The young man wished to speak with him in private.

"Mr. Scala, I just wanted to let you know that I care for your daughter very much." At nineteen, Al had grown into a frame that had been the benefactor of the many pounds of beef he cut at the butcher shop.

"You sound nervous my boy, what's up?" Vince had known Alfonse since he was Little Al. Always quiet and respectful, he had never acted flustered around him before.

"I'm a bit nervous. Sir, I just wanted to say that Rita and I are in love. I know she's only sixteen, but I'm crazy about her. Call me young and immature, but I know I want to marry her, so I just wanted to ask you for permission to do that." Then he laughed nervously. "Granted it will be a few years but since this is her special day, I thought it was a good idea to tell you how I felt about her."

Vince smiled broadly and cupped Al's sweating cheeks with his hands. He patted affectionately. "Let me tell you a story. The second I saw Teresa, I knew I would marry her. Love at first sight. She was even younger than Rita is now." He thought back to that day that had started out so wonderfully. "Now we knew we were perfect for each other, and we clicked right from the start ... I see that with my baby girl and you. You're a good kid. Teresa and I didn't have a fairy-tale romance, but let me tell you she was my reason for living and breathing. We finally got married, but not till much later ... I tell you what, I would have married her as soon as I laid my eyes on her if I could."

Al was one of the most intimidating-looking young men in the neighborhood. That is until you spoke with him and realized that he was a quiet kid who treated all with respect. He was a very familiar face every Sunday as he had been an altar boy at the Church of the Assumption and still rarely missed weekly Mass. He was also very emotional and started tearing as Mr. Scala gave his blessing that, yes, he would approve of Al asking Rita to marry him ... some day.

17

SABY'S HOUSE

August 12, 1998

THE ALTERNATING HUMMING, BUZZING, and vibrating of the air conditioner performed its part of providing the white noise and cooling capacity needed to assist in contributing to a good night's sleep. For the past week, a heat wave had swept across the New York City area and it had been unbearable to survive in a fifth-floor apartment. Damien Morris's two-bedroom unit would have been unlivable, and there would have been no way his girl would have spent the night there if the place had not been properly cooled.

He had picked Elaudys up at the McLean Avenue game around 3:00 a.m., and they went straight to his place. His testosterone level was through the roof after participating in a thorough beat-down of a drunk outside the strip club. His rage was fueled by the full dose of creatine and androstenedione he had taken hours before his afternoon workout.

Once he saw his Dominican honey's tight ass in her miniskirt, he let Big John know that she was done for the evening. She needed to conserve her energy for much more important activities. Damien and Elaudys made hot, sweaty love until the sun came up and he finally passed out in exhaustion. She left shortly after seven and left him a note saying that she would be going to the beach with friends and would see him later.

He finally woke a little after noon. While he had had only a few hours of sleep, he still felt refreshed. He had not drunk any alcohol the previous night. He needed to have a clear head whenever he discussed business or enforced the laws of the land. As a safer alternative to keeping his body massive and somewhat healthy, he had transitioned over the past year from injecting steroids to ingesting 20-25 grams of creatine powder in his daily meals and energy drinks. The added boost he received to his sexual appetite from his high testosterone level also provided an abundance of energy at all times of the day and night.

A high-protein meal of four egg whites and an energy smoothie was followed up with an intense heavy leg weight workout. All in attendance at the gym simply watched in amazement at the inhuman display. He maxed out on squats with 675 pounds for three reps and followed it up by commandeering most of the 45-pound plates when he moved on to the leg press. His last set consisted of twelve big plates on each side, a total of 1,080 pounds for four reps.

Later in the afternoon, he moved on to conduct some business. He stopped by the townhouse of the owner of the Hudson River Boat House. This restaurant on the water in Hastings-on-Hudson had a robust business. Damien provided much-needed protection to the high-scale eatery in case there was ever any criminal activity. Charlie McGuinness was very familiar with Morris's practices. He also owned two other successful restaurants in White Plains and had regularly paid him for his services. Quite frankly, an extra three dollars to the entrée selections more than made up for any headache he would surely have by fighting a fight he knew he would lose and lose badly.

After collecting the five grand, Damien drove down the Saw Mill Parkway and exited at Tuckahoe Road and then continued on to a warehouse on Nepperhan Avenue. He backed his silver Chevy Surburban into the garage. Three illegals proceeded to fill the back with twenty medium-sized cardboard boxes. A scruffy-faced white guy with a potbelly came over, and Damien handed him an envelope of cash. Then he drove off heading east to Tuckahoe. He parked in the Ressini's lot and walked in. They were in the midst of serving early bird specials to a packed house of geriatric couples. He walked past the hostess without acknowledging her presence and went through the kitchen doors.

"How are you, my friend?" Sal greeted his fellow gangster after wiping his hands clean on his apron.

"You got a sec, Sally? I got somethin', somethin' I wanna show ya."

"Sure thing." The two men walked out of the back of the kitchen to the parking lot. Damien knocked on the window of his truck and smiled. Sal looked in and nodded as though he were impressed.

"I got five hundred pirated movies. Friggin' *Saving Private Ryan*, *Mulan*, and *Shakespeare in Love*. All box office hits out in theaters now, a goddamn gold mine."

"Very nice my friend. How many can you spare? I could offload fifty or so."

"I can swing that, give me one fifty. Sell em' for five bucks. They should fly off the shelf … Hey, you remember when Santo had us copy movies back in the day?"

"How can I forget. I swear, we must'a seen *Back to the Future* and those Sylvester Stallone movies at least a hundred friggin times."

"You gotta admit, Big Tony made an impressive Rambo for Halloween. Why you chose to be Rocky, I'll never know."

"Hey, I had to. My girl at the time was named Adrienne. Yo, Adrienne!!" They both laughed reliving the old days when they had to do almost anything to gain their capo's trust and attention.

"You still seeing that chick? What's her name? Eue, Elle?" Sal asked.

"Elaudys. Yea, we're still having a real good time. Why you ask?"

"Thought you'd like to ask her to go to an event here with Ang and Vicky tomorrow. They liked her the time they met." Sal reached into his pocket and took out a folded red piece of paper.

"What's on tap?" Damien enquired as he accepted the piece of paper from Sal and began to read it. It was a flyer to a charity event to be held at Ressini's.

"There's a whole big fashion soiree for charity that a friend's hosting. A lot of women from town are going. Designer handbags, shoes, and whatnot. Free wine and booze. Of course my good food will be served." Sal always put a plug in. "Will cost ya a hundo to get in the door, though. Can you swing that, my friend?"

"I'll ask her. I gotta meet another guy who's gonna help with some distribution of the movies in Florida and another guy for Providence."

"You are a busy, busy man." They raised fists and gently banged them in a salute gesture.

"That I am, that I am. Gotta keep it moving. All seriousness, I feel like this chick is the one. Hope my mom doesn't mind me marrying a Latina." This was the first time Damien had confessed to anyone that he wanted to marry Elaudys.

"Hey, when you're ready, I know a guy that knows a guy that may know a guy that can get you a good deal on a rock for her." Sal laughed.

"Thanks, buddy, but I know a guy too." Damien playfully punched Sal's shoulder. "Hey, you know, the more I think about it, I'll definitely have Elaudys come tomorrow. I'll meet my guys at your bar." He reached into his pocket and peeled off a hundred-dollar bill. "This is for her ticket. I'm sure she'll spend more."

"No problem. We've got a game upstairs going on at the same time, so you're welcome to play. One thing, though …No heat … I do not like weapons of any kind when alcohol's being served." Sal pointed at Damien's bulge in the back of his pants.

"I'll behave." Damien gave a cocky smile. "Maybe I'll play a few hands, but I definitely wanta get my business transacted first. Know what I mean?"

"That I do, brother … that I do. See you tomorrow." Sal said good-bye and walked back into the restaurant.

Damien thought back to his friendship with Sal Esposito. Actually, if he thought of Sal, he also had to think of Tony Albanese. Those two were inseparable, and it was a major reason many wiseguys would never even think of being on their bad side. Damien had thrown many a beating in his day, but he had also witnessed the fury of these two guys working together to intimidate people and get their way. They never had problems collecting. Their games were clean and trouble-free, and law enforcement generally left them alone. This was not Damien's style, though. He felt more comfortable working alone and enjoyed the rush of living on the edge.

The Next Day
IT REALLY WAS A sweet gesture, even if it was from a professional killer. Last night, Damien had picked Elaudys-Dominique up at her faux apartment and surprised her. They drove directly to Neiman Marcus at the Westchester Mall to pick out something new to wear to the charity event. After trying on countless outfits, she left the mall more than happy with her selection of a matching Oscar de la Renta cream-colored blouse, a tan skirt capped off with a chic set of Jimmy Choo crystal-suede sandals with four-inch heels. The entire $3,168-bill was paid with a stolen credit card, of course, but it's the thought that counts.

Damien told her they would meet later at the restaurant, as he had much business to attend to. He always managed to tell her all the "boring" details during their pillow-talk time in between love-making sessions. She pretended to be naive and not very interested in his macho exploits, but in reality, she absorbed every word and took detailed notes the minute she left his place in the early morning hours.

Based on what she had been privy to so far—information that was later backed by verification from others at the agency—they had enough evidence to now put Damien away for the rest of his life. The clincher had been in May when agents dug up the body of a Mafia rat buried in a wooded field in upstate New York. Damien had been careless enough to bring Elaudys for a getaway weekend at the vacation cabin of his family friend in Greene County. He bragged to her that he loved the place because it was situated on forty undisturbed acres and they let him use it whenever he liked. Agents swarmed the area the following week and located the shallow grave of the Genovese rat who had been murdered three years prior.

Elaudys prepared for her evening out with the girls. She had met the wives of Sal and Tony once before at last year's holiday party. At the time, Angela Esposito was very pregnant and expecting twins. She and Victoria Albanese were cordial enough to speak with, but they provided no substance to her investigation. Agent Tejata would have much rather been glued to the side of her man as he spoke with friends of his.

Now in full character mode, she pulled her Lexus (another present from Damien) up to the front of Ressini's and waited for the door to be opened by the valet. The eatery was overcrowded with women of all ages. The charity event to benefit victims of sexual abuse looked like it was going to be a success.

"Hello, thank you for coming tonight. Is your name on our guest list?" an attractive early twenties brunette asked as she walked over to the reception desk.

"Yes, I believe my boyfriend paid for me yesterday. My name's Elaudys Reyes."

"Hey, girl, you look like a sexy mamma!" Angela tapped her on the shoulder and then gave her a hug and air kiss.

"Damn, girl, the baby weight came off fast … You look beautiful honey." Elaudys admired her new best friend.

"Back to a size six. I told Sal he better spring for a personal trainer, and bless his heart he did." She moved closer to whisper in her ear, "Next up is a boob job for Christmas. These girls are worn out." They both giggled as Angela grabbed her breasts with exquisitely manicured fingers.

As they made their way through the venue, both women sipped white wine and picked at a few of the appetizers being passed around.

"Don't you just love mini-quiche? Can you believe my husband makes these from scratch. Heaven!"

"Very tasty … Ooohhh, is that bruschetta coming our way. I'm starving." Dominique was playing the part, but in actuality the food was scrumptious. Italian food had always been her favorite.

Ressini's main dining area had been transformed into a mini-boutique. The outer rectangular perimeter was set up for local store owners to showcase handbags, shoes, accessories, and clothing. Sixteen shop owners had agreed to split profits equally with the charity organizer. This was the inaugural event for a new nonprofit organization named Saby's House, and the goal for the night was to raise $20,000.

They made their way around, viewing the finely made items. Just then, Angie moved her gaze across the room and smirked.

"Don't start with me, Ang. You don't know the crap I just put up with in order to get here." Victoria Albanese made her entrance in typical fashion, which was usually frazzled and an hour late. She hugged her friend and looked quizzically as Elaudys.

"We've met before, right? I'm Victoria, and you are?" Her last words were raised an octave.

"Yes, we met at a holiday party. I'm Damien's girlfriend, Elaudys."

"Honey, around these parts we call it a Christmas party. Right, right, I remember you now. I hate you, though, you know that … Your outfit is spectacular." Vicky teased then coaxed her to pirouette as she continued with the compliment.

"So why were you late this time?" Angela Esposito was eager to hear the latest escapades from the Albanese house.

"Oh Ang, I shouldn't complain to you. Jesus, you just had twins. But I'm telling you, my little Anthony's a terror. Three friggin' years old, and he just won't stop teasing his baby sister. Then Amanda Rose had a meltdown. Thank goodness, my babysitter showed up a few minutes early. That Jenny's a savior." Vicky breathed out heavily then felt much more relaxed after a few sips from her glass of white wine.

After a few minutes, the women were greeted by the event organizer, Sabina Ragonese. She thanked them all for their support.

"I am very impressed by how you put this together," Elaudys said after shaking Sabina's petite but strong hand. Even more impressive was that she had managed to put the event together while eight months pregnant.

Dominique could never envision being pregnant, let alone working endlessly at a task weeks before expecting to give birth.

"It really is for a good cause," Sabina said as she rubbed her stomach in an expected motherly way. "I am so grateful for the wonderful turnout. We should reach our goal, and for that I am so proud."

"I think your goal will be shattered, Sabe. Your sister-in-law just showed up."

"Why would you say that, Victoria?" Elaudys inquired as she looked over to the reception desk. She saw a beautiful blonde-haired woman wearing a spectacular red dress that was probably $2,000 more expensive than her high-end ensemble. The blonde had just finished writing a check. She looked Vicky's way, smiled, and waved.

"Megyn, you did *not* just have a baby! How on earth did you get your ass back in shape?" Vicky hugged her warmly.

"Two words: personal trainer." She showed off her hourglass figure and grabbed a martini off the tray a waitress was holding. "I hit so much traffic getting here. Dropped Samantha off at my parents in Queens at four and just got here. The Hutchinson River Parkway was insane."

"Ut-oh, Maria will be pissed that she didn't watch her granddaughter." Angela cautioned her.

"No, Mom really wanted to come here tonight, too. She's over there. Besides she's watching Sammy tomorrow." Megyn paused for effect. "As well as all of your kids too ... Cause Chris and I are taking all of you to Atlantic City."

They all squealed in excitement until Angela put a damper on the plans. "Meg, there is no way we're driving to AC for dinner. I'm not waking up with three kids after getting home at five in the morning."

Megyn took a sip of her martini then smiled broadly and spoke excitedly as she told them the big surprise. "You're not gonna be driving down there, honey. Chris chartered a helicopter. We're going in style. If you like, we could be home by midnight. Anyway, just to be safe, we have four babysitters lined up to assist: Jenny, Heather, and two of their friends."

Now they all squealed again.

Agent Tejata stood among them in fascination. For the next two hours they sampled and purchased much of the merchandise, while at the same time these women went on and on about their suburban lives and about who was pregnant, who had just had a baby, and who wanted to have a baby. She learned much about what was going on.

Tony's younger sister Joanne had just gotten engaged. She was twenty-seven years old, and the guy she was living with for three years had finally popped the question.

Besides the pending boob job, Angela recently had her tubes tied. Her three-year-old son, Mikey, was a bruiser, and while the twin baby girls, Brianna and Lexi, were precious, there was no way she was going to go through labor again.

Vicky was more than content and had sworn off spitting out any more kids. The baby factory was officially closed. She had her hands full trying to keep her mini-bowling ball Anthony Junior off of his baby sister.

Sabina seemed to be friends with everyone in the entire room. She was excited about being a mother. She had also survived a very difficult past. While all of the other women eagerly indulged in the free-flowing wine and martinis, Sabina only had a few sips of cranberry juice. This was not just because she was pregnant.

Megyn appeared to be a very nice woman and super smart to go along with drop-dead looks. To top it off, she had written a $10,000 check for the cause. Agent Tejata knew that she and Chris were portfolio managers who lived in Dallas and traveled to New York frequently. She did not know how successful they were until tonight.

While it was all very fascinating in a way, she anxiously wanted to say hello to Damien, who was sitting at the bar. She waved to him a few times throughout the night. He waved back more than once but seemed more interested in continuing his conversations.

The first took place at 8:15 p.m. with a tall, skinny black man named Marvin whom he had worked with a lot. The second discussion began at 9:30 p.m. and was with Hector, an overweight Hispanic gentleman wearing a green Boston Celtics jersey over a white T-shirt. Hector did very well for himself and kept his wife and four kids comfortable due to the relationship with Damien. That conversation was brief and concluded when they went outside for a few minutes to put a few boxes in the back of his beat-up Astro minivan. Damien then went up to the poker game for a little while. The third person he met with had shown up a little after ten. Damien was late to meet with him, and it was now almost 10:30 p.m., and the guy was still sitting with Damien at the bar. His back was turned the entire time, and she had not yet been able to profile him. Damien was laughing, talking to him, and having a few drinks, something he had not done during his earlier meetings. *He really does have a nice smile,* she thought before snapping out of it and reminding herself that she was still undercover and he was not her real boyfriend.

Well, she had had enough and excused herself. While contributing a few brief conversation topics and answering every question asked of her, she was way out of her league. A mother-wife-fiancée she was not. She was a special agent and had to return to the business at hand. Elaudys Reyes handed her three-quarter filled wine glass to the waitress and Agent Dominique Tejata made her way to the lounge. It was empty except for the bartender, Damien, and his anonymous business partner. She greeted her man with an affectionate kiss and then turned to say hello to his guest.

Around the Same Time

THE EXPENSES REQUIRED TO train, travel and enter arm wrestling competitions were much more than Felix Bannos had ever expected. He thought that after winning a few tournaments, he would obtain a sponsor that would then provide the capital needed to pursue his passion. It never came to pass, and he was now faced with a mountain of bills.

A street-smart guy to the core, he decided that the best way to fund his expensive hobby was to reach out to old acquaintances and see if they had swag he could peddle in South Florida. It could be anything, but in Felix's case, he did not want to blow his career and pension. He kept his side business under the radar and usually requested innocuous items that his superiors would not frown on and usually craved as well. He had a lot of success with hot children's toys at Christmas time, walkmans, VCRs, and tapes of just-released movies.

When he ran in shame from the Northeast, he left almost all of his former relationships behind. All except one; he had grown up on the same street as Damien Morris, and the two had remained close. The relationship had persisted even after Felix moved to the Sunshine State. Damien had reasoned that contacts throughout the country were a must, not just in the New York area. Felix had let him know after he became a state trooper that the badge provided access to many interesting people who could be helpful.

Bannos typically would drive up north every few months and load a friend's van with enough swag that could be offloaded quietly over the next few weeks. His take would usually be around fifteen grand for each score and provided him with more than enough cash to keep his quest for arm-wrestling immortality alive.

For this trip he had been summoned early and out of sequence. Usually, Damien would have the goods waiting at a drop point and the transaction would go off stealthy. Damien had just acquired a boatload of school supplies as well as pirated movie tapes of blockbusters that were currently in theaters. Felix simply could not pass this opportunity up, so he drove all night and reached the Yonkers Motor Inn just after 7:00 p.m. The place was a rat hole, located just off the Cross County Parkway. He didn't care. He liked to leave a small footprint, get in and get out. He would meet with Damien after a short nap. His plan was to be on the road heading south by early morning.

He checked in, beeped Damien, and then received a call back. He was told that ten o'clock would be fine to meet up. Felix pulled into the parking lot of Ressini's a few minutes early and sat quietly for a few moments. He knew this was Sal Esposito's place, and seeing those two scumbags in the Bahamas brought up some really horrible memories. He did not like them, but yet, here he was, literally afraid they would see him. His only satisfaction was that Domi had rebuffed their attempts to flirt with her. Then he had gone on to win the championship. *Screw those assholes.* Maybe he'd float a story to Damien that they were working undercover for the feds.

He walked in to the noise of a hundred women buzzing around. Thankfully, the bar area was quiet. He ordered a vodka tonic; actually, he decided he would probably have more than one drink tonight. Damien finally came walking down the stairs at twenty minutes after ten, after Felix had sucked down his third drink. From the long drive and his anxiety of being in his nemesis' establishment, he already had a slight buzz.

"Hey, Y-O, how you been?" Felix said to his old friend from "Y-Onkers." They shook hands, and Damien grabbed his shoulders.

"You're still fuckin' huge, Felix. How are things down south?" Damien motioned for the bartender to give his friend a refill and also ordered a drink; gin and tonic.

"Going real good. In line for a promotion, so that's gonna help out with pushing more merchandise. Arm-wrestling keeping me busy." Felix lifted his massive bicep to show it off. "Ain't got much time for anything else; haven't gotten laid in months!" He yelled and slurred the last line.

"How many of those you had tonight?" Damien smirked, pointing at the glass.

"Just a few, but drove all night to get here. Wired and haven't eaten much of anything all day … And I'm certainly not eating here." Bannos raised his voice again.

"Now, now, show some respect to our host. It's been a long time. Let the past go." Damien tried to calm his old friend down.

"I did let it go. You believe I actually saw those motherfuckers in the Bahamas. Talking shit to me and my friends. I should use this on them." Felix turned to show his service revolver tucked neatly by his side.

"Hey, Sal frowns on guns in his place. You better remove it, so there ain't no trouble. Go out and put it safely away … We're low profile here." If Damien had to follow the rules of the house so did Felix.

"All right. Be back in a sec." Bannos swayed as he got off the barstool. Then he walked out to the van and removed his weapon. Damien viewed the big man staggering around through the restaurant window.

"Bahamas, what are you talking about. Who'd you see?" Damien circled back to his earlier comment once Felix returned.

"Friggin' Sal and that piece of garbage Tony." Drunk and whispering, but getting irritated, he leaned in closer. "You believe they were at my arm-wrestling competition. Talking smack and disrespecting me. I was with family and friends. Tony had the nerve to call me out." Bannos drained his drink. On cue the bartender had another waiting.

Damien was now getting frustrated with his now clearly inebriated friend. "Look, buddy. I don't want to sound harsh, but I ain't no therapist, and I don't give a fuck if you got issues. Can we focus and talk business?"

"Yeah, yeah, whatever. You may want to watch yourselves around those two. I think they're working for the gov-a-mint … I mean the govvvermen … fuck, you know what I mean." Felix was slurring loudly, acting paranoid and rambling. "I'll make it easy for ya' and take ev-a-thing you got!" Again, he yelled and slurred the last words.

"Keep it down … Keep it down." Damien was facing close to Bannos and placed his right hand on Felix's left shoulder. At that point, Damien looked behind Felix's head and caught the eye of someone else.

"Hey, let's take a break. I do want to hear more about your Sal-and-Tony hypothesis. My girlfriend's here now. Say hello and then go compose yourself in the bathroom or outside." Damien stood, hugged, and kissed her. She turned to face Felix.

"Felix, this is Elau—"

"Dominique? What are you doin' here?" Felix cut off the introduction and also stood to face her. He swayed and his eyes were bugged out wide.

"What you talking about? Do I know you?" She looked irritated and confused as she turned to her boyfriend. "What's with the big drunk … He thinks all Latin women look alike." Elaudys kissed Damien again.

"Can we leave, baby? I bought a few things, but I'm bored with all these mothers. All they talk about are babies and shit." Felix watched the banter in silence until his drunken mind finally realized what was going on.

"I, I, I meant no disrespect … What you say yourrre name was? You do look familiar, but I'm from Florida, so I see a lot of attractive Cuban women."

"I'm not Cuban, big boy. No problem … So this guy has some hypotheses, baby? Looks like he got shit for brains to me." She looked at Felix with disgust.

Felix drained his drink once again. He exhaled, "Damien, I'll take it all. Same spot, I'll pick it up tamarra … Ob-visly I'm in no shape to do dis 'night, kay? Tell you 'bout those two assholes tamarra. Kay, ooooh-kay!" He slurred his words even more and then staggered away without saying good-bye. He bumped around then reached the bathroom door. Once inside, he was barely able to relieve himself. Wobbly and very drunk, he needed to leave this place immediately.

Bannos washed his hands and doused his face with cold water before leaving. When he finally pulled himself together enough to exit, he still had to hold on to the walls so he would not fall down. He glanced at the bar area; Damien and Dominique had already gone. Good, he did not wish to address this anymore tonight, and when he saw her in Florida, they could have a long discussion about this situation. He was torn. He really did not wish to put her in danger, but he wanted those two guys to be hurt.

Once out in the humid, midsummer night, Felix walked over to his van. Before he even put the key into the lock, a beefy hand grabbed his wrist from behind.

"You okay to drive, my friend?"

Felix stumbled around and lost his balance. Luckily, the side of the vehicle saved him from falling backward as he banged his head against the side. He breathed heavily, now looking directly at Big Tony.

"Hey, Sal, look what we have here. No drunk drivers leave Ressini's, my friend. Give me your keys. I'll get you to where you're going." Tony snatched the keys, opened the back sliding door, and guided him in. Bannos did not resist and simply slouched on the back bench and closed his eyes.

Tony got into the driver's seat and shut the door. He drove off. Sal followed in his Tahoe. They disappeared down Columbus Avenue.

18

THREE FAMILIES BLENDED

July 13, 1969

THERE WERE TIMES IN his adult life when Vincent was thrust back to his childhood, sitting with his father, uncles, and cousins debating the New York baseball wars. All of these frothy rivalry talks had ended after the Giants followed the Dodgers out west in 1957. New York became a one-team town, which left very little impetus for Vincent to debate former die-hard Brooklyn Dodger fan Greg Esposito and former diehard New York Giant fans Joe Cavazzi and Rocco Albanese.

Thankfully, the banter had sort of started up again after the New York Mets were founded in 1962. The new blue-and-orange team appeased the brokenhearted fans of the Dodgers (blue) and Giants (orange), giving them a reason to live again. While they lost more than a hundred games a year, these expansion-era Mets were just more fun to watch. The team from the Bronx had aged rapidly and was now an also ran American League franchise. Vincent's beloved Yankees had played so poorly in the mid-sixties, and with everyone else embracing the upstart Mets, he decided to switch allegiance to Queens.

His timing was perfect. After a hearty Sunday afternoon barbecue in the late summer sun, the men had all retired to the shade of a maple tree to watch the ad hoc entertainment center set up by Alfonse and Irish Mike. They had lugged out Greg's new television set (it had fallen off the back of a truck and found its way to Esposito living room) to his backyard. Then they arranged lawn chairs around it to view the last few innings of the Mets final game before the All-Star Break. Since the June trade for Don Clendenon, the team had caught fire and accomplished the unthinkable; they were on pace for their first winning season in the franchise history. With a dynamic pitching staff, which included Tom Seaver, Jerry Koosman, Gary Gentry, and a young fireballer named Nolan Ryan, they actually had a legitimate shot of competing against the Cubs for the National League Eastern Division pennant.

"Gregie boy, you mind tossing me a cold beer from that cooler now. I appear to be a bit parched." Irish Mike had picked up the game quickly and had officially changed his allegiance from European football to New York baseball.

He even ventured to take the three young ones— Little Chris, Sally the Nut, and Baby Anthony—to Shea Stadium all by himself to watch Saturday afternoon games. Most of the times, he could last only a few innings as he really could not handle keeping an eye on three toddlers at the same time.

"Friggin extra innings! Mets better pull this second game out." Greg had bet the Mets hard all summer and was on a roll, especially during July. If they won, they would be 15–7 for the month and he would be up over two grand in already-spent profits. He believed it was a good way for him to spend the time before the restaurant reopened.

All of the family businesses were temporarily closed as the Village of Tuckahoe was in the midst of a massive federally sponsored urban renewal project. Most of the buildings along Columbus Avenue and Main Street had been torn down and were being replaced by newer structures. Over one hundred shopkeepers and three hundred residents had been displaced during the process. Thankfully, all of their homes were untouched, so they did not have to move. The government had subsidized the families a bit, but they were all eager to reopen Ressini's Restaurant, Bella's Pasta, and Albanese's Butcher Shop before Christmas.

"Second games of doubleheaders are always a crapshoot, my friend." Vince tried to give Greg advice about not betting hunches all the time. But he was Neapolitan and thick headed, not Calabrese. So he had much more gamble in him than the more-conservative Scalamarri bloodlines.

"I rubbed the lucky head of my *compare* leprechaun before every game I bet them. No way I'm gonna lose this one." Greg leaped off his chair and good naturedly hugged Irish Mike for some additional luck.

They all watched intently as a ground ball to Buddy Harrelson recorded the second out of the inning. Before the next batter came to the plate, a news bulletin scrolled across the bottom of the black-and-white screen: The Apollo 11 Lunar Module Has Landed On The Moon.

"I finally have a piece of good news!" Rocky exclaimed. Then he explained his comment. "Guys, the Mets' first manager Casey Stengel said that my Mets would win the World Series when we put a man on the moon." He picked his grandson off the grass and hugged him.

"They're gonna do it. I can feel it. They'll do it for Ralphy and Jimmy Boy." Rocky hugged Baby Anthony and kissed him on the cheek. Then his eyes watered up. He maneuvered awkwardly as he lifted his body to go inside and compose himself.

Vince watched Rocky strain as he waddled into the house. While he had always been a large man, all were now very concerned about his rapid weight gain. He was now at least a hundred pounds heavier than a few years earlier.

The two friends, now bonded as Poppa Vince and Nonno Rocco to the same wonderful baby boy, had continued to remain close. This friendship and support had been much needed over the past few years. Rocky and his wife Isabella had a very difficult time dealing with the unfortunate trauma thrust upon them.

On one positive note, Alfonse had kept his promise and married Rita. They had a baby boy, and Al continued to work with his parents at the family butcher shop to support his family. That was where the good times ended. In May 1967 and again in March 1968, the family received heartbreak. Rocky and Isabella's two youngest sons, Ralph and James, had both been killed in action serving in Vietnam.

Ralph Albanese had joined the Army in 1966 when he was twenty years old. A sergeant in the Twenty-Fifth Infantry, he had been out leading a patrol when he stepped on a land mine in the Binh Duong province. Posthumously, he was awarded the Bronze Star for his actions that night.

Pfc. James Albanese had been a Golden Dragon of the Second Battalion, Fourteenth Infantry Regiment. He had joined the army right out of Tuckahoe High and served with his unit for only a few months. Jimmy Boy's Company C had been on a search-and-destroy operation in the Ho Bo Woods area. Fighting against the well-fortified North Vietnamese Army, he was killed by sniper fire, the only casualty that day.

Since his service in the Pacific, Vince had purposely shied away from revealing stories of his time in combat to anyone, in and out of the family.

The memories and nightmares were far too painful. He and Teresa decided well before he stepped off the train after his cross-country journey back home that there would be no additional words said. All that changed after Jimmy's and Ralph's deaths. Vince opened up to Rocky about how the brave men he had fought with had changed his life for the better and how he knew the Albanese boys would leave a long-lasting impression on the men they had served with.

They attended Mass regularly and took long walks around town, discussing how war, two very different wars, had changed their lives. It had been a long road. Rocky and Isabella were coming around a bit primarily because of the life-changing events of being grandparents, but they both had long ways to go. The pain of losing a son, let alone two, was difficult to recover from, and they probably would never heal completely.

"Yes, finally they win," Greg excitedly cheered about the Mets 3–2, 11 inning victory against the Expos as well as his one-hundred-dollar successful wager.

"Someone go tell Rocky they pulled it out." Joe Cavazzi smiled, realizing that any good news was a positive for the Albanese family.

At that moment, the back screen door crashed open with Alfonse barreling out in tears. "Someone call an ambulance. Dad's on the floor. I think he had a heart attack!"

August 8, 1974

THERE'S AN OLD SAYING: if you want something done, give it to the guy who is always busy. Vincent added to the long list of the names he was called—darling, Dad, Poppa, Vince, Uncle Vin—*Zio* Vincent and now coach. He had stretched his hours in the week to fulfill obligations with the sanitation department (only ten years to go till retirement), Ressini's (still bartending three nights a week), Bella's (Irish Mike covered most of the overflow hours, but he still liked to make his own macaroni on Sunday morning), and now the newest endeavor, head coach for the Eastchester Blue Devils.

He had been sort of tricked into volunteering three years earlier to be an assistant coach for the midget-level team after he drove the two older Esposito boys—Johnny and Robby—to practice one night. The long arm of the law had finally caught up to their dad. He was currently serving three years in a federal prison in Ohio for selling stolen goods and would not be out until the fall. Thank goodness he had not been caught in the restaurant, or they may have lost it too.

Uncle Vin had dropped the boys off when he noticed Jim Bell was running the program. Coach Bell's real job was as an insurance agent who had sold Vince his first life insurance policy ten years earlier. Through the years, he would see him around town, referred many relatives and friends to his practice, and in return, frequented Ressini's and Bella's on a regular basis.

The midget team had been in need of an assistant, and Coach Bell believed a rugged guy like Vince could help toughen the boys up. Vince loved the game and embraced the challenge to help transform the local youths into raging animals every fall Sunday. In the process, the Blue Devils turned the corner from a start-up ragtag bunch to an established program. Kids flocked to play for them. The organization grew from that one midget team and added a peewee team and, for this year, they also had enough interest to field a team for the real little guys, the junior peewees.

Vince was assigned as the head coach for the junior peewee squad, and he recruited Irish Mike and Big Al to assist him. They happily complied. Their rambunctious sons had been dying to participate for as long as they could remember. Cee Boy and Little Tony were joined by Sally the Nut. All three had recently turned eight years old, and they eagerly showed up on the first day of practice to fulfill the dream.

Coach Vince addressed the troops for the first time. "Nice to see all you boys here tonight. I see we've got about forty of ya'." There were fifteen ten-year-olds, eleven nine-year-olds, and fourteen eight-year-olds to work with. He tried to sound fierce to the group of scrawny kids but was careful not to believe they were marine recruits from his long ago past. "Now we'll teach you some football."

All the boys screamed in delight. "Now start running. Two laps around." They all groaned before bolting off.

Running was followed by stretching, drills, and fundamentals. Then, after they were good and tired, some football was taught. And then they ran again and again. By the end of the first week, before they had even been handed helmets, the roster had been whittled down to thirty-six players, including their three little guys.

"You can call us the Columbus Avenue Boys, Poppy. So you don't get us confused with the other kids," Little Tony proudly told his coach-grandfather as he anointed Chris, Sal, and him. The skinny terrors were holding their own with the others.

While the kids ran around the track, the coaches would talk about the practice schedule for the night but, for the most part, would pass the fifteen minutes of solitude discussing current events before going off to train the young athletes.

"I don't get those hippies. They all think they're still at the Woodstock thing from a few years back. Protesting and doing drugs, free love, and all that garbage." Vince was a traditional guy and had major reservations about this generation of youngsters.

Greg was due out of jail soon, and Vince was definitely going to speak with him about watching the older boys and being a better father. Johnny and Robby were both teenagers now, and with no father present they were susceptible to the lures of sex, drugs, and rock and roll. Vince already had his suspicions, but it was not his place to discipline.

"Forget them long hairs, it's the economy that's worrying me." Irish Mike may not been a citizen yet, but he loved the United States and followed politics and the economy closely.

"Better than last year when we had a wait for gas. My shop's still hurtin'." Big Al referred back to the gas rationing lines from last summer. Gas prices rose from thirty-eight cents a gallon to almost sixty cents, and the economy had turned down. The OPEC oil embargo had been punishment for US support of Israel during the Arab–Israeli war.

"We're all hurtin' fellas. That's why we gotta stick together. I lived through the Great Depression. I don't think it could get any worse than that." Vince put it in perspective but never told anyone the full extent of his teenage suffering.

"Coach, Coach Vin." Salvatore stopped prior to completing his final lap around the track.

"Yes, Sal. What is it, son?" Vincent eyed the boy inquisitively.

"I don't think I can run any more. I think I hurt my ankle," Salvatore said this while panting heavily through his oversized helmet.

"Well, son, I think we have a problem then. Seems to me you have forgotten where your ankle is." The kid had lamented about an ankle problem while pointing at his knee. "Run, boy, run till you drop," Coach Vin yelled and then looked over at Irish Mike and laughed uncontrollably.

Later that night, Maria Cameron prepared a hearty supper for the returning warriors. This Thursday night meal consisted of a frittata, a tomato salad fresh from the garden, a stick of *soppressata*, and a jar of *melanzana*. They always saved four loafs of Italian bread baked daily at Bella's and there was plenty of homemade wine.

A standard routine had been worked out. Maria would cook on Thursday and Friday nights, Rita prepared the Saturday and Monday meals (usually a barbecue of Albanese Butcher Shop's best cuts), and Dina would cull together two or three trays of assorted items from Ressini's for Tuesdays and Wednesdays. Sunday was still a special day, and after Mass, the three families bonded to prepare one late-afternoon feast.

The entire contingent of relatives and friends could not see the sixties and, for that matter, the first part of this decade end fast enough. While there were many blessed events with marriages and births, there was far too much despair. Two brave Albanese sons were lost fighting for their country, and their father died in the war's wake. The weak economy and high inflation had pushed their small businesses to the brink of bankruptcy, and now, with Greg Esposito away in jail, the stress was taking its toll on everyone.

To top it off, the older generation was getting smaller. At close to seventy, Dina's mom, Mary Scalamarri, had aged considerably and sadly was near the end. She spoke in a melancholy way about finally being with her beloved Antonio again. Mary's two sisters, Rosa and Angelina, had recently passed, which added to Mary's unwillingness to live. Julia Cavazzi recently lost her mother during the winter. *Zia* Sabina had lived to be eighty-seven and fulfilled the same wish *Zia* Mary now looked forward to fulfill. She lay next to her husband, Frank, at the Calvary Cemetery in Queens.

"I'll take her." Sabina scooped up baby Joanne. The three-year-old had been playing "London Bridge" with Uncle Pat. With him smoking during the entire game, it did not appear Sabina believed that was the safest place for a child to be.

"Saby, you're the best babysitter." Rita beamed.

"And the best cousin too. Thanks, Aunt Rita." Sabina smiled proudly as she playfully tickled Joanne.

Vince enjoyed the coming of age of the new generation. He watched quietly but keenly at how Sabina nurtured all the younger kids. Baby Joanne adored her, and Sabina never tired of playing. She was also not afraid to put the hammer down on her brother Christopher, or Salvatore and Anthony for that matter, whenever they got out of line. The adults would feed Sabina encouragement and allowed her to enact martial law whenever she deemed it appropriate. She had grown up early and looked more like a teenager than a nine-year-old. The boys may have been rough and tough football players now, but the three pups quivered whenever Saby came storming over to keep them in order.

"President Nixon's speech is coming on. Hush!" Mike and Al brought plates to the living room and looked at the black-and-white television screen as they ate from the coffee table.

The Watergate scandal had transpired in the aftermath of a break-in on the night of June 17, 1972. Five burglars had entered the Democratic National Committee office inside the Watergate complex and their subsequent arrest marked the beginning of a long chain of events in which President Nixon and his top aides became deeply involved in an extensive cover-up. Those activities had started in 1970 after the *New York Times* revealed a secret bombing campaign against neutral Cambodia was being conducted as part of the American war effort in Vietnam. Following the revelations, Nixon had ordered wiretaps of reporters and government employees to discover the source of the news leaks. The House Judiciary Committee then approved articles of impeachment charging the president with obstruction of justice and abuse of power. With a complete collapse of support from Congress, he was set to resign and avoid the likely prospect of losing the impeachment vote.

President Nixon began. "Good evening. This is the thirty-seventh time I have spoken to you from this office, where so many decisions have been made that shaped the history of this nation. Each time I have done so to discuss with you some matter than I believe affected the national interest. In all the decisions I have made in my public life, I have always tried to do what was best for the nation. Throughout the long and difficult period of Watergate, I have felt it was my duty to persevere, to make every possible effort to complete the term of office to which you elected me. In the past few days, however, it has become evident to me that I no longer have a strong enough political base in the Congress to justify continuing that effort. As long as there was such a base, I felt strongly that it was necessary to see the constitutional process through to its conclusion, that to do otherwise would be unfaithful to the spirit of that deliberately difficult process and a dangerously destabilizing precedent for the future ..."

"Do you think Gerald Ford will do any better now?" Irish Mike was always looking to learn more about American politics.

"We're in for a rough road. Don't expect things to change anytime soon." Al was traditionally a pessimistic person. His butcher shop was hanging on by a thread.

"We need to be able to trust our politicians, especially the president for Christ's sake!" Vince added his two cents. "Remember when President Nixon came to Tuckahoe in seventy-two. Gave a hearty speech on the spot of his urban renewal success story. All the while behind the scenes, those Watergate shenanigans are going on. Makes me sick."

"Word is Ford is gonna pardon him. He doesn't want a president to be going to jail." Joe had been reading about the situation for the past few months now. "I think it's the right thing to do."

"It probably is. Imagine if he were in some common jail … not what this country needs. Friggin' unemployment and inflation is strangling us. Looks like more rough roads ahead." Vince frustratingly made the statement and then walked to the kitchen to get a beer.

The sixties had started out so well with the families growing and their small businesses thriving. Since the escalation of the Vietnam War, there had been nothing but adversity and pain at every conceivable turn. Silently, they all prayed that they could stay afloat.

Scalamarri – Esposito Family
1887 - 1974

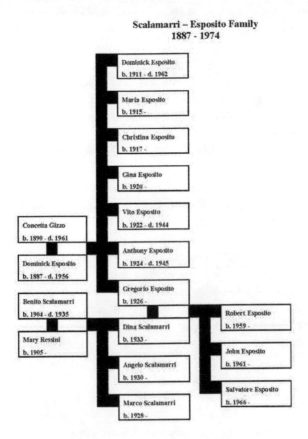

Scala – Albanese Family
1915 - 1974

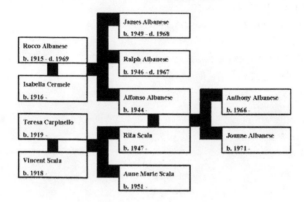

Scalle – Cameron Family
1912 - 1974

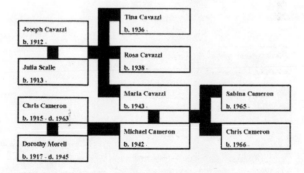

Part 3

Hit the Fan

19

A SMOLDERING WHITE VAN

August 14, 1998, Early Morning Hours

AGING RAPIDLY WITH A wrinkled, jowly complexion, it just never crossed Santo Tracino's mind to ever retire from the life. Now in his mid-seventies and a Grandpa Munster look-alike, Tentacles simply received too big of a thrill from even the smallest scams. The dossier compiled on the lifelong gangster was filled with brazen attempts to beat the system going as far back as when he returned from Europe after World War II. Incarcerated for the better part of his life, like a boomerang he would always circle back.

"I just can't help myself!" He'd boast to associates in his gravely, hoarse voice. "I'm even gonna pull a fast one on God. The big guy better watch his wallet when I get to the pearly gates." Tentacles had thought of and done it all to make an illegal buck.

"A little kid better hold his dollar tight waiting in line at the ice cream truck. Turn his head and that buck's mine!"

From the booth in the back room of his favorite diner, he would chain-smoke Virginia Slims while discussing new schemes with his crew. Whenever a brown paper bag filled with profits from his illegal ventures was handed to him, he would get visually excited, like he had just had an orgasm.

He was released from a federal prison in Oklahoma three years ago. His lawyer had convinced the parole board that his client was a frail and feeble man who was not a menace to society. "Your Honor, my client can barely get around without assistance."

The geriatric Tracino played the part to perfection. At his trial, he sat crouched in a wheelchair with a mask wrapped around his face, breathing oxygen, but the jury was not fooled in the least. When they reached the verdict, he was ordered to serve twenty to life for racketeering charges and bribing a police officer. Because of his condition, though, the judge granted leniency and reduced the sentence to five years. With the persistence of his well-paid lawyer, he even served his reduced time in the convalescent ward.

Once released, he immediately found the fountain of youth and began getting his hands into everything again. The party his son threw at the best steak place in White Plains when he was released was like a gangster venture capital convention. Associates gave him a taste of a myriad of activities, and he sanctioned them all, accepting the thousands of dollars in sweeteners like a tiger tearing into a piece of fresh meat.

Life returned back to normal. Then, a few weeks before Christmas in 1995, his wife of forty-two years suffered a debilitating stroke. His sweet Joanie had stood by him for the best and worst of it all. She took care of the house, kept cash flow lines active, and communicated regularly with his underlings when he was in the can. She even looked the other way regarding his *gooma* and constant late hours away.

The health care for the only woman he truly loved quickly took a toll, and it became difficult for a mobster with no insurance or long-term savings plan to absorb the staggering amount of rapidly piling up bills. The surgeries and rehabilitation required to keep his beloved functioning were more than even he could handle. She was admitted to a nursing home for around-the-clock care, and Santo was forced to sell the mansion. It was the only way he could cover the medical bills and also make the monthly nut for the expert staff of the residential facility at the Dumont Center Nursing Home.

Santo adapted. He rented a garden apartment in Bronxville and went into overdrive to find even more money-making opportunities. As her loving son, Jimmy was also squeezed by the old man to contribute. This constant need of large amounts of cash put added pressure on both of their crews to earn, and they became even more ruthless.

One of their most brazen schemes was conducted with the help of Jimmy's first cousins. Joanie's sister had lived out on Long Island with her two sons. Her oldest worked at the DMV, while his younger brother owned an auto body shop in Seaford. Through this relationship, they ran a complex auto insurance scam and fenced stolen cars.

"Just tell that guy who just brought in the blue Beemer that his transmission's shot." They would convince high-end car owners that they were in need of greater service and then submit the claim at an inflated price before the faux repair.

They also duplicated vehicle identification numbers and then forged the tags and stickers. The clean VINs would be placed on stolen cars and sold in other states.

"Yo, Dad, this is a gold mine. Fuckin' stupid computers don't even communicate. We could use the same VIN four or five times if we're lucky." Jimmy Tree was able to get away with this scam because state databases did not share information.

Santo Tentacles was a colorful and self-assuring wiseguy. He would brag to all in earshot that he was a part of La Cosa Nostra. He proudly told of getting his button. "Me and four other guys got inducted the same night. Paul Castellano called me in first. That'll tell you where I'm at!" He was a stand-up guy and never ratted or took a plea.

With his wife relegated to life at the Dumont, Tracino made the best of the situation. He visited her at the New Rochelle facility daily and also turned the entire nursing home into his own personal office. Many meetings were among its sick and elderly residents, but he also held court in the parking lot overlooking Long Island Sound and even around his sleeping wife's bed.

Santo would regularly stay late to read to his wife or watch TV. Thursday night was her favorite show, *Law & Order*. He laughed that the show tried to depict the most recent mob-related news into the story line. In these episodes the tough-guy actions appeared unrealistic, performed by over-actors who had never seen the dark end of a gun.

With the late-night news ending, he kissed his wife good-bye and walked out of the deserted facility. He ignored the teenage-looking security guard seated with his head buried in the *New York Post* at the front desk and hobbled down to his LeBaron parked under an oak tree near the water. A notorious creature of habit, he always parked in the same place. He spent many hours in its shade, admiring the picturesque views while chain-smoking and chatting with associates.

He opened the car door, sat in the driver's seat, and lit a cigarette before rolling down the window to let the smoke dissipate. On the gravel parking lot he heard footsteps. They began moving rapidly, getting louder. He tilted his head to see who was coming. Was it the security kid?

Pop! One shot at close range. The infamous life of Santo "Tentacles" Tracino was over.

Later That Day
FELIX AWOKE WITH HIS head pounding and chest on fire. He was sweating profusely and lying prone across the back vinyl seat. Early morning shade had given way to the late-morning sky. The van had been baking for an hour in the direct sun, and it was now unbearable to be enclosed in the vehicle any longer. Bannos maneuvered his body, raising his right arm behind his head and then twisting his immense frame. He grabbed the handle and slammed down hard. The sliding door opened with a blast of hot humid air.

He made his way to the sidewalk and staggered toward the Yonkers Motor Inn. Parked a block away, the van was on a street adjacent to an open field. After a few minutes, he entered his first-floor room and splashed cold water on his face. Then he grabbed his duffel bag and headed back out. A short drive later, he stopped at the warehouse, beeped the horn, and was let in. Two illegals filled the back of the van with his stolen cargo.

Felix remained seated in the driver's seat, waiting and collecting his bearings. He did not remember much from the night before. After Damien had greeted him, it all seemed to black out. *I could hold my liquor like a champ, so why am I feeling so shitty?*

He stopped at a Mobil for gas. Before he paid, he picked up a few bottles of water and a bunch of Tylenol packets. A couple of truck drivers who had stopped in for coffee appeared to be pissed at him. He had bumped them in the aisles. His icy stare and demonic, sweating face put a quick end to the abruptness.

It would be a long drive, and he needed to straighten out. Ten minutes later he crossed the George Washington Bridge heading south. Car horns blared and drivers passed by in frustration as he bled into the right and left lanes.

Damn it, gotta snap out of it! He slapped his face a few times and shook his head rapidly from side to side. With the air conditioner on full blast, he rolled down the window and plucked the ticket from the dispenser to enter the turnpike. He placed the ticket on the opposite seat. As he did, he noticed that his holster was peeking out from underneath the passenger-side seat on the floorboard, but his weapon was missing. *What the hell is going on? Where did I leave my revolver?* He leaned over and looked in the glove compartment. *Not there either. What the fuck! Is it in the back? … I'll check at the next rest stop.*

He opened the center console and felt around. Two bennies were wrapped in aluminum foil. The extra jolt was needed if he was to get the swag back home before his weekend double shift. He had already arranged to offload much of the supply with three Cubans who would be meeting him at a rest stop off of I-95 in Dade County.

Felix chewed and swallowed the pills. They began to work almost immediately, and he was soon alert and driving quickly. He pressed the accelerator to the floor, racing past ninety miles an hour and passing a plethora of slow-moving vehicles packed to the gills with luggage and bicycles, families heading to the Jersey Shore for their summer vacation.

He tried to piece through the events of the night and shook his head in disgust. *Was that the motherfucker Albanese who drove me back?* He thought more, backtracking in his foggy memory. From what he had comprehended through his stupor, Damien's girl looked a lot like Dominique. *Could she have been her?* All of this was too strange of a coincidence. He just knew those rats were working for the government, and he was going to let Damien know it. He just would not implicate Dominique.

Out of nowhere, Felix grabbed his chest with his free hand and squeezed his eyes shut in pain. Still traveling at an excessive speed, he was now unable to control the van. The wheels vibrated and rattled below as he bumped along, veering into the median. He was traveling dangerously close to the barrier and was out of control.

It was too late. His heart exploded. Felix Bannos let go of his grip on the steering wheel at the same time his life came to an end. The white van scraped along the concrete pylon for a few hundred feet before tipping. It rolled over three times before finally coming to a rest and exploding in a burst of flame just north of the exit 11 off-ramp.

That Afternoon

IT WAS A CROWDED fit and perilously close to the weight limit, but all six adults were comfortably seated in the Sikorsky S76. Like tourists, with wide eyes they peered down at the large W painted in the middle of the helipad as it lifted off from Westchester Airport. The circle got progressively smaller as they soared higher and darted in a southwesterly direction on a picturesque midsummer afternoon. In less than an hour they would touch down in Atlantic City and be on their way to Caesars for some gambling fun and a hearty meal.

"You lead some life now, my friend." Tony shook Chris's shoulder in appreciation for the complimentary trip.

"Hope it gets even better, buddy. I promise to not forget you guys, all you little people, when I'm among the rich and famous."

"I'll hunt you down myself if you end up eating caviar at some snooty country club and not cold pizza at my poker room," Sal chimed in to make sure Chris would never forget where he came from and who his friends really were.

After his tremendous success of being a portfolio manager at Conway Wealth, Chris was now in the final phase of opening his own investment fund. Cameron Investment Partners would be a hedge fund, and he was in negotiations with a group of prominent high-net-worth individuals who were eager to commit capital. His plan was to open his Dallas-based firm at the beginning of the year with a launch goal of a $100 million. There was already $65 million committed from Monroe Conway and a few of his wealthy friends. His boss had been instrumental in the launch, and he promised to have a good working relationship with his protégés' new endeavor.

"Monroe's been real good to me. Regardless of how this thing pans out, he's still gonna' pay me close to three mil this year, even before my new gig starts. I made Conway Wealth a lot of money these past years."

"Let's keep our fingers crossed. I have a lot of confidence in you." Megyn kissed him.

"If things go well, I guarantee, we all won't starve," he reassured his wife and buddies as they made their way south. The breathtaking view of the Manhattan skyline was upon them.

"Look at those towers, like two perfect columns heading to the sky." The World Trade Center was visible in the distance. As a construction guy, Tony loved to admire quality engineering.

"Chris honey, do you think my phone gets reception from up here? I want to give Amelia a call, have her look out of her office, and wave as we pass." Megyn's friend worked for a brokerage firm on one of the top floors of Tower 1.

"Give her a try. She'd get a kick out of it." Chris responded.

"Hello, hey … Amelia … Mia … Ms. Neill, are you there?" Megyn was frustratingly trying to make contact. She finally was able to get a clear connection. "Hey, girl, go wave out the window, we're zooming by you in a friggin' helicopter ... Heading to AC to gamble." They all waved out of the window as they cleared Lower Manhattan and the World Trade Center before zooming past the Statue of Liberty.

"She is such a sweet girl that Amelia. Love her."

"Thanks, Vicky, known her since college. My best friend."

As they left New York City airspace, the pilot followed the path of the New Jersey Turnpike. "Wow, good thing we didn't drive. Nice call, Cee. This'll be the only way we travel from now on." Tony had become quickly accustomed to first-class travel as he viewed what seemed to be a two-mile backup on the southbound side. The culprit was revealed less than ten seconds later: a smoldering white van surrounded by fire engines dousing out the blaze. The carcass of the vehicle was wrapped around a guardrail.

"Friggin' crazy drivers! Bet that dude was going a hundred ... Stupid dope could'a killed somebody. Thank God he was the only casualty." Sal made the sign of the cross and kissed the sky.

Because of the new start-up timetable, this would be one of the few times Chris would be able to see his buddies for the next few months. After this day trip, he and Megyn were headed out to Montauk to spend a week of quality time with their baby Sam. Then it was back to Dallas to raise more money, set up the new office, and meet with lawyers before the expected January start date.

This trip with the Albaneses and Espositos was overdue and well deserved. Based on conversations he had with Sal and Tony and corroborated by his discussions with Mitch Bassett in the Dallas field office, the FBI was extremely pleased with the information compiled so far. In two years, they had dossiers on over three times the amount of associates they had previously had on crime families throughout the Northeast. The names also extended beyond the traditional Italian mob to include the growing power of the Russian Bratva and Jamaican posses.

Last night had been very disconcerting, though. What were the chances Felix Bannos would show up out of the blue to meet with Damien, at Sal's restaurant no less? Again, just like in the Bahamas, the guys felt they had the situation under control. Based on the condition Felix was in when they dropped him off at his motel, there was no way Damien could take what he said with any reliability. Thankfully, Agent Tejata scurried her pseudo-boyfriend away quickly. She even called Chris in the morning to have him reassure Sal and Tony that Damien did not seem alarmed by the ramblings of the muscle-bound drunk. She would fly down to Florida to speak with Felix about the investigation and make sure he kept his nose clean and stayed away from the impending fireworks. She would make it perfectly clear that he would not interfere with the investigation any longer and that his days of working with Damien were officially over.

Late That Night

JUST AS MEGYN HAD planned, they touched down at Westchester Airport minutes after eleven. Angela's stupid husband could not take no for an answer. "Leave the blackjack table when you're ahead." Vicky was not happy either. "Friggin' Tony just don't know when to stop playing his favorite number in roulette … No, black four may never come out, maybe ever again."

As the engines came to a stop, Megyn shook Chris' shoulder and lightly tapped his cheek. No, her big lug wasn't a winner either. *He may be smart, but he cannot count a six-deck shoe, no matter how hard he tried or how cool he looked with his collar popped and sunglasses on indoors.* "Time to get up, babe. Rise and shine." Chris blinked his eyes a few times before stretching.

"Yo, dudes. Damn Ang, how long you been trying to wake him?" Chris said through a hearty yawn.

"Christopher, this man could sleep through an earthquake." Angela said as she shook her husband's shoulder.

"He did … once." Tony popped his eyes open to fill Angela in on information she had not known already about the love of her life.

Tony smacked the back of Sal's neck. It finally woke him up. "See, I'm like an alarm clock." He groggily laughed.

The group of very tired parents exited and made their way to the terminal gate. As they walked through the carpeted, air conditioned environs, two visitors were waiting.

"Hello, Chris … Sal … Tony … Can we speak with you for a few minutes." Agents Sikes and Nicholas escorted the trio to an empty seating area.

20

POWER WALK

November 28, 1980

ON THIS SUNNY BUT seasonably cool late-fall morning, they all set off with
gusto. All of the women were determined to embark on a new mission, an
exercise regime. The men had just packed up two station wagons and were
already on their way upstate to the hunting cabin. They had kissed love
ones good-bye and then watched three generations of Scalamarri women
disappear toward the direction of the trails along the Bronx River.

"My Michael said he was excited to go hunting, but all I saw him take
was a cooler of beer and his poker chips. Did your father even take his rifle,
Saby?" Maria Cameron sarcastically addressed her daughter, but made the
comment to all in pack.

"If he did, he'll have to borrow *Zio* Al's bullets, 'cause I hid his and
Christopher's." Saby was only fifteen, but she was all for animal rights.

Sabina was pretty much the poster child for almost all liberal causes.
The prior morning, while the mothers-grandmothers were preparing the
Thanksgiving Day feast, she yanked her brother out of bed before 8:00
a.m. Then the two of them literally pulled Sal and Tony out from under
their covers to assist in bringing donated food and clothing to the homeless
shelter on North Avenue in New Rochelle. The days of Sabina being
physically bigger than her brother and quasi-adopted brothers had officially
ended, but she still commanded her aura of authority. The boys cowed to
her wishes whenever she came calling.

"*Zia* Dina, I bet Sal won't even go out to hunt. He was having a ball serving food yesterday morning. He'll probably try and impress all the men around the grill." Sabina amusingly stated.

"You have that right, Sabina. That boy may love to act all bad and tough, but he loves anything to do with a kitchen." Dina had been very impressed with her youngest son. With his father away in prison for six of the past ten years, Salvatore took on the responsibility of serving meals for the family. She and her two oldest, Robert and John, had spent most of the day and nights at the restaurant. Now with Johnny away in the navy and Robby attending college in Ohio, Salvatore was finally old enough to get his wish, to help out at Ressini's.

"Do you believe he already asked for my veal saltimbocca recipe? Dina, he is such a delight to have around," Maria Cameron complimented her cousin.

"He thinks he's gonna run the restaurant. Big plans ... So cute, the big *chooch*."

Salvatore as well as Anthony had spent many hours under Maria Cameron's roof. Quite frankly, she had come to the conclusion that she now had three sons as the trio was inseparable. Chris would also tutor them both. They would tease him that he was a brainiac, but he was undeterred and aggressively pushed them to improve. Their barely C averages were now steady Bs.

The entire contingent of women were along for the power walk: the elders (Julia Cavazzi looking spry at sixty-seven and Teresa Scala beautiful at sixty-one), the mothers (Dina Esposito, holding strong at forty-seven; Maria Cameron, a young-looking thirty-seven; and Rita Albanese, thirty-three and reluctantly needing to lose a few pounds), and the girls (Saby was growing into a beautiful brunette and Joanne Albanese was nine, keeping up with the group but getting bored).

At Thanksgiving dinner, they had all vowed to get into better physical shape. The pie and cakes were pushed to the side, and a workout schedule was devised.

"We'll walk every day, in the morning or at night." Also fueling Rita was the results from her recent physical. Doctor Garson more than persuaded her to change her eating habits. She knew Big Al didn't get his nickname for nothing, so they agreed to start living healthier. Even their baby boy had transformed from Little Anthony to Big Tony right before their eyes.

Thankfully, the days of a room full of smoke were dwindling. Only Dina, Mike, Greg, and Joe still lit up. When Al and Rita quit, unfortunately they transferred the addiction to food. Surprisingly, most of the older generation bucked the trend of the time and had not succumbed to the allure of the cancer sticks. Even stationed in the Pacific during the war, Vince and Teresa never took up the nasty habit. Vince still snuck a cigar or two, but never more than that.

"Don't worry, ladies. My Vinnie told me that he would whip us all into shape, just like he did to those boys on the Blue Devils." Teresa amusingly let the girls know that her former drill sergeant would be on their butts if they slacked in this new initiative.

Vincent was sad to see his days of coaching behind him, but he had no more skin in the game. All the boys in his inner circle were playing for the junior varsity squad, and he would much rather focus his time watching them than coaching a fresh batch of unknowns. He was honored and touched when the Blue Devils thanked him for his years of service with a ceremony at the awards banquet. All of his focus from now on would be on the Tuckahoe Tigers, and watching the three Columbus Avenue Boys help bring the school some respectability on the sports fields.

"He's looking for some new victims, huh?" Rita smirked at the thought of her father demanding these ladies to do push-ups and sit-ups.

"Poppy said he's still sad," Joanne chimed in out of nowhere while doing cheerleading moves as they walked. All of them went quiet and looked down at the little princess.

"Yes, we're all sad, baby. Big *Nonna* loved everyone," Teresa consoled her granddaughter. Her little Jo-Jo had spent many hours with her grandparents and had never forgotten the emotion her grandfather displayed at his mother's funeral. Julianna Nurzia Scala lived to be ninety-three years old. While she endured much in her many years, she died a happy great-grandmother.

"How far have we gone? It's been like a half hour already. Wasn't that like five miles?" Rita joked to change the subject. In actuality, they had probably only finished their second mile.

There had been a refreshing change to the family dynamic over the past few years. Pat Fortuno was no longer around anymore and, of all the smokers, he had been the most brazen. Blowing the noxious fumes in the face of the children with no regard for their well-being was actually low on the list of his many offensive habits.

"Rosa's wedding was beautiful. I do hope second time's a charm. How are her and Mark doing? Have you spoken with them since the honeymoon?" Dina addressed Maria as they continued their power walk, which had now turned into a power stroll.

Before she could answer, Sabina broke in. "Uncle Mark's awesome! So happy *Zia* Rosa left that Pat … Second time's a charm for sure!"

"Now, now, Sabina, show some respect. Even though they're divorced, I don't want you saying that again." Maria Cameron was all about respect, even for those who did not show it back. Michael was not a fan of Fortuno either, but to keep peace with her sister they had to remain silent on this issue. That's just how it worked in the family.

"Saby, yes, I think we're all happy Pat and Rosa got divorced. He was a strange character, but your mother is correct." Her *nonna* made this comment as she tried to keep up with the younger group. All the women agreed in unison as they continued. The chatting and gossiping had really never stopped.

"My sister knew Mark since the early seventies. You know, he was her boss at that company she works for in the city. When they relocated the main office to White Plains, they'd commute together. We were not at all surprised they ended up together."

"Two weddings this year! My God, I hope Al don't have a heart attack. Our bank account is dwindling. Things better pick up, and fast," Rita added to the wedding talk but in a more moribund way. Her sister Anne Marie had also finally married her long-time boyfriend, Richard Ducker. The Albaneses were happy to not have any more boosts to hand out.

"Annie and Rich are comfortably living in Houston. He works for Exxon. That company moved a lot of workers out of New York. At least there's one part of the country that's doing good." Teresa was happy for her youngest daughter but missed her immensely. With high oil prices, Texas had been one of the few states that had added jobs in this very deep recession, and this was an opportunity they could not pass up.

The United States economy and political environment this past decade had mirrored all of their lives very closely. President Nixon resigned after the Watergate scandal in 1974, and the Vietnam War officially ended in 1975 without victory. Sex, drugs, and rock and roll had run rampant as had the unrest by the masses. Inflation and unemployment remained staggeringly high, and to top it all off, gas prices had risen once again to levels that choked the family budget. It was no wonder President Carter lost the election to Ronald Reagan.

"Through all of this, I am so proud of my Michael, though. Bless his beautiful green eyes. He's going to take his test to be a citizen." Maria was equally impressed that her son had eagerly stepped up to help his father study for the test. Chris loved American history to a point of being a fanatic. He and his father would constantly talk all types of world history and politics. This was just one of the ways a proud immigrant and his teenage son bonded.

"Daddy teased me that President Carter ruined the country. He said Reagan will do wonderful things." Even though Sabina was still not old enough to vote, she had volunteered on the local level for President Carter's failed bid to be elected for a second term.

"He's just bored, Saby, laid off from work and all. You know he loves to tease you, but that's 'cause you take it to heart so much. It's that sarcastic Gaelic humor." After a few seconds pause, Maria then added, "He actually thinks he is quite the funny Irishman."

The GM plant in which Mike Cameron worked had been closed for the past few weeks because of slowness in auto demand. He used the time to his advantage by studying for the citizenship test, but being so close to the holidays, he would much rather have been working double shifts.

"So, Dina, why didn't Robby come back for turkey day?" Julia changed subjects as they continued on.

"The boy's in love. He went to Indiana with his girlfriend to visit her parents for Thanksgiving. Not looking good that he comes back to good old Tuckahoe. He said he's interviewing for jobs as an accountant in Chicago. If he lands one, then he's going to marry her and move there. Nice girl, sweet. Her name's Carrie; think she's German."

The entire family had rallied around Dina as her life had been in turmoil for quite some time now. Two recessions during the past seven years had taken its toll on the restaurant, and her husband spending way too much time in jail certainly did not help matters. To make matters worse, her brother Marco was killed in a car accident last year and her mother died the year earlier after a long, draining battle with breast cancer.

"I just thank God I have all of you to help us. The way Vince helps out with the boys has been so wonderful." She reached back and squeezed Teresa Scala's hand. Her eyes were tearing. They did that a lot these days.

"We've had our drama, girls. And we'll all persevere and be there for each other, right?" Teresa had scooted to the front of the pack and impressed the women by facing them while walking backward as she spoke.

"Just think of all this family has gone through. It's been like a huge rollercoaster." Teresa was now starting to breathe a bit heavier.

"Too many downs, though. God in Heaven, watch over us!" Dina made the sign of the cross and kissed the sky.

"Now, we've made it this far. We'll get through this too." Teresa looked at Julia Cavazzi for agreement. Julia nodded back.

"Our family could be looked at as being cursed, but we have to view it as a blessing for having survived so much turmoil." Julia made the comment to Teresa knowing the full extent of the family pain. A pain that went back much farther than the other women even knew.

"Teresa, does this look familiar to you? This park hasn't changed in fifty years." Julia smiled as she reflected back to her infamous wedding day. It was the day Vincent and Teresa had fallen in love. It was also the day the Scalamarri family was shattered.

"Joanne, did you know Poppy and I had our first date right here?" Teresa smiled as she whispered this new bit of information into her granddaughter's ear. Then she looked in a melancholy way toward the direction of where the family's banquet hall had been located. In its place, a new establishment stood.

From Teresa and Julia's viewpoint, these younger women, the daughters and granddaughters, actually had been blessed. While they had had hardship financially and lost loved ones along the way, they had not endured what the two of them experienced growing up.

Because of her love for Vincent, Teresa eagerly entered the family. She embraced the challenge presented by him to rebuild the legacy. The Scalamarris had always been viewed by the newspapers and media of the day as a group of gangsters who "got what they deserved." The reality was that the community had adored them. The destitute, depression-era town folk poured out their hearts and, while most had very little, gave what they could to assist the survivors. This was truly a blessing and the main reason Julianna Scala never thought of leaving.

Teresa's parents, the Carpinellos, had the utmost respect for the Scalamarris. Their illegal business was built for survival during a time when there was not much of an alternative, and they gave back to the community in many financial ways. Teresa and Vincent had many discussions in later years that convinced her that the family would have eventually turned to be legitimate. Pasquale had aspirations for his son to attend college or, if he chose, to own the River House as a 100 percent legal entity. Those dreams were cut short that tragic night.

Teresa and Vincent alone shared all of the secrets of his past. These acts were committed in order to survive, and she knew to the core he was a good man, no, a great man. They still spoke frequently in private about the times he needed to kill, had to kill, and wanted to kill. For each he believed it was justified. Even to this day, Vincent continued to experience nightmares. He would wake in the middle of the night, screaming about an imminent banzai charge or cry uncontrollably about visions of the body of a buddy mutilated and desecrated by a Jap stealth attack. He never once, though, had nightmares of Bugsy Siegel or of the hobos he fended off.

Julia and Teresa would also speak secretly and quietly of the past, but they never wished to share the horrific details with the younger generation who had their own problems to deal with. During the Great Depression, Julia remembered times when they were barely able to eat. Joe would work for days at a time, sometimes not seeing his family for more than a few minutes. He labored at the docks in Brooklyn and cleaned the streets in Lower Manhattan to make ends meet. Before the end of the war, he had a wife, three daughters, and aging parents to support. Julia relished her family now, knowing that even though there seemed to be stress all around, they would find a way to make it through.

March 30, 1981
CITIZENSHIP WAS ONE OF the most coveted gifts that the US government could bestow. While most became citizens by birth, others could go through the process of naturalization. To do so, a foreign citizen or national had to fulfill requirements established by Congress in the Immigration and Nationality Act. These requirements included a period of residency within the country; the ability to read, write, and speak English; an understanding of US history; and demonstration of good moral character.

Michael Cameron proudly walked out of the White Plains courthouse. A mini-American Flag was flapping in his left hand. His right hand proudly clutched his citizenship papers. Once he reached the pavilion, a celebration ensued.

"USA, USA, USA!" Family and friends clapped hands and hugged him warmly as they chanted in a similar fashion as the crowd did when the US had upset the Soviet Union in the "Miracle on Ice" Olympic hockey game from a year earlier. The children were more than happy to be there. A well-deserved early absence from school would be overlooked by the faculty. All wanted to cheer on Irish-American Mike, the United States citizen.

"Hey, *compare*, does that paper make you an Italian too?" Greg laughed as he hugged and gave congratulations.

"Don't worry about him, Mike, my boy. I hear they're gonna take Greg's citizenship away if he has one more slip-up and he goes back in the can. Teresa and I are so proud of you." Vince hugged him and planted a hearty kiss on his cheek.

A commotion began to form. A sedan with its doors opened and parked a few feet away had the volume to the radio turned up high. People were conversing and in disbelief. Many were walking around nervously. Alfonse walked over to see what was going on and then came back a few moments later with the cause of the uproar.

"Holy crap! … President Reagan's been shot."

The jovial gathering quickly ended. Family members all ran to their cars to turn on the radio. Over the harrowing next few days, more details emerged. At 2:27 p.m., after a speaking engagement, the president had walked to his limousine outside the Washington Hilton. A gunman identified as John Hinckley Jr. stepped out from a crowd less than twenty feet from the president. He raised a .22-caliber pistol and fired. Press Secretary James Brady was hit by one shot; police officer Tom Delahanty was hit by another. Secret Service Agent Tim McCarthy had intercepted a shot that was on a vector to hit the president. After turning and shielding the president with his body, another bullet slammed into the door of the car as Secret Service Agent Jerry Parr was pushing President Reagan into the vehicle. The bullet glanced off the frame of the limousine and ricocheted, hitting the president under his left arm, puncturing a lung, and lodging an inch from his heart. Less than five seconds after the first shot was fired, the limousine carrying the president sped off toward George Washington University Hospital. Both Delahanty and McCarthy recovered from their wounds. Tragically, the shot to James Brady's head inflicted permanent brain damage.

As President Reagan was being prepped for what turned out to be two hours of life-saving surgery, he quipped to his wife, Nancy, "Honey, I forget to duck." Then to the surgeons he deadpanned, "Please tell me you're Republicans." The next day the president was reported to be in stable condition, and he even went back to work signing a bill.

"That, my boy, is a leader. I am confident he will do great things. God knows we need it." Mike Cameron sat watching the CBS newscast on the status of the president's condition. His son Chris was by his side. Ironically, Walter Cronkite had retired from broadcasting three weeks earlier, and this was the first historic event he had not reported on in the past thirty years.

"You think so, Dad? Saby said he's just an old actor that shouldn't have gotten elected in the first place." Chris was also doing his homework as they spoke.

"Christopher lad, our country, and I can finally say that, needs to get back to the world power we once were. I've been following this man's plan; President Reagan has a vision and I believe it. He wants to lower taxes, make it easier for small businesses like ours to get by."

"I hope so. We've been watching you grown-ups. Sal, Tony, and I see everything, you know. You may think we're just stupid kids, but we talk about it all the time. There's no way we're gonna let our livelihoods crumble!"

Mike hugged his son and smiled, hoping he was right. "Chris, whatever you do, just promise me that you will never stop trying. If you work hard, you could never disappoint me or your mother. We've been blessed with beautiful, good kids like you and Sabina. I know you've both got it in you to reach for the stars and succeed beyond your wildest dreams."

Mike Cameron was very lucky. His contentious and abusive childhood in Ireland was now long forgotten. He believed he had already been the luckiest man to walk the earth. How else could he explain a chance meeting with the most gorgeous woman he had ever seen, transpiring into being accepted into a loving and supportive group of friends? To top it off, they were proud parents of two wonderful children.

21

FUGAZI

August 15, 1998, Just Before Noon

The Dumont Center Nursing Home was located on a quiet peninsula overlooking Glen Island Park and Neptune Island. The grounds were spacious and provided a tranquil setting for its geriatric guests to spend their waning days in comfort.

Whether it was the beginning or end of his shift, it was not an uncommon sight for Harold Gayden to see the old maroon Chrysler parked under the big tree by the water toward the far end of the parking lot. Besides his other two jobs, Gayden worked days as a security guard at the Dumont. He was well aware of who that crazy old white dude was who drove the older model LeBaron, but this was by far his easiest gig, so he was damn well sure not going to make waves. No one cared when he disappeared to nod off during the day. There were also instances when he was lucky enough to be at the right time and place when the old Mafioso slipped him some cash to look the other way.

"Harry boy, you're a friggin' tall *mulignan*. Damn, you look strong as an ox. Hey, do me a favor, why don't you take a break. Here's a twenty, go run to the store and get me some smokes."

The racist, old geezer had a set of balls, but Harold never said a word. There were usually some bad-ass dudes with him as he made the comment, and it was not worth it.

He exited the bus on Pelham Road and walked toward the entrance to the nursing home. He checked his watch, quarter to twelve. Still a few minutes till his shift started, so he decided to stroll down and see if he could make some easy money. From the angle from where he was walking, he could see the old man sleeping in the front seat of his car. Harold figured he would go wake him and possibly be summoned to get a cup of coffee or something.

"Hey, Santo, my man. You oh-aight," Harold voiced loudly as he approached from the back of the vehicle. With no answer, he walked closer.

"Goddamn!" He spun around and bolted from the bloody scene. Seconds later, he pushed the doors to the nursing home entrance open, almost hitting an aide.

"Yo, call nine-one-one. There's a dude in the parking lot with his head shot off!"

Fifteen minutes later, a swarm of New Rochelle police enveloped the campus. Less than a half hour after the crime scene had been sealed, a crew from *News12* showed up and began to snoop around. The first report was broadcast to the region from the sidewalk in front of the facility at 1:45 p.m. The yellow tape with black lettering could be seen in the background as the cute young reporter shielded her eyes from the afternoon sun.

"A man was found shot to death, and police have sealed off the area. They are currently looking for clues to this brutal slaying. I have with me Mr. Harold Gayden." The camera panned to a two person shot. She placed a microphone in front of his face.

"Yeah, I found the dude. He comes here a lot, think his name's Santa, Santo, or something. His wife's a patient in the facility. Gruesome, just gruesome. I saw part of his brain splattered on his dashboard." Before he had agreed to be interviewed, Mr. Gayden provided the news crew with the alleged name of the deceased. After a fast bit of research, the producer had identified the body as the local crime figure.

"Police have yet to confirm the deceased, but there is speculation that he is believed to be Santo Tracino. Mr. Tracino was a reputed associate with the Gambino Crime Family. *News12* will stay on this story as we gather more information. From New Rochelle, I'm Christy Greene reporting."

An Hour Later

LOCAL POLICE SEALED THE area and ran the license plate and vehicle registration. In the search of the car, they located a wallet containing a driver's license. Due to the nature of the homicide, the name Santo Dominic Tracino was run through the database of the Organized Crime Control Board. When it was confirmed that the deceased was in fact the notorious underworld figure, a call was placed to the FBI.

Special Agents Nicholas and Sikes arrived shortly after 3:00 p.m. By that time, the facility had turned into a circus. Besides the *News12* crew, talking heads from three regional networks had also set up camp and were providing live reports.

"It appears Tentacles finally pissed someone off," Agent Sikes deadpanned as he viewed the body. Forensics were taking pictures and continuing to gather evidence.

"Have we heard back from Agent Tejata yet? I'd like to see if her boyfriend knows what's going on," Agent Nicholas whispered to him.

"We need to speak with her. I'd also like to hear what the two gorillas have to say." They peeled away and went back to their sedan. Agent Nicholas called the New York City field office. She was transferred to an emotional Dominique Tejata.

"Agent Tejata, are you all right? Do you have anything you can give us on the execution of your subject's boss?"

In a monotone and speaking slowly and deliberately, Agent Tejata replied, "I can confirm that Damien Morris was taken by surprise by the killing. He and I were at the gym together. He saw the report on TV and bugged out. He said he'd call me later, but he bolted before I had a chance to speak with him in detail." She noticeably sobbed.

"Dominique, what's going on?" Special Agent Nicholas raised her voice an octave.

"After ... After I left the gym, I received a personal call. This may or may not be related to the Tracino killing, but it's too coincidental to pass up." Agent Tejata paused.

"Go on!" Agent Nicholas pressed her impatiently.

"I had filed a report in February about a link between a family friend and the investigation I am assigned to ... this investigation. Unbeknownst to me, this friend happened to have ties to Damien Morris. When he was younger, he was a strong arm for both Tracinos ... Jimmy and Santo. Well, I was very close to this person, and I ... I ... I received a call from my brother that he was killed in an accident on the New Jersey Turnpike."

"I'm sorry for your loss, but what does this have to do with our investigation?" Agent Nicholas was not an emotional person and had little time for personal issues.

"His name was Felix Bannos, and he was a Florida State Trooper. I grew up with him … A friend of my brother." Dominique sobbed and covered the receiver with her hand.

"Okay … What's the connection?" Agent Nicholas asked in an irritated manner.

"He was corrupt. For years he had been buying and selling stolen goods through his association with Damien Morris. I found this out last night, and my cover may or may not have been blown. I was at the place owned by the gorillas." Tejata began to regain her composure.

"Okay … Continue." Agent Nicholas was now intrigued.

"Well, after Bannos almost fucked it all up, I left the establishment with Morris to get him away so no more harm could be done. As we were leaving, I saw Bannos trying to drive away." She paused for a few seconds. "But before he got into the car, I might add that he was very intoxicated. Well, as I drove off, I witnessed the two gorillas exiting the restaurant and moving toward the van that Bannos was driving." Agent Tejata was rambling but had to get it all off of her chest.

"Do you think they had anything to do with Bannos's and or Tracino's deaths?" Agent Nicholas asked, now in a more sympathetic tone.

Dominique added some more analysis. "That I do not know. I think you should ask the gorillas yourself. I also think it's time to locate Damien Morris and bring him in too. It's getting very hot, and he probably would be of no more use to us out on the street."

Agent Dominique Tejata was not upset that her romance was soon to be ending but was in a state of shock over the whole Felix situation. She hung up and made a series of calls from her cubicle on the twenty-third floor of Twenty-Six Federal Plaza.

Before speaking with the two agents heading the investigation, she had remembered back to her prior evening's festivities. Her calls were made to helicopter charter operations in the tri-state area. It only took a few minutes to locate the reservation made by Chris Cameron. The flight had landed in Atlantic City at 12:45 p.m. and was due back to Westchester Airport before midnight.

Early That Evening
DAMIEN MORRIS HAD JUST finished his last workout before the weekend; that is, he blasted out supersets of biceps and triceps until the blood flowed like a creek after a heavy rain. Unable to move his upper appendages, he went into the cardio room. Elaudys was reading some glamour magazine

on an exercise bike. He plopped down next to her, set the computer setting to level four and began to pedal while staring at the television monitor mounted above them.

"Can you come get me early tonight, baby? I don't feel like working too late." Elaudys patted her forehead with a towel and provocatively smiled.

"We'll see, we'll see. I got a few things to do later on. That drunken fool from last night was supposed to pick up a thing this morning. Wanna check that he went through with it. Stupid jerk!" Damien massaged his left bicep with his right hand.

"Yeah, well, come get me." Then she whispered, "My period's over." Then she seductively licked her lips.

Damien smiled back and readjusted his sweatpants. *Damn, my girl is so friggin' hot.* Then he moved his gaze toward the newscast above him.

"Holy fuck." He stopped pedaling and hopped off the bike. "Gotta go babe, I'll call you later." He bolted off.

Damien sprang up the stairs of the health club and emerged into the parking lot. He screamed out loud to no one in particular and got in his car and sped off, first heading north on the Bronx River Parkway and then west on I-287 before merging onto the thruway. He crossed over the Tappan Zee Bridge separating Westchester from Rockland County.

As he drove, he incessantly changed stations on his radio to find one broadcasting the news about the murder in New Rochelle. While the volume had been muted on the TV at the gym, he saw the caption on the screen that the deceased was alleged to be mob boss Santo Tracino. They even flashed to a picture of his capo to emphasize the point.

That was all he needed to surmise that he should hit the mattresses (lay low for a while). He sped north past Rockland and Sullivan Counties before stopping for gas in Kingston. After he filled his truck, he went to a payphone. He had to find out what the hell was going on.

He put a few quarters in and dialed. Jimmy Tracino answered and was noticeably upset. "Yo, Jimmy, it's Damien. I am so fuckin' sorry. How you holding up?"

Jimmy Tracino spoke somberly. "Not good, not good. My pop was a made man. Who would do this to him? Blew his fuckin' face off. Can't even have an open casket."

"I am clueless by all this. Far as I know, all was good. Who'd he piss off? There any Jamaicans he dealt with? They're some crazy bastards and don't play by our rules." Damien cupped his free ear with his hand and curled his head into the phone booth as he had a hard time hearing with the cars and trucks speeding by on the thruway.

"Nah, he didn't give a fuck. All he cared about was getting his taste. We were all pressin' harder since my mom got sick, but he wasn't goin' apeshit about it. Some of the Queens guys were being pricks, but screw them." Jimmy had lost his entire tough guy facade.

"Some of the Jiggles shit wasn't sitting well with a few folks, too, but your old man always went through proper protocol so the city bosses was cool. You're right, though; those Queens pricks were always a bunch of scumbags." During the drive Damien had been thinking about possible suspects to the unprovoked attack.

"Where you at, Damien?"

"On the road, bro, on the road. How 'bout you?"

"I'm at my chick's apartment. Went to the nursing home and then the police station but drove right by both of them. Friggin' reporters all over the place. Cop called me all sympathetically. Said they would have come in person, but all the news outlets had his name already, so they wanted to make sure I found out quickly."

"I'm getting out of here for a while. I got this place that no one knows about." Damien had already planned to hideout in his neighbor's vacation cabin.

"Once you get settled, if you got a safe phone, call the guys in my crew … I heard from Emile and Stevie Garbage already. Sal and Tony are MIA." Jimmy Tree had also been thinking long and hard about whom could have executed his father.

"Those guys were around last night. My girl said their richie-rich friend was in town, so they was headin' to AC. They'll be back soon," Damien told him matter-of-factly.

"Well, anyway, get somewhere safe. I'll get some calls into Manhattan to get the four-one-one." Jimmy Tree hung up.

Damien started driving again and did not stop until he pulled up to the gravel-and-dirt driveway of the cabin just north of Hunter Mountain. It was now 4:30 p.m. He jogged around the back. Underneath a large rock was the key to the door. He went inside and then opened the fuse box and switched on the electricity.

The cabin was tiny, probably only six hundred square feet total. There was a small bedroom in the left corner across the way from the kitchenette. The front area had a rectangular living space furnished with a couch, a coffee table, and an end table with a lamp. No shade was on top, just an exposed bulb. The room overlooked a picture window that provided a clear view of the broken-down porch and, importantly, the driveway leading up to the main road. This area rarely had traffic, so if a vehicle passed by, he would be ready.

He opened a kitchen cabinet and found a half-filled bottle of scotch. He cleaned a glass and then carried both to the couch. He placed his pistol on the coffee table. His make and model of choice was the *Beretta 9000S*. Its .40 S&W cartridge was filled and fitted with a twelve-round magazine.

"Aaahhh," he mouthed to himself as he took a one-inch shot of eighty proof. He looked at his watch; it was now a little after five. *Gonna be a long one.*

As he sat in silence, he thought about what to do next. Would Elaudys leave with him? Did she have relatives in the Caribbean they could crash with for a while? He had to get his stash of money out of the safe deposit box at the Chase branch in White Plains. Once he had that, he could live comfortably for a few years. *Damn, why am I thinkin' so crazy? This profession does make one paranoid.*

Another hour passed, and four more shots of Scotch were tossed down. As Damien sat in silence, he felt vibrations overhead. He could feel the unmistakable thwapping of helicopter blades getting closer and soon circling overhead. Two black sedans pulled up, stopped on the main road and parked back-to-back less than forty feet from the cabin. A cadre of figures in dark blue windbreakers with yellow lettering piled out. They remained safely behind the vehicles.

"Damien Morris … Come out with your hands where we can see them," a bellowing female voice commanded from a bullhorn. It sounded strangely familiar.

Staying low, he grabbed his pistol and crawled to the edge of the window. He looked closely. The sun was setting in the early evening sky, but he could clearly see who was calling for him to come out. He could not believe it. Elaudys had been stringing him on all along. *She's a federal fuckin' agent. I am one dumb bastard, told her every goddamn thing.* He shook his head in disappointment.

"Mr. Morris, this is the FBI. We have the place surrounded. Come out, we would like to speak with you." The voice was now that of a deep-baritoned African-American man.

Damien sat dumbfounded. His life was over. Even if he wanted to run, Elaudys was *fugazi*, and she had been the one he wanted to run with.

He stared at his pistol; the cool steel was heavy in his strong hand. He gently placed it on the floor in front of him. A few moments passed. Then he raised his knees to his chest and placed both hands over his face. The tough-guy mob enforcer who killed at will and who was feared wherever he went began sobbing uncontrollably.

The back door crashed open. Three heavily armed agents swarmed in through the narrow hallway. They took ready positions around the couch, but Damien did not resist. The *Beretta* remained on the floor. He never looked up as he raised both of his hands in surrender.

August 16, Just after Midnight

THE COLUMBUS AVENUE BOYS were sitting on uncomfortable folding metal chairs situated around a rectangular table in a sterile gray room in Westchester Airport. They had sent their wives home an hour earlier.

"What's this all about, Anthony? Who's the redhead?" Vicky had sharply asked her husband when Special Agent Nicholas walked up to them.

"Work-related baby. Angie, Meg, we may be a little while. Could you please take my missus home? Cee, we got a car waiting, right?" Tony responded. "It's probably nothing," he whispered in her ear before they accompanied the federal agents.

Special Agents Sikes and Nicholas were both sitting on one side of the table with Chris bookended by Sal and Tony on the other. After an offer of something to drink and to get a snack in the vending machine, the guys sat down to hear what was so urgent.

First, they were briefed on the untimely death of Santo Tracino. Sikes and Nicholas went over the details of his demise and asked each of them, three times no less and using slightly different wording for each instance, where they were between eleven and one the prior evening. Their stories remained the same for each of the three times the agents inquired about their alibi.

"I was indisposed of from elevenish to eleven fifteenish, if you know what I mean?" Tony matter-of-factly stated on all three occasions. "Then I was back in the card room till about four."

"'Indisposed of'? Can you elaborate?" Agent Sikes looked up from his notepad.

"You don't want him to elaborate. Friggin' guy was tooting so bad on our way from escorting a guy home." Sal gave a "you-make-me-sick" face at Tony.

"Who did you escort home?" Agent Nicholas pressed.

"This drunk, came to the bar and didn't even play cards. He just sat talking with Damien. I can't let a guy drive home in his condition, so our bartender flagged me and told me to get my butt down there fast." Tony gave the same exact answer for the third time.

"And all you did was drive him home?" Special Agent Sikes looked up from his notes.

"Yeah, actually he was out cold in the back of the van. I saw a Yonkers Motor Inn key on his console, so I put two and two together. Parked his ass right on the street. Sal followed me and we drove back together. Guy pissed me off so much I was gonna shit in his van, but decided against it!" Tony said proudly.

"We actually made good time. Drove him back around 10:40 p.m., and we were back before 11:00 p.m.," Sal stated. "Then the big guy makes a bee-line to the john, and the rest is history." They all giggled like little girls.

"Chris, where were you during all of this?" Agent Nicholas asked.

"Well, before they left I was playing cards. Then I was forced to leave the game to monitor the bank and chips. I was hot as hell, up about six hundred. That drunk cost me a lot of momentum! There were like twenty people there, Dawn."

"That's Agent Nicholas, Mr. Cameron. Were you guys aware that Felix Bannos was in a fatal car accident? Tests will be run in the morning, but the body's burned up real bad. How drunk was he at your restaurant?" Agent Nicholas seemed to be frustrated by the whole chain of events.

"We have no idea. Ask Damien Morris; he was with that idiot Bannos all night. I didn't even want that friggin' guy in the place to begin with, a little bad blood," Sal commented as he spread two of his sausage-like fingers an inch apart.

Chris then broke in and was furious. "Are you two ... is the federal government under the assumption that we killed Tentacles and Bannos in some elaborate undercover operation? You've gotta be kidding me. These guys worked so hard, and now you come crashing down on us."

"It came to our attention that Bannos may have spoken with Damien Morris about your association with Agent Tejata. We are simply checking to see if you guys may have gotten spooked by it and panicked ... Possibly reverting to the old days and tying up loose ends."

"Cover our tracks in a blaze of glory?" Tony gave his disapproval. "We trusted you guys to get us out if it got hot. I am not killing nobody, especially Santo, who I've known for a few decades. We had a bet the old man was gonna drop dead from natural causes any day now for Christ's sake."

"I had November in the pool. Damn, lost that one." Sal smiled and looked at Chris and Tony seeking approval for his perfectly timed punch line.

Just then, Agent Nicholas's mobile phone rang. She stepped away to take the call. In her absence, the guys tapped out Billy Joel's *Angry Young Man* with their hands on the top of the table. Agent Sikes was not amused by the well-choreographed banging.

She returned and whispered into her partner's ear. They looked across the table.

Agent Nicholas faced them smileless. "Gentlemen, you're free to leave."

"We're free to go? Don't keep us in suspense. Why, thought we murdered two guys with our split personalities while playing mind games." Sal was having fun with them now as he waved his hands trying to mock-hypnotize them.

Again, Sal had reverted to humor when he was actually quite hurt in a situation. As he told his therapist, whom he now saw weekly, "My friggin' life's been a cluster fuck!" Up to that point, he had only opened up completely to his two buddies, and not until recently had he begun to share with his wife. The question had always been asked, how could such a nice guy turn into a crazy man when angered? The answer: his youth was total chaos. Robert and John were treated the same way as he, and as a way to let off steam they used the opportunity to beat him senseless up until the time he was eleven. By that time, he had grown and began to fight back, in earnest. A truce was called, and the three parted ways. His two brothers moved across the country. They never even kept in touch with him anymore, and the last time he had seen them was when they came back for the funeral.

His father, "Dad of the Century" Greg Esposito, had dropped dead of a heart attack in 1986. The old man put up a good show in public but in reality, he had treated Sal horrifically behind closed doors by beating him senseless on numerous occasions. The happiest times of Sal's life were when his father was put away. *God rest his degenerate soul.* Then, to top it all off, his mother bugs out after his death and marries a guy she knew for like five minutes. She took off and moved to the west coast of Florida and did not care if the restaurant continued or not.

Sal had long since detached himself from the Espositos. No one ever called him "Espo," and that was for a good reason—but it was a reason that he was never inclined to share. He considered himself a de facto Cameron-Albanese. They were his family, and he aimed to please. He also loved to cook and never thought of losing Ressini's. In his formidable years, he had focused on earning money with Jimmy Tree so he could buy his mother out. The place was truly his, and he earned it, the hard way.

As they gathered their belongings, Agent Nicholas decided to tell them why the inquiry had ended. "They just ran the forensics on the bullet that killed Santo Tracino. It came from a Smith & Wesson, most likely the same model that was issued to the Florida Highway Patrol. They also found this type of revolver in a wooded area of the Dumont Nursing Home. One bullet was missing from the chamber … It was registered to Felix Bannos."

22

IT ALL DEPENDED ON HOW YOU
PLAYED YOUR HAND

June 15, 1984, Early Morning
IT WAS GOING TO be a hot day. Vincent arrived right before seven to set
up four lawn chairs under the only shady spot. These prime seats were
catty-cornered to the front row of folding chairs and a stone's throw to
the podium. The Tuckahoe High football field had been covered over to
provide this venue for the graduating class.

Vincent awoke as usual as the sun rose, and since it was less than a
week to the summer solstice, that meant he had already been awake since
5:15 a.m. After brewing coffee and eating a toasted corn muffin (*screw
the doctor, I like butter*), he showered and put on his best (and only) suit.
Confident he looked his best, he ventured off to secure the prime location.
The elders simply could not have the sun beating down on them for two
hours. Joe and Julia Cavazzi were now both over seventy, and he and Teresa
were also past retirement age.

Settling in, he perused the *New York Post*. He still had a couple of
hours to kill until relatives and friends of the other graduates would begin
to arrive for the ceremony. Teresa, Julia, and Joe would come right before
the start of the program, but he was the only one who could stand direct

rays of the sun for long stretches. He laughed to himself. *Why the heck are we all retiring to Florida then? It's hot there too!*

He had earned his pension from working for the town, and Joe had the good fortune of Bella's finally seeing light at the end of the tunnel and not the headlights from another train. After almost four decades of hard work, it was time. The economy had improved, and all of the small family businesses were now thriving.

The past Christmas and Easter seasons had been the best ever for Bella's. These two critical periods of time were traditionally the cornerstone for successful years. For the past twelve months, the Cavazzis had danced Irish Mike's jig. Young Christopher had calculated that Bella's would triple the amount of sales they had ever registered. Albanese's Butcher Shop and Ressini's Restaurant both experienced similar success, and the three families had been in a jovial mood all year.

Inflation's evil back had been broken by the monetary policies put in place by President Reagan. The first few years of the decade were extremely tough, just like in the seventies as interest rates rose dramatically to slow the money supply and put a strangle hold on rising prices. After topping out at 13.5 percent in 1980, inflation had begun to decline and was currently running at a 3.5 percent pace. The unemployment rate had also improved and was now below 8 percent. In response, gross domestic product rebounded heartily. After recessions in 1980 and 1982, economic growth had snapped back, and 1984 was on pace to expand an extraordinary 7 percent.

Reagonomics had four distinct parts: subdue inflation, reduce federal regulations, slow the growth of government spending, and lower income and capital gain taxes. With the economy humming along, inflation controlled, and much-needed tax relief, the small business owners exhaled for the first time in close to twenty years. Not rich by any stretch of the imagination, they now all simply slept much better at night.

With the healthier economic climate, Vince and Teresa now believed they could retire to the Sunshine State. Al and Rita were able to operate the butcher shop for the first time without her parents' financial assistance, and Anthony vowed to help out in between attending classes at Westchester Community College. Joanne was a very independent thirteen-year-old who was very busy with sports and the drama club, but she would also contribute when the time came.

"Pop, *Nonna*, we'll be okay. We saw how refreshed you looked when you came back from down there. You deserve to feel that way all the time … Besides, you know we'll visit you. Never been to Disney World, so you can take us," Anthony said this with tears in his eyes after Vince and Teresa had returned from scouting out retirement villages. They had spent nine weeks visiting with old friends in Boca Raton, Fort Lauderdale, Pompano Beach, and Jupiter before falling in love with a unit near the beach and adjacent to a golf course in Port St. Lucie. Joe and Julia also visited the location after Easter and even purchased a unit in the same complex.

It really was time. All of the younger family members had insisted they go and enjoy their golden years without social and economic drama. By being a thousand miles away, they would not be there to be guilted into work or to lend money. The younger generation would adapt without them.

To close the loop, Joe and Julia were presented an offer from Maria and Mike to buy Bella's. Still owned in the family, their retirement nest egg was monetized by the small business loan between family members. Sabina was going into in her sophomore year at Iona College, and she vowed to help. Christopher, though, would not. He was set to leave for the University of Texas after receiving a football scholarship and excelling in school. The boy had a good head on his shoulders and would take his father's advice to venture off to find himself away from his humble beginnings.

"Tuckahoe'll be here when ya get back, son, just give it a shot. If it doesn't work out, there's an apron and broom waiting for you now." Chris was excited and his family was very proud of him.

Dina and Greg Esposito were still young (*fifties is still young*) and had not even thought of retiring. Greg had kept his nose clean for five years now, but he still barely found time to go home as most of his hours were spent at Ressini's. Salvatore spent many hours there now too, but Vincent could see that the young man was not very close with his father. To no surprise to anyone, Robby and Johnny had not returned. Both had taken root thousands of miles across the country in Chicago and San Francisco.

A few hours later, the graduates tossed their mortar boards in the air, took a slew of family pictures, and said good-bye to teachers and friends. Then, Ressini's was closed to the general public, so the close-knit group could celebrate the momentous event as one. In total, nineteen relatives and friends were there for the occasion.

Ten in attendance for the luncheon were from the Albanese clan. Besides the immediate family, Rita's sister, Ann Marie, and her husband, Richard, had flown up from Houston. Vincent's sister, Amelia, had also made the trip from Brockton to congratulate her nephew. She still looked wonderful. At sixty, she showed no signs of slowing down and was taking the death of her husband of twenty-three years surprisingly well. Sadly missing was Al's mother, Isabella who had died the year earlier. Vince and Amelia's sister, Sophia, had also recently passed.

Poppa Vince was extremely proud of his big boy and the way he was turning his young life around. Anthony's friends now called him Big Tony, and he embraced the nickname. Always a "pretty boy," the kid constantly combed his hair and dressed to impress. But the self-anointed ladies' man was very self-conscious. While you would never think he was a troubled young man as you watched a smiling Anthony eviscerate a cut of beef, Poppa Vince knew the real story. Vince's grandson would constantly cry to him that he was embarrassed. Anthony hated being poor and while it appeared his skin was thick and he could take the verbal abuse and whispers from around town, he really could not. He would break down to his grandparents that many in the neighborhood laughed at his modest living conditions and that his parents were overweight. Vincent consoled his grandson as best he could. The pain grew more pronounced after his father was diagnosed with cancer of the parotid gland. This form of cancer was very rare and Alfonse had ignored the symptoms for far too long. In the summer of 1982, Tony remembered hugging his dad before he left to go to the hospital.

"It's nothing, son. I'll be home in a few days. Gotta get a darn growth removed."

A week and a half later, Alfonse came home with gauze wrapped around his head and half of his jawbone removed. Tony was in shock. While his father had been overweight, he was still a good-looking man. After the radiation and chemotherapy treatments, Alfonse became very self-conscious of his appearance. He lost his hair and was fitted for a toupee. His disfigurement was very noticeable. Customers to the butcher shop (mostly kids who had accompanied their parents) would snicker, treating him like a circus attraction, as a young Tony viewed these events from the back of the shop.

"Poppy, these kids make me so damn mad. How dare they disrespect dad. Do they have any idea what he's gone through?"

Anthony's rage continued to build at the same time he went through a growth spurt, and unfortunately, there were instances where he would blow his top. Many of those times when the rage was released occurred on the football field, but there had also been occasions when he would run into some of those kids whom he had recognized. Al and Rita were called to the local police station on more than a few occasions to come pick their son up. Thankfully, many law enforcement professionals and the chief of police were longtime friends.

After a long talk before school had ended, Poppa Vince told his grandson that he was a man now and should be proud of how he lived his life. While Anthony was strong and tough enough to shove a rich punk's silver spoon anywhere he chose, a real man commanded respect only after he had earned it. Anthony vowed to his beloved grandfather that he would command respect wherever he went.

January 1, 1988

As had been his ritual since graduating high school, Anthony always came down to Port St. Lucie to visit his grandparents immediately after Christmas. His grandfather knew that the week prior to the holidays was hectic and profitable at the butcher shop while the time immediately after was traditionally tranquil.

They loved this time. *Nonna* Teresa would venture to the Publix super market and stock up the refrigerator for her grandson. Anthony may have not been able to cuddle on their laps anymore (even though he still tried), but he was always excited to see them. *And that is what matters the most to two almost-seventy-year-olds.* He would drive them to visit faraway friends, move furniture, and help with small repairs that they had not gotten around to. Then, they would take a day and drive the two hours to Disney World. This would be repeated again in March, but at that time Anthony would visit with Salvatore, and they would spend time at the Mets new spring training facility rather than go to see Mickey Mouse.

Vince and Teresa had been looking forward to this visit even more than in the past. Both of their hearts were heavy after Joe Cavazzi had passed away in May, and Julia was now living in a convalescent home. Poor Joe had a stroke and died shortly after. Julia had broken her hip in December, and her prognosis was not good.

Their grandson was the window into Tuckahoe for the first half of the year. Then Joanne would switch places and visit a few times in the summer and fall. Sabina Cameron also came often as she had tended to her grandparents' needs. She had even pleaded with Julia to come back to New York after Joe died, so she could take better care of her. *That girl was a saint.*

As was the norm for New Year's Day, grandfather and grandson would park themselves on the couch for twelve hours watching football while *Nonna* Teresa cooked a pot of sauce filled with meatballs and sausage. For most of games, they had general interest, and Vince knew Anthony always had action on some team. One game today, though, meant more than the others, as the University of Texas Longhorns were set to kick off to the University of Southern California Trojans.

Currently pictured on the new twenty-seven-inch color TV screen, which Anthony had given to his grandparents for Christmas, was number ten, running in place and getting ready to sprint down the field for the opening kickoff.

Anthony was standing in front of the screen and taking a bite out of a sausage wedge. "Wow, great picture, so clear. Look, Cee's still playing special teams, even though he's captain of the defense. Friggin' guy just loves to hit people."

"I saw his game against Oklahoma the day after Thanksgiving. He clocked a guy. Nice of him to pick the kids' helmet up and hand it to him," Pops laughed. He tried to catch as many games as possible, and he always was a fan of hard-nosed defensive play.

Chris had not played much during his first two years, but toward the latter part of his sophomore season he got his chance. Since then, he had started in twenty-six straight games, and his teammates voted him to be one of their leaders.

"Hit him, Cee! Get that mother!" His buddy jumped off his seat and yelled at the TV as Cameron recorded the first tackle of the game. First and ten, USC from their own nineteen-yard line.

"Has Christopher decided what he's going to do after graduation? He's got a good head on his shoulders, that boy." Vince said this in a proud and complimentary way.

"He still doesn't have a clue. Guy aces all his friggin' classes but can't see himself wearing a tie and sitting in some cubicle. He'll figure it out. Gonna see him after I leave here, driving to Texas for a few days."

"What about the store? How long you taking this vacation of yours?"

"That's one of the things I needed to talk with you about Pops." Vincent actually liked the shortening of his name. *Poppa Vince is now Pops, whatever.*

"No one has told me anything yet. What's going on Anthony?"

"Well, it's all good actually ... All good ... Mom and dad are closing the store." Anthony began to cry, then composed himself and continued. "Some developer offered to buy the plot of land the store sat on, offered a friggin' half-million dollars."

Vincent whistled, "Tuckahoe real estate's getting expensive." He remembered Rocco, Al's father, telling him he had purchased the entire property in the forties for $6,000.

"Yeah, that's what I thought, too. A lot of retirement cash!" Anthony chuckled. "So Dad starts stuttering and Mom's all kinds of nervous. They're walking in circles, bumping into each other, mumbling. Jo and I just sat on the couch laughing, watching them trip over each other."

"Teresa, do you hear this? Hehe, Rita and Alfonse are rich." His wife walked over and received a quick summary from her husband.

"Oh my, Anthony, that is exciting." Teresa sat next to her grandson and patted his knee. "Are they going to retire or continue working?"

Anthony squeezed his *nonna*'s hand softly. "It's all too soon to tell, but dad said he could easily get a job as a butcher at Stop & Shop. Heck, that union got benefits and health care. He'd be set and mom's happy with her job at the bank."

"The mortgage is paid, too. I guess they can finally breathe a little. Good for them." When Vince and Teresa had moved to Florida, they sold the house to Rita and Al for a nominal amount. When he had purchased it in 1949, it cost all of $18,000, a huge sum back then.

The early afternoon continued. Texas and USC were locked in a tight game, and Chris had performed well: six tackles and two tipped passes from his strong safety position.

"So how much did you bet on, Christopher?" Vincent inquired to his grandson.

"He called me last night. Said they were real confident and no way USC should be four point favorites. They came up with a scheme to shutdown that back Len White."

"So?"

"So, I bet them heavy. Friggin' guy wins, and this little vacation is free, Pops." Anthony hugged him.

"And how's Salvatore doing?"

"He's all good. Working his ass off. Daunting task to own a restaurant at twenty-one. Know what I mean."

"That boy's had a lot thrown at him over the past few years. You keep a close eye on him." Vince felt as much love for the Esposito and Cameron kids as he did his own.

"No doubt, no doubt. Pops, we all look out for each other. Don't worry about us. Sal and I are even thinking of going into business together," Anthony confidently stated.

The Esposito family had been in disarray since Greg's death. When Dina packed up and moved away, Salvatore truly had to become a man overnight. He simply did not want to lose Ressini's and had worked his butt off to make it his.

"Holy crap! You see that hit, Pops. Cee lit his ass up!" Anthony clapped his hands rapidly.

"He fumbled too … Texas has the ball." Vince pointed at the screen with a big grin on his face. Chris had upended Len White inside the five-yard line. The Longhorns recovered and looked like they were going to preserve a five-point lead and win the Cotton Bowl.

Vince watched Christopher jumping up and down in excitement. It really was amazing that he, Salvatore, and Anthony always picked each other or others around them up. It truly was a special friendship between the boys, and he hoped they would continue to stay as close. There was a lot that happened as people matured from teen to early adulthood and then again after they married and had children. He thought back to his youth (or lack thereof) and wished he could have lived it different.

Instead of watching his buddy make a game-saving tackle, he watched them die. Talking through a friend's emotional distress after his father had a heart attack was replaced by applying pressure to a comrade's leg after being hit with shrapnel. Consoling a guy after he recently had his heart broken by a girlfriend was no contest to watching your entire family burn to death.

But you just cannot change the past. If he could, Vincent would have buried his father after a happy, healthy life, one in which he had prospered financially and witnessed his children, grandchildren, and even great-grandchildren grow up to make him proud. All in all, he had seen the worst and lived through it. Sitting now with his grandson, sipping a beer, and watching a football game, he thought that life really had not been that bad. As a longtime poker player, he knew you simply had to play the cards dealt to you, no matter how crappy they were. Even a busted flush draw could beat three of a kind. It all depended on how you played your hand.

23

DECADE AND A HALF

August 18, 1998

NEVER BEFORE HAD JIMMY Tracino been relieved so many people were now talking politics. The murder of his father had been front page and the lead news story in the tri-state area for the past three days, but it was finally usurped from the news cycle. Last night, President Clinton gave a nationally televised statement where he admitted to a relationship with a former White House intern, Monica Lewinsky. Now with calls for impeachment, the news outlets were having a field day and devoting all resources to the scandal.

Jimmy never followed the "Slick Willie" saga, but his girlfriend had been chirping about it, and it finally came to a head. What now felt like ages ago, Ms. Lewinsky's lawyers announced in late July that a transactional immunity deal had been reached. She admitted to having a sexual relationship with the president. This snowballed to President Clinton addressing the matter in front of the country.

With the television newscast on mute all day, Jimmy had been on the phone and meeting with associates from his living room. His father would be buried in a few days, but first, the medical examiner was running tests to determine the cause of death.

"Damien, he was fucking murdered and the ME still needs time to examine ... Bullshit ... I need to know who'd contract out an unsanctioned hit!" Damien Morris returned from his hideout and had been spending most of the time with his longtime friend.

"I got a feelin' it may have been related to his ratcheting up of squeezing people for money. I'm hearing the Colombos are not happy with their turf getting pinched," Damien stated somberly.

"Screw those guys. My pop has, Jesus Christ, my pop had more clout than that scum bag, Carmine Rezzo." Rezzo was a lower-level made member from Queens who had been making overtures to many of Tentacles' minions who had been outwardly voicing displeasure of having to kick up extra cash to support his medical and nursing home bills.

"Tony Bartucci's the key here. Word is that Rezzo had this whore give him lap dances all night, no charge … Then they sat down after he blew his load and asked him to jump ship. Said his split would be a heck of a lot better, and besides Santo's old and was gonna croak any day now. Wise-ass mother fucker!" Damien relayed information he had just received from Bartucci and were corroborated by other sources.

"Bart's a stand-up guy. It may be my mood that I'm going off half-cocked, but I don't give a fuck. You get your ass to Queens and put a bullet in Rezzo's head. I want this done and done fast. I need to send a message. I'll get this sanctioned after the fact. Junior already verbally told me that he would back it."

A Few Days Earlier

AFTER BEING PICKED UP by the FBI, Damien Morris had readily agreed to turn informant. Quickly taken to the Albany field office, Morris cried for the better part of the evening before finally getting himself composed. Agent Tejata and her associates could not believe that the killer had broken so easily. The other agents teased that Dominique's nickname was now "Music," as she had obviously been the one to sooth this savage beast. They watched him blubber for hours and could not imagine this tough guy was the ruthless killer his infamous dossier had made him out to be.

"Okay, Damien, this is how it's going to work. You'll wear a wire for the next few days. We need you to find out what actually happened here. Get evidence; we need to get to Jimmy Tree." Agent Tejata and two of her male associates presented him with his slim options.

"What's going to happen to me?" Morris was sitting somberly with the palms of both of his hands flat on the rectangular table. He was also nodding his head up and down ever so slowly and squeezing his eyes shut on numerous instances.

"Well, after you get us this information, and assuming you cooperate further—no bullshit—we want everything. Then you will go into witness protection." Agent Tejata said this to him as he looked across the table and into her eyes. Obviously his heart was broken, but she was now long past playing the part of Elaudys Reyes.

"Elaudys, baby, I'll cooperate. I have one thing to ask, though. Then I'll give you everything I got." Morris raised his hands and slowly reached across the table to touch her.

"My name is not Elaudys. I am a special agent, Mr. Morris. What is your request?" Dominique expressionlessly removed his hand from on top of hers.

After a long pause, Damien spoke with confidence. "I would like to know if I can have the contents of my safe deposit box. Then, fuck it … I'll rat on all of them."

"We'll see what we can do." Agent Tejata glanced at her male counterparts' bookending her then responded to his offer. "That should not be a problem."

Damien was whisked down to the New York City area, and he quickly took to the streets to find out who killed his capo and put his life in a death spiral. First, he went to Sal and Tony and met up with them for dinner at Ressini's. His fellow big men were visibly distraught over the loss of one of their mentors, and they vowed to help. Early the next morning, Tony called Damien with an interesting story.

"Dame' … did I wake you? Thought that honey of yours would be answering. … Know the roosters aren't even up yet, but this guy just left the club, played all friggin' night. Drinking a lot and what not, so I had to keep a close eye on him. Anyway, he's a buddy of Bart, and he's shooting his mouth off that Jimmy Tree's dad deserved it. Said Bart knew the guy that probably pulled the trigger."

"Thanks, Tee … Hey, you coming to Jimmy's later? He'd like to see you and Sal."

"We should be there. Sal's also sending over a platter of food for the family."

Damien also met with three others that day. After Tony's call, he chased down a slippery dude named Jose. Jose was Puerto Rican and ran a drug ring for Horace "Smiles" Johnson. Smiles got his nickname because he was all business, and Damien could never recall seeing him unveil his pearly whites. Jose was startled when Damien knocked on his door, but when he realized he was only after information, he loosened up. Jose was valuable because he always had his ear to the ground.

"Who dat? No one knocks up here. You gotta call first!" Jose yelled from behind his triple-bolted steel-enforced front door to his fifth-floor walk-up in Co-op City.

"Calm down, Jose. It's Damien. Let me in. If I was gonna whack you, I'd do it on the street."

"What you want, big man? We have no beef, know what I mean?" He was wearing an oversized pair of jeans shorts and a white wifebeater T-shirt on his skinny frame as he smoked a cigarette nervously.

"Lighten up. Settle a bit. Look, I just want to get assurance that Horace didn't hit Santo. Honestly, I don't figure he did. Just need to know where I gotta sniff. Enlighten me."

"No worries here, muscles. Horace be all business, but he's not crazy. Last thing he'd want is Jimmy Tree, or you to be putting him on a shit list. He likes money, not pushing up daises. Only one I heard that had a beef was across the Whitestone. Those guinea Queens boys are mad shit 'bout the Benjamins."

Informant Damien Morris came back to the unmarked sedan and sat in the backseat in between two agents who stood half his size. They were not intimidated by him, though. In fact, it was the exact opposite.

"Everything's pointing to Queens, and Rezzo's crew. Could all be supposition, because when the young guys hear something, they just make shit up. They only listen to half a story anyway, you follow?" Damien had lived and breathed the code of the streets his whole life. One thing he was certain about: for every grain of truth, there were a hundred lies. With that said, you still had to verify that the one grain was valid.

"Mr. Morris, we just received confirmation that Remo DeCarlo is at his pizzeria in Queens." The agent to his right looked at him sternly.

"Good, let's head there next." DeCarlo ran with the Colombos. He was a made member and had been a friend of Santo's for thirty years. Damien knew DeCarlo would say it straight and know if he would need to put a bullet in Rezzo's head.

The sedan crossed the Whitestone Bridge and doubled back below the span before parking on the corner of Eleventh Avenue and 152nd Street, next to PS 193. Damien walked a block east and nonchalantly entered Villagio's and ordered a slice.

"Where's Remo at?" he asked the young *guido* manning the counter. The reply was a nod to the back behind the brick oven. Without an invitation, Damien walked past the sweltering oven. He was not hungry anyway.

"Knock, knock. What's going on Remo?" Damien extended his hand and embraced the old-time Mafioso, who was sitting in a small, air-conditioned room. The *Daily News* was opened to an article about the murder. A picture of Santo Tracino with his arm around Carlos Gambino at Sandy Beach from circa 1976 was visible.

"Set a bit, sit down. How's young Jimmy holding up? So sorry for the loss. I liked Santo. Funny guy and a good earner." DeCarlo made the comment in his raspy gravely voice. His ever-present cigar was stuck between his fingers.

"He's pretty broken up. His dad meant the world to him. They've had to sedate his mother. She may not even last much longer ... Real sad." Damien relayed the somber news.

Remo got right to the point. "I know why you're here. All I can say is that there were some people who had been upset with Santo reaching deeper into their pockets. Can't get blood from a stone and all. Same old bullshit, but I hear where they're coming from. Santo always wanted more and more, even if his wife was sick or not. Most saw it as all nonsense and felt he was never gonna pay off those nurses anyway."

"Jim's pissed, all I'm saying. Think Rezzo's feeling his oats, making a move?"

"That's above my pay grade. I am an old man trying to survive now. From my years of experience, though ... " DeCarlo puffed his cigar and gave him a wry smile.

Damien left the pizzeria and walked south for three blocks. His ride pulled up and he quickly hopped in. He had connected more dots, and it was looking more likely that Carmine Rezzo was the motivating factor to the killing.

From there, Damien's personal federal driver took him back to Westchester, over the Whitestone Bridge and to Mount Vernon. This time he really was hungry. He was let out on Macquesten Parkway and walked the short way. He inhaled an entire small thin-crust pie at Johnny's Pizzeria. *Probably the last time I'll eat pizza this good for a long time.* At 6:00 p.m. he headed south for a few blocks on Fifth Avenue. Then he walked into Rose's Rendezvous. The strip club was sparsely filled with happy-hour regulars who sampled the mozzarella sticks and chicken fingers just as much as they partook in the merchandise dancing on stage and walking around seductively for private lap dances.

He walked toward the back and sat in an empty chair around a small oval table. All that could be seen on the other chair were two white hands vigorously caressing a perfect brown ass covered only with a red G-String. The woman was bent over and rubbed her breasts in front of the patron's nose. The song ended, and the young lady kissed her customer on the cheek. He slid a twenty-dollar bill into her garter.

She turned to face Damien. "You want some company, sweetie?"

"Na, I need to speak with your boyfriend. You are sweet as candy, though ... My, my, mmmm!" *Hope the place I get relocated to has a good selection of brown ass—better not be fuckin' Iowa.* Damien stopped smiling and turned his gaze to Joe Bartucci.

"What's up, Damien. What you doing here?" Bart meekly said as he readjusted his pants and buttoned his shirt.

"Like clockwork. If I wanted to kill you, I'd have an easy time finding your ass." Damien gave him an icy glare.

"Wuh ... Wuh ... Why you say that, buddy?" Bartucci fixed his disheveled hair and took a healthy gulp of his Budweiser longneck.

"What the fuck's going on with you, Bart? ... Word is you're jumping ship and being wooed by another team ... Tell it to me straight ... Santo ain't here no more."

Bartucci blew his breath out forcefully. He had known Damien for ten years, and their relationship had always been very professional. "Look, yeah, you could say that ... And fuck yeah, it was real enticing ... Santo's been jacking me since his old lady got sick. Not my problem, man ... I gotta eat too. Now it's hand over three grand a month. Last month it was twenty-five hundred. Damn, not made of money ... I don't crap hundred-dollar bills, Yo'."

"Been tough on all of us, but remember, Santo ran the show. You'd have absolute dick if he didn't sanction your biz."

"Whatever, man ... All a mute point now anyway ... But yeah, so Rezzo likes the way I operate ... came at me hard ... I hadn't given him my answer yet, but I know the way I'm leaning ... Sorry man, business is business."

"Jimmy's real pissed, all I'm saying. Watch yourself. Keep your head out of tits and keep it up. You may want to even watch that back of yours." Damien stood up and walked directly out of the establishment and into the early evening sunlight.

With these pieces to the puzzle coming together, Damien accompanied the agents to the New York City field office. He was then fitted with a wire and transmitter. From there, he was dropped off at his apartment. Fifteen minutes later, he left to pay his respects to the Tracino family.

August 21, Before Dawn

YESTERDAY HAD BEEN VERY somber and mourning was reserved for immediate family. Only Dominic Tracino and his wife and kids attended the funeral alongside Jimmy and his girlfriend, Laura. Their mother could not attend, she was far too fragile, and the summer heat made the decision final. After the ceremony at Cedar Grove Cemetery in Queens, the family remained sequestered in Jimmy's home. Without saying or doing much for the remainder of the day, Jimmy fell asleep on the couch in his den before dusk. Laura woke him to come up to bed at a little after two.

Two rings of the bell were followed by a gaggle of knocks on the front door. Jimmy popped his eyes open. He had seen this movie play out before. First as a child as his father was taken away (*it was always very early in the morning*) and then when he first got pinched, they busted him this way too. He had always emulated the old man, and had no regrets about it. Heck, his brother was fifty pounds overweight with a wife who was probably more than that. They never vacationed, they drove a used car, and he shopped at Walmart. Jimmy may have had to hustle, but he was a hell of a good earner and lived a life others only dreamed of.

As he slowly put on his shorts, he tried to calm down his girlfriend, a former stripper he might add. She had never lived through this before and began crying uncontrollably. *Friggin' Midwest girls. What'd she think I made my money from?*

"All right, I'm coming, I'm coming," Jimmy yelled down the stairs as he turned the hall lights on. He opened the front door. "What's up, scumbags!" Six FBI agents were waiting to take him away.

Later that morning, his cocky facade faded as special agents filled him in on current events. After hearing the recording of his voice order the execution of Carmine Rezzo and then being privy to the government proudly unveiling their star witness, he turned on a dime and was ready to deal. As with Damien Morris, James Tracino was now more than happy to speak about his dealings with the underworld and to detail names, places, dates and offenses committed over the past decade and a half.

Jackpot! Dawn Nicholas believed she may have earned a promotion.

November 13, 1998

IN A SERIES OF simultaneous, early morning raids spanning the entire tri-state area, seventy-seven alleged members and associates of four organized crime families were arrested. The charges included murder, extortion, loan-sharking, prostitution, and illegal drug distribution. In bail hearings, defendants included the young and the old. Some were obese; others frail, disheveled, fully coiffed, or balding. They stood expressionless in their pajamas or sweatpants or wore impeccably tailor-fitted suits. These indictments stemmed from a two-and-a-half-year investigation dubbed Operation Primate.

The six New Jersey residents included alleged members and associates of the Genovese organized crime family. They were charged with racketeering and related offenses. The twenty-one-count indictment filed in Newark federal court charged Richard DeGiorgio, a soldier in the Genovese organized crime family of La Cosa Nostra, and three of his associates—Aldo Rizzo, the former treasurer of the International Longshoremen's Association (ILA) Local 2248, Peter Nurzio, the former vice president of ILA Local 1994, and Richard LaFrance, the current vice president of ILA Local 4567—with racketeering conspiracy. These acts included predicate acts of conspiracy to extort ILA members on the New Jersey piers, bookmaking, and extortion collection of credit and illegal gambling. Nurzio and Rizzo were also charged with racketeering conspiracy involving the collection of unlawful debt.

The twenty-six-count indictment filed at the Stamford federal court charged twelve Gambino members and associates with crimes, including racketeering, weapons possession, tax evasion, bribery, murder, money laundering, and conspiracy. Rocco Vallone, the nephew of an alleged mob boss, had been charged with laundering money out of a string of pasta stores. Donato Vallone and Stephano Pagnotta were indicted for their alleged role in the panel that ran the organization from their homes in Connecticut.

A twenty-nine-count indictment that was unsealed at the Brooklyn federal court charged sixteen Lucchese members with murder, illegal drug distribution, extortion, and money laundering. John Cetto was formerly charged with the murder of John Gleason, who had been the owner of a sports club in Merrick. It was alleged that Cetto was dating the wife of the owner's partner and mistakenly murdered the wrong man in a failed attempt to cash in on a life insurance claim.

The eighty-one-count indictment filed at the White Plains federal court charged thirty-two members of the Gambino family with racketeering, illegal drug distribution, tax evasion, bribery, murder, money laundering, and conspiracy. Of those indicted were the current executive secretary treasurer of the Westchester Council of Carpenters (WCC), Kenneth Collins, and four of his associates—Victor Luongo, the former WCC vice president; Christopher Craft, the former WCC executive vice president; Gregory Williams, the former WCC comptroller; and Brian Graham, the current executive vice president of the WCC).

At the Manhattan federal court, the nineteen-count indictment alleged that eleven members of the DeCavalcante crime family committed bribery, prostitution, money laundering, murder, and tax evasion from a host of strip clubs and small businesses. Of those arrested were Joseph Maggia, who was charged with running a vast prostitution and illegal-drug operation out of a strip club in Lower Manhattan. Eighty-one-year-old Vito "Ocean" Panducci, who prosecutors say was a longtime boss in the DeCavalcante crime family, was arrested and charged with extorting protection payments from restaurant owners throughout the five boroughs.

In addition to the wide-sweeping arrests, the federal government announced that they had in custody high-level associates of the Gambino crime family. These made members had agreed to assist in the case against organized crime.

US Attorney General Janet Reno stated, "We have charged mob associates and mob bosses alike, including street bosses, acting bosses, and *consiglieri* of the most ruthless crime families ... Despite the high body count, none of the names were well known. I would like to commend all those agents and agencies involved for putting a major dent into the infrastructure of the most ruthless crime organizations in the country."

24

TOP OF THE BOX

February 10, 1999

SAL SEALED THE PERFORATED edges of two large aluminum trays. One was filled with freshly made veal cutlet parmesan; the other with sausage and peppers. He carried the tins out to his new Tahoe and handed them both to Chris who had been waiting outside the restaurant. Chris placed the hot items on the floor below on the passenger side of the vehicle as Sal scooted back to lock the back door. It was nine in the morning, and the wind was whipping fiercely along the adjacent train tracks. Grey-black clouds hovered low in the morning sky. It was a fittingly cold and uninviting day.

They drove out of the parking lot of Ressini's. A sign on the front door noted that they would be closed until Tuesday—Death In The Family. As they made the short drive to the Albanese house, Chris was somberly reading the *Reporter Dispatch*. Both men were dressed in black suits, but they did not have ties on, and the top buttons of their white shirts were unfastened. Two cashmere overcoats lay neatly across the backseat.

Rather than attempt to find a spot on the narrow one-way street, Sal made the left turn into the parking lot of the Church of the Assumption. He and Chris quietly made their way the short distance to 1 Circle Road. This was the home Tony had lived in all of his young life. His mother was also raised here, and even after she had married, they continued to live here. The home had been purchased by his grandparents in 1949.

While his grandmother, *Nonna* Teresa, had taken her last breath in a condominium in Port St. Lucie, Tony's grandfather had taken his last breath of life here.

Vincent Antonio Scala (1918–1999)

Vincent, 81, a lifelong resident of Tuckahoe passed away at home on Tuesday, February 9, 1999, with his family by his side.

Vincent was born in Tuckahoe, NY, to Pasquale and Julianna Scala. He attended the Tuckahoe schools. He served his country as a United States Marine from 1935 to 1944.

After returning from the war, Vincent spent most of adult life working for the Tuckahoe Department of Sanitation. He was an active member of the Republican Party, the Eastchester Italian American Club, and the Veterans of Foreign Wars Post 2285. He also coached football for the Eastchester Blue Devils from 1971 to 1980.

He was predeceased by his wife, Teresa Carpinello Scala, in 1995. He is survived by his two daughters, Rita and Anne Marie. "Pops" is also survived by three grandchildren—Anthony, Joanne, and Hailey—and two great-grandchildren—Anthony Jr. and Amanda Rose. Vincent was a devoted family man and a loving uncle to many and a friend to all.

Visitation will be Wednesday and Thursday, February 10–11, 1–3 p.m. and 7–9 p.m. at Westchester Funeral Home in Eastchester. The funeral mass will be at 10 a.m. on Friday, February 12, at the Church of the Assumption in Tuckahoe. Burial will follow at the Gates of Heaven Cemetery in Hawthorne.

Sal and Chris entered without knocking. The house was filled with grown-ups and children mulling around, preparing for the grueling and what was set to be a heart-wrenching three days. They set the food on the dining room table, next to a mound of other trays, gift baskets, fresh bread and cold-cut platters that had also been delivered by well-wishers. As was the norm, the small community had opened its heart to one of their original families and would definitely be there for the mourners in this time of need.

When they walked through the arched entry separating the dining room from the living room, Tony got up off the couch and reached over to embrace his two blood brothers.

"Gonna be a tough one; loved that guy," Sal said as Tony buried his head into his chest. He had stopped crying a bit, but once he saw his friends, he started up again.

"That man was so strong, in so many ways. His legacy will be felt for a long time." Chris grabbed the back of Tony's head and looked into his eyes. Both men were crying.

They sat together around the coffee table. Victoria and Joanne wore black dresses. Black shawls covered their shoulders. Both had tissues clutched in their fists. Tony sat between his wife and sister on the couch. Chris and Sal were next to each other on the loveseat. Not much was said. For the next fifteen minutes, they read the obituary and perused the pile of family photos strewn out on the coffee table.

"I want to make a few collages to place around the funeral home. There are great pictures of Pops and *Nonna* Teresa from back in the day," Tony somberly mentioned.

"Yeah, Angie and Megyn are at CVS now. I'll call them to pick up some poster board and glue." Chris stood up and left the room to make the call on his cell phone.

Sabina entered and took the seat Chris had relinquished. She exhaled and looked at Tony and then at Joanne. "Jo, should we start this? Poppy wanted Anthony to receive his present before the wake."

Tony looked at his sister and Sabina inquisitively. "What present?"

"You guys only thought Poppy liked to spend time with you three lugs. He and *Nonna* Teresa did a lot of things with us too. Sabina and I spent good quality time with them both in Florida. Then when he came back up after *Nonna* died, he relied on us to take him places and to do his daily routine." Joanne's eyes were red and swollen, but she was determined to make it through this request from her grandfather.

"He knew he had stomach cancer as far back as the summer of ninety-seven but implored Jo and me to not tell anyone. We took him to the doctor and the hospital for chemo. He fought like you would have expected. Guy was so darn tough." Sabina saw her brother standing behind her. He put his hand on her shoulders and massaged them.

"Poppy had his ending all planned out. He even wrote his own obituary," Joanne laughed sharply and then sobbed some more, raising the tissue to her eyes.

"Just like the old man, he was a planner, down to the last T to be crossed and I dotted," Tony said this with admiration.

"Right after the summer, he knew he would not last much longer. That's when he decided it was the right time to tell the family. Doctors were in disbelief. They had only given him less than a year to live when he was diagnosed." Joanne's eyes now began to tear. Tony put his arm around her.

Joanne looked directly at her big brother and squeezed his hands. "Well, anyway. Poppy put together a special chest for you. In it are items from his life, a life you and I never knew much about. He said he kept much of his early life private. He and *Nonna* Teresa talked about those times endlessly, and that was one of their special lovebird secrets."

"Pops and *Nonna* were quite the couple. That's where mom and dad get it, I guess." Tony thought back about how even as senior citizens, his grandparents would hold hands, go for walks, and lick from the same ice-cream cone. "Her death hit him hard!"

Life had been going along wonderfully in the Florida sun. For nine years Vincent and Teresa lived a carefree existence. Friends and family came to visit. They had ample time to share the tail end of their golden years together, and they never looked back. It was all very good. Then, in the fall on 1994, Teresa's hands began to shake, and she could not explain why. Her memory also became sketchy. After a battery of tests, her doctors determined that she had had a series of mini-strokes that had gone undetected, and she was soon diagnosed with vascular dementia.

The next few months became very trying on Vincent as the condition progressed. Teresa would wander around the complex at all hours, and she became extremely depressed. The woman he had adored since the moment he saw her had begun to deteriorate before his eyes. Vincent nursed her as much as he could, never agreeing to move her to an assisted living facility. Rita, Joanne, and Sabina spent many weeks rotating to help out, but in the end they had their lives in New York. Vincent devoted his days to caring for his beloved. His Teresa Lucia died by his side as he lay there with her in the early morning of May 25, 1995.

Joanne held out her hand and guided her brother down the hallway to the bedroom where their grandfather had slept. The bedrooms in the tiny colonial were all about the same size. Rita and Al never even thought of changing the living conditions even after her parents moved away. Tony and Joanne shared the third bedroom until he turned thirteen. Then, a section of the basement was converted into his abode.

The entire contingent of young adults followed Joanne and Tony to their beloved Pops' room. Once inside, Joanne dragged out a sturdy wooden chest from the closet. She handed her brother a key. Sabina and Joanne left the room, while Tony, Sal, and Chris stayed behind to open its priceless contents.

"Some cool things in here, hey guys?" Tony said after he opened it. Resting on top was Gunnery Sergeant Scala's dress-blue Marine uniform. Tony stood up and placed the jacket in front of him as he looked in the mirror. The guesstimate was that Pops had looked mighty sharp back in the day.

"Even you would be able to get a date if you showed up adorned in that impeccable uniform," Sal half-teased Tony.

Chris admired an eight-and-a-half-by-eleven-inch photo that he had plucked out. "Look at this picture of him and *Nonna* Teresa. He's wearing his dress blues, and she had on a uniform too. The writing on the back says it was their wedding day."

Sal reached in with both hands and lifted out a one-by-two-foot thin leather case. He placed it on the carpet and snapped open the latches. He whistled impressively. "Hehe, guy was a friggin' war hero, Tony. Look at all of these medals and ribbons. He ever mention this to you?"

Tony sat down in stunned surprise. He lifted a few and examined them in his hand. "No, ah no, actually." He was slightly embarrassed. "Well, I knew he served in World War II, but he never said he did much, only that he and *Nonna* Teresa helped with the war effort. Look, this here is a certificate saying *Nonna* Teresa was a WAAC. Wow, served in Guadalcanal. She never said anything about that."

"Look at all these. Silver Star, three campaign ribbons—Guadalcanal, Tarawa, and Saipan," Chris added.

Tony opened a small case. Inside was a gold star pendant. On the top was the American Bald Eagle with Valor imprinted below. A blue ribbon with white embroidered stars completed the impressive ornament. "The medal of friggin' honor!"

In 1861, Iowa Senator James Grimes introduced a bill designed to "promote the efficiency of the Navy" by authorizing two hundred medals be produced "which shall be bestowed upon such petty officers, seamen, landsmen, and marines as shall distinguish themselves by their gallantry in action and other seamanlike qualities during the Civil War." President Lincoln signed the bill and the (Navy) Medal of Honor was born.

The selected Medal of Honor design consisted of an inverted, five-pointed star. On each of the five points was a cluster of laurel leaves to represent victory, mixed with a cluster of oak to represent strength.

Surrounding the encircled insignia were thirty-four stars, equal to the number on the US flag at the time.

"Guys, I have to confess, he did mention it to me. After I won my Silver Star in Iraq, he opened up about the war and some of his accomplishments. He only said that he won the Silver Star too. He failed to mention that he was also decorated with the highest honor." Chris wiped a tear from his eye. "Sorry, guys, he swore me to secrecy."

"Just like Pops, to downplay things, all he cared about was the family and keeping us safe and secure. This tells a lot about the man." Tony could barely get the words out as he broke down again. This was all too much to absorb.

Chris reached into the chest and pulled out three old cigar boxes. They had all been taped shut, but instead of cracked yellowed tape, as you would expect, one was sealed with the new smoother style. "Open this; it looks interesting." He handed the box to Tony.

Tony scraped off the tape. Inside was a two inch thick bundle of envelopes held together neatly by rubber bands. "Look, there's a bunch addressed from my great-grandmother and my grandmother. These must have been from when he was in the service. I gotta take my time to read these. They look so friggin' interesting."

"Look, this one's definitely not from the forties. This envelope was just put in. It was placed in the top of the box. Say's 'Anthony, please read this!'" Chris handed it him.

Anthony:

If you're reading this, then you must be preparing to celebrate my life. Stop crying, for I am with my God in Heaven and side-by-side the woman I love. I know that my parents have also greeted me into the Kingdom. Bless me, and I will watch over you and Joanne as well as our entire family.

I lived a long and fulfilling life, and for that I am grateful. After my father and other family members were murdered, I devoted every day to rebuilding the Scalamarri legacy. By all accounts, we are strong again and will survive.

I kept my war years a secret from you because it was a very painful time in my life. I did not want to be unnecessarily glorified while my buddies had not made it back. I continued to have nightmares until the end; the horrors of the Pacific should never be underestimated. I am proud of defending my wonderful country and killing Japs. We are all better for beating back that evil. I also slept better knowing I beat Lansky and Luciano to the punch and rid the world of that nasty bug. To hell with him!

Anthony, I also have no regrets for what I did to protect you. I have to let you know that I was the one who put the bullet in Tentacles' head. I would do it again if I had the chance. I know he would have been a major obstacle in your quest to exit that horrid life. What may also shock you is that I was behind the demise of Felix as well. He came into the restaurant that night and was going to cause you harm. Luckily I was bartending. I poisoned his drink to make it seem like he was drunk. It worked even better than I ever imagined.

I have always watched over you. Now it is your turn to be the head of the family. Be a good strong person. End the nonsense and make me proud.

Your loving Grandfather.

On that fateful night, Vincent had volunteered to bartend for the charity event Sabina was hosting at Ressini's. There were three other bartenders working in the main room, and Vince was tasked to hold down the quiet lounge area.

He frustratingly watched as Damien Morris met with associates to go over his business. Then Vincent's internal alarm went off when he saw Felix Bannos barrel in. Sensing trouble, as Vincent had also witnessed the events firsthand in the Bahamas, he quickly devised a plan in his still sharp mind. His body may have been breaking down because of the disease that was eating him up, but he still had his street smarts.

Bannos had not recognized him, as Vincent was just an old man in the background when Tony stared him down at the arm-wrestling championship. After he ordered his first drink, Vincent knew what he had to do. He walked into the back with the ice-filled glass. On the counter in the kitchen was his bag containing his daily medicine intake. He reached in and unscrewed a thirty-milliliter-container of morphine. With the dropper, he squeezed in two milliliters and then went out and poured the vodka into the glass.

A normal person would have dropped right there, but because of Bannos's size and physical condition, Vincent had to continue to add the potent opiate analgesic to the next five drinks. Vincent had used the medication to relieve the pain associated with his stomach cancer. He was also very familiar with its quick results while on the battlefield. The effects still took its toll.

Vincent watched Bannos and listened to him lambaste and then accuse his grandson and Salvatore of being rats. Then he watched in silence as the female agent's cover was almost blown. At that point, Vincent asked one of the other bartenders to cover for him. He left through the back and made his way to the passenger-side door of Bannos's van. As he had seen Bannos remove his weapon a few minutes earlier, he checked the glove compartment, snatched the revolver, and walked away in the shadows. Circling around the back of the building, he got into his car and drove to New Rochelle.

Vincent had spent much time at the Dumont Nursing Home during the past year of his life. Two dear friends of his had been comfortably living out their last days at the facility, and he enjoyed spending hours on end chatting with them. In the course of his visits, he noticed the growing presence of Santo Tracino.

Whenever seeing the degenerate, Vincent would cringe and become visibly upset. On more than one occasion, he spoke with the attendants on duty. They let him know Tracino paid them well to look the other way and there was nothing that would make them change. Over the course of his time there, Vincent watched Tentacles closely and monitored his patterns and movements. After a few months, he knew when and where Santo would be even before he did.

He drove to the Dumont that night on a mission. As with Siegel's death, he knew the mob tended to panic after a made member was killed. The second he saw Bannos's revolver, Vincent's mind clicked. He would commit the perfect crime … again. Bannos would have little recourse, as he would be in no shape to disprove the events in the morning.

He parked a few blocks away, walked down, and waited by Tracino's car. When he saw him exit the nursing home, he crouched low in between two vehicles parked twenty feet away. Tracino started up the engine, and Vincent casually walked over. He hesitated while the window was being lowered, but the motion of the expert marksman was fluid, even after all these years. After one shot he threw the revolver into the brush and casually walked along the tree-lined landscape and out to Shore Road. He peeled off his surgical gloves and tossed them into the sewer along the road on his drive away from the crime scene. He was asleep by 1:00 a.m.

It worked out better than even Vincent could have planned. Bannos died in the car crash the next day. He probably should have not even awoken, as he was a dead man walking after the deadly mix of alcohol and morphine.

In addition, the panic in the aftermath of Tracino's murder rippled throughout the underworld. Jimmy Tracino had taken a stand and made a move to avenge the death of his father. The rats jumped ship and the federal government capitalized on the chaos.

Regarding Sal and Tony, both men were given stiff warnings by the FBI that they should never revert back to the underworld life. Tony continued to work for the Teamsters Union, but he focused his attention on developing his career. Now a business agent, he had grander goals and hopefully he could eventually be shop steward. Sal was more than persuaded by the government to sell the restaurant and end his high-stakes card games. He agreed and was currently weighing offers from three potential suitors. He was told to only sell Ressini's but was not precluded to open a new eatery.

Sal was already loudly hinting to their millionaire buddy, Chris, that besides investing money for a living, he should diversify the portfolio to also be the proud owner of the best restaurant in town.

Scalamarri – Esposito – Messini Family
1887 - 1999

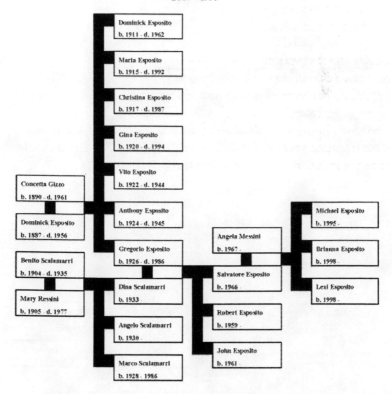

Scalle – Cameron - Kelly Family
1912 - 1999

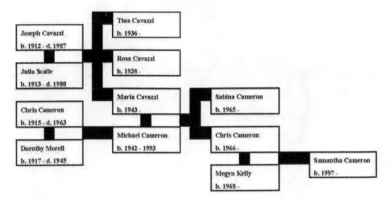

Scala – Albanese - Enrico Family
1915 - 1999

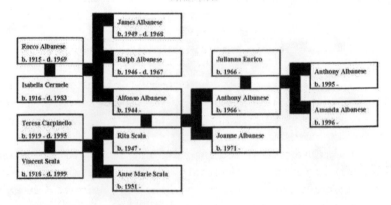

ACKNOWLEDGMENTS

OF COURSE, BEFORE ANYONE else, I have to thank the girls in my life. My Samajumia3—Samantha, Julianna, and Amelia—I love you, my babies. My wife, Teresa, was an incredible help with my motivation to write this story and a major inspiration for much of it. To my awesome dog, Cammie … Oh well, let me begin.

I began writing *Columbus Avenue Boys* as my first novel; *Cameron Nation* was being edited in January of 2011. I wrote the first few chapters of *Columbus Avenue Boys* and surprisingly came up with an outline pretty quickly. I even decided to work through the Scalamarri family tree, and I loved the shortened name of Scala (it was inspired by my Nicole side of the family, which also goes by Micole and Nicola).

All impetus to write came to a grinding halt on February 9. My beautiful, wonderful mother died that day and with her passing came the realization that everything was now different. My father had passed away in 1979, and I often thought how life could or would have been different, for me, my brother, sister and mother, if he had lived a full life. She loved that man more than anyone could imagine and lived with the pain of not being with him for thirty-two years. My mother always told me the family history, and we had many discussions about both sides, the Neills in Belfast and the Carraturos in New York. The direction of *Columbus Avenue Boys* immediately changed from solely a mob story about Sal and Tony to the saga of the Scalamarris.

As an Irish immigrant, my mother was taken into my father's Italian family as one of their own, and she loved every one of his cousins, aunts, and uncles. The memories of going to the many relatives' homes on Sunday afternoons were very special times. Mom, I adored our conversations and dream of the day in Heaven when we will see each other again.

Tuckahoe was the integral place of our family history, and I may as well just include my quaint village as a part of me. I have lived here now for forty-seven years. I absorbed these experiences and memories from my youth like a sponge. I walked by the depleted marble quarry regularly, always ate at Roma's (Ressini's inspiration) and Uncle Dom and Aunt Belle's Villarina's (Bella's inspiration) on Columbus Avenue. That small macaroni store was a major inspiration for my work. My father helped out there when he was not at the GM plant in Tarrytown (he liked his macaroni just as much as he did his cars).

Also, wonderful memories were with family friends who became more than friends, and you grew up like cousins or siblings. My father's best friend Phil Pinto and wife, Joan, will always be my Uncle Phil and Aunt Joan. Their kids were my "Italian cousins" even though we did not share the same blood. They have been there for every inflection point in my life.

I never knew I was poor. I always had a roof over my head, and my grandparents owned the house on Columbus Avenue that I grew up in. We were crammed together with my father, mother, sister, and brother in a two-bedroom section on the first floor. But we always went on vacation and drove a new station wagon, and I never starved. We were lucky to have grandparents who watched over us. Even though it was their house, they even sacrificed and moved into the basement apartment so their son's family could live comfortably, simply an amazing gift.

Life went on, and there were many bumps in the road. Death, alcohol abuse, disease, and economic hardship were all just an everyday part of my existence. The years 1974–83 were horrific, to say the least, to have lived through, but yet we persevered and survived. Lenny and Denise, we have made it through a very rough journey, but it could have been a heck of a lot worse. The dust could be settling; let's enjoy the last fifty years or so.

Through it all, I had my friends and relatives to help keep it together with Scotch tape. Throughout the story, you were mentioned either in a name, a great memory or an inside joke. Yes, I did embellish a few sports memories. If you write a book you can do the same. Just make sure I am still number ten!

A major inflection point was when I met my wife, Teresa. Her stability and love came at one of those points of the roller coaster ride when life was racing toward the bottom. It quickly turned up, and with that came the support and friendship of the Solano family. Each and every one of you, thank you for being there for me. I may be the only husband in the world who loves his mother- and father-in-law unconditionally, but they are truly special. Joe and Tina Solano—thank you. That message transcends to all of my brothers- and sisters-in-law and nieces and nephews. This story is a tribute to the hardworking and loving Solano family, just as much as it is for the Carraturos. I can taste the Sunday afternoon meal now … Yum.

Why am I a World War II buff? I trace it back to sitting with my father on a Saturday and Sunday afternoon watching *The World at War* narrated by Sir Laurence Olivier on Channel Five. Maybe it was also that my father served admirably on the *Intrepid* (1959–62) and by viewing his picture of the majestic carrier in my bedroom after he died that tragic cold January day that I had a calling to want to learn more about anything American history. Dad, you were only thirty-seven when you passed away; I was fourteen. I miss you so much every day. Take care of Mommy.

And this brings me back to my mother's death. I had begun to write this book at that time but stopped. As I looked out at the snowy field at the Gates of Heaven Cemetery, I noticed a mausoleum perpendicular to my parents' gravestone. The name on the mausoleum was Scala. I laughed and then began to cry as I looked down at the dirt that had yet to settle on the grave. Why had I, three weeks earlier, chosen the name of my main character to be Vincent Scala? Life has a way of sending you a message.

I hope you enjoyed this story as much as I enjoyed writing it.

NOTES

I CANNOT IMAGINE HOW anyone could have ever written a book or researched a story without the "worldwide Internet." I pulled from a myriad of sources in the process of my research gathering.

To Mary Nurzia, thank you for the English-to-Italian translations. You were a huge help.

To my daughter, Samantha, thank you so much for taking my author photo.

Thank you as well to the Village of Tuckahoe Historical Society for the picture of Columbus Avenue in the 1950s which was used on the cover.

I have to thank the people behind "Medal of Honor" (US Army Center of Military History website, www.history.army.mil/moh.html) for their work, which inspired many of my war sequences. Reading a few, the accomplishments by these brave heroes took my breath away. I came across this site while researching my father's cousin, Freddy Boy (SP4 Frederick James Carraturo, KIA in Vietnam in 1967), who received the Bronze Star and gave the ultimate sacrifice for his heroic service to our great country. E. B. Sledge, *With the Old Breed: At Peleliu and Okinawa* (New York: Oxford University Press, 1990), and Robert Leckie, *Helmet for my Pillow: From Parris Island to the Pacific* (London: Ebury, 2010), iBooks, were a huge help too. For my postwar Tuckahoe experiences, I had recently read the following for many themes and ideas: Alfred J. Mariani, *Columbus & Maynard* (Stratford, CT: Brew Printing, 2004). If you are from Tuckahoe, it is a must read.

The Bugsy Siegel fans were also a great help:

www.bugsysiegel.net, http://www.findadeath.com/Deceased/s/bugsy/bugsysiegel.htm.

Other sources I leaned on:

FBI website, "About Us," "News," "Stats & Services," www.fbi.gov.

"Local History," Town of Eastchester website, www.eastchester.org.

John Marzulli, "Gambino capo Greg DePalma's son Craig dies at 44 after eight years in coma," *New York Daily News*, January 17, 2011.

Jerry Capeci, "Greg DePalma, Pal of Sinatra and Willie Mays, Dies In Prison," *Huffington Post*, November 30, 2009.

Jeffrey Goldberg, "The Don Is Done," *New York Times*, January 31, 1999.

Charles Montaldo, "Charles 'Lucky' Luciano, Founder of the National Crime Syndicate," About.com, accessed January 15, 2012, http://crime.about.com/od/gangsters/a/luciano.htm.

"Lucky Luciano," *Wikipedia*, last modified January 15, 2012, http://en.wikipedia.org/wiki/Lucky_Luciano.

"Charles 'Lucky' Luciano," Answers.com, http://www.answers.com/topic/charles-lucky-luciano.

"Castellammarese War," *Wikipedia*, last modified November 1, 2011, http://en.wikipedia.org/wiki/Castellammarese_War.

"Bronx River Parkway, Historic Overview," www.nycroads.com/roads/bronx-river.

"USS *Intrepid* (CV-11)," *Wikipedia*, last modified January 15, 2012, http://en.wikipedia.org/wiki/USS_Intrepid_(CV-11).

USS Intrepid Association website, most recent revision April 5, 2011, www.wa3key.com/intrepid.html.

Andrew Glass, "President Reagan shot, March 30, 1981," Politico.com, March 30, 2009, http://www.politico.com/news/stories/0309/20628.html.

Charlie Johnson, "Church of the Assumption celebrates centennial mass," *Town Report*, September 29, 2011.

"Introduction," Siwanoy Country Club website, http://siwanoycc.com/public/frameset_public.aspx.

"History," Saint Andrew's Golf Club website, http://www.saintandrewsgolfclub.com/Club-Info-Guest/History-Guest.aspx.

"Babe Ruth," Leewood Golf Club website, http://www.leewoodgolfclub.org/Default.aspx?p=DynamicModule&pageid=333266&ssid=230471&vnf=1.

Monte D. Cox, "'Terrible' Terry McGovern: A Little Like Tyson," http://coxscorner.tripod.com/mcgovern.html.

Read more about the Columbus Avenue Boys

Cameron Nation: Going All-In to Save His Country
By David Carraturo

www.cameronnation.com

Prologue

BIG TONY AND SALLY NUTS

The Early 1990s

BROTHERS VINCENT AND JIMMY Petrillo, owners of the Oasis Café, were extremely happy with their now-profitable investment, which was past its critical three-year anniversary. Located just off the North Dixie Highway along the Indian River, the converted 1904 Victorian was the oldest structure in Brevard County and provided a breathtaking view from every table for patrons to comfortably spend their retirement dollars in snowbird paradise. Rave reviews stated, "The forty-two different beers on tap at Malabar's most popular restaurant are the perfect marriage to their signature Florida Fritters and Jalapeno Hush Puppies."

With fifteen years of loyal service, Pat Fortuno confidently believed Jim and Vinny had made the correct move to promote him from bartender and transfer him from their flagship location in Jupiter to run this newest venture. With two decades of life under his belt as a Floridian, the transplanted New Yorker had no regrets. Divorced and with no children, he never looked back on his past and embraced the opportunity presented to him when he hooked up with his two childhood friends from Yonkers. Even before the papers were signed by his ex-wife, Rosa, he was taking advantage of the plethora of transplanted widows populating the Sunshine State's senior living communities. Tall, lanky, well-tanned, and with the gift of gab, he bragged to all who would listen that he was the main reason the restaurant was always bustling.

Finished for the evening, Fortuno completed the last of his paperwork and stuffed the large manila envelope, fat with the cash and credit card receipts, into the drop safe below his desk on the office floor. While he was still upset he had to fire the cute waitress, he simply could not tolerate rude behavior to his best customers. She simply could not question a below-average tip from Jimmy's neighbor.

Alone now since the last busboy had finished sweeping the floor and left fifteen minutes earlier, he shut the last of the lights off, locked the backdoor, and completed his final end-of-night security check. Once outside in the mild winter air, he drained the last sip out of his Budweiser longneck and tossed the empty into the overflowing, rusted waste management container situated next to his BMW. Taking a whiff of the low tide twenty feet away, he shook his head and laughed. One of his executive perks: the smelliest parking space on the East Coast.

He lit a Winston Ultra Light and then stopped to glance at his watch; it was 1:00 a.m. on the dot. While taking a deep drag and fishing for his keys in the front left pocket of his Windbreaker, he thought about what to do during his three-day holiday vacation. Another new year; he could not believe it was already nineteen-ninty-f— *Whap!* Without warning, he was knocked on the base of his skull, and he crumbled forward to the gravel below.

Two burly Cubans carried the body to the small-craft dock and placed him in a waiting Carolina Skiff. The vessel was slowly guided away by a third accomplice, taking a slight northeastern course. The extraction was handled flawlessly. Working quickly, they undressed the six-foot-four-inch limp frame, roughly tied his hands and feet with duct tape, and finished by stuffing a rag into his mouth and further securing the orifice shut with the remainder of the all-purpose silver adhesive. A fourth accomplice, who had remained onshore, drove the abandoned sedan to a Hispanic neighborhood in Daytona. There would not be many salvageable parts for a rusted-out twenty-year-old import.

Under the Route 192 Bridge, connecting Melbourne with the Indialantic beach, a Tides fishing boat waited for the slowly approaching smaller watercraft. On the open stern stood two men donned head to toe in black; skullcaps masked their faces, sweatshirts tightly fit around their massive torsos, and steel-toed boots gave an extra inch of height to their already intimidating presence. With long latex gloves protecting their massive hands and arms, they effortlessly yanked the limp body on board. The larger of the men then tossed the Cubans a brown paper bag containing a compensation of $10,000—well earned for six hours of work.

With the cargo secured, the captain slowly eased the throttle forward and thrust the vessel away from the camouflage of the pilings. Picking up speed, they banked east and finally cruised into the vastness of the awaiting ocean. An hour later, the boat idled some ten miles out in the Atlantic. With sunrise still two hours away, the sky was as black as ink. It was going to be a brisk day for late December, but the water was unusually calm.

Fortuno groggily stirred a few minutes later after Big Tony placed the open end of a plastic jug filled with ammonia underneath his nose. Eyes still closed, he jerked his head, moving away from the smell of the noxious fumes. It took a few seconds for him to comprehend his restricted mobility before he popped his eyes open and became fully conscious.

Sally Nuts emerged from the lower galley. Orange fishing bib pants now complemented his black attire. As he reached the top step, he peered over and mocked Fortuno lying there with arms and legs hog-tied from behind, revealing an old, wrinkled body.

After an icy glare directly into his bugged-out eyes, Sally finally spoke.

"Not such a tough guy now, are you?" he snarled before completing the greeting by thrusting his right leg and extending it into the old man's chest. The heel landed squarely on its target and knocked Fortuno backward.

"Look, you slimy piece of garbage, do you know why you're here?" Big Tony's deep baritone voice commanded as he reemerged from the galley, rhetorically demanding an answer from their muzzled prey. He had also changed and now wore a full-body yellow nylon overall.

The old man shook his head rapidly, still not knowing why he was in this predicament. Then, uncontrollably, he relieved himself, urinating down the front of his jackknifed, bound lower body.

They glared down at the yellow stream, looked at each other, and laughed. "Ha. Look, Sal, he pissed himself."

Sal shook his head in a disapproving manner. "I always thought macho Don Juan–types like you would be tougher than that."

Big Tony crouched down and placed a small picture in front of Fortuno's face while his partner grabbed the matted, soiled gray hair from behind and then yanked it so his eyes would be level.

"Hey … Let me ask ya, my friend, you remember all of your conquests, right?"

On cue, Tony flicked on a small flashlight. The illumination showed clearly a picture of a girl, no older than six or seven, sitting on a younger-looking Fortuno's lap, his right arm wrapped around her shoulder. The little dark-haired beauty was peering up at him, lips pouting with a sad expression.

"Oh, so you do remember!" Tony seethed, watching as the old man suddenly realized what this torture was about.

From the galley, the captain emerged, peering at the quivering old man from behind Big Tony's massive shoulders. The captain then took the picture from his mate's hand and ignited the edge. As it began to slowly flame, it was tossed over the side, the monster's memory in time sizzling on top of the calm surface of the Atlantic.

Fortuno bucked his bound body, trying helplessly to escape his condemnation. Sally Nuts waited, entertained by the squirming for a few seconds, and then hauled back and kicked him again. This time the front of his boot impacted squarely on the tip of Fortuno's nose, breaking cartilage on impact and causing blood to explode from the mangled mess.

What a cowardly display, he thought. "Now, now, old man … We'll have none of that … It's time for you to go to hell, where you belong."

The shell of a man whimpered and curled up with the side of his face resting in a puddle of blood and piss.

Big Tony then got in on the action. "Field goal, three points!" After he kicked Fortuno in the groin, Tony laughed uncontrollably and then coughed as he tried to catch his breath.

Now working with Tony as a team, Sally Nuts's huge hands gripped Fortuno's bare shoulders and spun him around, his strength totally overpowering the old man. Big Tony smiled sardonically, proudly showing a foot-long meat cleaver. He moved the deadly tool up to his victim's face and, without emotion, effortlessly grabbed a sagging earlobe and smoothly sliced it off.

"Like butter, baby … Now that's how we do it, hey, Sally?" He tossed the appendage overboard.

"Hey, no fair, my friend … I get to throw the next one over."

They both let out devilish laughs.

Blood oozing down the side of his face, Fortuno's tortured body began to convulse. Big Tony took no mercy, the pleasure clearly apparent as he began the task of dismembering the still-live body.

Big Tony held down Fortuno's bound feet and chopped them off at the anklebones in one quick, forceful motion. Fortuno writhed in excruciating pain but was unable to make any real noise through the muzzle of the duct tape. The Cubans had done a very good prep job.

The trauma to his system too intense, with blood flowing quickly out of his lower extremities, he passed out seconds later, never to open his eyes again.

Systematically placing the bloody appendages into white plastic buckets, the burly pair threw the sealed and weighted canisters overboard every few hundred yards.

With the eastern sky coming to life, they picked up speed. The assassins meticulously scrubbed the boat clean, hosing down all the remnants of their victim into the dark, cold waters.

The vessel was left where it had been "borrowed" at the Cocoa Beach Yacht Club six hours earlier. The trio changed into sweat suits and then walked casually to the entrance, strolled past the chain-linked fence, and opened the door of a waiting Ford Bronco. They barely stopped during the twenty-hour trip back to New York.

Chapter 1

FIRST WE EAT AND THEN WE TALK

March 21, 2015

THE SUN SHONE BRIGHTLY in the eastern sky, but it was not the best day to be out along the border. With the late-spring morning wind whipping across the rugged south Texas terrain, the thermostat might have read thirty-one degrees, but in actuality it felt more like it was in the teens. Fort Bliss, the largest US Army Training and Doctrine Command installation in the country, was situated adjacent to the city of El Paso. The reservation, built in 1849 to protect the southern border from raids by Mexicans and Native Americans, served its country commendably, and it had a long history as a staging point for deploying military personnel to support conflicts around the world.

Ground zero was strategically located on the southwest quadrant of the military establishment. The US Army Corps of Engineers had erected a special six-story viewing tower that was secured directly into the pavement of the J. E. B. Stuart and Cassidy Road intersection. The eight-by-ten-foot rectangular platform protruded above a reception tent and provided a magnificent panoramic view for miles in all directions. The structure was purposely meant to look hastily constructed, but in reality it could withstand gale-force winds. As you looked east, the arriving and departing flights of El Paso International Airport could clearly be seen. To the north stretched the four-mile-long runway of Biggs Army Airfield. To the west, the city of El Paso blocked the expanse of Puerto de Anapra and the lands thereafter. Five miles to the south clearly showed the catalyst for today's event, Highway 375, snaking along the border with Ciudad Juárez. This Mexican city was home to one of the major hot spots for the crossing of undocumented aliens.

At 10:45 a.m. CST on board *Air Force One* during the flight from Washington, DC, to Texas, Christopher Joseph Cameron was sworn in as the forty-sixth president of the United States of America. He asked that the ceremony coincide with when they flew directly over Austin, or more specifically, his alma mater, the University of Texas.

While his transition team took these unprecedented forty days to work out succession details, his initial order of business was to focus his time on dealing with the escalating problems to the south.

You can't pick your neighbors; you can only choose your friends, the newly minted president thought to himself as he sat as a passenger in the new Stryker 250 armored personnel carrier next to a twenty-three-year-old motor transport officer from Palatine, Illinois.

As the sole vehicle traveling on Cassidy Road, this next-generation military transport was moving at close to full speed of seventy-two miles per hour. Set to be unveiled next month as the centerpiece of the ongoing army transformation, the "Quart," which had a range of 406 miles, operated with the latest C4ISR equipment and an integrated armor package to protect soldiers against a wide array of weapons and explosives.

Since his surprising election win two years earlier, Felix Lozario, the *presidente* of Mexico, spent a considerable amount of time condemning the actions of the United States and, in particular, outgoing President Harloe. With a strong left-wing political agenda, the sixty-one-year-old senior Party of the Democratic Revolution member devoted far more time to railing against US policy than focusing on stabilizing his fragile nation.

Now precipitously close to being declared a failed state, Mexico had been suffering for close to a decade mired in the grip of a never-ending recession. A crippling one-two punch was the culprit. Oil revenue was severely hampered by the precipitous drop in the price of the commodity, while at the same time, the flow of pesos from repatriated undocumented-worker earnings decreased significantly with the implementation of the initial phases of the FairTax. This monumental change in the US tax code did what had been previously thought of as impossible: it captured revenue from illegal sources. It was estimated that close to $2 billion that had previously been sent to Mexican families had now found its way into the federal tax revenue stream.

The knockout blow was the ever-expanding power of the cartels. The ruthless gangs exponentially increased the level of violence throughout the drug-smuggling corridors and continued their extortion of protection money and murder of local families and businesses. Even more disconcerting was that they now branched out to the political world and supplanted many government officials. This was most prevalent in Chihuahua, Coahuila, and Nuevo León, the states closest to the US border.

President Cameron arrived fifteen minutes before his invited guest and sat under the olive-colored canvas field tent in front of the viewing platform. He was casually chatting and comparing stories with the soldiers on duty about his time stationed at Fort Bliss before being deployed to Iraq in 1990 versus their current engagements. A table for two was set, waiting with some of his favorite Italian lunchtime selections laid out under silver tray covers. The two world leaders would start with a trio platter of sliced Parmesan cheese, thickly cut *soppressata,* and marinated *mulignani.* This would be followed by a tossed tomato salad with olive oil, basil, and oregano. When the appetizers were finished, there were family-style plates of broccoli rabe, fried veal cutlets, and roasted potatoes warming on a chafing dish. Of course, fresh Italian bread and a bottle of 2011 Drew Pinot Noir to wash it all down would go with every course.

The Mexican contingent, consisting of three silver Mercedes, arrived ten minutes after noon. Chris glanced at his Samajumia3-inscribed *minute repeater*; he really hated when people were late. Shrugging off the tardiness, he walked over and warmly shook the hand of Felix Lozario. Fourteen years his senior, Chris was careful not to squeeze too hard.

"*Bienvenidos, bienvenidos,*" he welcomed his guest. "Sit, sit, first we eat, and then we talk."

As he always did, Chris wished to make all visitors feel at home, even more so now that his home was the entire United States of America.

"This meal was specially prepared, and I present this to you in honor of my mother, so *manga, manga.*"

An hour later, after much small talk and a lot more eating, Chris drained the last drop of vino and stood up.

"That, my friend, should last me the entire day; I may not need to eat again until tomorrow night."

"*Si, si,* it was excellent and very unexpected. I thought we would not have time for a proper meal."

Chris laughed as he rubbed his stomach. "It's a wonder I'm not three hundred pounds; my mother cooked like this almost every day. Just your typical Italian family from the suburbs of New York."

"*Si*, my condolences for your loss."

"I really miss her a lot. She would not be happy if I had people over and did not feed them."

He then escorted his guest out of the tent and around toward the lift to make their six-story climb.

"*Perdon, amigos, solamente bastante cuarto para dos* (Sorry, folks, only enough room for two)," Chris said to the Mexican contingent following them, who attempted to squeeze into the four-by-four-foot elevator seconds before he locked the steel cage shut. He was glad to have picked up the language from his many years living in Texas. This meeting would be *mano-a-mano*.

After he pressed the green button on the control panel, the hum of the motor signaled their half-minute ascent to the viewing platform. As they inched higher, and once they cleared the top of the tent, the force of the wind grew more intense and the gusts whistled loudly through the exposed skeleton.

When they reached the top, Chris unlatched the door. Ever the cordial host, he motioned for his guest to exit first. Lozario tentatively pointed his head out and studied the rattling structure. Though he was bundled up nicely in a long cashmere jacket and wool gloves, at this moment in time he realized it was actually much colder than he had originally thought.

"No, no, no … after you, Mr. Vice President. It's still protocol for higher-ranking officials to exit last." He further delayed his exit by adjusting the collar to his coat and refitting his gloves to better shield him from the harsh elements.

"Heck, this is nothing. When I was a Ranger, we had a week of survival training in Alaska. I think it got to be ten below; froze my *cojones* off." Chris was amused because his counterpart, who obviously spent far too little time above the equator, was dressed in only slacks and a casual dress shirt.

He then firmly gripped Lozario's upper arm and guided him out into the elements. "Look around you, my friend. We both preside over beautiful countries."

Chris practically bounced around the structure, soaking in the panoramic views of the Texas border crossing. He turned to face Lozario.

The sun shone directly behind his head. "Oh, also forgot to fill you in on the changes. I'm officially the president, sworn in about an hour ago."

Like a child, Chris pointed left as a Boeing 747 effortlessly lifted off the runway at El Paso International. He then clanked right across the structure to admire the south end of the beautiful Franklin Mountains, which stretched north along the New Mexico state line. With each terrifying rattle, the *presidente* held the railing tighter and tighter.

"Isn't that the Juárez Mountains behind the Wells Fargo building?" He pointed and waited for a response.

"*Si, si* ... yes, it is," he meekly confirmed the location. "*Le ruego me disculpe*; I meant no disrespect calling you the vice president."

The wind howled, and the structure shook in response. Lozario tightly squeezed his eyes closed again. When they popped open a few seconds later, Chris had moved yet again. This early afternoon sightseeing tour was quite entertaining.

"No need to apologize, señor. You should be honored. You're the first person I've told as well as the first I've wanted to meet with." Chris smiled warmly and then changed gears and tested Lozario on his knowledge of the Treaty of Hidalgo, which had officially ended the Mexican–American War in 1848. Under the terms of the treaty, Mexico had relinquished all claims to Texas and ceded land in present-day California, New Mexico, and Arizona. They had also recognized the Rio Grande as the northern boundary, and in return, the United States had exchanged $15 million in reparations.

"Ironically, did you know this magnificent reservation was built soon after your government made us create the first generation of homeland security?" An additional provision to the treaty had included protecting property and civil rights of Mexican nationals living within the new boundaries, along with the promise of the United States to police its borders.

Lozario found a secure corner of the structure, and with the wind dying down a bit, his confidence from earlier in the day returned to his voice. "I believe you tend to stretch your facts. Maybe too many revisions as your country stole more of our land?" He exhaled forcefully and continued. "Mr. President, the people of my country need to work; we're suffering greatly. You're a wealthy country. We shouldn't be treated so harshly. Your predecessor, his policies toward my people were loco. You're a good man, healthy: your judgment is not clouded like his was."

Chris now went serious as he sternly walked past his guest toward the north end of the structure. "President Harloe's a good friend and an excellent man. It was the greatest honor to serve under him."

The roar of a C-5 Galaxy drowned out the Mexican *presidente*'s answer as the massive military transport passed above. At that same instant, the lift was lowered by personnel at the bottom of the structure, leaving the leader of the free world and the leader of the third-world country to the south stranded above.

He repeated the apology so Chris could now hear it. "Again, I meant no disrespect to President Harloe. It just appeared that he was not sensitive to how things work along the border. We cannot control this activity, just as your government cannot control young Americans' appetite for narcotics and selling guns back to our country."

"Look, my friend. Here's what's going to happen, okay? We've given you two years to figure out that we're upset with your behavior." He was now talking to Lozario like a child.

"Your policies have only crippled our economy more. Our people are suffering greatly."

"I respectfully disagree, Mr. *Presidente*. There have been many examples of unprovoked aggression from your military as well as the cartels. Heck, a few of your drones even crashed in Texas and Arizona."

"The aggression from our military only showed we are keeping the pressure on the cartels. We are fighting them even more than you could know."

President Cameron did not believe his counterpart at all. While on the surface it appeared there was a major crackdown, the largest and richest cartels appeared to be flourishing. The bribing of top government officials helped them consolidate power among the most powerful, ruthless organizations, making them stronger, while allowing the Mexican government propaganda moments to highlight the capture of the weaker, less important gangs.

"Felix, did you really think we were joking? This shit's serious. Our country's being systematically infiltrated by your people."

"With over five hundred years of history in this territory, there are many relatives and ancestors north of the Rio Grande," Lozario smugly replied.

"By this so-called 'territory,' would you mean Texas, New Mexico, Arizona, and California? Heck, Felix, over the past twenty-five years, your caucus in these states strengthened in Washington. There's more and more elected officials of Latin descent. Quite frankly, that growth rate was very concerning."

The two men were in a corner of the viewing area. They could not be seen or heard by anyone six stories below. Chris had planned for the discussion to be this way, as he wanted to dress down the Mexican leader for his failed policies and actions. At the same time, though, he did not want him to lose any respect or to have any witness to his bullying.

"Mr. Cameron—"

Chris cut him off. "That would be 'Mr. President' to you!" He raised his voice and then abruptly calmed down and pointed out at the army air base to the north. Far in the distance, you could see two doors of a massive hangar at Biggs Army Airfield opening.

"Let's look over there as we continue our discussion." He changed to a more normal speech pattern; he had vented enough. By coincidence, he handed his guest a pair of binoculars that just happened to be hanging on a corner railing. "Another surprise for you."

A transformer-like structure emerged from deep inside the hangar. Still miles away, it looked quite impressive rolling out on its massive treads. The electric gate blocking the exit to J. E. B. Stuart Road also began to swing open, providing an unobstructed path for the transforming figure to travel.

"Now listen up!" Chris totally changed his disposition, now speaking in a tone similar to the one he'd used while back in the neighborhood. "I'm giving you six months. When we get back down to the ground, get someone in your posse to write down 'November 9.' Circle that date. By then, you'll have made major steps on all of my demands."

Chris reached into his pocket. Out came a standard piece of paper, folded over four times. It looked like a note from his mother. He flattened it out and began to read the bullet points.

"*Numero uno*: By July, the Mexican government will begin to assist in the transport of all of your interred citizens at Gitmo. I expect to see the wake of your armada and at least fifteen thousand of your *ciudadanos* waving adios per month. Hey, they're your citizens; please take them back."

They both peered out again. The transformer began to move more quickly. It was now through the gate and heading south. "*Numero dos*: By August 1, the US government would like to receive our first installment of financial restitution for the medical treatment of Mexican citizens at our health-care facilities. I'd say it's about eighty million dollars, give or take a few million, so far accumulated since January 2014. The check should be made out to the US Treasury, and make the first one for twenty mil."

Seen in more detail now, the massive vehicle was beginning to gain speed as it continued down the cordoned-off eight-lane road, heading toward them. They admired it some more, and then Chris continued. "*Numero tres*: This one's pretty important, so stop viewing it for a sec, okay?"

Lozario was clearly not amused, and his blood began to boil. He became even more irate as he realized he could not get away from this pompous *gamberro*.

"Felix, Felix, pay attention. After the date I told you to circle …which was?" He raised the inflection of his voice at the end of the question.

"*Noviembre nueve*," Lozario disgustedly answered as he continued to stare at the approaching object still a half mile in the distance.

"Very good! Now, after this date, any border crossings by your citizens would be considered an act of war on the part of the Mexican government, and the United States would take military action to secure our border. Furthermore, as per the Roosevelt Corollary, we have a right to intervene in any way we choose to collect our outstanding health-care payment."

In 1905, President Theodore Roosevelt had expanded the Monroe Doctrine, which stated that European nations should not interfere with countries to the south of the United States and that doing so would require US intervention. The president had stated that the United States was justified in exercising international police power to put an end to chronic unrest or wrongdoing in the Western hemisphere. While President Franklin D. Roosevelt had later renounced this type of intervention in 1934 by establishing his Good Neighbor policy, President Cameron believed FDR's older cousin's ideas needed to be dusted off and modified for twenty-first-century events.

"*Capisce?*" He was tired of Spanish and needed to switch to Italian.

Lozario finally lost his temper. "You think you can bully my country and threaten us with outrageous demands. The United Nations will not allow it."

He began cursing rapidly in Spanish. Chris could not decipher Lozario's words and might have blushed if he could.

"*Presidente* Lozario, without the United States, the UN does not exist. My country holds all of its military and financial power. Besides, how could the UN object to a country defending its borders?"

"The world order would not approve of aggression from you. The UN would respond!" He ignored the explanation.

The president turned away from his guest to look directly at the six-story mobile observatory that had finally completed its journey. He checked his watch. "Fifteen minutes—not bad, huh? What's that, about fourteen to sixteen miles an hour?"

"What is this structure?" Lozario looked closely in amazement.

"Ahh. This, my friend, is the newest in US military ingenuity. It's amazing; we ask for the unachievable and our great citizens achieve it. It's quite remarkable, actually."

Soon after taking office, President Harloe had outlined his vision for protecting the southern border. After the failed implementation of the virtual border fence by the Bush and Obama administrations, he had learned from those mistakes and conveyed his vision for the best way to protect the country from intruders. By the end of 2013, Northman Hancock, one of the leading military contractors, had risen to the challenge, and in a highly competitive bidding process, had been awarded the $20 billion contract for their revolutionary design of the PERCH.

The dual-layered facility, powered by solar roof panels, was totally self-sufficient. Eight reinforced treads, with the flexibility to maneuver in all directions at speeds of up to twenty miles per hour, acted as the base of the unit. A crisscrossing array of titanium- and tungsten-infused steel rods supported the two one-hundred-by-sixty-foot oval-shaped floors situated above. The lower compartment housed the sleeping quarters, cafeteria, and entertainment center for the fifteen specially trained personnel on board. Further stabilizing the unit, a spiral staircase, made of the same space-age metal as the support rods, led up to the war room on the second level. The cockpit, controlling all movement of the unit, was located in the front arc of the second level. Behind it were video surveillance monitors and, more importantly, the command units to fire off laser-guided precision missiles. These missiles were stored in twenty facilities secretly hidden along the two-thousand-mile border. The clincher for Northman Hancock was their design of the ground-monitoring equipment. The Frisbee-shaped units—four thousand in total—were to be hidden along the border.

The latest in laser and solar technology allowed the spheres to capture energy from the sun and be self-powered, with no maintenance. The sophisticated infrared light was able to read the flow of human traffic and lock a position on multiple objects. The settings could be controlled to specify size and temperature of the bogey. These miniunits would be set to register objects over five feet in height and, more importantly, with a body temperature between 98 and 102 degrees. Once the position was locked, the precision unit would relay the data to personnel in the PERCH. From that point, a decision would be made to either engage with force or send the strike force on board to apprehend.

The alarmingly high number of mass border crossings of heavily armed drug mule convoys was almost impossible to stop. When fully implemented, this breakthrough surveillance and weapons technology would monitor the entire southern border.

"It's called a PERCH—you know, an elevated, advantageous place for sitting. We're going to have ten of these bad boys in operation over the next two years. The first one will be deployed by August."

"And what will these units do?" Lozario studied the monster. It was terrifyingly impressive. He looked up and then down to the ground six stories below. Army personnel were blocking any attempt of his contingent to get too close to the unit.

"I don't want to give away state secrets. Let's just say, we're going to stop the construction of the border fence because of this guy." He pointed over his shoulder like a proud father.

The clank of the lift interrupted their concentration. Chris turned his head and pointed his arm toward their exit point. "Shall we? It's time to go. I have to hurry back to Washington."

Chris escorted his guest to the small confines for their descent. Moments before they reached the ground, though, he looked at the president of Mexico and shook his hand. He squeezed it tighter than he had during their initial greeting and then moved closer and whispered into his ear, "Remember what I said. I've never been more serious before in my life. I will protect my country."

The president opened the door and bolted forward. He did not look back. As he approached the Quad, he blew past his aide and hopped over the side into the passenger seat. They sped off, leaving Felix Lozario to think about his new policy initiatives when he landed back in Mexico City. The clock was now ticking, and Chris hated when people were late.

Made in the USA
Lexington, KY
09 February 2013